WITHDRAWN

A
MOST NOBLE
HEIR

Books by Susan Anne Mason

COURAGE TO DREAM

Irish Meadows
A Worthy Heart
Love's Faithful Promise

A Most Noble Heir

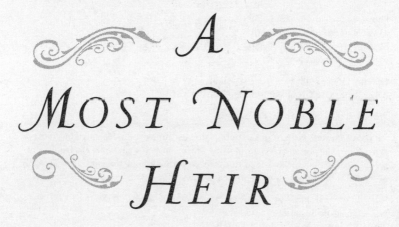

A MOST NOBLE HEIR

SUSAN ANNE MASON

BETHANYHOUSE

a division of Baker Publishing Group
Minneapolis, Minnesota

Published by Bethany House Publishers
11400 Hampshire Avenue South
Bloomington, Minnesota 55438
www.bethanyhouse.com

Bethany House Publishers is a division of
Baker Publishing Group, Grand Rapids, Michigan

Printed in the United States of America

Library of Congress Cataloging-in-Publication Data
Names: Mason, Susan Anne, author.
Title: A most noble heir / Susan Anne Mason.
Description: Minneapolis, Minnesota : Bethany House, a division of Baker
    Publishing Group, [2018]
Identifiers: LCCN 2017038830| ISBN 9780764230875 (trade paper) | ISBN
    9780764231391 (hardcover)
Subjects: | GSAFD: Love stories. | Christian fiction. | Historical fiction.
Classification: LCC PR9199.4.M3725 M67 2018 | DDC 813/.6—dc23
LC record available at https://lccn.loc.gov/2017038830

Unless noted, Scripture quotations are from the King James Version of the Bible.

Scripture quotations are from The Holy Bible, English Standard Version® (ESV®), copyright © 2001 by Crossway, a publishing ministry of Good News Publishers. Used by permission. All rights reserved. ESV Text Edition: 2011.

Cover design by Jennifer Parker
Cover photography by Aimee Christenson

Author is represented by Natasha Kern Literary Agency.

18 19 20 21 22 23 24   7 6 5 4 3 2 1

For Iris Irene Colver Farrell,
the grandmother I never had the privilege of knowing.

In researching your family history, I discovered my great-great-grandparents, Charles Henry Colver and Mary Hannah Burnan, were servants at Stainsby Hall in Derbyshire, England. The mystery of their romance and subsequent marriage became the inspiration for this book, and I am most grateful for the journey it took me on!

"The righteous shall inherit
the land and dwell upon it forever."

Psalm 37:29 ESV

CHAPTER

I

Derbyshire, England
March 1884

Nolan Price scanned the fields of newly budding greenery that stretched as far as he could see and slowly inhaled the scent of grass, soil, and freshly spread manure. Warmth curled through his chest with a feeling of such intense satisfaction that he wished he could ring the village bell to let everyone know of his joy. This moment would remain etched in his memory as the day he'd finally taken a bold step toward his future.

His future with Hannah.

Nolan turned to see Mr. Simpson, the farmer who owned the property, coming up beside him. He was a small, wiry man, still full of energy that belied his advanced years.

"It's been good doing business with you, son." Mr. Simpson stretched out his hand. "I'm glad to see the place go to someone who will love it and nurture it the way I did."

"Thank you, sir. I appreciate this more than you know." Nolan shook the older man's callused hand. The hand of a farmer, seasoned by years of hard, honest work. The type of life Nolan would soon become very familiar with. He held no illusions that his job as a groom in the Stainsby Hall stables these past eleven years had been in any way as arduous as the path that lay ahead. Still, he was prepared to trade in his life at the manor to become master of his own destiny and not the servant of a rich nobleman.

"You're a smart lad," the farmer said as they turned back toward the barn. "Saving up to buy your own land, a small piece though it might be. Me and my Sarah—God rest her soul—we had a good life here. I'm sure you and your young lady will too." The man's smile revealed several missing teeth. "You come by here at the end of the month, and we'll take care of transferring the deed to your name. A short trip into Derby will take care of that."

"I look forward to it." Nolan settled his cap more firmly on his head and untied the stallion's reins from the hitching post. "Thanks again, Mr. Simpson." He pulled himself up onto King's back and, with a quick nod at the farmer, set off down the lane toward the main road.

Partway along the path, he couldn't resist looking back for one more glimpse at the property that would soon belong to him. A rush of pride filled his chest. Imagine being a landowner at the age of one and twenty. Not many men born into his station of life could boast the same.

Nolan smiled to himself. Not many men had such a strong incentive—a girl of uncommon beauty named Hannah.

He could recall with stunning clarity the exact moment he'd first met Hannah Burnham. A waif of a girl with sad eyes the color of new spring grass, she'd captured his heart from the very first glance. Even then, at the tender age of fourteen, he'd vowed that he would one day make her his wife.

The black steed snorted and tossed his head, a sure sign that they were nearing home. Nolan tightened his grip on the reins and lifted his head. Sure enough, the tall peaks of Stainsby Hall became visible over the trees in the distance. Around the next bend, the estate's imposing structure—his home since his mother had come here eleven years earlier to take a position as housemaid—came into full view.

For the first time, Nolan found he could be objective in his assessment of the mansion and observe it as someone who would soon no longer call it home. Stone walls towered high above the tree line—the mansion's many turrets and peaks seeming to scrape the sky. Nolan would never describe the building as beautiful. Majestic, yes. Imposing, certainly. But there was nothing comforting or endearing about the structure. No warmth or sense of welcome.

Just like its owner.

The overbearing Earl of Stainsby was one person Nolan would *not* miss when he left Stainsby Hall.

Nolan glanced at the sun overhead and tried to gauge the time. A little before noon, if he calculated correctly. His half-day off was over. Time to get back to work. He gave King a gentle nudge and set the stallion to a swift trot. Soon, they had traveled the main road that led to the estate. On reaching the stables, Nolan swung down from the saddle and led King into the impressive building. The finest stable this side of London, Bert always said. And Nolan couldn't disagree.

Bert had been the blacksmith on the estate for over thirty years, and a better man Nolan had yet to meet. His chest tightened at the realization that leaving Stainsby meant he wouldn't get to see the burly Scotsman every day. He'd surely miss the big man and his words of wisdom.

Nolan grabbed a brush from the hook and began to smooth out King's black coat. Another shaft of regret sliced through him. "I wish you could come with me too, boy. But even if I could afford to buy you, we won't have need for a stallion on the farm. Working horses only. Besides, I could never see you pulling a plow." He smiled at the ridiculous thought.

On a burst of fresh resolve, he grabbed a pitchfork and threw some clean straw into the stall. He would not allow any trace of disappointment to ruin this day for him. Instead, he focused on the happy fact that he'd soon be able to take his dear mother away from the hard life she endured here. As head housekeeper, she put up with long days, overseeing not only the underlings, but every detail of life in the manor. It was hard work, and her health had suffered as of late. This winter had been especially harsh, leaving her with a cough she couldn't seem to shake.

Nolan put King in his stall and latched the door, then returned the grooming brushes to their proper spot. If luck were with him, he might catch Hannah coming outside to sit under the tall elm for a break. He couldn't wait to give her the news that Mr. Simpson had agreed to sell him the farm and that they could soon be wed.

He hurried over to the water trough, scooped a handful of cool liquid, and splashed it over his dusty face. With damp fingers, he attempted to tame his wild locks into some semblance of respectability, then went to stand at the open stable door, his spirits lifting even higher at the possibility of a few stolen moments with the girl he loved. By all rights, he should have a ring for Hannah and propose to her properly. She deserved that much at least.

Well, ring or no, once they were both off duty tonight, he would tell her how much she meant to him and ask her to be his wife.

"Dinna tell me you're mooning over young Hannah again?"

The booming voice snapped Nolan to attention. He turned to find Bert McTeague standing behind him, grinning.

"I'm not mooning over anyone." Nolan fixed him with an annoyed glare.

The big man belted out a laugh, his blue eyes twinkling with merriment. "Ach, there's nothing wrong with eyeing a bonny lass. Wouldn't be normal if you didn't notice her. Especially now that spring's in the air." He winked at him. "Have you kissed the girl yet?"

Nolan jerked back from the doorway, heat infusing his neck. "No."

"What are you waiting for, lad? You're not getting any younger."

The broad-shouldered blacksmith had taken Nolan under his wing soon after Nolan had started as a stable boy. Maybe it was because he'd learned Nolan had no father, or maybe because he and his wife, Franny, had not been blessed with children. Whatever the reason, Nolan had forged a strong bond with Bert, who'd eventually become more friend than mentor.

Usually Nolan tolerated Bert's good-natured ribbing, but for some reason today it chafed.

"That's a private matter between Hannah and me. Besides, you know how his lordship feels about the servants . . . fraternizing." Nolan bent to pick up a forgotten piece of rope coiled on the dirt floor and returned it to its peg. "Sneaking a few moments to talk each day is risky enough."

"Ach, I'm sure there are many below-the-stairs romances going on under his lordship's nose," Bert said.

"Well, I'd never compromise Hannah that way. Nor bring shame to my mother." When Nolan and Hannah left Stainsby Hall, it would be on their own terms, not because the heartless earl had sacked them.

Bert's expression softened. "One of these days you'll learn to put your own needs ahead of your mother's."

"Nothing's more important than Mum. She's all the family I've got." Nolan itched to tell Bert that he'd soon be able to rescue his mother from this life of drudgery, but he owed it to Hannah to hear the news first.

"You're not still fretting over your lack of a father, are you? Because you're a fine man in your own right." Bert crossed his arms over his large chest, pulling the material tight on his muscled arms. "Finding out who sired you canna change that."

The familiar ache that resided deep within Nolan reared its ugly head, fueling a rush of insecurity. Why couldn't Bert understand Nolan's need to learn the identity of his father? Sometimes he felt he'd never have peace until he knew where he came from. But Nolan didn't intend to rehash that subject again. "You needn't worry, Bert. I've put the issue to rest."

For now.

Three years ago, Nolan had been prepared to leave Stainsby to seek the answer of his paternity, one his mother refused to disclose, but Hannah had begged him not to leave. Only his love for her had kept him from going. But one day, when the timing was right, he intended to travel to the town of his birth and solve the mystery of his parentage, no matter what the outcome.

A sound in the distance made Nolan's pulse sprint. Eagerly, he scanned the expanse of lawn and spotted Hannah starting across the yard toward the chicken coop.

A slow grin stretched Nolan's lips as he clapped Bert on the back. "If you'll excuse me, my friend, there's something I need to do before I get back to work."

With a few minutes to spare after the midday meal, Hannah strolled across the grass, hoping the sunshine and the gentle afternoon breeze would lift the worry from her soul. She ducked around the side of the chicken coop and took a seat on a wooden crate beneath the welcoming branches of the stately elm.

For a moment, she looked over at the lush Stainsby gardens with the majestic reflecting pond at its center and wished she could take refuge there among the fragrant spring flowers. But servants weren't allowed to linger in the gardens in case the master or one of his guests wished to partake of its loveliness. Perhaps one day she'd have a garden of her own, where she could sit and admire the blossoms whenever she wished.

Hannah's thoughts turned from daydreams of the future to the unsettling news contained in her mother's latest letter. The knot in her chest tightened as she removed the envelope from her starched white apron and drew out the pages she'd all but memorized. She skipped the beginning of the correspondence, which contained the usual description of life on her stepfather's farm, and skimmed to the part where her mother mentioned Molly.

Now that your sister is of marriageable age, Robert has picked a suitable husband for her. Mr. Elliott lost his wife last year and needs someone to help with his children and the farm. Robert is most pleased to join with his neighbor to the south, since the combined acreage will be of benefit to both. Their betrothal will be announced very soon.

Hannah's fingers tightened, crumpling the pages. It was bad enough to pledge Molly in marriage, but did it have to be to Mr. Elliott? Hannah had met the man briefly on her last visit to the farm. The image of a man with a straggly beard, a sweat-stained shirt that barely covered a large belly, and teeth blackened from tobacco came to mind. Worse than the man's appalling personal habits was the fact that he had to be approaching forty.

Just as Hannah feared, Molly had become a bargaining tool for her stepfather, sold to the highest bidder. How could her mother allow such an atrocity?

Are you really surprised? a bitter inner voice taunted. *Did she not ship you off into servitude around the same age?*

But back then, her mother had been desperate—widowed, penniless, and turned out of their home. She wasn't desperate now. She was the wife of Robert Fielding, farmer of over two hundred acres. This had to be *his* idea—that dreadful man who always put his own welfare above all else. Now he would condemn Molly to a loveless marriage with a man who would likely view her as his property. Much like how Mr. Fielding treated Mum.

Hannah lowered her face into her hands. *Please, God, help me to save Molly from such a terrible fate.*

Nolan rounded the side of the henhouse and stopped cold. The sight of Hannah seated on a chicken crate with her head in her hands had all thoughts of his happy news flying from his mind. Was she praying or crying? Either way, she seemed far from her usual cheery self.

"Hannah? What's wrong?"

She raised misty eyes to his and blinked several times. "Nolan. I didn't hear you."

"No wonder. You seem rather preoccupied." He pulled a handkerchief from his trousers and passed it to her.

She dabbed the white square of cotton to the corners of her eyes. Loose strands of blonde silk escaped her cap and clung to her damp cheek.

Tension coiled in Nolan's stomach as he crouched in front of her. "It's not that Bellows character, is it? If he's bothering you again—"

"It's nothing like that, I promise."

A small measure of comfort eased the tension in his muscles. Nolan would be glad when he could claim Hannah as his wife, so all the eligible men, especially a certain shady footman, would leave her alone.

Hannah sniffed and returned the handkerchief to him, then twisted her hands in her lap, offering no explanation for her tears.

"If it's not Bellows, then why are you crying?"

She lifted a letter from her lap. "It's Molly."

"What about her?" Hannah tended to worry overmuch about her younger sister, but not usually to the point of tears. "She's not ill, is she?"

"No. It's my stepfather. He's arranged a marriage for her and is set to announce the betrothal very soon."

Nolan frowned. "What is he thinking? Molly's too young for marriage."

"Mr. Fielding doesn't seem to care." Hannah slid the letter into the pocket of her apron. "I wish Mum would let her come here with me. At least then she could have a decent life, without having to look after some old farmer and his brood." Her bottom lip trembled.

The need to comfort Hannah overcame the need for propriety. Nolan rose, tugged her to her feet, and with a quick glance around to make sure they weren't being watched, he gathered her to his chest. She laid her cheek against his shoulder with a sigh.

His arms tightened around her, a fierce protectiveness rising up through him. How he wanted to promise her the world. Yet all he could offer was life as a farmer's wife. He hoped it would be enough.

He rubbed her back in a soothing manner, inhaling the

scent of fresh bread and apples that always seemed to sur-round her. "We'll find a way to help Molly. I promise. As soon as—"

"I know. As soon as we leave here." She sniffed again, then her head snapped up. "Oh, I haven't even asked how it went with Mr. Simpson."

Despite Hannah's distress, Nolan couldn't withhold a giddy grin. "He accepted my offer. The farm will be mine at the end of the month."

"Oh, Nolan. That's wonderful. I'm so proud of you." She squeezed him in a tight hug, then pulled away, a soft hue color-ing her cheeks.

The admiration shining on her face humbled him. How had he ever earned the affections of such an incredible woman? He'd wanted to wait until a more opportune moment to propose, but maybe now was the perfect time. He turned her hand to press a kiss into her palm. A soft gasp escaped her lips, and her eyes widened.

Have you kissed the girl yet? Bert's question echoed through his brain as Nolan's gaze focused on her mouth. He knew he should resist, but heaven help him, it was way past time. His heart beat double time in his chest. He could almost imagine the sweet taste of her lips. His pulse thundered as he lowered his head toward her.

The swish of approaching footsteps in the grass beyond the henhouse snapped him to attention. Quickly, he released Han-nah and took a step away. Surely the earl wouldn't come looking for him here.

"Nolan! Are you there?" His friend Mickey's urgent call echoed across the open air.

Relief trickled through Nolan. At least he needn't worry that Mickey would fuel the servant gossip mill. His friend and fellow stable hand abhorred gossip as much as Nolan. He stepped out into the open. "Here I am. What is it?"

Mickey Gilbert turned and jogged over, his linen shirtsleeves flapping in the breeze. Instead of his usual jovial grin, a frown creased his brow. "I'm sorry, Nolan. It's your mother."

The air in Nolan's lungs thinned. "What about her?"

"She collapsed in the kitchen. They've taken her to her room and sent for the doctor." Mickey's eyes filled with sympathy. "You'd best hurry. She's asking to see you."

CHAPTER

2

Taking the steps two at a time, Nolan rushed up the narrow back staircase to the third-floor servants' quarters, concern tumbling through his brain. He'd spoken with his mother just yesterday, and she hadn't seemed ill. Though now that he recalled, she *had* looked pale, but he'd put it down to her lingering illness.

Yet to collapse like that, her health must have taken a sudden turn for the worse . . . unless she'd been hiding her infirmity for fear of losing her job. In all likelihood, she'd been pushing herself too hard, not letting her body fully heal from the constant bouts of bronchitis that had plagued her all winter.

Nolan silently gave thanks for the good news he could now share with her. That her days of slaving for the unfeeling Lord Stainsby would soon be over. That she could live with Nolan and Hannah, filling her time with pursuits that brought her pleasure. Planting flowers, reading, sleeping whenever it pleased her to do so, and looking after the grandchildren he and Hannah would give her. With her health restored, they would all live together as a loving family.

Nolan strode down the dank corridor to the very last room. Outside his mother's door, he paused to contain his emotions, pushing back the waves of worry. He had to be strong—for her sake, if nothing else. After two deep breaths, he knocked on the door and stepped inside.

Heavy drapes had been pulled to cover the windows, leaving the room shrouded in darkness, save for the flickering candle by the bed. Nolan squinted to find his mother under the patchwork quilt. The sight of her frailty hit him as hard as a stallion's kick.

A desperate prayer whispered through his mind. *Dear God, I know I've been remiss at conversing with you lately, but I'm asking you now to please heal my mother. Help her withstand this illness and regain her health.*

She opened her eyes and gave a weak smile. "Nolan. Thank goodness you've come."

"I'm here, Mum." He moved to the side of her bed and took her hand in his.

"There are some things I need to tell you whilst I still can."

"You mustn't talk like that." He dragged a chair over to the bed and sat down, attempting to ignore the musty odor that permeated the room. "Now that the winter's over, you'll soon be feeling better. In fact, I have some news that should help your recovery." He dredged up a smile for her benefit. "Remember the farm I told you about?"

Surprise and what might have been regret flickered in her eyes. "I remember."

"I met with Mr. Simpson today and made arrangements to purchase it. In a few weeks, you'll have a place of your own where you can rest and recover your strength. And when you're feeling better, you can plant a vegetable garden. I know how much you've missed that—"

"Nolan, please. I need you to listen." Bony fingers gripped his like a hawk's talons.

The urgency in her tone raised the hair on the back of his

neck. "All right, Mum. I'm listening." He struggled to gain a foothold over his emotions. He needed to be his mother's strength in her time of need, as she'd always been for him.

With a tender look, she smoothed the hair from his forehead as though he were still a boy. "Though I may not have birthed you, Nolan, you are my son in every way that matters. I love you more than anything in this world. I hope you know that." Two tears slid down her pale skin.

His throat threatened to close. Why did this sound like she was saying good-bye? "I love you too, Mum," he said hoarsely. "More than my own life."

"I know you do. But there's much I need to explain. I only hope you can forgive me when I tell you everything." The anguish in her eyes took Nolan's breath away.

"It's all right, Mum." He reached out to take both her cold hands in his, her skin as thin as parchment.

"I should have told you the truth long ago. Now there's no time to cushion the blow." Her voice quavered. "I need to tell you about your father."

Nolan's mouth fell open. Over the years, Mum had rarely spoken about her sister, who'd died giving birth to Nolan. The few times he'd dared to ask about his father, Mum had told him she didn't know who his father was. And because the subject had always seemed to trouble her, Nolan had left it alone, figuring that when the time was right, he'd search for answers on his own.

"Before my sister died, Mary got to hold you for a few precious moments. She made me promise to look after you but never to disclose the identity of your father." Another tear followed a path down her cheek. "Though I struggled with that promise, I've kept it to the best of my ability."

The blood leached from Nolan's brain, scrambling the thoughts in his head. "I-I don't understand."

"As time went on, I didn't know how to tell you. Or if I had the right."

A dark suspicion took shape, one that had lingered in the back of his mind all these years. Was he the illegitimate offspring of a shameful union? Worse yet, could his father be a criminal? Held in jail these last two decades? Chills raced up and down his spine. His world and everything he knew about it was unraveling before his eyes. He swallowed the bile in his throat. "Just tell me, Mum. Who is my father?"

Her gaze slid to the quilt, and a look of utter misery washed her pale features. She licked her dry, cracked lips, not meeting his eyes. "He is a nobleman. Your mother was a maid in his family's employ. Theirs was a forbidden love, and when Mary found herself with child, your father married her in secret, against the wishes of his family."

Nolan struggled to focus. His parents had been married at least, which lifted the burden of illegitimacy from him. But how had Mary ended up giving birth at her sister's home without her husband? And what made her want to hide his identity?

"Why didn't my father claim me when she died?" he demanded. "Did he not wish to raise his son?"

Her hands gripped the blankets. "There was an estrangement. Your grandparents did not approve of the union and refused to accept—" She clamped her mouth shut and shook her head.

Nolan waited while she seemed to wrestle with herself. What was she so afraid of?

A sharp knock broke the uncomfortable silence.

"Mrs. Price? It's Dr. Hutton." The door opened and the rumpled, gray-haired physician entered.

The lines on his mother's forehead eased as though relieved

at the interruption. "Thank you for coming, Doctor. You remember my son, Nolan?

"Yes. Hello, Nolan." The man set his leather bag on the dresser near the bed. "If you'll excuse us for a minute, I need to examine your mother." His features looked pinched as if he didn't expect a good outcome.

"Of course. I'll go down and see to your horse." Nolan rose from the rickety chair and gave his mother a pointed look. "We'll continue our talk later."

Outside in the courtyard, Nolan untied the reins of the doctor's dapple gray, led him into the barn, and went to fetch fresh water. As he performed his tasks, Nolan struggled to come to grips with the enormity of what his mother had told him, all the while fighting to quell the anger that brewed beneath his skin.

All the assumptions he'd made about his lowly heritage had been wrong. It appeared noble blood ran through his veins. Now it remained to be seen if Mum would disclose the name of his father, and if so, what would that mean for Nolan? Would he go in search of him?

Remnants of his fondest boyhood wish flickered to life. Nolan used to dream that one day his father would come to find him and sweep him up in a boisterous embrace, regaling him with tales of bold adventure that had kept him away these many years. Then his father would take Nolan and his mother away from their lives of servitude to abide with him in familial bliss at long last.

Could any part of this long-held dream come true?

Nolan's boot squished beneath him, and a foul odor met his nose. He bit back an oath and found a stick to scrape the offending dung from his sole.

Reality returned with an equally sickening thud at the mere thought of confronting a nobleman with news that Nolan was his son. Perhaps his father was dead. Surely that would explain why he'd never attempted to contact Nolan, never reached out to establish a bond.

Still, from the little Nolan knew about the rules of succession in the noble ranks, if he were the true son of a titled man, he could be wealthy in his own right.

The horse neighed and tossed his head against Nolan's shoulder.

"You're right, boy. What would I do with a title and wealth?" The thought of the chaos involved in attempting to prove such a claim made Nolan cringe. Better to leave well enough alone and continue on the path he'd chosen for his life. Forget he even had a father.

He closed his eyes against the rush of resentment that bubbled just under the surface. Against the sense of betrayal that his mother had lied to him all this time. Why hadn't she told him the truth years ago? What difference could it have possibly made?

He inhaled and blew out a long breath. Knowing his mother to be an upstanding Christian woman, there had to be a good explanation for her actions, and until he'd heard the whole story, he would give her the benefit of the doubt, without judgment.

The crunch of carriage wheels over gravel penetrated the haze in Nolan's brain. Lord Stainsby, who'd been out most of the day, must have returned. Nolan would need to see to the horses. He tugged his cap into place as he rushed through the open stable doors. The earl's carriage came to a halt in front of him, the horses snorting in welcome.

Nolan pushed back his shoulders and clasped his hands behind him as he waited for the coachman to jump down and open the carriage door.

Seconds later, the earl emerged.

For a man in his forties, his lordship remained in excellent physical condition. Tall, lean, and vital—most likely a result of his love of the outdoors. Dressed in a black greatcoat and top hat, the master created a formidable picture.

Nerves skittered in Nolan's stomach as he gathered his courage. As much as he disliked his employer, he needed to put his feelings aside—for his mother's sake. Her health had to take precedence over everything else right now.

"Excuse me, my lord."

"What is it?" The earl's dark brows shot together in undisguised annoyance, apparently aggrieved at being bothered by a stable hand.

Nolan swallowed his impatience. "My mother, Mrs. Price, is ill again. She collapsed and was taken to bed."

His lordship muttered an oath beneath his breath and took a few strides away.

"The doctor is with her now," Nolan called after him. "But she may need to go into Derby to the infirmary."

The earl careened to a halt and turned to stare at him with incredulity. "And you expect me to pay her medical bills, is that it?"

"Surely as your head housekeeper—"

"My head housekeeper," he snapped, "has been woefully negligent in her duties these past months. She's lucky I haven't replaced her with someone younger and healthier." His handsome features twisted into something ugly.

Only concern for his mother kept Nolan's temper from spilling forth. Biting back the retort that burned on his tongue, he pulled himself into the proper servant's stance but fixed hot eyes on his employer. "I'm sorry to have bothered your lordship."

"Yes, well, make sure the horses are well watered." He shot an irritated look at Nolan before striding off.

It took all Nolan's restraint to remain still, but once Lord Stainsby disappeared into the house, he stalked across the lawn to the servants' entry. Hatred grew with every step. His mother gave every ounce of her energy to ensure the smooth running of the earl's estate. And what thanks did she get for her years of loyalty?

Nothing. No words of compassion. No offer of assistance.

Nolan flung the rear door open and entered the mansion. He would find out what the doctor had to say, and if his mother needed to go to the infirmary, Nolan would pay for it himself.

Even if it meant he would have to forfeit his farm to do so.

CHAPTER
3

Edward Fairchild swallowed a last sip of wine, patted the linen napkin to his mouth, and laid it over the china plate in front of him. Seated with proper posture on the cushioned chair, he stared out over the expanse of table that stretched the full length of the ornate dining room.

Eighteen feet of table with only one place setting at the end.

Edward's gaze moved up the gilded walls to the decorative swirls on the plaster ceiling. All this luxury—a twenty-room estate with a full complement of staff—for a sole inhabitant.

He exhaled loudly. Maybe the second glass of wine tonight was making him melancholy. For once, he actually missed the presence of his daughters. Yet whenever Evelyn and Victoria came to visit, Edward couldn't wait for them to leave to return to his solitude.

He scowled as thoughts of Evelyn and her infantile husband brought to mind the letter he'd received yesterday from his London solicitor. Its contents had only served to reinforce Edward's belief that Evelyn had made a colossal mistake marrying Orville, solely—he was certain—because Orville was now the heir presumptive to the Fairchild holdings. He'd already proven completely unreliable, racking up large amounts of debt from his gambling habit, as well as from indulging his outlandishly expensive taste in horses and fine brandy. He hadn't even bothered to wait for Edward's demise to start undermining the family fortune. What would become of the Fairchild legacy under Orville's incompetent leadership?

Edward pulled the letter from his pocket and reread Mr. Grayson's unsettling message.

Lord Stainsby,

I'm writing to apprise you of a recent visit paid to me at our London office by your son-in-law and heir, supposedly at your behest. Forgive my mistrust, sir, but I did not believe his claim for a moment. My suspicions were confirmed when Mr. Fairchild asked me for a financial reckoning of all the Fairchild holdings, with particular interest in Stainsby Hall and the surrounding property. When I declined to comply with his request, stating that unless I had your express authority to divulge such information I could not do so, young Fairchild then asked whether the Stainsby lands could be sold off in the event that the future earl needed an infusion of cash. I managed to put him off with a slew of legal jargon; however, I thought you should be aware of his intentions toward your family property. Given his propensity for gambling, I should imagine you would find this information troubling to say the least.

Troubling? Edward snorted. An understatement if ever there was one. The idea that everything he'd sacrificed in order to keep the Fairchild earldom intact could be squandered away by Evelyn's sniveling husband had Edward fisting his hands in helpless frustration.

A footman approached the table. "Will there be anything else, my lord? Dessert perhaps?"

"Not tonight."

"Very good, sir." The man jumped into action to remove the covered food dishes.

The candles in the center of the table flickered with his movements.

Still ruminating over Orville's nefarious intentions, Edward folded the letter and returned it to his pocket. If only cousin Hugh hadn't fallen victim to a hunting accident, they wouldn't be in this mess. Hugh Fairchild had been a perfectly acceptable heir, whereas Hugh's spoiled son was anything but.

Edward absently rubbed the finger that had once borne his wedding band. After ten years being a widower, the indent had long since faded, as had the desire to ever repeat his wedded folly. But recently, he found his certitude wavering, and his decision to remain single weighed on his conscience. If he'd done the dutiful thing and found another wife to give him a son, this whole situation might have been avoided. True, his marriage to Penelope had been a disaster, but did a bad experience give him the right to shirk his obligation to ensure the family title went to a responsible heir?

Even now, at the age of forty-two, the possibility still existed that Edward could marry and conceive a son. But there was no guarantee of begetting a male child. What if he married another woman who turned out to be as vain and selfish as Penelope? One who gave him only more daughters to worry about?

A shiver went through him. No, he'd be wiser to spend his energy on managing the present heir, on trying to groom Orville for his future duties. If Edward impressed upon him the significance of the family history, the importance of the earldom, and the necessity to keep the Stainsby property in the family, surely he could make Orville understand the magnitude of the responsibility he would carry.

Perhaps the time had come for Edward to move back to his London house and keep a closer eye on his son-in-law. Renew acquaintances with some old friends and business associates who could help mentor Orville. The weather had turned nice at last after a long, dreary winter. The hustle and bustle of London might be just the thing to change Edward's bleak outlook—at least until he grew bored of the endless social engagements.

Yes, he'd make the arrangements tomorrow.

Slightly cheered by his decision, Edward pushed his chair back, nodding to another footman who hovered nearby. "I'll have brandy in my study now."

"Very good, my lord." The young man bowed and hurried to uncap the decanter as soon as Edward stepped away from the table.

With a purposeful stride, Edward exited into the main hallway. Halfway to his study, he became aware of footsteps behind him—footsteps that were decidedly feminine, and not the staid footfall of his butler, Dobson, who usually lurked about the halls.

"Excuse me, my lord."

Edward pushed back a wave of annoyance and turned to see one of his senior housemaids come to a halt, her breathing ragged as though she'd been running a race.

"What is it, Miss Hatterley?" Edward tugged the sleeve of his dinner jacket in place.

"I'm sorry to bother your lordship." The normally composed woman appeared flustered. "As you know, Mrs. Price is very ill."

"So I understand." Impatience crawled over his skin. The

blasted woman was always under the weather. If she could not perform her duties, he would have to consider someone else for the head housekeeper position.

"Mrs. Price has requested to speak with you, my lord. In her bedchamber, since she's too weak to make it downstairs." Miss Hatterley clasped her thin hands together.

Edward frowned. "This is highly unusual. Did she indicate the reason?"

"No, sir. But from all accounts, she's not expected to last much longer. Maybe she wishes to make arrangements . . ."

Edward raised a brow. "It's that serious then?"

"It is, my lord."

Guilt pinched like an uncomfortable cravat. He hadn't realized the woman's illness was so severe. Edward huffed out a sigh. His staff might accuse him of being a hard taskmaster, but to deny his housekeeper's dying request—well, even he couldn't be that unfeeling. His brandy would have to wait. "Fine. Lead the way."

After climbing to the third story, where he hadn't set foot since childhood, Edward followed Miss Hatterley down the corridor.

She knocked once on the last door and opened it, nodding for Edward to enter.

The stench of the room enveloped him the moment he crossed the threshold. He paused until his senses adjusted to the onslaught, aware of the soft click of the door behind him. His nerves jumped as though a guard had just locked him in a jail cell.

With dread roiling in his stomach, he approached the bed. The barely recognizable form of his housekeeper stared back at him.

"Thank you for coming, my lord," she whispered.

Edward shifted, an unwelcome sensation of guilt seeping through his system. How had he failed to notice this woman's dire condition? "I'm sorry to hear of your indisposition, Mrs. Price. What can I do for you?"

The pale eyes, sunken in a gaunt face, shone with what looked like fear. Emaciated hands clutched the faded quilt. "You may wish to sit down for this, my lord. I expect what I have to say will come as quite a shock."

Nolan seethed with frustration as he made his way to his mother's bedchamber at last. His earlier attempt to see the doctor had been thwarted by an emergency with a lame horse that needed new shoes. And then, once he and Bert had taken care of the animal, Mr. Dobson had asked for his assistance moving some furniture. Now he'd sacrificed his dinner to finally get to speak with the doctor, a fact his stomach seemed determined to scold him for. At least he knew Dr. Hutton hadn't left, since his horse was still safely stowed in the barn.

Halfway down the long corridor that led to his mother's room, he spied the man seated on a chair, medical bag in hand. He rose as he spotted Nolan.

"Mr. Price. I'm glad you're here." The doctor's face was grim.

"How is she?"

The flame in the wall sconce flickered, casting eerie shadows over the floor.

Dr. Hutton shook his head. "I wish I had better news. It appears your mother has developed pneumonia."

Alarm shot through Nolan's system. Pneumonia was decidedly worse than bronchitis. "What can you do for her?"

"I'm afraid there's not much anyone *can* do . . . except pray." He patted Nolan's arm, his words weighted with sadness.

Pray? This was the man's best medical advice? "We must get her to the infirmary. I'll ask his lordship for use of—"

"It won't do any good, son. Her lungs and heart are too weak to withstand the journey." Sympathy swamped the older man's features. "I'm sorry to say it's only a matter of time. You may wish to call a clergyman, if your mother is so inclined. It might bring her comfort in her final hours."

An invading coldness seeped through Nolan's chest, spreading outward until his whole body seemed encased in ice. His mother was dying? How could this be possible?

"I'll be in the parlor if you need me." The doctor shot a glance down the hall. "You may wish to wait before you go in. Your mother has a visitor."

As soon as Dr. Hutton disappeared, Nolan sagged against the stone wall. Tears burned his eyes, blurring his vision. His mother couldn't die. He wouldn't allow it. He gulped in a few breaths, determination giving him purpose. They'd seek another opinion, a specialist perhaps. He'd do whatever it took, whatever it cost, to save his mother's life.

As he approached the room, a loud male voice breached the heavy wooden door. What on earth was Lord Stainsby doing up here? Had he doubted Nolan's claim about his mother's health and come to see for himself?

Harsh anger laced the earl's words, and though Nolan couldn't make out what he was saying, the man was obviously berating her. Pressure built in Nolan's chest. How dare he yell at an incapacitated woman? Without knocking, Nolan pushed open the door and strode inside. "What is going on here?"

Lord Stainsby whipped around, his features pinched, eyes hard. He held himself as rigid as the statues in his garden, yet outrage quivered in the air around him. In his hand, he clenched the Bible that belonged to Nolan's mother.

"Surely you're not reprimanding my mother. Can you not see how ill she is?"

"It's all right, Nolan." His mother's eyes appeared huge in her gaunt face, darting from the earl and back to him.

"No, it is not. I won't allow him to bully you." Nolan glared at the man, for once not intimidated by his position, not even caring if he got sacked.

The earl's nostrils flared. "You have no idea what you've interrupted."

"I don't care. Leave us now. My mother needs peace and quiet."

A muscle in the earl's jaw flexed. He leveled a long look at Nolan and then turned to address his mother. "Very well. But we will talk again." He set the book on the nightstand and marched from the room.

Nolan waited until the door closed, and then crossed to the bed. With extreme willpower, he pushed down the toxic swirl of emotions rioting through him. His mother needed calmness and strength, and that's what he would give her.

She lay against the pillows, deathly still, all the energy drained from her.

"Mum, I want to take you to the infirmary in Derby. They'll have better medicines there. Ones that can cure—"

She shook her head. "There's nothing to be done. I've suspected for a while now that my health had gotten worse, but I didn't want to burden you." She gave a weak smile and lifted her hand.

He caught it between both of his and squeezed as though he could infuse her with his own vitality.

"All I've ever wanted is your happiness," she whispered through blue-tinged lips. "Promise me you'll go on with your plans. Buy your farm and marry Hannah. Live a good life."

His throat seized, rendering him mute. How could she just give up like this? Why wouldn't she fight to stay alive?

She gripped his fingers. "I need to tell you why his lordship was here."

"I don't care why. He had no business yelling like that—"

"Nolan." The authority in her voice silenced him.

Icy chills invaded his heart. He knew without a doubt he did not want to hear what was to come.

She waited until his gaze met hers. "Nolan, Lord Stainsby is your father."

CHAPTER 4

Hannah wiped the last trace of moisture from the work surfaces with a rough towel. All the chores were done for the moment, yet she couldn't bring herself to leave the kitchen. Truth be told, she was waiting for Nolan to come down from his mother's room.

Her heart squeezed at the anguish he must be facing. Word had spread throughout the house that Mrs. Price was dying, and Hannah knew her demise would devastate Nolan. She pushed the stray wisps of hair off her damp forehead. How she wished she could do something to ease his pain.

"You're still here? I thought you'd be done by now." Mrs. Edna Bridges shuffled into the kitchen. Without her apron and cap, she appeared more like a grandmother than a cook.

Warmth curled through Hannah at the sight of her. Edna had certainly been both a mother and grandmother to her. Her dearest champion since Hannah's first days at Stainsby.

"You're supposed to be resting," she scolded the older woman.

Edna took out the small copper kettle, placed it on the range, and stoked the fire. "My mind is stewing over things I can't control."

Hannah hung the towel on a hook near the oven to dry. "I know. I'm trying to keep busy so I don't worry about Nolan and his mother." She swooped in to take the kettle from Edna. "Let me do that. You sit and put your feet up for a few minutes."

Edna nodded, and with a long sigh, pulled out a chair at the table.

A wave of sympathy hit Hannah as she watched the older woman sag onto her seat. Nolan might be losing his mother, but Edna was losing her best friend. Elizabeth Price had touched many lives during her time here.

"Would you like me to help you upstairs?" Hannah asked softly. "To see Mrs. Price?"

Edna pulled a square of cotton from her pocket and dabbed her moist eyes. "You're a good child. Always thinking of everyone else." She patted Hannah's arm. "I'd like that very much."

Hannah moved to take the kettle off the heat. "We'll have our tea later."

The older woman leaned heavily on Hannah as the pair climbed the back staircase with slow and steady steps. On the second level, they stopped for a rest.

Edna mopped her brow with the handkerchief. "These old knees can't take the stairs anymore." She huffed and puffed for a few minutes until she motioned for Hannah to help her continue. "Good thing my quarters are off the kitchen. I'd never make it to bed at night."

As they ascended, Hannah strained her ears for any approaching footsteps, hoping she might see Nolan on his way down. When they finally made it to the top story, Hannah led Edna to a bench before tackling the long hallway.

"You rest here a moment. I'll go and see if Mrs. Price is alone." Edna nodded and waved her off, still struggling for air. As Hannah made her way down the long corridor, her shoes made little noise on the carpeted floor. She paused outside Elizabeth's door, listening for any voices inside. All appeared quiet. She'd raised her fist to knock when the door burst open before her.

Nolan stopped short of barreling into her. He said not a word, but stared wide-eyed, like someone who'd just received a terrible shock.

Hannah's hand flew to her throat. Surely his mother hadn't passed away? "Nolan. What's happened?"

He blinked and focused on her, as if suddenly realizing her presence. His hands curled into fists at his side. The veins stood out in his neck.

Hannah recoiled as comprehension seeped through her. He wasn't sad—he was filled with *rage*.

In all the years she'd known him, Hannah had never seen Nolan in such a state.

He didn't answer her, merely shook his head and pushed by her, boots pounding the floor in his haste.

Hannah bit down on her bottom lip to keep from calling after him. What could possibly have made him so angry?

She turned back to the door of the bedroom and peered inside. Mrs. Price held a fist to her mouth, silent tears coursing down her cheeks. She didn't even notice Hannah in the doorway.

For a moment, Hannah wavered on what to do. Then with grim determination, she headed back to where she'd left Edna. If anyone could comfort the distraught woman, it would be her best friend.

Hours later, Hannah slipped through the silent night, across the damp grass that separated the barn from the main house. The light of her lantern bobbed with each step until she reached the stable entrance. Once inside, she paused to allow her eyes to adjust to the dim interior and to make sure no one lurked in the darkness. The powerful scent of manure and hay filled her nostrils.

Her heart beat hard against her ribs. Whether Nolan realized it or not, he needed her, and if he wouldn't come to her, she had no choice but to seek him out.

On noiseless feet, she moved toward Nolan's quarters at the back of the stable. A thin beam of light shone under the crack in his door. Hannah hung her lantern on a nail by the last stall and pressed a palm to her stomach to squelch the butterflies fluttering there.

Please, Lord, let Nolan allow me to help him through this troubled time. Give me words of wisdom to comfort him and ease his pain.

After one more deep breath, she knocked lightly on his door.

"Go away, Mickey. I'm in no mood to talk." Nolan's deep voice pierced the silence of the barn.

Hannah licked her dry lips. With determination, she rapped again.

Footsteps clattered across the floor and the door flung open.

"I told you—" Nolan stopped dead, his mouth agape. He wore trousers and an unbuttoned shirt, suspenders hanging loosely at his sides. His eyes brightened for a brief second, replaced almost instantly with a deep frown. "Hannah. You shouldn't be here. 'Tisn't proper."

Proper or not, Hannah refused to be deterred. But she averted her gaze from his hastily donned shirt, still open at the chest, and brushed by him into the small room. A candle flickered wildly on its stand. Wrinkled blankets on the cot told her Nolan had been lying there moments ago. "I need to speak with you."

Nolan raked a hand through his tousled hair, releasing dark

curls that sprang across his forehead. "It's too great a risk. If anyone sees you in here, your reputation will be ruined."

"This is too important to worry about such trivialities." She crossed her arms and waited.

Nolan blew out an exasperated breath, then grabbed his worn jacket from a hook. "If you must talk, we'll do it outdoors where it won't be as scandalous to be discovered." He eyed the bed with a meaningful glare.

Hannah was grateful for the faint light to hide the blush on her cheeks. "Very well."

Nolan took her by the hand and led her out the back door. "We can sit out here."

The moonlight provided enough illumination to see each other clearly as they took a seat on the rough wooden bench. Hannah pulled her shawl more firmly around her shoulders. In the spring chill, goosebumps rose on her arms.

"Now, tell me what's so important that you came out in the middle of the night? It's not more news about Molly, is it?"

The gentleness of Nolan's tone brought a lump to her throat. He thought she had some problem of her own—not even considering that his pain would keep her awake.

"I'm worried about you. Something is wrong—more than your mother's illness, I mean. Won't you tell me what it is?"

His eyes turned dark. His mouth tightened into a grim line.

Fearing he would turn her away, she forged on. "Nolan, if we are to share a future, you must learn to trust me. To confide in me when you have a problem. Wouldn't you want me to do the same?"

A blast of air escaped him. "Yes, of course I want to share your troubles."

"Then allow me to do the same for you." She laid a tentative hand on the sleeve of his thin jacket. Even through the material, the heat of his skin warmed her palm.

He hesitated for a moment as though weighing his options. "If I tell you, you mustn't breathe a word of it to anyone. Not even Edna."

"I swear it." Hannah kept no secrets from Edna, but for Nolan she would.

He grasped one of her hands in his. The rough calluses on his thumb caressed her skin like a kiss. "My mother gave me some distressing news. I haven't even had time to determine the meaning of it yet." He paused to look directly into her eyes and lowered his voice. "She told me that Lord Stainsby is my father."

Hannah's free hand flew to her mouth, but it couldn't hide her gasp. "Oh, Nolan. How is that possible?" Tears welled as she tried to grasp the enormity of what he was telling her. No wonder he'd been so distraught. "Surely he hasn't known all along, has he?"

"No. Apparently he's as shocked and angry as I am." Nolan leaned his arms on his knees, head bent.

"Why would your mother keep this secret so long?"

He sighed. "That's what I've been trying to figure out. Perhaps she'd planned to tell him someday, but kept putting it off—until the illness forced her hand." He got to his feet and paced in front of the bench. "I've always longed to know the identity of my father, but I never dreamed . . ."

"That you were the illegitimate son of a nobleman?" Hannah asked softly.

His head jerked up. "I'm not illegitimate, Hannah. I don't know all the details, but I do know that my parents eloped before I was born."

Nolan was the *legitimate* son of an earl?

Hannah's heart seized as the terrible truth seeped into her

40

consciousness. Their plan to marry had long been an understanding between them, but now her vision for the future evaporated, much like the filmy mist that hung over the fields would dissipate in the morning light.

She pushed to her feet, tears blooming beneath her lids. Lord Stainsby would never allow his son to marry a mere kitchen maid. Not if Nolan was proclaimed the Fairchild heir.

Nolan jumped to her side, concern creasing his brow. "The news is shocking, but it's not as bad as all that." He pulled her into his arms and laid his chin on her head.

For a moment, she allowed the warmth of his body to ease her trembling. She clung to him as though she'd never let go and breathed in the outdoor scent of him—horse and hay and lye soap.

Oh, God, how could she bear to lose him? A sob hiccupped through her body.

Nolan kissed her forehead and pulled her gently away from him. "Is it so terrible to love the son of an earl?"

His amused tone meant to tease, but she was in no state of mind for jests.

"You do love me, don't you, Hannah?" The vulnerability in his eyes tore at her.

"Aye. More than anything."

Relief spilled over his features. "Then you've nothing to worry about. Because I love you even more."

He bent his head toward her, but she pressed a hand to his chest. "Don't you see, Nolan? His lordship will never allow us to be together. If he claims you as his heir, which I'm certain he must, you'll be expected to marry within your rank." Her voice faltered. "The son of an earl could never marry a servant."

Nolan's features darkened and his dark brows drew together. He gripped her arms with bands of steel. "I don't care what the earl says. I love you, Hannah, and I intend to marry you. Nothing will change that. Trust me."

Oh, how she longed to believe those beautiful words. Two large tears escaped her lashes to trickle down her cheek.

"If I cannot make him understand, then we will leave this place. I will not lose you, Hannah."

He pulled her to him, and his mouth captured hers in a storm of passion.

Her heart sprinted like a rabbit racing over the meadows. How bittersweet that he'd found the courage to kiss her at last—now that he would surely have to leave her. With a low moan, she wrapped her arms around him, relishing the taste of his lips, the strength of his arms, the scent of his skin. In a reaction born of sheer desperation, she returned his kisses, measure for measure.

Tonight she would accept as much of his love as he gave, for tomorrow everything would change.

CHAPTER 5

After a sleepless night, Nolan rose before dawn and made his way to the main house. Dr. Hutton had insisted Nolan try to get some rest, saying he would need his strength for the vigil to come, promising to send for him if his mother's condition worsened. After all the shocking discoveries that day, Nolan should have realized that sleep would be impossible. His thoughts had chased round and round his brain until he thought he'd go crazy. If not for the few stolen moments with Hannah, he might have.

The hours of soul-searching, however, had made one thing perfectly clear—no matter what lies his mother had told, no matter what truths she had withheld, it could never outweigh all she'd done for him. From the moment of his birth, her sole purpose had been to give him the best life possible. Whatever her reasons for keeping the knowledge of his paternity a secret, she must have believed it to be in his best interest. He owed her his loyalty and his love. And he would do everything in his power to give her comfort in her time of need.

Yet, deep down, his whole being balked at the knowledge that his mother's days were numbered and that only a miracle could restore her to health. Would God deem them worthy of bestowing such favor? Though Nolan had been raised with his mother's staunch faith, his own belief now faltered like a seed that had never taken root.

Fatigue weighted each step as he trudged up the staircase and entered the room. His mother lay unmoving under the quilt. Her lips, still tinged blue, stood out against the paleness of her face.

Dr. Hutton dozed on a wooden chair by the bed. At the sound of the door, he opened his eyes.

"How is she?" Nolan whispered.

The physician rose and adjusted the glasses on his nose. "I'm afraid her fever has worsened. And she's having greater difficulty breathing."

Nolan's throat tightened. It seemed a miracle was not to be. "If you'd like to get some food, I can stay with her now."

"Thank you. I'll be in the kitchen if she . . . if anything changes." Dr. Hutton buttoned his waistcoat and quietly left the room.

Nolan took a seat beside the bed and lifted his mother's hand. The fingers lay cold and limp against his. "Please, Lord, help her get better. Don't take her, now that I finally have the chance to give her the life she deserves." He bowed his head and fought to stem the sorrow that rushed through him. There would be time for grieving later. Right now, he needed to remain strong.

At a movement in the bed, Nolan raised his head.

His mother's body shook, and the air rattled in her lungs as she attempted to draw breath.

"Nolan?"

"I'm here, Mum."

Staring right at him, her eyes shone with an unnatural light. "Forgive me, son." The words rasped from her throat.

"There's nothing to forgive, Mum. You did what you thought was best."

She clutched his arm with a look of desperation. "Promise me something."

"Anything."

"Promise you'll let go of your anger. Don't blame God for taking me. His will is beyond our understanding, but perfect in its execution. Don't let this shake your faith."

Nolan held back a bitter reply. How could she speak of faith when their prayers went unanswered?

She took another tortured breath. "No matter what the earl does, put the past behind you. Trust what the Lord has in store for you."

His body shook with the enormity of emotions racing through him. How could she ask that of him when he was about to lose her? But he had no choice. He had to let her go in peace. "I'll try my best, Mum. For you."

A smile of almost perfect serenity spread over her face, the lines of tension easing. "I love you, son. You were my greatest blessing. From the moment I held you, you were mine."

"I love you too." His voice cracked, and his strength crumbled. He clutched her hand hard as though by the sheer force of his will, he could keep her here with him.

He sat holding her hand for what felt like hours, listening to her breathing grow more and more shallow. His own lungs cramped in sympathy. He drew in long breaths, as though he could somehow help her draw air.

At last, a final shudder wracked her body. She became very still, her chest no longer moving, as though her soul had shed its skin.

With a strangled cry, Nolan dropped to his knees, burying his face against her side. He draped his arm over her frail form and wept.

He didn't even hear the doctor enter. When he raised his

head, the man had his stethoscope out and was listening to his mother's chest.

Dr. Hutton closed his eyes and slowly removed the instrument. "I'm sorry, son. She's gone."

Nolan wiped his face with his sleeve and rose. His gaze bounced from the dark drapery to the bare nightstand to the stark gray walls. The bleakness of the space matched the state of his soul. Nothing would ever be the same with his beloved mother gone from him.

Lines of fatigue framed Dr. Hutton's mouth as he stepped away from the bed. "I'm sorry," he said again. "I wish I could have done more." He closed his leather bag and straightened.

"You did your best." Nolan's voice didn't even sound like his own.

The dank air of the room was suffocating. He had to get out of the illness-infested space and into the clean air. He bent to kiss his mother's cheek one last time, let his fingers linger on her hair, then strode from the room. With each step, the numbness receded and the pain intensified, until his lungs felt like they would collapse. Partway down the hall, he came upon Reverend Black scurrying toward him, Bible clutched in one hand.

"You're too late. She's gone," Nolan growled and pushed on past. The raw, empty grief made it impossible to care about being rude.

"I'm very sorry for your loss." The minister's words echoed off the stone walls, mocking him.

His mother was dead.

Nolan's gut twisted in painful spasms. He needed air. He needed . . . Hannah.

In a blind state, he tore down the servant staircase and burst into the kitchen. Like a drowning man, he searched the room until he spied Hannah at the far end of the table, kneading dough on a flour-covered surface. He grasped the edge of the table and paused to drag air into his lungs.

"What on earth?" Mrs. Bridges rose from her seat in the corner. As her eyes met his, her wooden spoon clattered to the floor, and she let out a harsh cry.

Hannah's head whipped up. She wiped her hands on a rag at the sink. "Is she . . . ?"

His breathing still ragged, Nolan could only nod.

Mrs. Bridges lowered her bulky frame to a kitchen chair and held a tattered handkerchief to her nose. "God rest her soul," she murmured.

In two strides, Hannah was at his side. Seeming to sense his fragile state, she took him by the hand and led him out the back door to the yard. In a daze, he followed her. Out of sight of the main house, she stopped under a tree and wrapped her arms around him.

"I am so sorry, Nolan. Your mother was a fine woman. I admired her a great deal."

Hannah's soft words of comfort unleashed a torrent of emotion that rose through his chest and congealed in his throat. He clutched Hannah to him. Hot tears spilled from under his closed lids as his grief poured out. Hannah was his haven—the safe place where he could reveal every truth of his soul. Nothing would embarrass or confound her.

When at last the tears ceased to flow, he mopped his face with his sleeve and looked down at her.

"Thank you" was all he could manage.

She nodded and wiped her own face. "Come back to the kitchen, and I'll make you some tea."

Like his mother, Hannah believed a cup of tea could cure anything.

"Just for a few minutes. Then I have to make arrangements for the funeral."

As they crossed the lawn, Nolan let out a shuddering breath. He would need to inform Lord Stainsby of his mother's passing. Nolan hadn't seen or spoken to the man since he'd practically thrown him out of his mother's room. He had no idea what the earl was thinking after learning that Nolan was his son. Did he believe the claim, or would he dispute it, convinced that Nolan would only be out for the wealth and status a title would bring?

Yet what if his lordship did acknowledge him publicly as his son? Did Nolan even want that? How would he handle the changes that would accompany such a status?

Nolan pushed these new worries to the back of his mind. It was all he could do to put one foot in front of the other right now. He'd let the events play out as they would and make decisions as he went.

Edward stood, feet apart, hands clasped behind his back, staring at the simple wooden cross rising from a patch of grass in the poor section of the St. John cemetery. The words *Mary Breckinridge* had been carved into the wood, as well as the years of her birth and death. The irony of making this trip now, twenty-one years later, to his first wife's rural village struck Edward hard, weighing him down with long-forgotten guilt. The village was only a day's ride away. Why hadn't he tried harder to find her all those years ago?

Forgive me, Mary.

His heart twisted at the whisper of the cherished name that still resonated in his soul.

How he had loved her—with the passion of youth and the dangerous thrill of the forbidden. If only he'd been brave enough to fight for their love, to suffer the consequences of his father's wrath, perhaps they could have been happy.

He'd made so many mistakes back then. First by allowing his passion to overtake them and being careless enough to get her with child. Then, once he made the situation right by marrying her, not putting her and their unborn child first. He'd let his fear of his father outweigh his good sense.

And unbeknownst to him, his father had bullied Mary, his threats the real reason she'd run off. Would she have died in childbirth if Edward had been with her? If he'd been able to procure the best medical care his wealth and position could afford?

That question would haunt him for the rest of his life.

Now, all these years later, it seemed inconceivable that their child hadn't perished with her. That Edward, in fact, had a grown son. Whispers of doubt curled around this heart. Before he dared trust Elizabeth Price's claim, before he dared hope it might be true, he needed proof.

Only then could he allow himself to believe he had a son—a tangible connection to his one true love.

Only then could he allow himself to believe he had an heir—one who would surely prove more fitting than Orville.

The wind whipped Edward's greatcoat tight against his legs and stung his eyes until tears formed. Movement behind him caught his attention. Edward turned to see the vicar coming down the path from the road toward the small stone church. The elderly man tipped his hat at him and continued inside.

Edward pulled his own hat more firmly onto his head lest the wind seize it, then made his way to the building and climbed the rickety few steps. Inside, the warped wooden boards groaned beneath his feet as he walked up the main aisle to where the clergyman stood lighting a pair of tapered candles.

"Reverend Daniels?"

The man blew out the match and set it in a small container of sand on the floor below the iron candelabra. "Aye. I'm Reverend Daniels. Can I help you?"

"I hope so." The comforting smell of burning sulfur filled the air as the candles flickered to life. "I'm looking for some information about a family who used to live here." Belatedly, Edward removed his hat and tucked it under one arm. "Have you lived in the area long, sir?"

"I've been the vicar here for thirty-four years." Reverend Daniels gave him a curious look, fingering his trim gray beard. A shaft of light from the arched side windows danced off his wire spectacles. "What exactly would you like to know?"

"The girl, Mary Breckinridge, buried at the back of the cemetery—did you know her?" Edward willed his face to remain immobile, to reveal none of the emotions warring beneath the surface.

"Ah, yes. Young Mary. Sad story that. Died giving birth to a son."

Edward's heart pumped harder. "Do you know what happened to the child? I understood he perished with the mother."

"No. I baptized the boy myself right here in this church. Mary's sister Lizzie took him to raise as her own. A very brave thing, considering she was a struggling widow herself."

Edward stiffened, his jaw tight. Elizabeth Price's story appeared to be true. The ramifications waged war in his chest. He clenched and unclenched the fingers of his left hand. "What happened to them? Do they still live nearby?"

"Last I heard, Lizzie couldn't keep up her late husband's farm and moved away to take a position as a lady's maid. Never heard where she went from there." The vicar moved over to lean on the first pew, his knees cracking loudly in the silence. "I imagine the boy would be about twenty by now."

"I'd like to see the baptism register for that time period."

Reverend Daniels gave Edward a long look. "Are you some relation to the boy?"

"I might be. Which is why I need to see the official record." The scrap of paper in Mrs. Price's Bible hadn't meant a whit to him. It could have been forged by anyone.

"And your name, sir?"

"Edward Fairchild." He declined to give his title. Simpler that way.

A flicker of something akin to recognition flashed in the clergyman's eyes. He pursed his lips and nodded. "I see. You'd best come with me then, and we'll see what we can find."

Edward released the breath he'd been holding as he followed the older man through a side door and down a narrow hall to a back room. Reverend Daniels took out an iron key, fit it into the lock, and opened the door. They entered an office with a scuffed wooden desk and walls of books.

The vicar shuffled to the far side of the room, picked out a large leather volume, and set it on the desk. Adjusting the spectacles on his nose, he flipped several pages until he found the one he wanted. "If memory serves, the birth took place in the fall of either 1862 or 1863."

"It was '62." Edward could never forget the year. It was etched into his memory along with his sorrow.

The man ran his finger down the page. "Ah, Breckinridge. Here it is."

Edward leaned over the desk for a better view, barely able to make out the script. "What does it say?" He shoved his shaking hands into his coat pocket.

"A son born November 18, 1862. Christened Nolan Edward

on November 25. Mother: Mary Breckinridge. Father: Edward Stuart Fairchild." The vicar peered over his spectacles, his stare scraping at Edward's nerve endings.

"Is there any way this information could be false?"

"None. I entered this record myself. If it would help, I could write a statement swearing to its veracity."

"That might be prudent. Thank you."

As the clergyman went to the drawer to retrieve a pen and paper, Edward released a long breath.

Faced with irrefutable proof, he could no longer deny the truth.

Nolan Price was indeed his son.

CHAPTER

6

"Ashes to ashes, dust to dust." Reverend Black's solemn voice drifted over the group gathered around the gaping hole in the ground that contained Elizabeth Price's plain wooden coffin.

Somber clouds trudged across the sky, threatening to unleash a torrent of rain, but for the moment the ground remained dry. A gust of wind teased the minister's long black robes and lifted the scent of freshly dug earth to Hannah's nose.

She dabbed a handkerchief to her damp eyes while fixing her gaze on Nolan, standing so tall and stoic across from her. She wished she could stand by his side, holding his arm as he bore this tragedy. But for appearances' sake, she must pretend no relationship to him other than a fellow servant. Thankfully, Bert and Franny McTeague kept silent vigil beside Nolan, along with Mickey Gilbert and a few of the other hands.

Nolan remained dry-eyed and still, staring at the ground before him with no expression to give away the pain Hannah knew was tearing his soul apart. Elizabeth Price had been the only relative Nolan had ever known. Now she was gone, and Nolan must feel adrift, like a ship without an anchor. Hannah wanted to be his steadying force, his refuge—just as he'd become hers since the first weeks she'd come to Stainsby.

She remembered being that terrified thirteen-year-old girl, alone in a monstrous house with strangers all around. One morning, not long after she'd arrived, she accidentally dropped one of Mrs. Bridges' best serving dishes. The crockery had split in two, cracked right down the middle. Certain that the misdeed would earn her a severe reprimand, if not punishment, Hannah had taken the broken pieces out behind the chicken coop and tried to dig a hole to bury the evidence. The small gardening shovel had little effect against the hard ground. Tears had streamed down her face, mingling with the streaks of dirt as she'd tried to cover up her crime. It was then Nolan had come upon her and, learning of her dilemma, had unearthed the pieces and taken them to the stable, promising to bring the restored dish back the next day.

The following morning, she'd found the crockery sitting on the kitchen table, glued back together so well that she could scarcely see the crack. Nolan had come to her rescue, and from that day on, Hannah knew she had one person she could count on no matter what.

The thud of the shovel hitting the earth brought her out of her thoughts. Reverend Black had said the final blessing and the men were throwing dirt into the hole to fill it. Most of the servants approached Nolan to speak their words of condolence on their way out of the churchyard.

As much as she wanted to stay with him, Hannah had to get back to the kitchen and help with the food for the small reception. Surprisingly, the earl had ordered refreshments to be served in the main dining room for those attending the burial. For once, the servants were invited to eat with the family. A rare day indeed.

Later, when most of the food had been sent upstairs, Hannah turned to Edna. "You go on up and join the others. You've more of a right to be there than a lot of the other servants." Most of whom would show up mainly for the food. And for the opportunity to spend time in the main part of the house.

Edna sighed and untied her apron. "Only if you'll come with me, child."

Hannah's heart gave a tiny lurch. She'd hoped to go upstairs and maybe catch a closer look at the earl's daughters, Nolan's half-sisters, who had come in for the funeral at their father's request. Years ago, Mrs. Price had gone above and beyond her duties as housekeeper when the girls' mother died, and apparently his lordship felt it only right they should pay their respects, though secretly Hannah thought it had more to do with their new brother than anything else. Hannah had no doubt that once the earl verified Mrs. Price's story, he would name Nolan as his son and heir. If the claim were true, he'd have little choice. But what would his daughters think when they learned of Nolan's parentage?

Hannah pushed away a rush of apprehension, praying his lordship would not break the news just yet and allow Nolan this day to grieve in peace.

Nolan stood beside the serving table in the main dining room, holding a plate of untouched food in one hand, a linen napkin in the other. It took every ounce of willpower not to bolt from the room and flee to the solitude of the stable.

He did not belong in this ornate room, even filled with servants like himself. The oddity of having Lord Stainsby and the members of his family mingling with the staff made the situation far more awkward than it should have been. The fact that

Nolan suspected the real reason for the earl's solicitude only compounded his discomfort.

Nolan set down his plate of now-cold food on the long dining table and reached for a cup of ale. As he took a sip to ease his parched throat, he noticed Evelyn, the elder of the earl's daughters, and her gaunt-looking husband staring at him from across the room. Nolan's stomach twisted, but he gave a polite nod.

In the days before the funeral, Nolan had managed as little contact as possible with Edward Fairchild. An urgent business matter had called the earl away from Stainsby for several days, which had been a welcome relief. Now, however, Nolan dreaded the inevitable confrontation with his father and prayed the earl would wait a while longer before approaching him.

Nolan set his cup on the sideboard and looked up as Hannah and Mrs. Bridges entered the room. A wave of relief crashed through him. With her fair head uncovered, Hannah shone like a ray of sunlight, piercing the darkness of the gloomy gathering. Before he could cross the room, Timothy Bellows slid beside her and took her by the elbow.

Nolan's hands tightened into fists at his side. No matter how many times Hannah rebuked Bellows's advances, the redheaded footman would not leave her alone. Hannah tried to free her arm, but the barnacle remained attached. A low growl rose in Nolan's throat. He took a step forward, only to feel a large hand clamp down on his shoulder.

"Best not to create a scene, lad. Your mother wouldn't have wanted that." Bert's mild warning rang in Nolan's ear. "That rascal canna do much with all these people here and the earl himself in attendance."

Nolan's nostrils flared like a stallion boxed in a pen, pawing the ground, wanting to charge. "That lout has his hands all over Hannah like she's his possession." Nolan had heard tales of Bellows's frolicking with the local tavern girls, as well as several illicit dalliances with the kitchen maids, and Nolan vowed Hannah would never be one of his conquests. Hannah's lack of interest, however, only seemed to fuel the man's determination to have her.

"Don't let him goad you into doing something daft." Bert squeezed Nolan's shoulder none too gently.

Nolan inhaled and slowly let out the breath. He noted Mrs. Bridges' vigilant presence beside Hannah and fought to reclaim his sense of calm. "Thank you, Bert. My emotions are a bit raw today."

"And well that lad knows it. He's probably counting on you doing something outrageous to discredit you with Hannah—and the earl."

Nolan watched as Hannah edged away from Bellows, picked up a plate from the table, and began to spoon potatoes from the large serving bowl. Bellows appeared miffed but didn't follow.

Nolan made his way to Hannah's side. "Can I help you with that, Miss Burnham?" he asked, sending Bellows a frosty glare.

Hannah smiled and handed him the plate. "Yes, thank you, Mr. Price. That's very kind."

"No trouble at all."

"How are you bearing up?" Hannah whispered as she added a biscuit to the dish.

"As best I can. Though I'd feel a lot better if Bellows would leave you alone."

"Just ignore him. He's not worth a moment's thought." Suddenly, Hannah froze and then dropped a small curtsy. "My lord."

Nolan turned to find Lord Stainsby, unsmiling, beside him.

The man inclined his head toward Hannah, then directed his steely eyes to Nolan. "Mr. Price, I'd like a word with you in my study, if it's convenient."

Nolan's chest tightened. "Can it not wait until the morrow?"

"I'm afraid not."

Nolan kept his gaze even. He refused to allow the man to think he intimidated him. "Very well." He passed the plate back to Hannah, whose expression mirrored the anxiety he was trying hard to tamp down. He smiled briefly, hoping to reassure her. *I'll see you later*, he mouthed, and turned to follow the earl out of the room.

Nolan walked behind Lord Stainsby across the corridor and into the study. Silently, he vowed to get through this conversation without losing his composure. He would show his father that even a stable hand could behave in a civilized manner.

Inside the room, Nolan paused to take in the space. Except for the kitchen and the servants' quarters, he'd never had occasion to see much of the interior of Stainsby Hall—and certainly not the earl's private office. Leather chairs sat before a gleaming desk that took up a large portion of the room. Row upon row of bookshelves lined the walls. The lingering scent of tobacco hung in the air.

Lord Stainsby crossed to the huge stone fireplace and grabbed a poker to stoke the waning fire. He gestured to the chairs across from the desk. "Please have a seat."

"I prefer to stand."

"As you wish." The earl crossed his arms over his chest. "It's time we discussed the issue we've both been avoiding." His face remained as stony as the fireplace. "I have done some investigation to verify your mother's claim, and it appears she was telling the truth. You are indeed my legitimate son, and as such, you are the heir apparent to the earldom, which includes Stainsby Hall as well as all the other Fairchild holdings."

For the first time, the reality of his birthright hit him like a slap to the face. Nolan swallowed hard. "Perhaps I will have that seat after all."

He sank into an armchair near the fire, surprised when the earl took the chair opposite him.

"I take it this news causes you some distress."

Nolan wet his dry lips. "This whole situation has come as an enormous shock. As it no doubt must have for you."

He stared at the man before him, to whom he bore a striking physical resemblance—now that Nolan took the time to notice. The same dark hair, the same slash of eyebrows over vivid blue eyes, the same square jaw with a cleft in the chin. A huge part of him resented the fact that this man, once his feared employer, was now his father. That he'd lived under the same roof all these years and hadn't known it.

Did his father feel the same way?

The earl fiddled with the collar of his shirt, as though his cravat had become too tight. "I will admit that this turn of events has unsettled me." He regarded Nolan with a level look that softened. "On closer inspection, I see qualities of your mother in you. It's a shame you never knew her. Mary was . . ." He paused to clear his throat. ". . . an exceptional woman."

"As was the woman who raised me." Nolan attempted to bank his resentment, knowing his father must not think well of Elizabeth for lying to him all these years. Though Nolan still didn't understand her motives for doing so, he would defend her with his dying breath.

The earl gazed into the fire for several moments, lost in thought. Finally, he glanced over at Nolan. "I want you to know I had every intention of honoring my marriage to your mother. And that I was very much looking forward to the birth of our child." He steepled his fingers, his brow furrowed. "My father was a hard man whose sole interest was his reputation and his position in society. Naturally, he disapproved of my association with Mary. But I was a headstrong young man. I wasn't concerned about my father's opinion, nor about my responsibility to the family name. I only cared about being with Mary."

"I can understand that," Nolan said, his mind on Hannah.

"My mother—your grandmother—was not a well woman, prone to bouts of angina. While I waited for her to become strong enough to relay the news of my marriage, Mary left Stainsby with no warning. I did not know my father had threatened her, and I mistakenly assumed she'd gotten cold feet about the marriage." He pushed up from his chair and walked to the window. "I sent letters to her parents' home, thinking that was where she had gone, but they went unanswered. Finally, around the time our child was due to be born, I was preparing to go in search of her when we received word from Elizabeth that Mary and the child had died." The veins in Edward's neck stood out as he worked hard to contain his emotions.

As much as Nolan wanted to despise the man, a tug of sympathy wound through him. Perhaps he had truly loved the woman and had been devastated by her death.

"With Mary gone, there seemed little point in defying my father. He had a suitable bride picked out for me, and so I married Penelope six months later."

From his dour expression, Nolan doubted the union was a happy one. Though Nolan was still a long way from accepting this man as his father, perhaps he could begin to understand the reason behind the earl's bitterness and anger. "As I recall, your wife died quite some time ago." He had a vague recollection of a funeral at Stainsby Hall, but being so young, he hadn't paid it much attention.

"She did. Not long after you and Mrs. Price came to live

here." Lord Stainsby moved away from the window and turned to face Nolan. "But that is all in the past. What I wish to discuss with you now is how we move forward from here. Your whole world is about to change, and I'd like to help you adjust to your new position."

Nolan tugged at the lapel of his Sunday suit. What he wouldn't give to be mucking out a stall right now. But there was no point in putting off the inevitable. "Before I agree to anything, I'd like to know what would be expected of me."

The earl resumed his seat, one brow raised as if questioning Nolan's intent. "To start, I've had a suite of rooms prepared for you on the second floor, down the hall from my own quarters. You can move in when it is convenient for you. Tomorrow, I will send for the tailor to measure you for suitable clothing." He scanned Nolan's attire with a barely disguised grimace. "You will need to dress the part in order to act the part."

Nolan grunted. More uncomfortable clothes. Just what he needed. "What else?"

"You will be groomed in the ways of the aristocracy, and when you are ready, I will introduce you to society as my heir."

"I see." Nolan gripped the armrest as though to keep him anchored there. What on earth would "being groomed in the ways of the aristocracy" entail?

"I plan on breaking the news to my daughters this afternoon. Once they've had some time to digest the shock, you can meet your sisters."

Nolan stiffened. What did one do with sisters who came from a completely different world than he? Perhaps Hannah could help him in this area.

As though reading his mind, the earl's eyes narrowed. "There is one other important subject I must speak to you about right away."

Tension coiled in the back of Nolan's neck. Instinct told him he would not like what was coming next.

"As my son, you will no longer associate with the staff. Except to issue orders, that is."

Issue orders? To his friends and fellow workers? He opened his mouth to argue, but the earl held up a hand.

"In particular, any romantic liaisons you might have formed with any of the servants must end. Immediately." He leaned forward as if to emphasize his point. "After you have learned all that is involved in being a member of the noble class, we will find you a suitable bride from a well-bred family. One who will benefit us socially and financially, of course."

The crackle of flames in the fireplace became the only sound in the room. Coals fell in the hearth, and a flurry of sparks spurted outward, matching the fiery throb in Nolan's temple. He jerked to his feet and paced in front of the window. Fat drops of rain slid down the pane of glass, mimicking his future that now seemed to be slipping through his fingers—exactly as Hannah had predicted.

He sensed Edward come up behind him. "Nolan, I must have your word on this. A nobleman might get away with the odd dalliance, but he may never marry beneath him. The rules of our class dictate that."

The last thread of Nolan's control snapped. "You dare say this after everything you've been through with . . . Mary?" He couldn't bring himself to call her his mother. "The heartache and the loss? Two lives shattered because of a title?"

"Believe me, I'm only trying to spare you the lesson I had to learn the hard way. I will never forgive myself for what happened to Mary. In my arrogance, I chose to ignore the constraints of my world, not fully considering how it would affect her. Yet even if my father had relented and accepted our marriage, I'm not certain Mary could have withstood the societal pressures she would have faced." A flash of pain appeared in the earl's steely eyes. "You need to accept what life is like for those of us with noble blood. With great wealth comes great sacrifice."

Nolan barked out a harsh laugh. "You mean with great wealth comes the shackles of imprisonment."

"I'm sorry you see it that way." A nerve ticked in Edward's jaw. "I had hoped you would be pleased to be my son. Perhaps once you experience the advantages nobility can offer, the sacrifice won't seem as great."

Nolan turned away, attempting to calm the blood pounding in his ears. Sacrificing Hannah was not an option—of that much he was certain. By all rights, he could refuse Edward and waive his birthright. Continue with his plan to become a farmer and marry Hannah.

Yet hadn't one of his greatest wishes since boyhood been to learn his father's identity and establish some type of relationship? The opportunity had now been handed to him—by fate or by God, he didn't know. Would he reject it outright without even trying?

Nolan's mind whirled faster than the wind in the outer courtyard. He needed time to come up with a strategy. Time to determine the best course of action. He schooled his features, then turned back to his father. "It seems you have left me little choice. For the time being, I will abide by your wishes."

Lord Stainsby looked like he was about to challenge Nolan's statement but instead gave a slight bow. "Very well then. I will expect you to dine with me tonight, at which time I will introduce you to your sisters."

CHAPTER

7

Standing at the parlor's service cart, Edward poured an inch of whiskey into a crystal tumbler and took a stiff drink before he turned to face his family. As with most unpleasant tasks in life, he found it best to get on with it as quickly as possible and deal with the consequences afterward.

His youngest daughter sat on the sofa, a book of poetry on her lap. The dreamer in the family, Victoria seemed oblivious to the underlying tension in the room. Evelyn, on the other hand, perched on the very edge of her seat, and though still classified as a newlywed, she paid not the slightest attention to her husband. Orville stood apart from them, absently swirling the cocktail in his glass.

Evelyn rose to cross the floor. Dressed in a garish dress of red and gold, she reminded Edward of a Christmas tablecloth. "Tell me, Father, is there more to this visit than our former housekeeper's funeral? Because for the life of me, I can't see why you'd insist we attend. You've never given a whit about a servant's death before."

Edward should have known Evelyn would suspect something. Nothing much escaped her keen notice. "As a matter of fact, there is. I have some rather important news to impart to all of you."

Orville's gaze snapped to Edward. "What is this about?"

Edward stilled, conscious of the blow he was about to deal this man. Though immensely relieved that Orville would not be able to ruin the Fairchild's assets in the future, Edward didn't quite trust what Orville's reaction might be to this news. He made a mental note to speak to Mr. Grayson about curbing Evelyn's allowance, as well as taking steps to ensure Orville's debts be contained.

"Please take your seats, and I'll explain everything." Edward took another sip of liquid courage and set the glass on the mantel. "Prior to her death, Mrs. Price asked to speak with me and made a startling revelation, which I'll admit has shaken me more than a little."

"Whatever could a housekeeper say to startle you, Father?" Victoria closed her book, a curious expression lighting her face.

In contrast to Victoria's endearing naïveté, a scowl creased Evelyn's brow, emphasizing her sharp features. Orville stood behind the sofa, shoulders stiff, as though ready for battle.

"Before I continue," Edward said, "I must tell you something of my past." Nerves dampened his palms. How he hated dredging up the folly of his youth, especially in front of his daughters. "When I was young—before I wed your mother—I was married to someone else for a brief period of time."

Evelyn eyed him with suspicion. "We've heard rumors to that effect. Aunt Ophelia admitted there was an elopement, but not much else. Except to say that the girl died, and then you married Mother."

"That much is true. However, Ophelia left out some rather pertinent details." He took a breath and then as succinctly as possible relayed the details of his short-lived relationship with Mary Breckinridge. "Until a few days ago, I believed the child Mary carried had died with her. Mrs. Price, as it turns out, was Mary's sister. She helped deliver the baby, who in fact survived, and she then raised the boy as her own."

The color drained from Orville's already pasty face. He clutched the back of the sofa. "You have a son?"

"It appears so."

Evelyn jerked to her feet, eyes wide as she apparently put two and two together. "The stable boy is your *son*?" She thrust out a hand. "Surely you don't believe a servant's lies."

"I'm not a fool, Evelyn. Of course I verified her story. I saw the entry in the church register with my own eyes. Spoke to the clergyman who knew the family and who performed the baptism. There is no doubt about the boy's parentage."

"Then why didn't she come forward long ago? Why wait until she was dying?" Evelyn's voice grew to a screech. "It's . . . it's preposterous." She flailed a hand in her husband's direction. "Orville, do something. Defend your position."

Orville squared his shoulders. Patches of red stood out on his thin cheeks. "If your father was legally married to the woman at the time the child was born, there's nothing to be done. Price is the heir apparent."

Edward almost felt sorry for the chap. To have his future snatched out from under him in such a manner . . .

"But—but—" Evelyn whipped her attention back to Edward. "How can you possibly expect someone like that to become your heir? He knows nothing of the aristocracy."

"He will have to learn," Edward said calmly.

Victoria rose, her hands clasped together. "What if he doesn't want the title?" she asked.

"Are you daft?" Evelyn's features twisted in a most unladylike fashion. "What peasant would turn down a life of luxury? Why, he's probably packing his belongings as we speak."

Edward ran a hand over his jaw and suppressed an oath. He'd expected surprise, shock, anger even. But he'd forgotten about Evelyn's mean streak and her predisposition to melodrama.

"Does Price know he's your son?" Orville came around the sofa. Though pale, his eyes held a steely quality.

"He does. And he's as shocked as all of us." Edward raised a hand and let it fall. "I'm sorry, Orville. This is a rather unfortunate turn of events for you."

"Save your false sympathy," Orville said coldly. "I know you were never thrilled to have me as your heir. Looks like the fates took pity on you and gave you the son you wanted after all."

Edward couldn't deny the truth to his statement, so he remained silent.

Evelyn moved between them. "You never answered my question, Father. Why did Mrs. Price keep it a secret all these years?"

Why indeed? Edward still didn't understand her reasoning. "At first, she kept silent to honor her sister's dying request. But as the boy grew older and began asking questions, Mrs. Price came here in order to assess my character before deciding whether to reveal his parentage. Apparently, she found me lacking in several key areas, and for that reason, kept her secret."

"I'm sorry, Father." Victoria laid a hand on his arm. "You must be angry that she denied you your son all this time." Sympathy swam in her eyes.

Along with being a dreamer, Victoria was by far the most compassionate member of his family.

He shrugged. "There's nothing to be gained by dwelling on things we cannot change. What we need to do now is move forward, and to that end, I've asked Nolan to dine with us this evening."

"What?" Evelyn's eyes became twice their usual size. "That's absurd. I will not share a meal with a stable hand."

Edward's patience came to an abrupt end. "Not only will you eat with him, you will treat him with respect. Like it or not, he is your brother and a member of this family. It is our job to help him acclimate to his new role." He swung his gaze to Orville, then Victoria, and back to Evelyn. "Do I make myself clear?"

"Perfectly." Evelyn practically hissed the word. "But don't expect me to like it."

As Evelyn stomped to the far side of the room, Edward clamped his lips together. If he were a religious man, he'd pray for the strength to get through this upcoming meal with his sanity intact.

Nolan stepped away from the angry voices coming from the open parlor door and leaned against the corridor wall. His heart thudded painfully against his ribs. He'd only caught the tail end of the conversation, but that was enough to determine that things were not going well. He'd accepted that his siblings would likely not be happy about the news of his existence, but he'd never expected such blatant hostility. The hatred spewing from the older girl nearly knocked his feet from beneath him.

Lord, I don't know how much more I can take. First my mother and now this? What is it you want from me?

He took in a long breath and blew it out. Apparently he hadn't given the earl enough time to break the news to his family. Should he return to the barn and come back later? The temptation to scurry back to his quarters burned hotly in his chest. But he was no coward. He would do his best to face this lion's den or die trying.

Nolan tugged his brown tweed vest in place. He'd donned his best Sunday suit for the occasion, though he doubted anyone would notice. With a final deep breath, he stepped through the door. "Good evening, everyone."

All heads swiveled in his direction. Nolan got a brief impression of masculine furnishings and dark wood décor. The pleasant smell of pine logs and pipe tobacco scented the area, and though a fire roared in the hearth, a definite chill invaded the room.

"Nolan. Come in." The earl came forward, lines bracketing his mouth.

After the snippet of conversation Nolan had overheard, it was no wonder the man was tense.

"I hope I'm not early."

"Not at all. Allow me to formally introduce you to your sisters." He gestured to the taller of the two women, dressed in a vivid red and gold gown. "This is my eldest daughter, Evelyn. Evelyn, this is Nolan."

She stared at him, unsmiling. "We have met the stable hand before, Father."

The earl whipped around to glare at her. "Not as your brother, you haven't. Now kindly greet him properly."

Since Nolan had no idea what a proper greeting entailed, he remained still, awaiting his cue to react.

She dipped a small curtsy. "How do you do?" The words were ground out between clenched teeth.

He gave a bow. "A pleasure to meet you, Evelyn."

"And this is Evelyn's husband, Orville Fairchild. Orville is a third cousin, which is why he shares the same last name."

Nolan hesitated. Did he offer a hand to shake?

Orville merely inclined his head.

"I guess that makes us distant cousins as well," Nolan said.

"So it would appear." The hardness of Orville's stare did nothing to make Nolan feel welcome.

Edward stepped forward. "And this is my youngest daughter, Victoria."

Nolan turned his attention to the other woman. She was indeed an attractive girl, much more so than her sister, with soft brown curls and luminous amber eyes. Nolan guessed her to be about eighteen.

She came toward him with a tentative smile. "Welcome, Nolan. It's a great shock to learn we have an older brother. But I'm sure I'll get used to the idea soon enough."

He smiled in return and bowed. "Thank you, Victoria. Since I am unused to having siblings, I shall ask for your patience as I grow accustomed to the situation."

"As long as you grant me the same concession." She gave a light laugh.

The tightness in his chest loosened a notch. Perhaps one of his sisters didn't hate him after all.

The butler appeared in the doorway. "Dinner is served, my lord."

"Thank you, Dobson. Shall we adjourn to the dining room?" Edward gestured for the women to precede him into the hall.

They passed by in a whirl of silk and lavender. Orville stomped out after them.

Edward lifted a brow. "I hope you're made of sturdy stuff, Nolan. You'll need it for tonight."

The air whooshed from his lungs. "Indeed, I believe I shall."

CHAPTER
8

Hannah sat on the side of the bed, her Bible open on her lap. The candle on her table flickered, casting restless shadows on the walls. Outside, the incessant cascade of rain on the windows seemed in keeping with her mood. If only she could concentrate on the words before her, they might bring her a measure of comfort. But her agitated state made concentration impossible.

She hadn't seen Nolan since the earl had summoned him away from the funeral reception. He'd indicated they would talk later, and she'd expected him to come down to the kitchen after his meeting, but he never appeared. Not even to take his dinner with the rest of the servants.

Now, sometime after midnight, Hannah tried to imagine what could have happened. She didn't have to be a scholar to know that Lord Stainsby would expect great changes in Nolan's life. That as the earl's son he would no longer be allowed to associate with the servants, nor live in the stable.

Would the newness of the situation cause Nolan to set aside his own plans for the future to please his father?

The selfish part of her hoped he would choose a life with her over his noble roots. But would that really be fair to him?

She sighed, laid the Bible back on the table, and crossed the room to the plain wooden dresser where she picked up her hairbrush. Perhaps the soothing strokes would help calm her nerves. Hannah sat back on the thin mattress and loosened her braids until her hair fell in waves to her waist. As she brushed the silken strands, her thoughts turned to Molly. How Hannah used to love to comb her baby sister's blonde curls when she was young. Did Molly even remember that now?

It had been several years since Hannah had traveled to her mother's farmhouse. The last trip had been a disaster, and she hadn't had the courage to repeat it since. Her mother's husband had made her feel most unwelcome, and Mum had flitted around trying to placate him. In addition, when it was time for Hannah to leave, Molly had begged to come with her, and that more than anything had broken her heart.

A flash of guilt surfaced. In all the upheaval with Nolan, she hadn't had much time to dwell on Molly's predicament. With Nolan's whole future hanging in the balance, it didn't seem fair to remind him about his promise to help her sister. Even before any mention of Molly's upcoming betrothal, they had talked about bringing her to live on the farm with them. But if Nolan now chose to forfeit the purchase, Hannah would have to come up with another solution for her sister.

A sharp knock sounded at her door.

She jumped, and the brush slipped from her fingers. "Who's there?"

"It's me," a familiar voice whispered.

Nolan? What on earth was he doing here at this late hour?

"Just a minute." Hannah grabbed her robe off the hook on the door and quickly wrapped it around her. Nerves skittered along her spine. If anyone found Nolan here on the third floor, in the female quarters no less, they would both be in the worst kind of trouble. Going to see Nolan in the barn hadn't felt half this risky.

She inched the door open with only the smallest of creaks.

Nolan stepped inside and closed the door behind him.

The room seemed to shrink with the breadth of Nolan's shoulders taking up most of the space. She clutched the neckline of her robe and stepped back. "Nolan, you shouldn't be here."

"Forgive me, Hannah, but I had to speak with you. I waited until I thought everyone would be abed for the night and snuck in the back door." He scanned her from the top of her head to her bare feet, his Adam's apple bobbing as he swallowed. When his eyes met hers, they held a hint of wildness that unnerved Hannah.

"Where have you been? You missed the evening meal."

Her question snapped him out of his trance. "Sit down, love. You're trembling."

Her knees were indeed shaking. Not daring to sit on the bed, she perched on the wooden chair in the corner. Hands clutched together on her lap, she waited for Nolan to explain himself.

For several moments, he paced the tight area. "When are you next free for a day or two?"

Her mouth fell open at the unexpected question. "I—I have a few days owing to me. I hadn't planned when to take them."

"Can you tell Mrs. Bridges you need them as soon as possible? Say that you're worried about your sister and wish to make the trip to see her."

The urgency in his voice created spasms in her stomach. "Why? What is this about?"

Nolan's behavior was not at all in keeping with his usual calm demeanor. Her unease must have shown, for he bent one knee on the floor before her and took her hand in his. "You deserve so much better than this, Hannah. I promise I will make it up to you."

Her throat constricted. Had his father forbidden them to be together? Was he telling her good-bye?

"Hannah, I love you, and I cannot picture my life without you." His intense blue eyes bore into her. "Will you do me the honor of becoming my wife?"

She gasped. A thousand thoughts swirled through her brain, fighting for a foothold. On all the occasions she'd hoped he'd reveal his heart, this time she was not prepared. "What about Lord Stainsby?"

"This has nothing to do with him." He scowled, but then let out a sigh. "I had planned to propose the night I made the deal with Mr. Simpson. But circumstances with my mother intervened." He caressed her hand with his thumb, his eyes softening. "So I'm asking you now. Will you marry me, Hannah?"

A few days ago, she would have answered without hesitation. But after everything that had happened and all the uncertainty between them, she needed reassurance. "I'll not give my answer until you tell me what went on between you and the earl."

His clenched jaw told her more than his words ever could.

"Nolan, did his lordship acknowledge you as his son?"

"Yes." He pushed to his feet.

Hannah's stomach sank. Of course the man would be thrilled to have a legitimate son and heir—even if he was a stable boy.

"He told me about my . . . about the woman who bore me, how he'd married her against his family's wishes. That she'd run away, and he'd tried to find her, only to learn of her death. And mine—or so he thought." He shook his head. "He seemed to genuinely care for her. That, at least, is a comfort."

She rose to face him. "What else did he say?"

His gaze slid to the floor. "He invited me to dine with the rest of the family. That's where I've been for most of the evening."

Hannah covered her mouth with her hand. She couldn't imagine Nolan eating in the grand dining room with the earl's family. "You met your sisters? How did that go?"

"It was an awkward affair, to say the least. Victoria was gracious, but Evelyn and her husband clearly resent my existence." Nolan's features hardened as he gripped the metal foot rail of her bed. "Not unexpected, I suppose. But neither they, nor the earl, will dictate my life. Which leads me back to my proposal." The tension eased from his face as he moved toward her. "I want to marry you, Hannah. And start our lives together, whether it be on our own farm as we'd planned, or as part of the aristocracy if I decide to accept my title."

Nervous energy pulsed through her. She took a step in retreat, afraid that his nearness might sway her decision. "But if you do accept it, the earl will never . . ." Suddenly his haste made sense. "That's why you want to marry now, isn't it? Because you know his lordship won't allow it."

He reached for her hand, his rough fingers gentle on hers. "Do you trust me, Hannah?"

She sighed. "You know I do."

"Then take a leap of faith with me, love. Together, we can face any challenge life brings us."

"And if your father rejects you because of me?" Her hands shook at the idea that she might be responsible for Nolan losing the opportunity to know his father. Surely he would resent her for it one day.

"Then he will make my choice very simple. I will go ahead with the purchase of the farm as planned, and we will live an honest, hardworking life."

Hannah bit her lip, her insides twisting with indecision. Then she raised her eyes to stare into his earnest face, the face she'd loved since she was a girl, and saw only honesty, integrity . . . and love. How could she refuse him?

"After we're married," he continued, "we'll go straightaway to fetch Molly and bring her back with us. She can stay with Bert and Franny if need be until we determine the course our lives will take."

"Oh, Nolan. Truly?" She hardly dared believe that everything she'd ever wanted was within her reach. Marriage to Nolan, her own home to tend, and Molly safe with them. The dream danced before her eyes like a mirage.

"I'd do anything for you, Hannah. Just say you'll be mine forever."

A bubble of joy—one that overrode every logical argument—threatened to lift her from the ground. The heat of his hand anchored her, steadying her as he always did, and she knew what her answer would be. "Yes, Nolan. Yes, I'll marry you."

"Praise be!" A huge smile broke over his face. "You are the light in this dark time of my life, Hannah. I don't know where I'd be without you." His lips came down on hers with a fierceness that shook her to the core.

He kissed her until her knees went weak, and she finally broke away, gasping for air. "Nolan. We mustn't."

He rested his forehead against hers, his breathing uneven. "Forgive me. I got carried away."

She tried to remain miffed, but her own happiness overflowed into a stifled laugh. "When will we be wed?"

"I'll see Reverend Black tomorrow and make the arrangements. Will you be able to get away at the end of the week?"

"I think I can convince Edna to let me go for a few days. But what will we do after the ceremony?" Her heart raced at the thought of their wedding night.

A slow grin crept across his handsome features, giving him an almost rakish air. "You leave that part to me, Miss Burnham."

A blush heated her cheeks, and she looked away.

"I'd better go now—before I push my luck too far." He crossed the room, then paused with his hand on the knob. "One more thing. Let's keep our plans to ourselves. No one else need know—especially Edna. You know how she loves to talk."

Hannah clutched the neck of her robe. Though she hated the thought of deceiving the dear woman, Nolan was right. "I promise."

"Good." A determined gleam shone in his eyes. "We'll meet on the road to the village at dawn two days from now. Until then, remember how much I love you."

He dropped a quick kiss on her lips and disappeared out the door, leaving Hannah wavering between elation and terror.

CHAPTER 9

The next morning, Nolan completed his chores in the barn as usual. Despite the fact that his father wanted him to immediately give up all aspects of his old life, Nolan was not yet prepared for such a bold declaration of his parentage, and chose instead to continue his normal routine.

He'd just finished cleaning the last stall when Bert appeared in the main corridor.

"I see you've finished in record time this morning. Did his lordship light a fire under you with his talk last night?" Along with the twinkle in Bert's eyes, sympathy radiated from his features. He was the one person, besides Hannah, who Nolan had told about the earl being his father.

"I'd rather not discuss him, if you don't mind." Nolan closed the stall door and shoved the pitchfork into a bale of hay.

"So, your opinion of the man hasn't softened any?"

Nolan shot the Scotsman a black look. "Did you really think it would?"

Bert stroked his reddish beard. "I thought once you spent some time with him as your father, and not your employer, you might see the man in a different light."

Nolan strode toward his quarters at the rear of the stables, Bert following close behind. With a loud exhale, Nolan stopped and crossed his arms. "If you've something to say, please spit it out. I have an errand to run."

"There's something I think you should know about his lordship. In fact, there's something I need to show you."

Nolan scowled. He had far more important matters to attend to this morning. "I don't have time—"

"It won't take long." Bert exited out the rear door, his long strides kicking up dirt behind him.

Knowing his friend wouldn't rest until he'd had his say, Nolan reluctantly set out after him.

Bert headed across the meadow toward a sharp incline in the east.

Nolan jogged to catch up. "Where are you taking me?"

"Not far. Just over the rise."

Silently, they climbed the hill, and at the top, the black spires of the fence surrounding the Fairchild cemetery stood out in stark relief against the light blue sky. It hit Nolan then that these were his relatives buried here. "You brought me here to show me my ancestors?"

"Not exactly." Bert continued to walk at a fast pace, forcing Nolan to keep up. They passed the entrance to the burial ground and kept going.

Around a slight bend, Bert slowed to a more normal pace, then stopped altogether. Nolan followed the line of sight to where the Scotsman stared ahead.

Nolan's breath caught. A magnificent cherry tree in full bloom filled the horizon, its branches spreading up to the sky. Certainly a beautiful sight, but why had Bert brought him here?

"Is there some significance to this tree?"

"Aye. His lordship planted it himself, the day he learned

of his first wife's death." Bert fisted his hands at his hips. "It was her favorite tree, or so he said when I was installing the markers."

Nolan squinted against the sun's rays. He found it difficult to believe the earl would have confided in his blacksmith.

Bert jerked his head toward the tree. "Come on."

Once again, Nolan followed the burly man until they came to a thicket of bushes. A wooden trellis marked the opening in the shrubbery, and a sign above read *Mary's Grotto*. Beneath it was carved *In loving memory of Mary Breckenridge Fairchild*.

Huffing from exertion, Nolan dragged a sleeve across his clammy forehead. Edward must have truly loved the woman to create a shrine in her memory. As a sign of deference, Nolan removed his cap before entering through the trellis. A bench sat among the greenery, and some of the bushes were beginning to bud. In the center of the grotto was the cherry tree. Immediately below were two pewter crosses: one larger, engraved with the name Mary Fairchild, and the other much smaller, obviously meant for a child.

Nolan inhaled sharply, realizing that the cross was actually intended for him, since at the time the earl had believed him to have perished.

"His lordship asked me to fashion these markers, which I was happy to do," Bert said. "The day I brought them up here, that tree was no more than a sapling the width of my finger." He pointed to the array of rocks that lined the area. "The earl carried all those stones up here himself and arranged them like that. Every year, he adds a few more. And in the nicer weather, he plants flowers among them."

Nolan bent to examine the crosses, running his finger over the intricately engraved patterns. "They're beautiful, Bert. Did you know my . . . did you know Mary?"

"Aye. She worked for his lordship's father as a housemaid before his son took a fancy to her." Bert turned to look at Nolan. "She was a fetching lass, kind and loyal. I tried to warn her about the folly of getting involved with Master Fairchild, as I called him then. But it was too late. She wouldn't heed my words of caution."

Nolan straightened as a sudden thought occurred. Had Bert known all along who Nolan was? He opened his mouth to form the inquiry, but Bert shook his head.

"Nae, lad. I had no idea you were the result of that ill-fated union. I only learned of it the day of Elizabeth's funeral." Bert laid a hand on Nolan's shoulder. "I thought it might bring you comfort to know that your father loved Mary beyond all reason. Never known a man to show such grief over a loss. Still comes here every year on their wedding anniversary and on the date of her passing." Bert crossed his arms in front of him. "His lordship told me once that when the cherry blossoms start to fall, it's as if the tree is weeping for her as well."

Nolan swallowed a rise of emotion. Maybe there was more to his enigma of a father than he knew. Perhaps under all Edward's harshness lay a redeemable human being. "Thank you for bringing me here. At least I know I'm the product of a genuine love."

Bert nodded. "Thought you might understand your father better if you saw how profoundly Mary's death affected him. Changed the course of his life, it did."

"It does help. Thank you, Bert."

Nolan shoved his cap back on. How different would his life have been if Edward had gone after Mary sooner? Perhaps she would have lived, and they'd have shared a true family bond— not this fractured, hostile relationship.

He took one last look around the intimate grotto. Could he and Edward ever develop a true father and son attachment?

Nolan prayed that, despite everything, he might still have the opportunity to find out.

When he got back to the stables, Nolan went to his quarters to don a clean shirt and tidy himself up. Then he saddled King for a ride into the village. He'd expected to have left before now, but he didn't regret visiting the grotto. Bert was right. Nolan needed to see it in order to better understand his father. A beating heart might actually lie beneath the earl's cold chest after all.

Nolan gave King a slight kick, urging him to a faster pace. Normally he took the time to savor his surroundings, but today all he could think of was the task at hand, as well as the necessity to be back before the tailor's arrival alerted Edward to Nolan's absence.

A niggling sense of guilt chafed Nolan. He'd told his father he would sever ties with Hannah, and now he was about to go completely against his wishes. Yet he had little doubt that his lordship would do whatever it took to ensure Nolan complied with his plans, even if it meant sacking Hannah and forcing her away.

This mistrust was the reason Nolan felt the need for secrecy. He would hold off making a decision about being Edward's heir until he and Hannah were married. Then if Edward refused to accept her as Nolan's wife, they would have the option of leaving Stainsby to live on the farm.

The sun shone brightly after the rain the night before, and the scent of blossoming flowers drifted by him on the breeze. A perfect spring day. A good omen, perhaps, that things would go his way.

When he reached the small stone church, he guided King

down the flagstone path that led to the rectory. There he tied the horse to a tree and knocked softly on the front door.

Mrs. Black answered with a welcoming smile. Soft gray curls framed her round face. "Good morning, Mr. Price. How are you holding up? I was ever so sorry to hear about your mum."

Her sympathetic tone jarred him from his mission. He'd had so much on his mind, he'd pushed his grief to the background, but now it crashed back over him. "I'm doing as well as possible under the circumstances, Mrs. Black. Is your husband available?"

"Of course, dear. Come in, and I'll fetch him."

He stepped into the tiny cottage. The smell of eggs and bacon hung in the air, making Nolan wish he had eaten breakfast.

A few seconds later, Reverend Black lumbered down the hall. "Nolan. How are you getting on, my boy?"

"I'm fine, Reverend. Could I speak to you for a few minutes?"

"Of course, lad. Come into the parlor."

Sudden shame filled Nolan as he recalled his behavior on the day of his mother's death. With all the fuss at the funeral, he'd never had the chance to apologize. He removed his cap and followed the stooped man into the sitting room, which was furnished with an overstuffed sofa and two armchairs. An open Bible and a pipe sat on the table beside one of the chairs, where the reverend had likely been sitting.

"What can I do for you?" he asked after they had taken their seats.

"First off, sir, I owe you an apology for my disrespect the day my mother passed away. I was wrong to take my anger out on you."

Reverend Black shook his head. "Think nothing of it. I've had much worse said to me in a moment of grief."

"I appreciate your understanding." Nolan hesitated, trying

to choose the best way to approach the next topic. "I need your help with another important matter."

"I'll do my best."

"This may sound odd, given my . . . circumstances," he drew in a breath, "but I want to get married as soon as possible."

The older man choked back a cough, eyebrows raised.

"It was my mother's dying wish to see me settled down. She knew I intended to marry Hannah and made me promise to do so. I feel it only right to honor her wishes and continue with the path I'd chosen for my life." Nolan ran the tweed cap round and round through his fingers and held his breath. Would the minister accept his explanation?

"Well, this is highly unusual, I must admit." He hesitated until Nolan met his gaze. "Is the young woman in question agreeable?"

"Yes, sir, she is."

"And there are no impediments?"

"No, sir." Not the kind he meant, anyway.

"Who will stand up for you?"

Beads of sweat pooled under Nolan's collar. "I was hoping Mrs. Black could be our witness."

"An elopement then?"

"Of sorts, I suppose." It struck him then the sacrifice Hannah would be making, forfeiting a real wedding with her family and friends in attendance.

Reverend Black cleared his throat and peered at him over his wire spectacles. "You can tell me the truth, young man. Have you gotten the girl in trouble?"

Heat burned up Nolan's neck to enflame his ears. How easy it would be to say yes and force the minister's hand. But he wouldn't do that to Hannah; he would not compromise her reputation. "No, sir. I would never dishonor Hannah that way."

"I see." Reverend Black picked up his pipe and tapped the barrel with one finger. "What about family, then?"

Nolan chose his words with care. "It's always been just me and Mum. And Hannah's family lives a day's journey away. Even if they lived closer, they couldn't really afford time away from their farm." He paused. "We're planning a short trip to see them right after we've wed—to share the good news." He forced his mouth into a smile.

A few seconds of silence ensued.

"I guess I can't offer any binding reason why you shouldn't be married," the minister said. "After the banns have been published for three Sundays in a row—"

"Three weeks? Is there no faster way?"

Suspicion returned to the reverend's demeanor. "The upper classes sometimes purchase a special license, but they're quite costly."

"Where would I get such a license?"

"Closest place would be the clerk's office in Derby."

"Good. I'll set out straight away then." Nolan unclenched his fingers. "If all goes well, could we be wed tomorrow?"

"I suppose, if everything is in order." His eyes narrowed, making Nolan squirm in his seat. The unspoken question hung in the air, but the reverend wouldn't likely give credence to village gossip about Nolan's parentage. And even if the clergyman suspected the earl would disapprove, he would have no concrete reason to refuse Nolan's request.

"We'd like an early ceremony, so we can make a good start on our journey afterward."

"The missus and I are early risers ourselves. However, according to the law, eight o'clock is the earliest hour to perform a marriage."

"That would be fine." Nolan expelled a soft sigh of relief.

He rose and extended his hand. "I can't thank you enough, Reverend."

The rector clasped Nolan's hand in a tight grip. "I hope you're taking this sacrament with the seriousness it deserves, young man. Marriage is holy in the eyes of God."

"Trust me, sir, I've been planning this union since I was fourteen years old."

On Friday morning, Hannah paused in the hallway outside the kitchen to calm her unruly nerves. A prayer seemed the only way to do so.

Lord, forgive me for having to deceive the people I love, especially dear Edna. But I trust you understand the need for secrecy. If you're so inclined, please give me a sign that this union is in Nolan's best interest, that he won't forever regret it. If it be your will for us, please grant us your blessing on our marriage. Amen.

With a final deep breath, she entered the kitchen.

Edna looked up from the table where she had rolled out a length of pastry for the day's pies. "There you are, girl. I was wondering when you'd come to say good-bye."

Hannah forced a bright smile. "Don't worry. I won't be gone long. Only a few days." She hoped that was the case. She wasn't really sure what Nolan had in mind.

"You don't have to pretend with me, dearie. I know the real reason you're leaving."

Hannah's feet froze on the stone floor. "You do?"

"How could I not, when it's the talk of the house." Edna wiped her hand on a rag and leaned closer. "Word has it that Nolan is really his lordship's son. And that he's been told to have no contact with any of us belowstairs."

The air stilled in Hannah's lungs. What could she say to that?

"I know you were hoping to marry the lad. You must be devastated, poor dear." Edna pulled Hannah in a tight hug. "A little time away will do you good."

For a woman who normally didn't show affection, this was most unexpected.

"Thank you, Edna. I'm sure things will seem a lot different when I return." If only she knew how much.

"Say hello to your mother for me. It's been an age since I've seen her." Edna sniffed and shuffled back to the table.

"I will. You're sure you can manage without me?" Hannah smoothed down her cotton skirt, wishing she could wear her Sunday dress. But Edna would be suspicious if Hannah were to travel in her best outfit. So unless there was an opportunity to change at the church, she would be married in her serviceable blue skirt and high-necked blouse.

"I'll manage just fine. The other girls will fill in while you're gone." Edna picked up a basket covered with a red cloth. "Here, take these biscuits with you. Always a favorite of your mum's."

"Thank you. I'm sure she and Molly will love them. And thank you again for giving me the time off."

"No need to thank me. You've earned it, and you deserve a break."

Hannah tried to smile, but guilt made her lips tremble. "Well, I'd best be off."

"You sure you don't want one of the lads to take you into the village?"

Alarm surged through Hannah's body. She couldn't risk anyone seeing her with Nolan. "No, no. I've got plenty of time before the coach. And I'd prefer to walk. It's such a lovely morning." She picked up her bag, positioned the basket on the crook of her arm, and forced a smile. "Take care of yourself, Edna."

It wasn't until Hannah had walked the length of the Stainsby property and stepped out onto the road that led into the village that she allowed herself to take a full breath. Once around the bend and completely out of sight of the estate, she looked for the lane where Nolan had promised to be waiting.

Sure enough, a small buggy, barely visible through the brush, stood at the appointed spot. The horses stamped their hooves as though impatient to be off.

"You made it." Nolan jumped down to assist her. His smile beamed across his face, his blue eyes dancing in the morning sun.

"Of course I made it." Nerves dampened Hannah's palm as she took note of his attire. He was dressed in his Sunday suit, complete with tweed waistcoat, pocket watch, and matching cap. He looked so handsome, her heart hurt. She passed him her basket.

Nolan placed it on the seat of the carriage and turned back to take her bag, his smile replaced with a slight frown. "You haven't changed your mind, have you?"

"No. I'm just nervous . . . about everything." Her lashes fluttered down to cover her discomfort. How could she explain that not only did she fear being found out, but that she was terrified of the wedding night? If she'd been able to, she would have asked Edna what to expect. Before becoming a widow, Edna had enjoyed a very happy marriage. "What about you? You're certain this is what you want?" She'd give him one last chance to back out of this crazy scheme.

He took one of her hands in his. "I've never been more certain of anything. I love you, Hannah. Nothing will change that.

Definitely not a father I barely know, nor a title I care little about." He kissed her fingers. "Now, leave the worrying to me. Everything will go just as we planned. You'll see." He set her bag beside his in the carriage and assisted her onto the seat.

When he leapt up beside her and grabbed the reins, a measure of calm returned. How could she not trust Nolan? Hadn't he always protected her? His solid presence beside her gave her the security she needed. That and the many heartfelt prayers she'd offered along the way.

After making sure that no one else traveled the road, Nolan guided the horses toward the village.

"Won't you get in trouble for taking the buggy?"

He raised one brow with a grin. "I can't get in trouble for taking my own property, now can I?"

Soon Nolan pulled the horses to a stop in front of the rectory, and Hannah's nerves returned in full force. As if sensing her unease, Nolan took her gloved hands in his. The warmth of his skin seeped through the thin fabric to her icy fingers.

"I love you, Hannah. I can't wait to make you my wife. I've dreamed of this moment from the first day I met you." His blue eyes shone with sincerity.

Tears burned behind her lids, but today of all days, she would not let them fall. "You always say the perfect thing to make me feel better."

He dropped a light kiss on her lips. "Good. Since that will be my job from now on." He hopped down and reached up to assist her.

Together they approached the rector's door, and Nolan knocked. A few moments passed before Reverend Black opened the door.

"Good morning, Reverend." Nolan beamed at the man, who strangely enough did not smile in return.

"Good morning. Please come in."

Hannah pressed a palm to her abdomen, willing the nausea to ease as they stepped inside the quaint cottage. Was every bride this nervous?

"Shouldn't we head over to the church, Reverend?" Nolan asked. "Nothing against your fine home, but we'd like to be married in God's house."

The minister didn't quite meet their eyes. He clutched his hands together in front of him. "I'm very sorry, Mr. Price, but I won't be able to perform the ceremony today."

Hannah's knees threatened to buckle. She gripped Nolan's arm and willed herself to remain standing.

Nolan's dark brows drew together in a frown. "Has some emergency arisen?"

"No."

"Is there a problem with the license then?"

"The license is fine." Reverend Black now appeared decidedly uncomfortable. His pale face held a hint of fear as well as compassion. "Lord Stainsby came to see me yesterday. He forbade me to marry you without his express permission, as well as his attendance at the ceremony."

Hannah raised a hand to hide her trembling lips. It was just as she feared. His lordship would do everything in his power to control Nolan's life from now on.

"The earl," Nolan bit out, "has no say in the matter."

For the first time, the minister met Nolan's eyes with a frank stare. "I think we both know why he has the right to an opinion on any prospective bride you might choose. Especially if you plan on marrying beneath your new station." He turned an apologetic glance to Hannah. "No offense intended, dear."

Hannah's tongue remained glued to the top of her mouth.

She blinked to hold back the threat of tears and risked a glance at Nolan. The veins in his neck stood out beneath his clenched jaw. She sensed he was using every effort to control the outrage that must be burning inside him.

"Did you tell him I'd been to see you?" Nolan's terse tone gave credence to his anger.

"No. I felt our conversation was a private matter. I did, however, pray long and hard into the wee hours to discern what I should do."

"And I suppose you cannot go against the earl's wishes."

The older man sighed. "Not when the residents of Stainsby Hall and the surrounding properties make up half my congregation. Not to mention the fact that the earl contributes large sums of money to keep the church running." Reverend Black gave a small shrug. "I'm sorry, son. But perhaps it's for the best. If this marriage is the will of God, it will happen one day. Give it some time and prayer."

His sympathetic expression did nothing to ease the band of tightness in Hannah's chest. She clutched Nolan's arm harder to steady herself.

"I understand the difficulty of your position, sir," Nolan said slowly. "Might I trouble you for a glass of water for Hannah? I fear she's had somewhat of a shock."

The minister's brows shot up. "Of course. Please excuse my bad manners. I've kept you standing in the hall. Have a seat in the parlor, and I'll have Mrs. Black bring you some tea."

Hannah's heart beat against her ribs. Nolan's tight smile may have fooled the minister, but it didn't fool Hannah. She knew him far too well for that. She gave him a hard stare before she made her way into the parlor and perched on the edge of one of the armchairs.

Out in the hall, Reverend Black called to his wife. Then the murmur of male voices drifted into the parlor. Hannah strained her ears but could not make out a word of what was being said. From her reticule, she took out a handkerchief and dabbed at the moisture on her forehead and upper lip.

What was Nolan up to now?

CHAPTER 10

Nolan paced the narthex of the country church, trying to ignore the beads of sweat forming while he waited for Mrs. Black to bring Hannah over from the rectory. Despite the early hour, the hot sun had raised the temperature to an unseasonable level. It didn't help that the church had been closed up tight since Sunday, and the air inside hung thick and suffocating like a shroud.

Nolan looked around the hushed building, seeing the wooden pews and stained-glass windows with new eyes. If it had not mattered so much to Hannah to be married in a church—not to mention his devout mother's feelings on the matter—Nolan would have set out to find a magistrate in another town whom he could bribe to marry them. For Hannah's sake, though, he was glad he'd been able to persuade the good reverend to his way of thinking.

Nolan had used every line of reasoning he could imagine, appealing to the man's sense of compassion and honor, begging him to do right by Hannah. After all, Nolan had argued, the minister had known him since he was a boy and Hannah since girlhood. He'd seen them in church almost every Sunday. And Nolan promised to take full responsibility with the earl for the matter, assuring Reverend Black that the monetary contributions to the parish would remain the same. When the man still wavered, Nolan thanked him, told him he understood, and that he and Hannah would keep going until they found a minister who would marry them.

Nolan had asked for the license back, at which point Mrs. Black had intervened. Her added plea for the cause of true love had been the deciding factor that had finally swayed Reverend Black, and at last, he'd agreed to marry them.

Nolan continued to pace the small vestibule, nerves getting the best of him. Had the minister changed his mind—*again*? He peered out the side window, dreading to discover that the earl had found them out. Nothing, however, looked out of the ordinary.

Even though Nolan's faith had wavered in recent days, he paused to offer a fervent prayer heavenward. *As much as I've always wanted to know my father, Lord, I can't say I'd have picked this particular man. But I trust you. I know you have a plan for me. I'm asking you to let that plan include Hannah, for I don't think I could bear my life without her. I promise I'll be a good husband to her for the rest of my life.*

At the loud creak of the church door, Nolan's head flew up. He blinked at the vision of Hannah in the doorway. She'd changed into a different dress, one the shade of the lush Stainsby lawns. Her green eyes shimmered, and her hair rippled over her shoulders in shining waves, adorned with daisies that danced around her head like a halo. Never had she looked more beautiful.

Nolan swallowed hard and held out his hand. With a tremulous smile, she stepped forward and placed her trusting fingers in his. He gave her a reassuring squeeze that he hoped conveyed the depths of his feelings.

Reverend Black strode past them up the main aisle of the church. "Let's get started before I come to my senses."

Mrs. Black and the couple's housekeeper, who had agreed to serve as a second witness, came up beside Hannah.

"Don't mind him," Mrs. Black said. "He'll be fine. Now, let's get you two lovebirds married."

Nolan escorted Hannah to the altar and they stood before the minister, their hands joined. Above them, sunlight streamed through the stained-glass windows, bathing them in a wash of color—almost as though God himself had reached out to bless their union. A measure of peace spread through Nolan, calming his jumbled nerves.

After a slight pause, Reverend Black opened his prayer book. "Dearly beloved, we are gathered here in the sight of God, and these witnesses, to join together this man and this woman in holy matrimony; which is an honorable estate, instituted of God, one that should not be entered into lightly." He raised his head to look at Nolan and Hannah. "Have the two of you come here freely, of your own accord, to commit yourselves to this union for the rest of your lives?"

Nolan nodded. "We have."

"We have," Hannah repeated.

The minister paused to study them both. "Very well then. Let us proceed." He turned to a marked page in the book and cleared his throat. "Nolan, wilt thou have this woman to thy wedded wife, to live together after God's ordinance in the holy estate of matrimony? Wilt thou love her, comfort her, honor, and keep her, in sickness, and in health? And forsaking all others, keep thee only to her, so long as ye both shall live?"

Nolan looked directly into Hannah's eyes. "I will."

"Hannah, wilt thou have this man to thy wedded husband, to live together after God's ordinance in the holy estate of matrimony? Wilt thou obey him, and serve him, love, honor, and keep him in sickness and in health; and, forsaking all others, keep thee only unto him, so long as ye both shall live?"

Tears flowed down Hannah's cheeks. "I will."

Nolan squeezed her fingers, his throat tight.

"I now ask you to pledge your troth to one another."

Nolan took a breath and solemnly vowed to love and cherish her forever. Hannah followed, stating her vows in a voice so sure and true that the depth of her devotion humbled him. His chest swelled with a tide of pure love, matched only by the emotion that shone from Hannah's eyes.

In addition to his pledge, Nolan gave Hannah the simple metal band Bert had fashioned for her. "With this ring, I thee wed. With my body, I thee worship and with all my worldly goods, I thee endow. In the name of the Father, and of the Son, and of the Holy Ghost. Amen." He then slipped the ring onto her trembling finger.

The rector peered over his spectacles. "Thereto having given and pledged your troth to one another and having declared the same by the giving and receiving of a ring, I now pronounce that you are man and wife. Those whom God has joined together, let no man put asunder."

A reverent hush fell over the group, as Nolan and Hannah stared at each other in giddy disbelief.

They were married!

Nolan could scarcely contain the joy that burst through him. *Thank you, Lord. I promise to spend the rest of my life making Hannah the happiest of women.*

And without waiting for permission, he bent to kiss his wife. The joining of lips in their first married kiss was as holy as the vows they had just spoken.

Then, with swift slashes of ink over paper, they signed the

marriage register and accepted the congratulations of the rector and his wife.

Nolan pressed the agreed fee, along with a nice bonus, into the minister's hand. "I can never thank you enough, Reverend. You've made Hannah and me the happiest pair on earth."

"You're welcome, lad. I only pray God spares me from the wrath of Lord Stainsby." He snapped the prayer book shut. "When will you tell him the news?"

Nolan's lips twitched. "Not just yet. I think my wife and I need a few days alone first."

Reverend Black adjusted his glasses on his nose and nodded. "May God bless you both."

Hannah floated on a wave of sheer bliss so heavenly she didn't even feel the bumps of the carriage as they traveled the rough side streets. *She was a married woman.* Her dream of becoming Nolan's wife had come true. Maybe not exactly as she'd hoped, but the unfamiliar weight of the silver ring on her finger spoke of the vows they had exchanged before God. Promises that bound them together for life.

All that remained to seal the union was the wedding night.

A shiver of nerves rippled down her spine. Where would they spend it?

Nolan smiled over at her with such warmth that her cheeks heated. "Almost there, Mrs. Price."

A sudden thought struck. "Am I Mrs. Price or Mrs. Fairchild?"

His frown made her rue the question.

"We signed the register as Mr. and Mrs. Price. I'll not worry about names right now."

"I'm sorry. I shouldn't have mentioned it."

His features softened. "Don't be sorry, Hannah. You need never fear speaking your mind to me. It's best to have things out in the open rather than let them fester."

A smile trembled on her lips. "That's how I feel as well. A husband and wife should be able to share every thought, every feeling, in complete safety."

"Agreed."

"So, in that spirit, where are you taking me, husband?" The lovely word fell from her tongue like she'd been married for years.

They'd been traveling for several hours now, and the early afternoon sun beat down on the top of her bonnet. Only her stomach rumbled in complaint, reminding her that she'd not eaten any breakfast. "I could use some refreshment sometime soon."

"You're in luck then, because I believe we've arrived at our destination." He slowed the carriage to a halt outside an old stone inn.

The moss-covered building was set back from the road, surrounded by a low brick wall and a gate that led into the courtyard. The sign above the door read *The Thornbridge Manor Inn*.

"I'll see to the care of the horses, and then we'll have ourselves a wedding feast," Nolan told her as he leapt nimbly to the ground.

Hannah accepted Nolan's assistance out of the carriage and waited as he paid the stable boy to look after the horses and another boy to bring in their bags. She cast nervous glances at the elegant people entering the establishment. "This place seems a trifle costly. Can you afford this?"

"You leave the money worries to me." Nolan offered her his arm. "I plan to spoil you as much as I can."

She attempted a smile as she allowed Nolan to lead her

through the main doors. Inside, the place bustled with activity. To the right, boisterous guests filled the elegant dining room, enjoying the remnants of their midday meal. To the left, a wooden desk spanned the wall under a sign that read *Register*. Straight ahead, a golden oak staircase curved up to the second story where the bedrooms must lie. A flush moved from Hannah's neck into her cheeks at the thought of sharing a room—and a bed—with her new husband.

Nolan stepped toward the desk and spoke with a gentleman. Hannah remained standing in the open, not wanting to hear whatever Nolan might be telling the man. Her acute embarrassment that the people in this establishment might know they were on their honeymoon was almost too much to bear.

The boy from outside appeared with their bags.

"Room 23," the desk clerk instructed.

Nolan tossed the boy another coin, and the lad bounded up the stairs. Hannah watched as Nolan crossed the polished wooden floor to her side and held out his elbow. "I believe a table is waiting for us in the dining room."

Moments later, seated at the small cloth-covered table adorned with china cups, saucers, and sparkling silverware, Hannah felt she should pinch herself to make sure this wasn't all an elaborate dream. Here she was, a mere kitchen maid, being treated like a fine upper-class lady. With trembling fingers, she removed her gloves and placed them in her reticule.

Nolan reached for her hand under the table and gave a gentle squeeze. "Please try to relax, Hannah. I want you to be able to savor this moment and remember it for years to come." His earnest blue eyes met hers.

Why couldn't she relax and appreciate Nolan's generosity? After commanding herself to stop worrying, she managed to enjoy the experience of being served a fine meal. The roast pheasant, mashed potatoes, and apple pie for dessert rivaled Edna's finest feast. With a full stomach and the restful surroundings, Hannah's anxiety finally receded. Still, every so often, her attention shifted to the entrance of the dining room, sure the earl would come bursting in and ruin this wonderful day.

She leaned forward to speak softly in the vicinity of Nolan's ear. "Do you think Lord Stainsby will be after us by now?"

Nolan regarded her with a steady gaze. "Not unless Reverend Black went against his word. I told his lordship that I needed a few days to travel to my mother's hometown and inform her relatives of her passing. He agreed with little objection."

"But what if he realizes I'm gone too?"

Nolan raised her hand to his lips. "Let's not borrow trouble, my love. I have much more important things on my mind right now. Like taking my wife up to our room." A rakish grin creased his handsome face.

Hannah's heart sprinted in her chest, and she could only stare at him.

"Ready?" he asked gently.

She swallowed hard and nodded. *As ready as I'll ever be.*

Together they climbed the winding staircase to the upper level. Hannah was sure every eye followed their ascent, every guest whispering behind gloved hands as to what the young couple was up to. She looked straight ahead as she walked down the carpeted corridor to the end room. The sweet scent of cinnamon and apples wafted up the stairs from the kitchen below. The lighting grew dimmer the farther they walked, just as Hannah's courage faded with each step.

At last, Nolan stopped outside a wooden door. He took out a brass key, fitted it into the lock, and with a loud click, swung the door inward.

Hannah's feet froze to the floor, immobilized with fear. Nolan turned back when she didn't follow him in, a question in his eyes. Did he sense her uncertainty?

He walked back into the hall. "Of course. I almost forgot." With a swoop of his arms, he lifted her high and stepped across the threshold of their room. He dropped a light kiss on her cool lips. "Welcome to the honeymoon suite, Mrs. Price."

A large four-poster bed dominated the cozy room. Heavy drapery flanked the rectangular window that faced the back courtyard, and a large stone hearth took up most of the adjoining wall. Their two bags sat on the braided mat.

Nerves fluttered in Hannah's stomach as she looked everywhere but the bed.

Nolan moved to the washstand where he inspected the pitcher. "There's water and clean towels here if you'd like to freshen up." A reddish tinge colored his neck. "I'll go check on the horses and give you some privacy."

As he moved past her, he dropped a kiss on her cheek. "I'll be back very soon."

"I'll be waiting," she promised.

As soon as the lock sounded in the door, Hannah removed her hat, dress, and shoes. She made use of the chamber pot, washed off the dust from the day's travels, and dabbed her skin dry with the softest of towels. She opened her bag and took out the few articles of clothing she had brought with her, hanging some in the wardrobe along with her good dress. Quickly she changed into her white cotton nightgown. While she brushed out her hair, she gazed at her reflection in the warped mirror. If only she had something nicer to wear than her high-necked cotton gown. Would her husband find her appealing or plain?

Nolan checked on his horses, made sure they were comfortable with food and clean water, then spent a few minutes staring up at the late-afternoon sky in the back courtyard of the inn. The wind had picked up since they arrived. Overhead, clouds swirled in hypnotic patterns, as if trying to outrun the impending rain. He pulled up the collar of his jacket against the sting of dirt in the air as thoughts of Hannah tugged at his conscience.

He couldn't deny the abject fear he'd sensed in her since arriving at the inn. If he had his way, he'd ease his beloved into the physical aspect of marriage, woo her over time until she felt comfortable with him. Unfortunately, time was a luxury they did not have. He needed to make sure their union was validated, so that an annulment would not be possible.

Despite the confidence of his decision, a degree of unease plagued him. Had his arrogance, his desire to circumvent the will of the earl, caused him to push Hannah into marriage too quickly?

For the second time that day, Nolan turned his thoughts to the Almighty. *Lord, forgive me for my recent anger at you and for my arrogance with Hannah. Please ease Hannah's fears and help me to be a sensitive husband to her.*

With a long sigh, he straightened, pulled his cap low on his forehead, and headed back inside.

When Nolan returned to the room, he knocked softly before he inserted the key into the lock. The interior was shrouded in darkness, save for the flare of a lone candle on the night table. Hannah had pulled the heavy drapes across the window, effectively blocking out all remaining daylight.

Where on earth was she? She wouldn't have gotten so nervous that she bolted, would she?

A small shift under the voluminous quilt on the bed pin-pointed his attention to the eyes peering out at him.

"Did I give you enough time?" he asked softly.

"Yes."

The one-word answer did little to ease his mind. He turned the lock on the door, then peeled off his jacket, coat, and vest. The eyes watching him got wider by the moment. He breathed out a soft sigh and asked the Lord for guidance.

"Do you mind if I wash up a bit?" He kept his tone as casual as if he'd asked her to pass the potatoes.

"No. Go ahead." She pulled the covers over her head to engulf her completely.

Nolan raked his fingers through his flattened hair. With a resigned grunt, he opened the collar of his shirt and moved to the washstand. Quickly he washed his face, neck, and hands, and dried off with a towel. Not a sound came from the bed.

His shoulders slumped. How many times had he dreamed about making sweet love to Hannah? Too many to count. And never once did this particular scenario enter his mind—his bride cowering under the coverlets, afraid to even look at him. What should he do?

Remember to put the Lord in the middle of your marriage.

The minister's parting words came back to Nolan, giving him a burst of inspiration. Still clad in his white shirt and trousers, he went to sit on the side of the bed. Hannah's quick intake of breath beneath the covers gave away her nerves. Gently, he took the edge of the blanket and drew it down to reveal her anxious face.

"Hannah, give me your hands." He kept his voice calm, as though soothing a skittish mare. Bert always said Nolan had a way with nervous horses. He hoped he had a way with terrified women as well.

Her fingers held a frozen grip on the linens.

"You can do this, love. Take my hand. We're just going to talk a while."

"Talk?" The air whooshed out of her lungs in one great gust.

"Yes. I want you to feel comfortable with me, if nothing else. And to do that, I'd like us to pray together. Would that be all right with you?"

"I've been praying all day." The words were no louder than a whisper.

"That's fine. But I'd like us to start our marriage by praying together. It could be something we do every night, if it suits you."

Relief visibly flooded her features, and a tremulous smile appeared. "I'd like that very much."

Carefully, she peeled the covers back. Nolan's pulse sprinted at the sight of the long golden hair that spilled over her shoulders. He caught a glimpse of a white lace bodice before she tucked the covers under her arms and reached out to clasp his hands. Taking a deep breath, he fought to keep his heartbeat under control.

Give me the right words, Lord.

He bowed his head and began with the simple Lord's Prayer, which they recited together. Then he spoke from the heart. "Thank you, God, for the gift of Hannah as my wife. May I always be a kind and gentle husband. Help me to show her how much I treasure, cherish, and respect her—in all ways. May our love be perfect in your sight. Amen."

When he lifted his head, he saw moisture glistening in her eyes. "Oh, Nolan. That was lovely. I—I'm sorry I'm not behaving like a proper wife on her wedding day." A lone tear escaped her lashes and rolled down to her lip.

He reached up to wipe it away with his thumb. "There's

no proper way to act. You can't help your feelings . . . or your fears." It occurred to him then that she'd had no mother to prepare her for what to expect after the wedding. "We're both nervous, Hannah. But we have our whole lives to figure this out. Do you . . ." He cleared his throat. "Do you understand what happens between a man and woman?"

"I think so," she mumbled, looking at the bedspread.

"You must be able to at least look at me. There is nothing to be ashamed of or embarrassed about."

Hands still captured in his, she slowly raised her eyes.

"After tonight, there will be no awkwardness between us—only joy. I promise. We will truly be one. Just as God intended."

Though her cheeks flamed, she didn't try to hide her face. He lifted one hand to run his palm down the silky length of her hair. How many times had he longed to feel its texture? "You are so beautiful. I don't know how I got lucky enough to claim your heart."

"You've had it since I first arrived at Stainsby and you fixed that broken dish for me. Other than Edna, you're the only one who's ever really cared about me."

Nolan went still, incensed that his beloved felt less than the wondrous woman she was, and he silently vowed to spend his days making up for the lack of love in her life. He ran a knuckle down the velvet skin of her cheek. "I have loved you since I first saw you, though I didn't know it then." He leaned his face forward to fan soft kisses on her forehead, her temple, her eyelids. He inhaled the clean, pure scent of her, cheered that she didn't flinch from his touch.

He pulled back to look deeply into her eyes, to make sure she was willing to proceed. He was grateful to see no fear, only love shining there. His gaze fell to her parted lips, and his breathing grew shallow. "I'm going to kiss you now, if it's all right with you."

She swallowed and slowly nodded.

His pulse pounding in his veins, he cupped her face in both his hands and lowered his mouth to hers. It took only a moment for her cool lips to warm under his. A soft moan vibrated in her throat. She clutched his shoulders like a woman drowning and fused her mouth more firmly to his.

Sweet heavens, he hadn't dared hope for such enthusiasm.

Her eager lips lit a flame in his body that leapt and sputtered like the embers in the grate beside them. "I love you more than life itself," he whispered, trailing kisses down her jaw to her throat.

And when he laid her back on the feather mattress, all traces of her fear had been erased.

CHAPTER II

Morning light roused Hannah from a heavy sleep. She blinked and sat up in bed, pushing her tousled hair over one shoulder. Why hadn't she bothered to braid it last night? The sudden recollection of the reason sent a flood of heat to her cheeks. She covered her mouth as sensations flooded her, recalling how her tender, sweet husband had made her his wife in the most intimate way possible. Though she'd understood the mechanics behind it, she could never have dreamed the joy involved in sharing oneself so completely.

Movement at the side of the bed claimed her attention. Grinning at her, Nolan tugged a drape back from the window.

"Are you going to sleep all day, Mrs. Price?"

"What time is it?"

"The morning's practically over, and I, for one, am starved." He gestured to the small table beside the hearth. "I took the liberty of bringing up breakfast, since I thought you might not wish to eat in the dining room this morning."

"How thoughtful. Thank you." She fought the feelings of awkwardness that tried to take hold.

He brought her a tray with a plate of toast and marmalade

and a cup of tea. While she balanced the offering on her knee, he sat down beside her and devoured a half slice of toast in one swallow.

"After we eat, I'll ready the horses while you dress, and if you're agreeable, we can set out toward Cobourg."

Cobourg. The nearest sizable town to her stepfather's farm. She took a hasty sip of tea to wet her dry throat.

"We'll find an inn to stay in for the night and show up fresh tomorrow morning at the farm. That will give us enough time to get Molly's things in order and return to Stainsby by nightfall."

Dread curdled the tea in her stomach at the mere mention of the estate. The thought of returning to face the earl's wrath was not something she looked forward to. "Could we not stay here for a few more days on our own?" She hated to sound like a whining child, but she finally had Nolan to herself and was loath to let their time end just yet.

"Does my bride wish more practice in being married?" The twinkle in his eyes combined with his low chuckle made her pulse quicken.

"Nolan!" She jerked, sloshing tea over the side of her cup.

He only laughed at her outrage. "I have no objection to spending the afternoon right here in this bed, if you'd like."

She swatted him. "Behave yourself."

"I'm teasing you, Hannah. Whatever you wish, we will do."

He may have been teasing, but the love in his eyes told her he was serious. "Your plan sounds fine," she said. "Though I hate to leave such a lovely place."

"I've already asked at the desk and got the name of an equally fine establishment in Cobourg." He popped another piece of toast in his mouth and washed it down with a slurp of tea.

He certainly seemed in good spirits today. She wondered

how he managed to put thoughts of his irate father out of his mind so easily.

"Nolan?"

"Yes, my love?" He twirled a strand of her hair around his finger.

"Your father can't . . . I mean . . . our marriage can't be dissolved, can it?"

He lifted his palm to cup her cheek. "No, sweetheart. We are well and truly married now. And I intend for us to stay that way for a very long time."

Then his lips claimed hers in a kiss that promised an eternity of love to come.

"Blast it all." Edward slammed the ledger closed on top of his desk. The urgent business matter his solicitor had brought him yesterday would not be easily resolved. Edward had already spent far too long going over and over the figures. He simply could not force his mind to concentrate on the situation at hand when all he could think about was the fact that he now had a grown son.

One who had fled the manor before Edward could even begin training him.

Nolan had claimed he needed to travel to his mother's hometown and inform her relatives of her passing, but it seemed more like an excuse to leave. Perhaps the boy simply needed time to gain perspective on this monumental change in his life.

Edward pushed his chair back from the large mahogany desk and moved to the window behind him. Once again, memories of the boy's mother returned to taunt him.

Mary. His heart breathed her name and squeezed with sorrow. The woman he'd loved more than twenty years ago, who'd died bearing his child. *His son*. Had Mary really asked her sister to keep Nolan from him, or had Elizabeth simply made the decision on her own?

Edward was trying hard not to despise Elizabeth Price for her deception, but red-hot anger still consumed him every time he thought of her treachery. The rational side of his brain told him it was ridiculous to harbor such animosity toward a dead woman.

For Nolan's sake, Edward would have to get past it.

He strode to the fireplace and stoked the embers until a small flame flared. For his own sake, he needed to bury his resentment and concentrate all his efforts on forging a relationship with his son. The future of the Fairchild family rested on Edward's ability to turn a stable boy into a proper heir.

For certain, Nolan was a strong-willed lad. Edward hadn't missed the air of defiance surrounding the boy whenever Edward issued orders. Yet Nolan obeyed without question, giving Edward no cause for reprimand. The only time the lad had dared defy him was when his mother had taken ill. It was then Edward became aware—in no uncertain terms—of Nolan's disdain. Edward would have to tread carefully in his attempt to break his son of his servant's upbringing and mold him into a nobleman.

The first course of business would be the hardest—severing all ties between his son and the kitchen maid who had him so bewitched. The irony of the similarity to his own history was not lost on Edward. But he would do everything in his power to ensure a happier outcome for his son's future. It occurred to Edward that Nolan had not actually agreed to end his relationship with the girl, and so it fell to Edward to make sure his wishes were followed.

He set the poker back with a clang, his mind racing. What better time to speak with the maid than while his son was away?

He was sure the girl could be made to see reason before his son would. Especially if her job was on the line.

Isn't this exactly how your father treated Mary? Edward pushed away the guilt that threatened to surface. The two situations were not as similar as they seemed. After all, from what he'd observed, the young couple was merely flirtatious. Nowhere near as serious as he and Mary. He needed to take action now, while there was still time. Before, heaven forbid, the girl ended up with child.

He'd already dealt with Reverend Black and ensured his co-operation.

Now to make his position abundantly clear to the maid.

With a purposeful stride, Edward left the study and headed to the main hall where the butler always hovered.

The thin, balding man appeared from the shadows and offered a bow.

"Dobson, get the kitchen maid for me—the blond one—and send her to my study at once." Without waiting for a reply, Edward stomped back to his office.

When footsteps sounded in the hall several minutes later, followed by a rap at the door, Edward looked up from the papers on his desk. "Come in."

His plump cook wedged her way in the door and bobbed a curtsy.

"Mrs. Bridges? I sent for the kitchen maid. What is her name again?"

"Hannah Burnham, my lord."

"Yes, well, where is she? I need to speak to her about an urgent matter." He ignored the fact that it was highly unusual for the master of the house to speak to a mere maid.

"I'm sorry, sir. That's what I came to tell you." The woman clutched her apron as though agitated. "Miss Burnham had a few days' leave coming. She's away visiting her family."

Edward jerked, jolting the pen in his hand. A slow rage spread through his torso, matching the splotch of ink that bled onto the page before him.

The chit of a girl was away at the same time as his son. This could not be a coincidence.

Edward focused to contain his emotions lest they intimidate the older woman. He inhaled and let the air out in an even release. "I see. And do you have any knowledge of where Miss Burnham's family lives?"

"Oh, yes, sir. I know exactly where they live." The woman's air of anxiety dissipated and a wide smile creased her cheeks. "Ann Burnham and I grew up in the same neighborhood. She married a farmer and lives not far from there."

The tension in his shoulders uncoiled a notch. "Excellent. Have a seat, Mrs. Bridges, and tell me everything you know."

Nolan hummed under his breath as he guided the carriage off the main road onto the dirt lane leading into Cobourg's outlying farm territory. The faint scent of manure, combined with fresh cut hay, floated on the breeze.

Nothing could dampen his good spirits today. He was legally, physically, and spiritually wed to the woman he loved. A woman who quickened his pulse with only a glance. He turned to find her watching him and winked, causing a blush to pink her cheeks. Was she thinking of their passionate interlude at the Swann Inn? Much to his delight, Hannah's fear from their wedding night had vanished completely and last night, she seemed to enjoy their time together as much as he.

Heat crawled up his neck at the memory. He took out a handkerchief and mopped the beads of sweat from his brow.

As the road became less even, he slowed the horses' gait. In the distance, two distinct farmhouses stood out. He nodded toward the horizon. "Is one of those farms your mother's?"

Hannah's slight form stiffened beside him. "No. It's the next one, over that ridge." Her mouth tightened, and little lines of worry creased her forehead.

If only her mother didn't upset her so. Nolan gathered the reins in one hand and reached for her fingers with the other. When he saw the tears on her lashes, he realized the depth of her distress went far beyond what he'd imagined.

He slowed the horses to a halt at the side of the road. "Are you worried about telling your mother we're married?"

"A little. She always makes me feel that I'm wrong. That I'm not good enough, not important enough."

The sorrow in her voice tore at Nolan. He gathered her to him in a fierce grip. "Well, you are the most important person in the world to me. You are kind, loyal, and honest." He kissed the top of her head, vowing never to let anyone hurt Hannah again now that he was her husband.

She turned her face to give him a watery smile. "I thank God every day for you, Nolan, because when I lost my family, God gave me you." With a small sigh, she brushed her lips to his.

His heart swelled with love and the desire to protect her. Never again would Hannah feel abandoned or unloved. He would make sure of it.

Twenty minutes later, they crested a hill, and a colorful patchwork of farmland spread out before them. Hannah pointed to a barn in the distance. "That's the one."

He clucked to the horses, and they forged ahead. The closer they got to the farm, the more Nolan's skin prickled. Would Hannah's family be happy about their union or upset? Would they agree to let Molly come with them, or would Nolan have to use all his powers of persuasion to convince them?

Hannah, too, was tense and withdrawn as the carriage swung onto the Fielding property. A large cloud now obscured the sun that had beat down on them the whole morning, throwing shadows over the road ahead. A small wooden farmhouse appeared to their right, while the dirt lane veered to the left toward the barn. Nolan guided the horses there, hoping to get some hay and fresh water for the overheated steeds.

As they rounded the side of the barn, shock froze Nolan's hands on the reins. His insides hardened to stone, squeezing the breath from his lungs.

Hannah gasped and clutched his arm.

In the shade of the Fielding barn sat the Earl of Stainsby's personal carriage.

CHAPTER
12

Hannah's hand, encased tightly within Nolan's, trembled like leaves caught in a gust of wind. Her first instinct had been to flee. Get back in the carriage and keep on going—anywhere but into that house to face the earl and her mother.

But Nolan's good sense had prevailed. They had to face his father sometime, he'd reasoned. It had just happened a little sooner than expected.

Hannah willed her legs to move up the few rickety steps to the farmhouse door. Nolan's fierce scowl did little to ease her anxiety. What would he say to the earl? She prayed he would keep his temper in check.

Lord, give me the strength to get through this. And help Nolan to stay calm.

Her mother answered on their first knock. Hannah's heart rate sprinted at the sight of the woman she both loved and resented. Her mother had aged over the years, her brown hair now streaked with gray. An array of fine wrinkles wreathed the skin around her tired eyes, and a plain dress hung loosely on her thin frame. She must be working herself to the bone to keep up with the house and the children.

"Hello, Hannah. We've been expecting you."

No smile of welcome, no embrace for a daughter dearly missed. Only lines of worry hugging her mouth, and nervous energy that came off her in waves as she peered out over their shoulders to the fields beyond—no doubt making sure her husband was not in the vicinity.

Hannah stepped inside the door, which opened into the kitchen. The lingering scent of the morning's bread hung in the air. Hannah gave her mother a brief nod. "Hello, Mum." She turned, almost colliding with Nolan behind her. "This is . . . this is Nolan Price." She threw him an apologetic glance, not sure if she should reveal their marriage now that the earl was here.

Nolan stepped forward. "Nice to meet you, Mrs. Fielding."

Her mother shook Nolan's hand and motioned them to come farther inside. She leaned closer to Hannah, gripping her arm. "Maybe one of you would care to explain why there is an *earl* in my sitting room? Lord Stainsby arrived an hour ago and told me you would be coming." Her tone held a hint of accusation, as though Hannah had forced him here.

She flinched from the iron grip of her mother's fingers. "It's a long story." She turned miserable eyes to Nolan who stood rigid beside her, his jaw clenched.

"You two had better come with me." Her mother turned on her heel and disappeared down a hallway.

Hannah stared after her. The heat from Nolan's hand at the small of her back cued her frozen feet to move.

"It's all right, Hannah." Nolan's warm breath stirred the tendrils of hair at her temple. "He can rant and rave, but he can't change the fact that we are legally married."

She nodded, wanting to believe those comforting words, yet a deep, cold part of her worried that his father would find some way to tear them apart.

The earl unfolded his tall frame from the chair by the hearth and rose to his full height, eclipsing Ann Fielding, who stood beside the faded sofa.

Keeping Hannah to his side, Nolan stopped in the middle of the room, feet wide, prepared to do battle with his father. Nolan held his head high—no servant's submission would he show. He was a married man now, protecting his wife. "What are you doing here, sir? Why are you imposing on Hannah's family in this manner?"

"Mr. Price. Miss Burnham." The earl gave a slight bow. "So nice you could join us." Though his features remained neutral, his tone oozed with subtle intimidation.

"My lord." Hannah dropped a curtsy, then straightened. She kept her head bent, gaze fused to the braided rug at their feet.

Nolan clamped his back teeth together, his jaw muscle tightening. How dare he make Hannah feel inferior in her mother's home? "You haven't answered my question," he said.

"I have been enjoying Mrs. Fielding's company. I also had the opportunity to meet her younger daughter, Molly. Such a pretty child." The earl lingered on the last word, his eyes narrowed on Hannah. "It seems congratulations are in order on Molly's upcoming nuptials."

Under Nolan's arm, Hannah's frame stiffened.

A flicker of awareness flashed in Edward's eyes, almost as if he'd been baiting Hannah on purpose in order to gauge her reaction.

Nolan had no idea what game the earl was playing, but he

wouldn't allow his bride to become a pawn. "Hannah, would you and your mother excuse us, please? I'd like to speak to Lord Stainsby in private."

Mrs. Fielding looked to the earl as though seeking permission, and Hannah threw Nolan a desperate look.

Despite Edward's glare, Nolan placed a hand on his wife's shoulder. "It will be fine. Go and visit with your mother and sister."

She bit her lip and nodded, then dropped another slight curtsy before following her mother out of the room.

The moment the women left, all false niceties fell away.

"By all that is holy, tell me you have not gone and married that chit." Edward's eyes glittered as hard and cold as the glass bowl in the center of the gateleg table.

Nolan held his fists at his sides to avoid the temptation of using them. "You, sir, will speak of my wife with respect."

"So, my suspicions are correct." The quiet words packed more punch than a bellow.

Nolan held his stance, refusing to be intimidated. "Yes, we are married—legally and before God."

Edward paced in front of the hearth. "No matter. Your mistake can still be undone."

"No, it cannot." With supreme effort, Nolan kept his temper in check. "We are united in all the ways that will matter to a judge."

The earl stopped and seared Nolan with a hard look. "Do not presume that I am without the means or the influence to fix this. I have the power to pull whatever strings necessary to dissolve this union."

The threat hung in the air between them.

Nolan's last thread of hope that he would be able to foster a real relationship with his father unraveled faster than the ball of yarn in Mrs. Fielding's knitting basket. All his life, Nolan had dreamed about having a father to look up to, to be proud of. Now it seemed he'd been better off not knowing his father at all.

Nolan took a measured step forward. "Do not presume," he said, his tone just as threatening, "that I value your paternity, your position, or your wealth above the love of my wife." He spoke with a calm that belied his inner rage. "Because if you force me to choose, I will take Hannah and leave Stainsby—for good."

"What manner of trouble have you gotten into now?" Hannah's mother lifted a shaky hand to peer through the curtain at the kitchen window. She looked left and right, then let the lacey panel fall back into place. When she turned, her mouth was pressed into a grim line.

Hannah stood in the center of the room, fingers clasped together in an effort to calm her wayward nerves. "I'm sorry, Mum. I had no idea the earl would come after us here."

"What have you done to make him chase you? Stolen his property?" She jabbed a finger toward the door. "That buggy out there belongs to him, does it not?"

Hannah couldn't quite meet her mother's glare. "Nolan borrowed it . . . for our wedding trip."

"Wedding?" The high color in her mother's cheeks faded to gray. She clutched the kitchen table and lowered herself onto a chair. "Don't tell me you married that boy."

Hannah fingered the metal wedding band, trying to let the sting of disapproval roll off her. She would not let her mother make her feel like she'd done something wrong, not about this. She lifted her chin. "Yes. Two days ago at the church in Stainsby," she said quietly. "I love Nolan very much."

"Fat lot of good love does you." Her mother scowled.

Hannah winced. Was she thinking of Hannah's dear father? How he'd promised to provide for her, but died unexpectedly, leaving them with nothing?

"That still doesn't explain why an earl would bother chasing after two of his servants. If he didn't approve of the marriage, he'd simply sack you when you returned." Her hard eyes narrowed. "What aren't you telling me?"

Hannah shifted her weight from one foot to the other. "It turns out Nolan is the earl's son. His mother revealed the news on her deathbed not long ago."

Understanding dawned. "And Lord Stainsby is none too happy that his son ran off with a maid." She heaved a great sigh and pushed up from the table. "Well, this is a fine mess you've made of your life."

Hannah winced. Whatever happened to the mother she used to know, the one who used to laugh and bake cookies with them, the one who wanted the best for her daughters? "You were happy once, weren't you, Mum?" she asked softly. "When Papa was alive, and we were all living at the rectory?"

"Aye, once." Her mother pinched her lips together as though trying to keep any emotion from leaking out. "But that was long ago, and there's no use living in the past." She darted a glance at the door. "I'll ask that you be gone before Mr. Fielding returns for his dinner. We don't need to upset him with all this." She reached for a basket on a shelf above the sink. "I have beans to pick for our midday meal."

"Can't you be happy for me, Mum? At least a little?" Hannah hated the pleading note in her voice and swallowed hard to dislodge the tears threatening to surface.

Her mother stilled, a flash of pain crossing her features. "I hope your marriage is everything you want it to be, daughter," she said. "But from experience, I doubt very much that it will. I'll send Molly in to see you." With a swirl of cotton, she left the house.

Hannah sank onto one of the hard kitchen chairs, grateful for a moment to compose herself, free of the tension that had suffocated the room. For an instant, Hannah had hoped her mother might soften, but bitterness had reared its head once again. After the death of Hannah's father, followed closely by the loss of Hannah's younger brother, Mum had become a hard, broken woman with little joy in her life. The thought saddened Hannah almost as much as the idea of Molly living in such an atmosphere.

The sound of footsteps pounding up the rickety stairs made Hannah jolt from her seat.

"Hannah, you're here!"

The kitchen door slammed, and a slim girl hurtled herself into Hannah's arms, almost knocking her over with her zeal. Molly's greeting brought warmth to Hannah's chest, easing the pain of her mother's indifference. She returned her hug, lingering longer than necessary, then held her sister at arm's length to study her. "Molly, is that really you?"

Long golden hair hung over her shoulder in a thick plait. The girl was almost as tall as Hannah, and her face had lost its baby roundness. Only her vivid blue eyes remained unchanged.

Hannah swallowed her regret at how much she'd missed of her sister's life. "My goodness, you've grown into a fine young woman."

"And you look like a grand lady." Molly smiled, transforming her youthful face into that of a beautiful girl on the brink of womanhood.

"Apparently you haven't seen too many ladies. I assure you, they are much grander than I." For the moment, Hannah forgot her troubles and laughed with her sister. Molly's arrival proved a welcome distraction from what might be happening between Nolan and his father in the other room. "Come and sit down."

Molly took a seat at the table and sobered at once, her eyes becoming anxious. "I'm so glad you're here. Promise you'll speak to Mum and Mr. Fielding. Tell them I don't want to marry that horrid man." Her nose wrinkled with distaste. "Mr. Elliott's old, Hannah. Nearly forty, I think."

If the situation wasn't so dire, Hannah might have laughed at Molly's exaggerated reaction. But no matter the age of the groom, the fact remained that Molly was too young to be married—to anyone. Hannah's stomach gave an uneasy roll. She wasn't sure what to expect once they returned to Stainsby, but she hoped Nolan could secure Molly some type of position. If the earl was too angry to allow it, then Hannah would prevail upon Mrs. Bridges to help find Molly work at a neighboring estate. Anything would be better than marrying Mr. Elliott.

"That's why we're here." Hannah leaned close to her sister, the fresh scent of grass and sunshine wafting off Molly's hair. "We want to bring you back to Stainsby Hall with us." She kept her voice low for fear of being overheard.

"Oh, Hannah. That would be wonderful." Then Molly's eyes clouded over. "But I don't think Mr. Fielding will allow me to go. The wedding's set to take place in two weeks' time."

"Two weeks?" Hannah gasped. "Why so soon? They haven't even announced the betrothal."

"Mr. Elliott's housekeeper just gave her notice. She'll be moving away to live with her son. That's why they're rushing the ceremony."

Hannah bristled. Couldn't the man simply hire another woman? Or did he want Molly for the free labor she'd provide?

"Well, then," she said firmly, "we'll have to make sure you

leave with us today." Hannah rose to pull back the curtain at the kitchen window and peered out over the property. In the distant field, the toiling figures of three men and a horse told her the Fieldings were still at work. There was no sign of her mother. She returned to the table.

"It won't be easy," she told Molly. "You'll likely get a position as a maid, and you'll have to work hard each day. But you'll receive a wage and have a room of your own."

Molly grasped her hand. "The work can be no harder than all I do here for no wages at all. Plus I have to share a room with Mr. Fielding's daughters. My own room sounds like heaven."

Hannah pressed her lips together to contain her emotions. All these years she'd envied Molly being allowed to stay with her mother and become part of a large family. Suddenly Hannah's life at Stainsby appeared to be the better one.

"I must tell you my news," she said. "I have recently married. His name is Nolan and he lives at Stainsby as well." She paused. Best not to swamp the girl with all the details of Nolan's situation right away. They would have plenty of time for her to learn the whole story. "Right now, Nolan is speaking with the earl about letting you come back with us."

The anxiety lifted from Molly's features. "I hope he manages it. It will save me from having to run away like I'd planned."

Horror filled Hannah at the thought of what could become of her sister. There were fates worse than marriage for a young girl with no means to support herself. "That won't be necessary, dearest. One way or the other, we'll figure something out. I promise."

Hannah set her jaw. She would not allow Molly's life to be ruined. If their own mother would do nothing to protect her, then Hannah had no choice but to step in and do whatever it took to guard Molly's innocence.

Nolan waited for the earl to respond to his ultimatum. Instead of becoming angry, the man had turned pensive, watching him with catlike eyes.

A clock on the mantel ticked out the seconds.

Nolan shifted his weight, wishing he were wearing his comfortable boots. His Sunday shoes pinched his toes, but he refused to take the weight off by sitting down. That would give the earl an edge, and Nolan needed every advantage he could get.

At last, Edward spoke. "I take it Miss Burnham is not pleased by her sister's upcoming marriage."

Of all the things he'd prepared for the earl to say, this hadn't even crossed Nolan's mind. "No. Hannah feels Molly is much too young to wed."

"I gathered as much. And in that vein, I have a proposition for you."

Apprehension slid down Nolan's spine. "What sort of proposition?"

The light from the window reflected off the silver strands at Edward's temple as he adjusted the sleeve of his navy coat. "I will offer Molly a post at Stainsby, and she may accompany us back, if"—he paused—"you agree to annul this farce of a marriage."

A volcanic heat rushed through Nolan's chest. He should have known the man could not be reasoned with. "Absolutely not. This conversation is over." He started for the door.

"Wait."

The hint of desperation in his father's voice gave Nolan a momentary victory. He schooled his features and turned to face him.

"If you agree to come back," Edward said slowly, "and receive the training necessary to become a proper earl's son, I will find a position for the girl."

"And what of my wife?" Nolan lifted his chin and held his breath. Whatever the earl said next would sway Nolan's decision on how their relationship would go from here on out.

Edward squared his shoulders. "I would ask that you not make your marriage public until I've had the chance to introduce you into my social circle. It will be difficult enough to explain your existence without complicating matters with a low-born bride."

Nolan's nails bit into the flesh of his palms, and a growl rumbled in his throat.

Edward held up his hands, as if in surrender. "I only speak the truth."

The air hissed from Nolan's lungs. "How long will this training require?"

"Four weeks—maybe more—depending on how quickly you learn everything there is to know."

"And where would Hannah and I live?"

"You may move into the suite I have provided, but I would ask that Hannah remain in the servants' quarters for now." The earl shrugged. "It would defeat the purpose of keeping the marriage a secret if you lived together."

Nolan did his best to rein in his anger. He needed to keep a clear head, think logically. If he could get his father to ignore their marriage for four weeks, Edward would have time to grow accustomed to the idea. Surely then he would relent and accept Hannah as Nolan's wife.

If not, Nolan would be in possession of the Simpson farm by then. With a means to provide for Hannah and Molly, Nolan could part ways with the earl in an amicable manner.

Yet Nolan couldn't seem to abandon all hope that he and his father could come to a reasonable compromise.

"I need to discuss the matter with Hannah before I agree to anything." He moved to the door. "I'll be back in a few minutes."

Without waiting for a reply, he headed back to the kitchen where Hannah and a young girl sat at the table.

Hannah immediately got to her feet. "Is everything all right?" Her green eyes searched his.

He tried to smile, but his lips refused to cooperate. "This must be your sister. I'm Nolan, Hannah's husband."

"Hello, Nolan." Molly giggled and glanced at Hannah. "I wouldn't mind having to marry if Mr. Elliott looked like him."

"Molly, hush." Hannah's cheeks reddened.

Nolan turned to his wife. "I'm sorry to interrupt your visit, but I need to speak to you in private for a moment."

When Hannah nodded, he led her out the front door and down the steps onto the grass.

"What is it?" Her light brows pulled together in a frown. "Does your father know we're married?"

"He does now. Though I think he suspected as much and that's why he came here." How he hated that their idyllic days together had turned sour so quickly. Nolan reached for her hand to calm his inner turmoil as much as hers. "He's made us a proposition, which I won't agree to unless you do too."

Hannah blanched but lifted her chin. "Go on."

"He wants me to undergo training in the ways of the aristocracy. In return, he will give Molly a position at the manor."

"I see. And what about our marriage?"

Nolan paused to weigh his words. Telling Hannah that the earl had wanted their marriage annulled would only make her feel worse. "He's asked that we keep our union a secret for now, until I've been introduced to his peers as his son."

"What will that accomplish?" She seemed genuinely perplexed.

"I'm not entirely certain, but agreeing to his stipulation will buy us time. The training will take about four weeks, during which time Edward will surely grow accustomed to the idea of our marriage." At least Nolan hoped so, though he couldn't shake the feeling that Edward hadn't totally given up on dissolving their union. "If having a son is so important to him, he'll have to understand that he can't have me without you."

Hannah bit her bottom lip and frowned again.

He laid a hand on her shoulder. "If you don't wish to do this, we can return to Stainsby, pack our things, and leave." The more he thought about it, the sweeter the idea became.

"Where would we go? You don't own the farm yet." She waved a hand. "We certainly can't stay here. Mr. Fielding would never allow it."

"I'll find a way, Hannah, if that's what you want. Your happiness is the most important thing."

Tears formed in her eyes. She paced away from him and stood staring out over the landscape. At last, she squared her shoulders and walked back to him. "Very well. I'm willing to accept the earl's offer, if you are. It will get Molly away from here at least. And if things don't go the way you hope, by then you will be in possession of your farm, and we can move there."

"You're sure?"

She nodded. "I can wait four weeks to resume our life together if it means saving Molly. And I can give you that time to determine if being a nobleman is the type of life you wish to live."

A rush of relief filled Nolan's lungs. "You are a very wise woman, Hannah Price." He pulled her into a tight hug and kissed the top of her head. "Let's go and break the news to Lord Stainsby. Together."

CHAPTER 13

An hour later, Hannah waved to her mother as Nolan clucked the horses into motion. Standing on the porch, her mother gave no response, probably due to the presence of her husband standing rigidly beside her. Hannah shivered. The years had not been kind to Robert Fielding. His brown hair, now mostly gray, along with his sun-wizened skin, gave him the look of a much older man. The perpetual scowl on his face and the thick brows that hovered over his sunken eyes did not help matters.

Seated between Nolan and Molly in the buggy, Hannah breathed a quiet prayer of thanks that matters had transpired so smoothly and that Molly was able to leave with a minimum of upheaval.

After witnessing her stepfather's harsh reaction to their presence, Hannah had been relieved when Lord Stainsby asked the ladies to leave the men to discuss business alone. Whatever the earl had said to Mr. Fielding in private had finally persuaded him to let Molly leave with them. Perhaps a large sum of money had been involved. That seemed the only possible explanation to have changed her stepfather's mind. No matter, Hannah was grateful to have Molly safely in her care and away from the dreaded Mr. Elliott.

As the horses lumbered down the road, Hannah fingered the piece of paper in her pocket, slipped to her by her mother upon parting. Mum had actually hugged her, thanked her for helping Molly, and whispered in Hannah's ear, "If you ever find yourself in trouble, seek out Iris. She will help you."

Hannah had a vague recollection of a tall, striking woman who'd visited them years ago, before her father died. As soon as Hannah got a moment of privacy, she would read the note and attempt to piece together the connection. Not that Hannah expected to contact the woman. She had to believe that Nolan was right and things would work out in their favor.

It was dark when the carriage pulled up to the Stainsby stables many hours later. Nolan helped Hannah and Molly alight.

"Why don't you go inside and get Molly settled? We'll talk later." The intensity in his eyes made Hannah think there was an underlying message there. He moved a step closer and reached for her left hand. "Remember, we must keep our news to ourselves." He slipped the metal band off her finger and pressed it to his lips. "I will keep this in a safe place until I can put it back on your finger myself."

Hannah fought the disappointment that engulfed her as she stared at her now bare finger. With that small gesture, it felt like her marriage had come to an end. She lifted a silent, desperate prayer skyward that such would never be the case.

"Don't forget," he said to Molly, "your sister's and my marriage must remain a secret for now."

"I won't." Molly threw her arms around Nolan in an enthusiastic hug. "Thank you, Nolan. You saved my life."

Nolan broke out the first real smile Hannah had seen since

they had found the earl at her stepfather's farm. "Welcome to Stainsby Hall, Miss Molly. I hope you'll be happy here."

"I'm sure I will." With the enviable optimism of youth, Molly linked arms with Hannah.

Although she wasn't entirely comfortable with how things had turned out, having Molly here with her lifted a huge burden from Hannah's spirit. "Thank you, Nolan. I'll see you later, I hope."

He nodded, a shadow of regret in his eyes. "I need to see to these horses." With that, he turned to open the stable doors.

Hannah let out a small sigh, wishing she was bold enough to give her new husband a kiss right out in the open. It felt too long since they had shared even that small intimacy. Maybe Nolan could sneak up to her room tonight once everyone was asleep. She allowed herself a thrill of anticipation, thinking of the possibility that they would surely share more than a kiss. Perhaps she'd suggest a midnight tryst when she saw him later.

Hannah led Molly into the kitchen through the servants' entrance.

Mrs. Bridges looked up from the sink, gave a strangled cry, and bustled over to envelop Hannah in a smothering hug.

"My dear girl, you have no idea how worried I've been." She dabbed her apron to her eyes, about to launch into a further explanation when she stopped. "And who do we have here?"

Hannah draped an arm around Molly's slim shoulders and pulled her forward. "This is my sister. Molly, this is Mrs. Bridges, the head cook and your new supervisor."

"This is wee Molly? Why, you're a young lady now."

Molly giggled and dropped a half curtsy. "Hello, Mrs. Bridges."

Edna peered over her half-spectacles. "Did you say Molly is working here now?"

"Yes, the earl has given her a position as scullery maid."

Edna's brows rose. She gave Hannah a knowing stare. "He has? Well, you'll have to tell me how all this came about. But first you can show Molly to her room. Miss Hatterley will tell you which one she can take."

Hannah's smile faded. How would she explain Molly's being here? The thought of not being able to tell Edna the whole story didn't sit well. "Yes. We'll talk later."

"Count on it, miss." Edna gave her a stern stare, then looked pointedly at Hannah's left hand as though she could see an imprint of the ring that had been there.

With a blush heating her cheeks, Hannah turned away to usher Molly up the stairs.

Through the ever-present gossip mill, Hannah soon heard various servants discussing the fact the earl had given Nolan a whole suite of rooms on the second floor. Of course, the other maids had been quick to tell Hannah how flabbergasted everyone had been that one of their own had risen to new standing as the earl's son. The girls' inane chatter only increased Hannah's unease at the huge secret she kept.

Now, while helping Edna with the evening chores, Hannah braced for the woman's inevitable questions, praying she could find a way to explain how Nolan and Lord Stainsby had ended up at her mother's farm.

"You two ran off together, didn't you?" Edna's question jarred Hannah from her thoughts. "That's why his lordship had me tell him where Ann lived. What other reason could there be?" The woman fisted a hand on her ample waist.

Hannah kept her focus on the dish in her hand. "Before Mrs. Price took ill, Nolan promised to help me get Molly away from our stepfather and his marriage schemes. When the earl realized we were both gone, he jumped to a different conclusion about our absence." There, not quite a lie. The truth cloaked in innuendo.

"I still don't understand how Molly came to be here." Edna swished the water in the sink.

"Nolan agreed to come back and take his position as the earl's son if his lordship gave Molly a position here."

Edna gave her a suspicious look. "That doesn't explain where you both were for two days before the earl left."

"I'm sorry. I really can't talk about that." Heat flooded Hannah's neck and cheeks. She ducked to place a bowl in a low cupboard.

Deafening silence filled the kitchen.

"Excuse me," Edna said stiffly. "I need to check the larder for tomorrow's meals." She shuffled toward the back door, leaving Hannah with a bucket load of guilt. She'd hurt the only person other than Nolan who'd ever cared about her well-being.

Forgive me, Edna. I promise to make it up to you one day.

Molly came into the kitchen, her apron filled with potatoes. "What's the matter with Mrs. Bridges? She about bit my head off." Molly dumped the vegetables into a large wooden bowl on the table.

"She's just tired. She'll be in better humor tomorrow. Come and help me finish up here."

The evening shadows shrouded the room as she and Molly washed the remaining dishes. Molly seemed to sense Hannah's need for quiet, and they worked in silence.

A few minutes later, the sound of heavy boot steps descending the back staircase had Hannah's heart racing. She turned to see Nolan's broad shoulders filling the opening from the stairs.

Her hands fluttered to her apron. "Nolan. How are you? Have you eaten?" They'd arrived past the supper hour, but Mrs. Bridges had given her and Molly some bread and cheese.

"Yes. I ate with my . . . with the earl." He nodded in Molly's direction and gave her a smile. "How are you settling in, Molly?"

"Very well, thank you."

"I'm glad." He gave her a distracted smile, then turned to Hannah. "May I have a word with you in private?"

Was it her imagination, or did he already sound different? More like an upper-class gentleman than a servant? "Of course." She untied the apron and pulled it off. Anticipation quickened her pulse.

"Let's talk outside." He moved to the back entrance and held the door for her.

Hannah's stomach dipped at the grim line of his mouth and the tension in his shoulders. Gone were his easy grin and the teasing glint in his eyes.

She stepped out into the cool night air and followed him to a wooden bench beside the door. He gestured for her to sit.

"Nolan, has the earl done something to upset you?" She searched his face for a clue to his odd mood.

He reached over to take one of her hands in his. The warmth of his fingers helped ease the chill that had invaded her heart. "No more than usual. I wanted to see how you were faring with Edna. Did she question you?"

"Of course she did. I told her you were helping me with Molly, and that the earl jumped to a wrong conclusion." She sighed. "I fear I hurt her feelings when I wouldn't explain further."

"I'm sorry. I know this is difficult for you."

"I'll manage." She smiled. "Knowing Molly is safe and happy more than makes up for it."

His callused thumb rubbed circles over her palm. "This isn't how we planned to start our married life, and I'm truly sorry for that. But I do feel an obligation to try to get to know my father." He tipped her chin up to look into her eyes. "Giving Edward this one concession will work in our favor. It will give him time to adjust to our marriage, and perhaps if we cooperate with him, he will do the same for us."

It was only natural that Nolan would want to forge some sort of relationship with his father. Hannah could never deny him that. She gave his fingers a squeeze. "I understand. I can surely wait four weeks to resume our marriage. It's the least I can do after all you've done for Molly."

"Thank you, Hannah." He heaved out a great gust of air. "You have no idea how much I hate having to be apart from you. Please do not doubt my feelings. Nothing has changed that."

His arms came around her then, and he pulled her tight to his chest.

Her heart thrilled as his lips came down on hers in a lingering kiss.

"Oh, Nolan." She raised a hand to his jaw, the stubble pricking her palm. "I will miss you, now that I've gotten used to sharing"—she flushed—"so much time with you."

"So will I, my love," he said in a husky voice. "But it won't be for long. I promise."

Hannah prayed he was right. "When will I see you again?"

"I'll try to meet you at the elm tree for your afternoon break. Maybe we can steal a few moments together then." He kissed her again. "For now, I'm afraid that will have to do."

CHAPTER 14

Anticipation tingled through Hannah's system as she crossed the back lawn. Would Nolan be waiting for her today?

For the past two weeks, they'd managed to sneak a few precious moments together each afternoon and steal a few heart-stopping kisses in the cluster of bushes behind the tree, out of sight of anyone who might wander by. It wasn't much, but it kept Hannah from losing hope that their marriage could survive this huge change in Nolan's life.

When she turned the corner, a spurt of disappointment washed over her. He wasn't sitting on the chicken crate as usual. She slowed her pace until she reached the tree. She'd wait here and hope that he'd show up before her break was over.

The hens in the nearby chicken coop clucked loudly, fighting over some feed no doubt. She must remember to tell Edna that Lucy, the oldest bird, wasn't laying as many eggs lately.

A hand grasped Hannah's waist. She let out a strangled cry and whirled around to find Nolan grinning at her. "Mickey came by so I had to hide. Though I must say it's great fun to surprise you." His lips came down on hers before she managed to get her breath back.

She pushed him away to gulp in some air. "Nolan Price, you almost gave me heart palpitations." A huff of laughter escaped as he led her into the shelter of the bushes.

Hannah still couldn't get used to his new clothing. The fine linen shirt and fancy waistcoat, the untied cravat that now hung from his neck. Even his hair was different, combed back from his forehead.

"How are things going?" It was a question she'd avoided for some time now, almost dreading the answer. Was it selfish of her to hope that he might decide *not* to accept this new lifestyle? That he'd go ahead with his original plan to secure the farm?

"Tedious. I've never listened to so many unimportant details about dukes and earls and the nobility. Never had to learn so many names of relatives and business associates." He shrugged. "I imagine I'll figure it out eventually, but I don't know if it's possible to learn everything before the ball."

The ball. The affair that had the whole staff in an uproar. The event of the season during which Nolan would be presented to society as the earl's son and heir. She dredged up a smile. "I'm sure you'll do fine."

"We'll see." He pulled her back against his chest. "Let's not waste our time talking about trivialities."

When his lips met hers, she allowed the delicious thrill to silence all the worries tumbling about inside her. Allowed the warmth of his hand on her waist to override the fact that he didn't smell the same anymore. That the comforting scent of horse and hay and leather had been replaced by the smell of sandalwood soap and pipe tobacco. Had Nolan started to smoke a pipe?

"I miss you, Hannah. I miss Bert and the horses." Nolan looked up at the manor house, just visible beyond the tree line. "Will I ever get used to this? Do I even want to?"

She held her breath, not daring to guess his answer.

"In a few more days, I'll have the deed to the farm. And if things don't go well with my father, at least we'll have another option."

She reached up to lay her palm against his cheek. "We need to pray, Nolan. Pray for God's wisdom to guide you. To show you the path you're meant to take."

"I *have* been, love. On my knees every night. I don't know how much I harder I can possibly pray."

She wrapped her arms around his neck and pressed her cheek to his, wishing she could ease his tension. "It will all work out, you'll see. I'm sure once the ball is over, you'll know where things stand with your father. We just need to be patient a while longer."

Seated on King's back two days later, Nolan inhaled the fresh morning air and released a contented sigh. Dressed in a simple shirt and trousers, his favorite cap on his head, he felt more confident than he had in the past two weeks. More certain of his place in the world.

Today he would finalize the deal with Mr. Simpson, and the farm would belong to him. Then Nolan would have the comfort of knowing that he and Hannah could walk away from Stainsby Hall any time he chose and start their life on the farm.

As he rode on, the piece of paper in his pocket rustled, reminding him of the one thing that had put a damper on his good mood. This morning Nolan had found a message on the floor of his bedchamber, obviously slipped under the door in the middle of the night.

If you know what's good for you, stable boy, you'll leave Stainsby Hall and never come back.

The implied threat didn't scare Nolan, only angered him. What sort of coward would leave an unsigned threat? Only one person came to mind—one who hated Nolan enough to do such a thing. Not only was Timothy Bellows jealous that Nolan had claimed Hannah's heart, but now that Nolan was a member of the noble class, Bellows must surely be seething with resentment. Nolan would have to keep a close watch on him—especially around Hannah.

Nolan looked up at the sky and mentally calculated the time it would take to meet Mr. Simpson, travel into Derby to conduct their business, and return. If things went well, he'd be back before Edward had even come down for breakfast.

The closer he got to the Simpson property, the more certain Nolan became that this was the path God intended for his life. After all, wasn't this what his mother had wanted for him too?

"Promise me you'll go on with your plans," she'd said. *"Buy your farm and marry Hannah. Live a good life."*

He'd fulfilled one of his promises when he and Hannah had wed. Today, he would fulfill the other. A measure of peace settled over him at that thought.

The only thing marring his confidence was the knowledge that Edward would certainly be upset if Nolan chose not to take his rightful place as heir. The part of Nolan that still wished to please his father cringed at the thought of disappointing him, but Nolan could not determine the course of his life based on Edward's expectations. His talk of duty and sacrifice meant little to Nolan, since he hadn't been raised in Edward's world and didn't feel the same sense of obligation, the same connectedness to the Fairchild heritage.

Nolan would always be grateful he'd learned the identity of his father, that the mystery of his birth had been solved. But life as a nobleman didn't sit well with him. It was as uncomfortable a fit as the new clothes he was forced to wear. He doubted he could endure living that way for the rest of his life. So the question remained: should he inform Edward of his decision today or should he go through with the ball as intended and break the news afterward? Perhaps it would be kinder all around if he was honest and spared Edward the humiliation of introducing his son to his peers and business acquaintances, then having to explain why Nolan had left.

When the Simpson farm came into view, Nolan guided King down the lane toward the house, relieved to find the farmer seated on the porch step, waiting for him.

"Good day, Mr. Simpson," he called out. "'Tis a beautiful day for a ride."

The man rose but offered no greeting in return.

A thread of unease wound through Nolan's system. He pulled King to a halt and slid from the saddle. "Are you ready for the trip into Derby?"

In his overalls and stained shirt, the man didn't appear dressed for a business meeting.

Mr. Simpson shook his head. "Something's come up, I'm afraid." His gaze skittered to the fields beyond.

"I see. Well, I can come back another day then." Nolan fought the rise of disappointment. He'd counted on having ownership of the property today.

The farmer came down the steps toward him, scratching the back of his neck. "There's no easy way to tell you this, son. I've found another buyer for the farm."

Nolan jerked, jolting the reins in his hand. King snorted and tossed his head. "What do you mean? I thought we had an agreement."

"We did, and I hate to go back on my word." He squinted off into the distance, still not meeting Nolan's eyes. "But I received another offer. One more than double what you were willing to pay. I knew you couldn't match the amount, and frankly"—he gave Nolan a sheepish glance—"I can't afford to pass it up. I'm sorry, son. But business is business."

A chill settled over Nolan. "Who made such a generous offer? It must have been someone quite wealthy."

"Aye, that's the truth."

Nolan waited for him to name the buyer, but he only shrugged.

"I hope you find another property to your liking, Mr. Price. And again, I'm sorry for the way things turned out." Mr. Simpson headed back toward the house.

"It was Lord Stainsby, wasn't it?" The bitter words flew from Nolan's mouth of their own volition.

King gave a soft whinny, protesting Nolan's tightened grip.

The farmer stopped, his back rigid, then without a word, continued up the steps and into the house.

Nolan flung himself into the saddle. He didn't need Mr. Simpson's confirmation when his gut already knew the truth.

Somehow his father had gotten wind of Nolan's intent to purchase the farm, and had taken steps to ensure that would never happen.

Leaving Nolan with no second option, no avenue of escape. The Simpson property had been the only one in the area that Nolan could afford. He'd cultivated a relationship with Mr. Simpson for several years now so that the man would sell to him—to someone he trusted—when the time came. Funny how integrity fell by the wayside the moment large sums of money became involved.

Bitterness clawed at Nolan's chest. What would he do now? And how would he ever break the news to Hannah?

Nolan burst into the dining room and stomped across the floor to where the earl sat at the head of the table. Nolan glared at the footman standing by the sideboard. "Leave us."

The young man bowed and rushed through the servants' door.

"Is something wrong?" The earl patted a napkin to his mouth and laid it on the table. "You seem out of sorts."

"Why did you buy the Simpson farm?" His words were raspy, his lungs still heaving from the frenzied ride back.

"I don't know what—"

Nolan slapped a palm on the table so hard the china rattled. "Don't lie to me!"

"Very well." Edward pushed his chair back in a deliberate manner and rose. "It's true. I recently acquired a piece of acreage nearby. The owner was grateful for the tidy sum I offered."

The blood pounded between Nolan's ears. "You don't care about owning a farm. You only bought it because you somehow found out that I had an agreement to purchase it. Why would you do that to me?"

"I'll admit that when one of my footmen brought it to my attention that you intended to buy the Simpson farm, I felt a certain sense of betrayal." Edward walked slowly around the table toward him. "I thought we had come to an understanding, and yet all along you planned to leave. To become a *farmer*." He stopped to level a cold stare at Nolan. "I had to assume that you were merely humoring me. That the only reason you agreed to take your place as my son was to rescue your wife's sister."

Nolan's mouth gaped. He sputtered, then clamped his lips closed, because he couldn't totally deny Edward's claim.

"So in order to level the playing field, I removed the safety net." Edward's features hardened. "Although to truly level the field, I should remove the biggest obstacle of all."

Nolan surged forward. "You leave Hannah out of this. I won't allow—"

"Relax. I will do nothing to Hannah—as long as you continue to honor our agreement." He moved past him. "But I will have to insist you stop your clandestine meetings by the henhouse. A definite violation of my terms."

Nolan's hands shook. How could his father know about that? Did he have someone spying on them? He opened his mouth, but no words came out.

"Remember, the ball is less than two weeks away. Without the farm and Hannah to distract you, I trust you'll now have greater incentive to focus on your duties as my son." With a haughty incline of his head, Edward strode out the door.

A volcano of fury exploded through Nolan. With an unholy roar, he picked up one of the chairs and smashed it against the wall. Fragments of splintered wood flew in all directions.

He stood in the middle of the room, his chest heaving with the force of his rage, until a footman appeared.

"I'll clean that up for you, sir." The frightened look on the lad's face drained the last of Nolan's anger from him.

Attempting to control his ragged breathing, Nolan looked down at the shard of wood in his hand and carefully set it on the table.

"That won't be necessary," he said slowly. "I'm responsible for this mess. I'll clean it up myself."

CHAPTER 15

The loud clang of Bert's hammer striking the anvil sounded as Nolan entered the smithy. Still seething with resentment over Edward's treachery, he found himself in dire need of Bert's wisdom. Perhaps his friend could help him make sense of the mess his life had become.

Nolan's first instinct had been to take Hannah and Molly and leave Stainsby immediately. Yet, even in his heated state, he realized the futility of that plan. Though he still had the money he'd saved to buy the farm, it wouldn't last long, and in the meantime, he had nowhere to live, no means to provide for the women in the long term. He couldn't just rip them out of their security here on a whim of temper.

"Nolan, hello." Bert set down his tool and wiped his hands on his apron. "What brings you out here at this time of day?"

Nolan crossed the stone floor and leaned against a wooden post, inhaling the smell of fire and hot metal. "You're busy. I shouldn't have come."

"The work can wait," Bert said mildly. "But I dinna expect you can. I can see something's troubling you."

Nolan had only spoken to Bert once since he and Hannah

had returned to Stainsby. Unlike Edna, who couldn't keep a confidence to save her soul, Bert was the one person Nolan trusted with the news of their wedding, knowing he wouldn't even tell Franny if Nolan asked.

"Is his lordship giving you a hard time then?"

"That's an understatement of monumental proportions." Nolan lifted a metal spike from a pile of tools and turned it over in his hand, unable to hide his bitterness. "He bought the Simpson farm out from under me. Offered double my price. Of course, the man couldn't turn down that much money."

Bert came forward and laid a hand on Nolan's shoulder. "I'm sorry, lad. That was a rotten thing to do. But it tells me his lordship is scared."

"Scared?" Nolan sneered. "I don't think anything scares that man."

"You'd be surprised." Bert turned back to his workbench and picked up a set of tongs. "When a man has so much at stake, he sometimes takes extreme measures to hold on to it. Especially someone like the earl, who's used to getting his own way."

"That doesn't excuse him trying to manipulate me." Nolan blasted out a loud breath. "I don't know what to do, Bert. I don't think I'm cut out for this life. And if it means I'll turn out like him, then I want no part of it." He threw the spike back onto the table. "But where am I going to find another property I can afford within the next few weeks?"

Bert moved to the brick hearth, where several pieces of metal glowed in the fire. "Running away might be the easiest thing to do. But staying and figuring this thing out, now that takes real courage."

"Are you calling me a coward?"

"Nae. Just a mite hot-tempered and quick to jump to conclusions." Bert wiped his forehead with his sleeve. "Have you

144

considered the bigger picture of what being the earl's son could mean?" Using the tongs, he repositioned the metal, and then set the tool down to fix Nolan with a pointed stare. "Think of the good you could do for the servants and the tenant farmers. What better advocate could we have than someone who's lived in our shoes?"

"An advocate? To improve the conditions of the workers, you mean?"

"Aye. Not that Stainsby is a bad place to work. But there are always improvements that could be made." A sheen of sweat shone on Bert's flushed face. "For instance, it seems to me that staff members who spend their whole lives here should be rewarded for their service. I've asked his lordship several times about starting a collection for us older workers—a retirement fund, if you will—but he's never taken the request seriously."

"Haven't you saved for the future, Bert?" In the past, Nolan had questioned Bert as to when he planned to stop working, but the man had always avoided answering.

Bert shook his head. "Not enough. Not with having to help support Franny's widowed sister and her crippled niece. The truth is I'll probably have to work till I die—if I'm able. Speaking of which, I'd better get back to it while I still have a job." He bent to pick up the hammer. When he straightened, a look of alarm leapt into his eyes. He swayed and clutched the workbench.

"Bert!" Nolan rushed to steady him.

"I'm all right, lad. Just stood up too quick is all." He waved off Nolan's help. "Think about what I said before you burn any bridges with his lordship. Bridges you might need one day." He turned back to retrieve a piece of metal from the fire.

Nolan glanced around the meticulous smithy, the place Bert had made his own for over thirty years. Perhaps Bert was right. Perhaps Nolan hadn't considered the bigger picture, too focused on his own selfish desires. As the earl's son, he would have the opportunity to affect many lives here. Not only his and Hannah's, but Bert and Franny's, as well as all the servants and the tenant farmers who relied on Stainsby for their livelihood. If he could manage to put aside his resentment, he might be able to use his influence with his father to affect some positive changes for the people he'd grown up with.

With a quick wave to Bert, Nolan left the smithy and made his way back to the main house. For the first time, he forced himself to consider that losing the farm might have been part of God's plan to show him his true path. A path he hadn't intended to take.

Perhaps Nolan owed it to himself—and to God—to put his best effort into seeing if this was where his destiny truly lay.

Hannah paced the grass beneath the elm tree, trying to quell her growing apprehension. More than twenty-four hours had passed since Nolan's meeting with Mr. Simpson, and she hadn't seen or heard anything from her husband. She couldn't shake the sensation that something had gone horribly wrong.

Had the earl discovered their secret meetings and put a stop to them? It wouldn't surprise Hannah if he had sent some of the servants to spy on them.

Perhaps that was it. But then why did Nolan not get word to her somehow?

A rustling in the bushes beyond the tree had Hannah's heart leaping with breathless anticipation. He'd come after all. Finally she would be wrapped in his arms, receive his intoxicating kisses, and find out exactly what was going on.

The bushes parted, and Mickey Gilbert stepped out.

Hannah's stomach swooped. She grasped the base of the elm tree to support her.

"Sorry, Hannah. It's only me." Mickey gave a shrug. "Nolan asked me to tell you he's sorry he couldn't come and to give you this." He held out a folded piece of paper.

She took it from him with shaking hands. It contained bad news, she was certain.

"I've got to get back. If you want to send a reply, leave it in the barn. I'll see that Nolan gets it." He tipped his cap and bounded off through the foliage.

Hannah lowered herself to the chicken crate and bit her bottom lip. *Lord, please help me accept whatever Nolan has to tell me.*

With trembling fingers, she opened the paper.

Dearest Hannah,

I'm afraid I have some unpleasant news. Mr. Simpson has sold the farm to someone else for a higher price. Words cannot express how disappointed I am, as I'm sure you are too.

I also have to tell you that Edward has somehow discovered our meetings and has put a stop to them. He claims it's in violation of our agreement. So, for Molly's sake, I will abide by his wishes.

Have faith, my love, and try not to worry. Once the ball is over, if Edward does not accept our marriage, I promise I will come up with another way for us to be together. Until then, remember how much I love you.

Yours, Nolan

A tear dropped onto the paper. Hannah sniffed and took out a handkerchief. She wiped her cheeks and then blotted the page lest it ruin Nolan's words.

Poor Nolan. His dearest dream of owning the farm—gone. How could Mr. Simpson go back on his word like that?

Hannah swallowed the sour taste on her tongue as the bitter truth became apparent. She'd bet a month's wages that Lord Stainsby was behind the loss of the farm. How had he discovered Nolan's intention? Did the man have spies everywhere? And if so, how could she and Nolan ever fight such relentless efforts to control their lives?

Hannah folded Nolan's letter and shoved it deep into the pocket of her apron with the firm resolve not to allow fear to overcome her. Tonight she would write a note of encouragement to Nolan, reminding him of her faith in him, and drop it off at the barn for Mickey to deliver tomorrow.

No matter how dire things seemed, she needed to trust that God was on their side and that everything would work out according to His plan.

CHAPTER 16

Nolan grumbled under his breath as the tailor fitted the side of his jacket. He did not enjoy being used as an oversized pincushion.

"One more and we should be through, sir," the short, stout man mumbled through a sea of pins held between his lips. Nolan wondered how he managed not to swallow them.

It had been a little more than four weeks now since he'd begun learning his new role. Four weeks of constant attention to the most trivial of details—which fork to use, which tie to wear, when to bow, when to shake hands, the names of all the earl's acquaintances, their wives, their children. Constant fittings were only some of the many annoyances men of the nobility were forced to endure. The ball tonight was another.

Nolan's brain swam with the mundaneness of it all. And his heart ached for Hannah.

"These few alterations won't take long, sir. The jacket will be ready for this evening."

"Thank you, Mr. Smithers." Nolan shrugged out of the offending piece of clothing, only scraping his arm twice on the pins. He bit back an oath and donned his everyday gray jacket from the new wardrobe the tailor had already fashioned for him. It took some getting used to, all the starched shirts, the cravats, and the obligatory coat. Would he ever stop wishing for the freedom of his stable clothes?

His valet hovered at his elbow, brushing imaginary lint from Nolan's sleeve. "The earl would like you to join him in his study as soon as you're able, sir."

Nolan sighed. He'd hoped to have a few minutes of peace before any more last-minute instructions on how to behave tonight. He was still having a hard time forgiving his father for the loss of the farm, though Bert's advice, as well as a sweet note from Hannah, had helped lessen his wrath. Hannah had figured out that Edward was behind Mr. Simpson's change of heart, yet she hadn't given in to despair, and had instead declared her faith in Nolan to find the right solution.

Nolan pressed his lips into a tight line. Would she feel the same when she learned that Nolan may have decided to accept his role as a member of the aristocracy?

Over the last two weeks, Bert's advice had taken root, and Nolan had begun to see how he could be an advocate for the less fortunate, and for the servants and farmers in the area. Didn't he have an obligation not to squander the opportunity he'd been given?

"Thank you, Jeffrey," he said to the valet. "Tell his lordship I'll be right down."

As Nolan descended the main staircase a few minutes later, he prayed that if the ball was a success and his father's peers accepted him, Edward would see fit to return the favor and recognize Hannah as his daughter-in-law. Nolan had kept to the terms of their agreement and hadn't seen Hannah in two weeks. Surely that deserved some kind of reward. And if Edward didn't see it that way, Nolan was prepared to insist he endorse their marriage as a stipulation for continuing in the role as his son. Edward wasn't the only one who could use manipulation to get what he wanted.

Nolan knocked on the study door, and the earl bade him enter. As he stepped in, Edward rose from his chair, as did the man seated in front of the desk.

"Nolan, please meet Mr. Wallace Grayson, our family solicitor."

Mr. Grayson was a hefty man of average height with bushy sideburns. A hint of suspicion hovered on the edge of Nolan's mind as he shook the man's hand.

"It's a great pleasure to meet the son of my dear friend." Mr. Grayson's jowls wobbled with the force of his handshake.

Nolan inclined his head in what he hoped was a noble manner.

"Please have a seat," Edward said. "I've asked Mr. Grayson to draw up some papers for us."

Nolan sank into the leather chair, eyes narrowed. "What type of papers?"

"Don't look so worried. These are a mere formality to name you as my son and heir. They require both our signatures to make it legal." He gave a small, somewhat nervous gesture with his hand.

Legal? Was Nolan ready for such a permanent step without discussing it with Hannah? He leaned forward. "May I read them over?"

"Of course." Edward passed him a small stack of papers. "Might I take this opportunity to mention how relieved I am your mother taught you to read and write? This whole business would have been so much harder if she hadn't."

Nolan looked at the pile and cringed. It would take him hours to read every word. He scanned the first few paragraphs, dismayed to note that much of the legal terminology escaped him. "Is this a document to change my name?"

"Yes. A mere formality since your birth certificate already bears the name Fairchild. However Elizabeth did give you her surname when she became your guardian, so this will serve to clarify the issue."

An uncomfortable sensation banded Nolan's chest. He'd always gone by Nolan Price. How could he give up the name he'd had all his life, the last tie to his beloved mother? "I—I'd like some time to think about this."

The earl inclined his head. "It is also customary for an earl's eldest son to receive a courtesy title. I've chosen Viscount Price for you, in deference to your present surname. You will be known as Lord Price."

Nolan swallowed, unsure what that meant and too embarrassed to ask for further clarification. Apparently he still had a lot to learn about the nobility.

"The Fairchild family name is what you'll be inheriting and all that comes with it." Edward flattened his palms on the desktop. "I would hate to think I've wasted Mr. Grayson's time coming here today—all the way from London."

Nolan recognized Edward's bullying tactics. Still, his argument made logical sense. After all, these papers only stated an already documented fact—that Nolan was Edward's son. "I will agree," he said slowly, "to a hyphenated surname. I cannot reject the good name I've had all my life."

"Very well. I will concede to Nolan Edward Price-Fairchild." Edward turned to the solicitor. "That will satisfy all legal requirements, will it not?"

Mr. Grayson cleared his throat. "I believe it will."

"Excellent. We have compromised and come to an agreement. That seems to be the way our relationship is destined to be."

Though he smiled, Edward's eyes glittered with a hardness that matched the slick wood beneath his hands. "Now if you would be so good as to add your signature to mine on the last page of the document, I'm sure Mr. Grayson would like to rest up before the festivities tonight."

Trying to ignore the tightening of his gut, Nolan took the pen that Edward gave him. He leaned forward and flipped a few pages, scanning random words as he went, yet nowhere did he see any mention of his marriage or of Hannah's name. Surely he was being overly suspicious, thinking something more sinister was afoot. Yet after the farm fiasco, who could blame him?

He turned to the last page, signed his name, and laid the pen down. "Is that all?" Nolan straightened his jacket as he rose.

"For now, yes. Don't forget to be on time for our first guest's arrival this evening."

How could he forget?

"I'll be there." Nolan shook Mr. Grayson's hand, bowed to his father, and left the room.

If only he could leave the unsettled feeling behind him as easily.

It was well past midnight before Mrs. Bridges released Hannah and Molly from their duties for the evening. A few of the more senior maids had been kept on hand in the event that the master needed something else from the kitchen, but Hannah was relieved to be able to escape to her quarters. After seeing Molly settled, Hannah retired to her own room, but remained dressed, knowing sleep would be impossible. How could she sleep, consumed as she was with thoughts of the event taking place downstairs? The whole house buzzed with the energy of the hundreds of guests at the ball.

A ball in honor of her husband from which she was banned.

In an effort to quell her resentment toward her father-in-law, who seemed bent on keeping Nolan from her, Hannah fell to her knees on the worn rag mat beside her bed, as she did every night, and bowed her head in prayer. Prayer for help in accepting these circumstances and prayer for assistance in becoming a patient, loving wife to Nolan no matter what direction their lives took.

A small measure of calm ensued once she had run out of petitions to the Almighty. Still, a niggling sense of unease and curiosity wore her nerves to a fine thread. She couldn't help but wonder what was happening below. After what felt like an eternity of pacing, she gave in to temptation. She told herself she only wanted a glimpse of Nolan in his finery—that she would then be satisfied and come straight back to her room.

But deep down, she knew better.

Hannah moved on soundless feet down the corridors to the west wing where the ballroom was located. Keeping in the shadows of the hallway, she made her way around to the rear entrance, the one staff used discreetly when serving. The muffled combination of voices and music wafted through the air. Hannah waited to make sure she would not be seen before advancing to the door and nudging it open a crack. The moment she broke the seal to the room, the roar of the music almost overpowered her.

Her heart beat a painful thump against her ribs as she scanned the sea of colors and frenzied movement. Dresses of all shades and materials whirled by on the dance floor, interspersed with the black of the men's formal attire. How would she ever spot Nolan in this crowd?

She focused her attention on the center of the room where a dark head gleamed under the chandeliers. The man turned, smiling widely at the lady by his side, and Hannah's breath caught in a gasp. Could that dashing gentleman be Nolan?

She almost didn't recognize him in such formal attire. He wore a black tailcoat, a striped waistcoat, and a white ascot tied in an intricate manner. His hair had been slicked back in some dandyish style instead of being allowed to fall over his forehead as usual.

She forced her gaze away from Nolan to examine his female companions—all stylish, well-to-do young women garbed in the most elaborate gowns and hairstyles. Jewels gleamed around every throat and wrist. One dark-haired beauty grasped Nolan by the arm and twirled him onto the dance floor. Hannah watched them spin in circles until Nolan threw his head back and laughed with unrestrained abandon.

A sob rose in her throat. Hand to her mouth, she retreated and closed the door, leaning her back against the cold stone wall.

The very thing she'd dreaded all along, she'd now witnessed with her own eyes. Her husband had changed, and she no longer fit into his world. How could he ever be satisfied with a mere maid, when in that room alone, he could choose from any number of rich, fashionable beauties?

In a haze of pain, she stumbled down the carpeted hallway, heedless of her surroundings until the murmur of male voices met her ears. Quickly she ducked behind a large potted tree in a corner alcove.

Two men, one of whom she recognized as Lord Stainsby himself, strolled into view. The man with him wore a loud striped suit that matched his outrageous sideburns.

"It's all set then?" the earl said in a low tone.

"Yes. The documents are legal and binding. Your son's marriage will be dissolved as soon as I file them."

Hannah bit her lip to keep from crying out, sinking farther into the shadows.

"I was afraid the boy wouldn't sign," the stout man continued. "Thank goodness your logic swayed him."

The earl chuckled. "I knew Nolan would come around. It was only a matter of time."

Both men laughed and continued down the hall. Once they were out of sight, Hannah's legs crumpled beneath her and she reached out to grasp the wall. Tears spilled unheeded down her cheeks.

Her worst fears had come to fruition.

Nolan had signed annulment papers, and soon their short-lived marriage would be over.

CHAPTER

17

Nolan slept late the next morning. The dancing had gone on into the wee hours and, being the person of honor, it would have been rude to leave before the last guest had retired. Many of the earl's friends were being put up in the Stainsby guest quarters in the west wing, which meant he would have to dine with them this morning.

As he pushed himself out of bed, Nolan reflected on the success of the previous evening. Edward had appeared pleased at how well his peers had taken the unexpected news of his grown son. Even though they had treated Nolan with respect, he'd sensed a chilly reserve behind their eyes, as though they didn't quite trust him. Edward had kept quiet the fact that Nolan had been a servant at the estate all these years, deeming it unnecessary information. And the guests had been too polite to question Nolan directly. What would they say when they learned he'd been a stable boy until now?

He frowned as his valet helped him dress, dreading the necessity to entertain those people again today. He only hoped they'd all be on their way right after breakfast.

Luck, however, was not on his side. About thirty guests

planned to remain for another day and night, meaning Nolan would have to put off his reunion with Hannah a little longer. After breakfast, the earl met with Nolan to inform him of the day's scheduled events, complete with a formal dinner and musical entertainment in the evening. Nolan sincerely hoped these extravagant social gatherings would not be expected too often. Once or twice a year would be more than enough for him.

On the positive side, his father assured him that the fact that so many guests had stayed on was indeed a good sign that his peers had accepted Nolan's given place in the family's hierarchy.

After an excruciating midday meal, during which every young woman present postured for his attention, Nolan sought out the peace and quiet of his father's study. He doubted any of the women would dare follow him there.

He'd just flopped into a chair by the hearth when the door opened and the light tap of female feet sounded. Nolan turned his head to see if perhaps a maid had come in to clean the room, only to find his two half-sisters hovering inside the doorway. As manners dictated, Nolan got to his feet and bowed. "Good afternoon, ladies."

Dressed in an outlandish velvet creation, Evelyn reminded Nolan of a large blue ostrich. Victoria, smaller in stature with light brown hair, wore a modest yellow gown. She always seemed rather intimidated by her older sister, remaining in the background as though she were somehow less important.

Evelyn snapped her fan closed. "Good day, Mr. Price. My sister and I would like a word with you, if you don't mind."

"Of course. And please call me Nolan." From her steely expression, he doubted she wished to congratulate him on the success of his first ball. He hadn't seen his sisters since the night of their initial awkward introduction, after which time they'd returned to London.

Nolan remained standing until the two women crossed the floor and took seats around the hearth. "To what do I owe this unexpected pleasure?" he asked.

Victoria kept her gaze fixed on the fire before them, while Evelyn stared at him as though in silent challenge.

"We want to know your intentions regarding our family." Evelyn's toe tapped against the carpet.

He frowned. "I'm afraid I don't know what you mean."

Evelyn rose and flicked open her fan. "This must all have come as a shock to you. A mere stable boy suddenly thrust into the world of the nobility."

"It is challenging, I won't deny." Nolan chose his words with care, as though avoiding a trap. "And it takes some getting used to."

Victoria continued to keep her eyes averted. Nolan waited to see where the conversation was headed.

Evelyn whirled to face him, passion blazing. "You realize that your being heralded as our father's heir has effectively ruined both our lives." Her dark eyes shot daggers at him, all pretense at civility falling away.

He expelled a long breath. Hostility veiled in politeness baffled him. Anger, however, he could deal with. He stood with quiet dignity, determined to keep calm. "Believe me, I have no intention of eclipsing you or Victoria from our father's life. And I will always make sure you are well provided for." It was the least he could do for them. Growing up, he'd always wished for siblings, but these women before him were strangers. It would take time to establish a relationship.

"My husband is not at all pleased at this occurrence," Evelyn snapped. "He married me with certain expectations. To have them yanked out from under him by a mere . . ." She clamped her mouth shut.

"A mere stable hand."

She had the grace to flush.

He stepped forward to meet her as an equal. "I'm sorry your husband is distressed over this development. However, I have no desire to yank anything from anyone. Surely it is better that the title goes to me rather than some distant relative with no vested interest in keeping harmony within the family. Or keeping the Fairchild holdings intact."

Victoria wrinkled her nose. "Didn't Father tell you—"

"Never mind that now, Victoria. There'll be time enough to delve into the family lineage at a later date." Evelyn pressed her thin lips together, her features pinched. She shot her sister a pointed look, one that held implied meaning.

Family secrets?

"I assure you both," Nolan said, "I will do everything in my power to have the Fairchild assets distributed evenly." He turned to Victoria. "Amongst all of us."

"But I don't care a whit about the money." Victoria threw out her hands, her features becoming animated. "All I care about is my beau, Sebastian Coverton. He was about to propose marriage, but ever since he learned about you, he hasn't called on me in weeks." She broke into sobs. "This scandal has ruined my chance to marry."

Nolan's mouth fell open, unsure how to deal with such hysterics. Once again, he fell back to his training with horses—advance with caution, show no fear. He approached the distraught woman and passed her a handkerchief.

She snatched it from him and blew her nose.

"I'll admit, I'm out of my element in the matter of suitors, but if I can help in any way, I'd be happy to do what I can." His soothing tone had the desired effect, and her sobs subsided into sniffles. "Would it help if I met with the gentleman in question?"

Victoria's chin trembled, and before she could answer, Evelyn placed a territorial arm around her shoulder. "I should think not."

"Why not, Ev? It couldn't hurt." A light of hope glowed on Victoria's face. "Maybe if Sebastian got to know Nolan, he'd realize there's nothing to fear by marrying into the family, despite the circumstances surrounding Nolan's birth."

"That sounds like a splendid idea." Nolan gave her an encouraging smile. "Simply name the place and time, and I'll be there."

Hannah glanced down at the crumpled piece of paper in her gloved hand as the coach bounced over the rough roads. Beside her, Molly took in the sights of Derby from the curtained window.

"Hannah, look at all the grand ladies with their parasols." She giggled, seeming in that moment to revert to the six-year-old girl Hannah remembered.

"Yes," Hannah murmured. "They're lovely."

She returned her gaze to the paper in an attempt to quell her nerves, though right now anxiety was the only thing keeping her from wallowing in grief.

After witnessing Nolan's transformation at the ball, Hannah had spent the rest of the night sobbing into her pillow. At the break of dawn, with her emotions finally spent, she had come to a decision. She could not stay at Stainsby and watch Nolan marry some beautiful heiress. The thought of seeing him with another woman, after she'd lain with him as his wife, was more than she could bear.

In desperation, she'd found the note her mother had given her when they'd left Mr. Fielding's, and Hannah had latched onto the one route of escape open to her.

"Iris Hartford, the Duchess of Hartford, Hartford Hall, Derbyshire." The name dredged up long-ago memories of a distant relative, a grand lady they'd seen sporadically over the years before Hannah's father died. According to Mum's note, she was her mother's stepsister, a woman who had married well for her station in life, and who would be willing to give Hannah aid in time of crisis.

Hannah swallowed. Was she being too presumptuous to arrive unannounced on this relative she hadn't seen in years? She glanced over at Molly's happy features and knew she had no other choice. Perhaps, at the very least, this woman could offer them employment in one of her homes. It was all Hannah dared hope for.

The driver stopped at the center of town to ask for directions to the Hartford estate, and soon the carriage lurched into motion again. Hannah pressed a handkerchief to her nose to block the unpleasant odors, which, combined with the motion of the carriage, had turned her stomach sour. Once past the outskirts of the city, the landscape became greener and the air easier to breathe. Several miles of rolling countryside later, the driver turned through a stone gate onto a winding drive that led up to a residence that rivaled Stainsby Hall in grandeur. The ivy-covered brick dwelling loomed above them on a slight incline, like a sentinel standing guard. The carriage stopped in front of the main entrance, and the driver helped them alight.

"Please wait for us until we're sure the duchess is at home," Hannah instructed.

"Very good, miss." The slight man bowed and stood at attention as Hannah and Molly walked to the front door.

"What a beautiful house," Molly exclaimed.

She was so full of enthusiasm at this unexpected visit that Hannah hadn't wanted to worry Molly with the real reason for this trip until she knew what to expect from their aunt. With trembling hands, Hannah knocked on the front door. Seconds later, a man, presumably the butler, opened the door.

"May I help you?" The tall man peered at them over his spectacles.

Hannah pulled herself up to her full height, willing a confidence she didn't feel. "Good day. Is the Duchess of Hartford at home?"

He frowned. "Whom shall I say is calling?"

"Her nieces, Hannah and Molly Burnham."

He raised a brow, then bade them enter. They stepped into a spacious vestibule, tiled in white and black squares. While they waited for the man to return, Hannah scanned her surroundings. High ceilings with wide crown moldings and an enormous chandelier dominated the area. Green paneled walls led down two different hallways, one of which Hannah presumed led to the back of the house. Before them, a wide staircase curved upward.

Hannah blinked. How was it that their mother led such a meager existence when her stepsister obviously enjoyed great prosperity? And why wouldn't Mum have asked the duchess for help when she was widowed? Had she been too proud?

As Molly gaped in awe at the splendor before them, Hannah checked her image in a large gilded mirror to ensure that no strands of hair had escaped her straw hat and that she looked presentable as a relative of such a wealthy woman.

The sound of quick footsteps on the tiled floor brought Hannah whirling around. She grabbed Molly and pulled the girl to her side.

A tall, willowy woman rushed into the vestibule, an expectant expression lighting her wide gray eyes. Dressed in a fashionable green skirt and high-necked blouse with her chestnut tresses coiled at the nape of her neck, she was indeed a striking woman. Hannah gauged her to be somewhere in her early forties.

"Don't tell me these are Ann's two girls?" She clasped her hands in front of her like a youngster herself.

Hannah dropped a slight curtsy. "How do you do, ma'am. I'm Hannah, and this is my sister, Molly."

The duchess gave a small laugh and rushed forward to envelop them in a hug.

Hannah remained immobile, in shock over such enthusiasm. When her aunt pulled back, Hannah straightened her shawl. "I'm sorry to impose on you unannounced, but my mother said you might help us. Molly and I are in need of a place to stay temporarily." Hannah ignored the puzzled frown on Molly's face. "If it's inconvenient, our driver is waiting out front. We can find lodgings in Derby." She held her breath, hoping she wouldn't have to use the last of her savings so quickly.

Mock horror filled the woman's eyes. "Absolutely not. I insist you stay with me." She waved a hand, and the butler appeared from the shadows. "Carstairs, please collect the girls' luggage and take care of the driver."

"Oh no. I can pay for the coach." Hannah fumbled with her reticule, cheeks burning that her aunt might think she was angling for financial assistance.

"Nonsense. Carstairs will handle it. Now come with me. You must be tired and thirsty after your journey."

Hannah bit back words of argument and motioned Molly to follow her down the hallway. Behind the duchess, they entered a sitting room, decorated in pinks and greens with floral cushions and vases of fresh-cut flowers. The soothing atmosphere instantly put Hannah's nerves at ease. "What a lovely room."

"Why, thank you. My late husband never dared venture in here. Said it was far too feminine for his tastes. Which is exactly why I love it." She indicated the green satin sofa. "Please have a seat."

It was then Hannah noticed the large dog lying on the carpet beside a wing chair. The animal raised its head and gave a swish of its tail.

"This is Daisy. She's a chocolate Labrador, a gift from my late husband, Edgar. She's very gentle, so you needn't worry about her." The duchess bent to pat the dog's head and its tail wagged harder.

Hannah and Molly sat and removed their gloves. Within moments of her aunt pulling the bell cord, a maid appeared in the doorway.

"We'll take tea now with a plate of cucumber sandwiches and biscuits. Thank you, Maggie."

When the maid left, their aunt turned to them and smiled. "How is your dear mother these days? I'm afraid I've been remiss in keeping in touch."

"She was well the last time I saw her." Hannah fidgeted with the cuff of her blouse. She longed to voice the questions circling her brain, but wasn't sure how to begin.

The duchess folded her hands in her lap. "You likely don't remember me since I didn't visit very often. The last time I came, you were still living at the rectory. Long before your dear father and brother had perished."

Hannah bit her lip and nodded. "I remember."

"I don't," Molly announced. "But then I'm much younger than Hannah."

The woman smiled. "I think you were only three at the time, Molly dear."

"If you're our aunt, does that mean you're Mum's sister?"

"Actually, I'm her stepsister." She turned to Hannah. "Did your mother never tell you about her childhood?"

"Not really. Mum rarely spoke about her family." Hannah leaned forward, eager to learn more, thankful for Molly's uninhibited ways. "I got the impression there was some type of falling-out with her parents."

Just then, the maid entered the room with a cart topped with a silver teapot, china cups and saucers, and a platter of sandwiches.

"Please help yourself before I tell you the long, sad tale."

"Thank you, ma'am." Molly darted forward to take a plate, while Hannah hung back.

The duchess chuckled. "And please, you must call me Aunt Iris. *Ma'am* makes me feel so old."

Hannah's tense muscles began to relax. She'd pictured her aunt as an austere older woman with little sense of humor. What a refreshing difference her aunt was proving to be. Hannah chose two small sandwiches and a biscuit while her aunt poured the tea.

"Now where were we?" Aunt Iris asked, teacup in hand. "Oh, yes. You probably don't know this, but your mother and I grew up together."

Hannah swallowed a bite of sandwich. "Really?"

"That's right. Ann's mother, your grandmother, married my father, Sir Arthur Templeton. Father was a baron, a widower with my brother, Ronald, and me to care for. Ann and her mother moved in with us, and I was delighted to have a little sister to play with."

Hannah frowned. "Then why have I never heard of this?"

"When Ann was eighteen, she met your father, George Burnham, a penniless curate. Father refused to consider his offer of marriage, deeming him too far beneath our family socially. I was already married to Edgar by then and didn't realize how serious things had become until I learned that Ann had run off with George. My father, in turn, disowned her." She set her cup on the tiny table beside her with a sigh. "I always wondered whether I could have changed the outcome of the situation if I'd been around. Perhaps tempered my father's reaction."

Hannah sipped her tea, trying to imagine her mother and father entering marriage in such a fashion. Not unlike her own, in some respects.

"Even though Father forbade us to have any contact with Ann, I managed to keep in touch on and off. I never was very good at following the rules." She winked at Hannah. "Unfortunately, at the time your father passed away, I was laid up with an illness that lasted the better part of a year. By the time I caught up with Ann again, she'd married Mr. Fielding."

Hannah clenched her teacup. If her aunt had known of their dire circumstances, how different might their lives have been?

Iris rose to refill the cups. Despite Hannah's warning glare, Molly helped herself to several more sandwiches. "Molly, mind your manners."

"No, please. Eat as much as you'd like. I don't stand on ceremony." Iris reclaimed her seat across from the sofa. "Now, why don't you tell me why you've come?"

Though her tone was soft and hinted at sympathy, Hannah found the complicated turn of recent events left her tongue-tied. She'd left Stainsby Hall so quickly, she'd barely had time to think. All she knew was that she had to leave before Nolan found her. She couldn't bear to listen to his false explanations. The very thought of his conspiring with the earl to end their marriage brought tears to her eyes.

Her aunt's shrewd gaze missed nothing. She rose and rang for the maid, who promptly appeared in the door. "Maggie, please show Miss Molly to the guest quarters. Molly dear, you may bring your biscuits with you this once. I'd like a moment to talk to your sister alone."

Molly gave Hannah a questioning look.

Hannah nodded. "Go ahead. I'll be up in a few minutes."

Molly paused long enough to grab two more biscuits before she followed the maid into the hall.

Iris came to sit beside Hannah in the spot Molly had vacated and patted Hannah's knee. "Now, my dear, you must tell me everything. Whatever the problems plaguing you, I'm sure that together we can come up with a solution."

CHAPTER
18

Nolan ripped the cravat from his neck and hurled it onto the bed. He'd only been gone for three days, yet it felt like an eternity. His father had insisted they accompany Evelyn and Victoria on the train back to London, and while there, to stay at Edward's house in the city and meet Nolan's Aunt Ophelia. During their short visit, Nolan had also met Victoria's beau, Sebastian, who seemed a pleasant enough chap. He only hoped the man's objections had been laid to rest and that he would resume courting Victoria.

Nolan learned that Fairchild Manor, the family's impressive townhome near St. James's Square, was occupied by a small staff under the direction of Ophelia Fairchild, Edward's spinster sister. Her frosty reception of Nolan had rivaled Evelyn's and left him feeling like a fish out of water. Edward had tried to allay his discomfort, claiming that both his eldest daughter and his sister shared a somewhat prickly nature, but that Nolan would win them over in time.

Still, the sojourn to the city had done nothing to ease the transition into his father's world. The rounds of business and social acquaintances made Nolan's head spin. He was beginning to doubt anew that he was cut out for the life of a noble gentleman, since he'd far rather spend an evening with Bert and the horses.

And Hannah.

His stomach lurched at the thought of his beautiful wife. After Edward had banned him from seeing her in the yard, his yearning for her had only intensified. Once, he'd actually attempted to sneak up to her attic room, but his valet had stopped him on the earl's orders. No sneaking off to consort with the servants, he'd said.

As of the ball, however, the four weeks he'd promised his father were more than over. Nolan planned to find Hannah and move her into his suite tonight. Nothing would stop him this time. Not his valet, not even the earl himself. And if his father still refused to accept their marriage, Nolan would leave Stainsby and find work elsewhere. For as much as he'd come to terms with his new station in life, if it could not include Hannah, then Nolan wanted no part of it. Of that, he was one hundred percent certain.

He stripped off his jacket and waistcoat, relishing the freedom to move unhindered. After a quick wash to freshen up, Nolan made his way down the back staircase, whistling in anticipation of Hannah's sweet kisses.

He bounded into the kitchen, noting the darkness with surprise. Clearly he hadn't paid enough attention to the time. Had Mrs. Bridges and the maids already retired?

"Can I help you, sir?" Mrs. Bridges' voice was as cold as the stone floor.

He turned to see the large woman standing with her arms crossed over her night robe. "Mrs. Bridges. Yes, I'm looking for Hannah. Is she finished for the night?"

The woman pinned him with a cold stare that made the hairs

on his neck stand on end. "Oh, she's finished all right. Finished with the likes of you."

She took a menacing step toward him, and though he stood a head taller than the woman, he stepped back in retreat.

When her words finally penetrated, he scowled. "What is that supposed to mean?"

"It means you've gone and run her off—for good." The woman's chin quivered, belying a tide of emotion that bewildered him.

A ball of dread curdled the leg of lamb he'd eaten for dinner. "I don't know what's going on here, but I've done nothing to Hannah. I haven't even talked to her in over two weeks."

Mrs. Bridges advanced again. "And is that any way for a man to treat his wife?"

Shock rendered him mute. So Hannah had gone against their agreement and told Mrs. Bridges about their marriage. Did the whole staff know then? His muscles stiffened as he fought the anger that swirled in his chest. "She told you?"

"Aye. I dragged it out of her before she left."

His stomach clenched again. "Where did she go?"

"I wouldn't tell you even if I knew. What I do know is that she quit her post. Took Molly and left, and she's not planning on returning."

Nolan reached out to grasp the back of a chair as the room swam around him. This couldn't be true. Hannah would never leave him like that, without a word. "When?" The word barely rasped out through his thickened throat.

"The morning after the ball. I've never seen her so upset."

Nolan gulped in a huge breath and pushed himself upright. Mrs. Bridges may not know the reason Hannah left, but there was one person who might.

And heaven help Edward if he had played any part in this.

Hannah awoke slowly, relishing the feel of the silk pillowcase against her cheek. She opened one eye, then bolted upright in the bed, not recognizing the room in which she lay.

She moved aside the thick drapery surrounding the bed and startled at the bright morning sun that streamed through the parted curtains. The maids must have come in and pulled them open already.

What time of day was it?

Hannah rose and rushed through her morning routine. Breakfast might well be over at this late hour, and though her stomach still hadn't recovered from the carriage ride yesterday, a piece of dry toast and a cup of tea would be most welcome.

As she passed Molly's room, she peered in to find it empty, and the bed neatly made. She prayed Molly wasn't making a nuisance of herself. Though her aunt had been more than gracious last night, listening to her story with sincere empathy, Hannah did not wish to wear out their welcome. This morning, she intended to broach the topic of gaining employment here or in Derby.

Hannah made her way down the stairs to the front hallway, where Mr. Carstairs stood at attention.

"Follow me, miss, and I'll take you to breakfast."

"Thank you." How odd it was to have a butler attending her in such a manner when, back at Stainsby, the butler was so much higher up the servants' ladder than she.

In the grand dining room, she found Molly and Aunt Iris already eating. Her aunt looked even lovelier this morning, as fresh as the flowers that adorned the table. Her hair was swept up in a soft style on top of her head with a few curls framing her face. Her gown of muted lilac brought out flecks of color in her gray eyes. If Hannah didn't know better, she'd swear Iris was a girl of two and twenty instead of a widow in her forties.

"There you are, my dear," her aunt called from the end of the long polished table. "I trust you slept well."

Hannah inclined her head. "Forgive me for sleeping so late. I'm usually up before the sun."

"There's nothing to forgive. You were obviously tired from your trip. Please join us for eggs and bacon."

A maid took the lid off one of the serving dishes, and Hannah's stomach rolled at the pungent smell. She must have paled, for her aunt rose and rushed to her side.

"Are you quite well, Hannah dear?"

"I'm fine. The carriage ride yesterday did not agree with me." She sat in the chair Iris pulled out for her. "Just a slice of toast for me, please."

Molly shoved a mouthful of scrambled egg into her mouth. "You must have caught a flu, Hannah. You haven't been feeling well all week."

"It—it must be the strain. I'll be fine once we get settled."

The maid poured a cup of tea and slid a plate of toast before Hannah.

Iris returned to her seat. "It's a beautiful day. Why don't I show you the famous Hartford gardens after we finish? Daisy loves to go for a morning walk."

"That sounds wonderful," Molly said cheerfully. "I've always wanted a dog, but Mr. Fielding would never allow it."

Hannah swallowed her bite of toast. "Actually, I wanted to speak to you about finding employment for Molly and me. Perhaps you could recommend where to begin?"

Iris frowned over her teacup. "I won't hear of any such thing. You are family, and you're welcome to stay here as long as you wish."

"But we couldn't impose on you indefinitely. We need to earn our keep." Hannah's fingers worried the collar of her dress.

Iris set her cup down with a clink and studied Hannah with a thoughtful expression. "Very well. When the time is right, I shall be delighted to help you find employment. In the meantime, you are under strict orders to relax and enjoy your time here."

Tears clogged Hannah's throat more than the dry toast. How could she ever repay her aunt for such kindness? Even her own mother had not treated her half as well.

Nolan's buggy flew into the drive of the Fielding farm. The muscles in his arms strained as he pulled the horses to a sharp halt and vaulted down from the seat. Edward had sworn he'd had nothing to do with Hannah's abrupt departure, only learning of her resignation that very morning. This was the only place Nolan could think of that Hannah might have gone.

With several long strides, he reached the farmhouse door, where he paused to rein in his emotions. If Hannah was indeed hiding here, he needed to show patience and listen to her side of the story. Whatever the misunderstanding between them, he was sure they could resolve it face-to-face.

Before he knocked, he said a quick prayer, realizing as he did so, that he'd been remiss in his relationship with the Almighty as of late. Remorse flooded his soul as he remembered his vow to make nightly prayer something he and Hannah would share. In reality, he hadn't done very well by any of the promises he'd made to her. With firm resolve to do better, he rapped on the wooden door.

After a second knock, the door opened. Mrs. Fielding stood holding a dishcloth, frowning. "Mr. Price. What are you doing here?"

"I'm here to collect Hannah and take her home where she belongs."

The frown turned to alarm. "What do you mean take her home? Where is she?"

"She's not here?"

"No, of course not. What gave you that idea?"

His stomach sank like a rock in a pond. If she wasn't here, then where on earth would she have gone? The blood drained from his head, bringing an unwelcome rush of vertigo. He grasped the doorframe to steady himself.

Mrs. Fielding opened the door wider and scanned the fields behind him. "Come in and sit down. You don't look well at all."

Nolan stumbled inside and sank onto a hard kitchen chair. Mrs. Fielding handed him a glass of water, which he drained in one gulp.

"Maybe you'd better tell me what's going on between you and my daughter." She took a seat across the table from him.

Her sharp look did nothing to inspire sharing a confidence, nor did the fact that Nolan resented the way she had treated Hannah in the past. But what other choice did he have since he had no further ideas as to where his wife might be?

Nolan quickly relayed a shortened version of the story, and when he finished, he shook his head. "I didn't realize until now how hard this must have been on Hannah. I've neglected her in order to fulfill an agreement with my father."

"Did this agreement have anything to do with Molly?"

Nolan held back his surprise. The woman was more astute than he realized. "In part. The earl realized how anxious Hannah was over Molly's upcoming marriage and promised to take Molly on as a servant if I agreed to his terms."

Mrs. Fielding's hard features relaxed. "Though I'm not happy with the way you've treated Hannah, I am grateful for you providing this opportunity for Molly. The considerable sum of money your father offered has also been most welcome and has done a lot to ease the strain on my husband." She squared her shoulders. "That being said, if Hannah chose to leave, why should I help you find her?"

Nolan leaned across the table. "Mrs. Fielding, I love Hannah more than my own life. I've handled things badly, but if you'll help me find her, I promise I'll spend the next forty years making it up to her."

She held his regard, then lifted one brow. "Only forty years, Mr. Price?"

The Hartford gardens were as beautiful as Iris had promised. Surrounded by tall, well-trimmed hedges, the beds of roses swirled in a kaleidoscope of colors around the interior. At the center of the garden, a stone fountain held a place of honor, filling the lovely space with the murmur of gentle water.

After several turns around the perimeter, Iris passed Daisy's leather leash to Molly. "How would you like to take her for a run on the far lawn?" She pulled a rubber ball from the pocket of her skirt. "Daisy loves to chase this, and most times will even bring it back to you."

"I'd love to." Molly's eyes shone.

It warmed the cold places inside Hannah to see Molly so carefree. Rescuing her sister from a terrible fate had to be worth the price of her own heartache.

"Come and sit with me." Iris's tone broached no objection. She led them to a bench in front of the fountain. The gurgle of water competed with the sweet trill of the birds in the trees.

Hannah wished she could stay in this garden forever. "It's so peaceful here," she whispered.

"I've always found this to be the best place to talk to God. He seems to listen better when I'm out here." Her aunt winked.

Steeped in sadness, Hannah could not muster an answering smile. "Then perhaps I should stay and pray here for several hours, since He doesn't seem to be listening to me anymore." Why were tears so near the surface at every thought lately?

Iris laid a warm hand on her arm. "Hannah, my dear, Edgar and I were never blessed with children, so I am greatly enjoying having you and Molly here. I hope you'll find peace during your stay with us."

"Thank you, Aunt Iris. I don't know what Molly and I would have done without you."

"You would have found a way to do the right thing." Her gray eyes became serious. "Just as I know you'll do the right thing now."

Unease stiffened Hannah's spine. "What do you mean?"

"Don't you think you should at least attempt to work things out with your husband? A marriage sanctioned by God is not something to be discarded lightly."

Hannah pressed a hand to her heart as though she could stop the constant ache that resided there. "I fear the marriage will be annulled by now. Remember the papers I told you about?"

"Papers you only heard about secondhand." Iris squeezed Hannah's arm. "One thing I learned early on with my Edgar was that clear communication is the key to harmony in a marriage. Whatever Nolan may or may not have done, wouldn't it be better to have a frank discussion and clear the air? Find out where he stands on your relationship?"

The thought of confronting Nolan so directly twisted Hannah's stomach. Yet she couldn't deny the truth of her aunt's observation. In hindsight, running away did seem somewhat cowardly. "I suppose you have a point, but the thought of going back there . . ." Hannah bit her lip.

A pair of squabbling sparrows drew her attention to a tree across the way. They flapped their wings at each other until one darted off, the other soon flying after its mate. Even the birds, it seemed, were trying to teach her a lesson.

"There's something else you may need to consider," Iris said gently. "Is it possible you could be expecting a child?"

Hannah's throat constricted. She couldn't seem to catch her breath. "I-I don't know." She forced her mind to think back. When had she last had her monthly occurrence? She could not remember it since before her marriage. One hand flew to cover her mouth. The sickness, the tears, the fatigue—all the symptoms began to make sense.

Iris took Hannah's hand, a sympathetic smile creasing her face. "My dear, I believe you may be carrying the next Fairchild heir—all the more reason to speak with your husband as soon as possible."

CHAPTER 19

Nolan knocked on the front door of a great ivy-covered residence and clasped unsteady hands behind his back. A tall, lean butler answered moments later.

Nolan gave a stiff bow. "Good afternoon. I'd like to speak with Mrs. Price, please."

"I'm sorry, sir, I believe you have the wrong address." The man's thin face remained as bland as his livery coat.

Nolan's temper sputtered to life. He'd been traveling for hours. Hot, tired, and exasperated, he would not be put off. "I know my wife is in there. You cannot keep her from me."

"Sir, I do not know your wife, but whoever she is, I assure you she is not here."

He went to close the door, but Nolan jammed his foot in the opening and forced his way inside.

The butler's face reddened. He grabbed Nolan by the sleeve. "Look here, if you do not leave at once, I will be forced to call the constable."

"I'm not leaving until I see her."

"Carstairs, what is all the commotion?" A tall, elegant lady appeared from one of the rooms off the hall. Her skirts swished as she came closer.

"This man forced his way in the door, Your Grace. Says his wife is here, but I told him he had the wrong house."

The lady stepped forward to level Nolan with a steady stare. "Mr. Price, I presume?"

"That's right." Nolan pulled his arm from the grip of the wizened butler.

"I'm the Duchess of Hartford, Hannah and Molly's aunt." She watched him with undisguised curiosity. "But then you must already know that since you're here."

"Hannah's mother told me she might have come to see you." He adjusted his jacket. "I need to speak with Hannah, please."

The woman turned to the butler who looked ready to pounce. "That will be all, thank you, Carstairs." She gave a sweep of her arm. "Please come in, Mr. Price."

As much as he wanted to charge through the house until he found Hannah, Nolan had enough sense to realize the foolhardiness of that idea. Instead, he followed the duchess down a hall to a formal parlor. He entered the room, his pulse jumping in the hope of seeing Hannah seated there. The room, however, was empty.

Impatience coursed through him. "Where is Hannah?" She must be here. Why else would the duchess have invited him in?

In a calm manner, the woman crossed to one of the wingback chairs. "Please have a seat, Mr. Price. Can I get you some refreshment?"

"No, thank you. I just want my wife." Nolan clenched his hands at his side.

"So you have said repeatedly. Right now Hannah is resting. While we wait for her to awaken, I think it's a good idea for us to get to know each other better." With a slight smile, she sank gracefully onto the chair.

Nolan took a deep breath and forced the blood surging through his veins to slow down. He moved to the sofa and lowered himself onto the uncomfortable-looking piece of furniture. "I'm sorry, Your Grace. I don't know what Hannah has told you, but I can assure you—"

"First of all, I'd be pleased if you called me Aunt Iris. Second, Hannah has told me everything."

Nolan swallowed. "Everything?"

"I believe so, yes." She smoothed the hair from her forehead. "Now I'd like to hear the story from *your* point of view."

Though she smiled, Nolan sensed the underlying steel in her words.

The clatter of feet in the hallway stalled his next words. Molly entered the parlor, followed not by Hannah, but by a large brown dog.

Molly came to a halt when she saw him, her eyes lighting with pleasure. "Nolan. What a nice surprise." She rushed to embrace him. "We are having such a lovely visit with Aunt Iris. This is her dog, Daisy. Isn't she beautiful?"

Despite his problems, Nolan couldn't help but smile. The change in Molly since she'd left the farm had been remarkable. The quiet, reticent girl had blossomed into a happy, cheerful young woman. He bent to rub the dog's head. "She is indeed a beauty. So you and Hannah are having a nice time?"

She scrunched her nose. "I am. But Hannah's been under the weather and a little sad. She'll feel better now that you're here."

Iris rose from her chair. "Molly dear, would you take Daisy into the kitchen for some water? She always gets thirsty after a long walk outside. And ask Cook for some sugar cookies while you're there."

"Of course. Thank you, Auntie." Molly called to the dog and led her out the door.

Nolan whirled around. "What did Molly mean? Is Hannah ill?"

The woman's expression didn't change, except for a slight flicker in her eyes. "She's sick at heart more than anything. Come now, sit down and tell me all about your new life as the son of an earl."

A weight shifted on the bed, stirring Hannah from her light slumber. She blinked and stared up into Molly's beaming face.

"Wake up, sleepy. You have a visitor." Molly's laughter echoed off the walls.

Hannah struggled to sit up, clutching the covers to her chin. "Nolan?" The word came out as a whisper.

"Yes. He's talking with Aunt Iris right now."

Hannah's treacherous stomach rolled. Beads of sweat broke out on her forehead. She never dreamed he would find her here. What was she going to do now?

Molly's smile faded. "Why don't you look happy to see him? I thought you loved him."

Hannah swallowed the lump in her throat. "I do love him, Molly. But it's complicated. Nolan's the son of an earl now, and I—I'm still a kitchen maid."

"I don't see why that matters since you're already married."

Hannah repressed a sigh. If only life could be that simple. "Did Aunt Iris send you to fetch me?"

"No. I'm supposed to be having cookies in the kitchen, but I wanted to surprise you."

Hannah dropped a kiss on her sister's head. "Thank you. You surely did surprise me. Now help me get up. I suppose I must go down and talk to him."

Ten minutes later, Hannah sent Molly to the kitchen and

made her way on shaky legs down the main staircase. She paused in the corridor to take a deep breath, silently willing the nausea to leave her for a few minutes. Time enough to get this conversation over with and send Nolan on his way. One thing she knew for certain. She could never let Nolan suspect she was with child, for if he knew she was carrying his father's heir, he would never leave her. And she would never be certain of his true motivation for being with her.

Pasting on a false smile, she entered the parlor.

Nolan bolted up from his seat on the sofa. "Hannah."

The torture in that one word almost brought Hannah to her knees. "Hello, Nolan."

He looked haggard, yet wonderful. Dark stubble hugged his jaw and smudges of purple shadowed his eyes. His dark hair, tousled like it had often looked when mucking out the stalls, fell over his forehead. It hurt to see the misery on his face, so she turned her attention to her aunt.

"Aunt Iris, I see you've met Nolan."

"Yes, my dear. We were just getting acquainted. Won't you join us?"

"Of course." Hannah chose a chair across from the sofa. Not sure how to proceed, she folded her hands in her lap and waited.

Nolan faced her aunt. "May I speak to my wife in private, please?"

A slight hesitation followed. "As long as you promise not to upset her."

Nolan nodded. "I'll do my best."

"Very well." Iris smoothed her skirts as she rose. "Hannah, if you need me I'll be next door in my sitting room."

Hannah fixed her gaze on the tapestry of the carpet until she heard the door click. Her heart beat a terrible rhythm in her chest as Nolan's boots entered her line of vision. Then he knelt before her. An overwhelming urge to throw herself into his arms seized her, but she held herself as rigid as the legs of her chair to keep from making a complete fool of herself.

She forced herself to recall that he had signed papers to annul their marriage.

"Hannah, look at me."

She stared into the soft pinks and greens of the carpet, barely breathing.

He captured her chin and gently forced her face level with his. "Why did you leave without so much as a word to me?"

Her eyes met his and slid away. "Isn't that what you wanted?"

"Of course not. Why would you think such a thing?"

She looked up at him. "I saw you with all those fancy women in the ballroom, dancing and laughing . . ." Her throat tightened and she couldn't go on. She shook her head as if to erase the taunting images. All those women vying for the attention and favor of her husband.

"How? Were you there?"

"I watched from the servants' door." She bit down on her bottom lip. She could not give in to her emotions now. She needed Nolan to give her answers without the influence of her tears.

He huffed out a tired-sounding breath. "That was all an act, carefully rehearsed by my father on what to say and how to behave. Believe me, it was sheer torture having to endure that evening."

She forced herself to continue, to make him see what she had seen. "You looked so different, like a rich gentleman—one who belonged with those beautiful ladies. Not with a maid like me, someone who doesn't matter." Sadness gripped her hard and twisted. Here was the truth she'd always known. She would never be enough to matter to those she loved. By choice or by heavenly design, everyone left her. First her father died, then her mother abandoned her, now Nolan would leave her too.

"You matter to me, Hannah." His dark brows plunged into a fierce frown. "I don't want any of those silly, simpering women. I want a woman of substance. That's why I fell in love with you. You're everything I need . . . and more."

Her heart squeezed. How she longed to believe him. Yet she couldn't forget the influence his father had over him. Couldn't ignore the deep wounds she'd sustained.

Not trusting herself to answer him, she remained silent.

Nolan cringed at Hannah's wounded expression. He placed one hand over her fingers that lay fisted in the material of her skirt and caressed the satin of her skin with his thumb.

"I've neglected you these past few weeks. For that I am truly sorry. But you knew the conditions my father placed on me—the conditions I agreed to for your and Molly's sake. I had to keep my word and stay away from you for the rest of the allotted time."

She raised her head, sudden anger snapping in her eyes. "Time enough for your father to convince you to annul our marriage, you mean."

His chest tightened, restricting his air. "Whatever gave you that impression?"

"I heard your father talking to some man outside the ballroom. He said you'd signed the annulment papers—that you'd finally come around to his way of thinking and that once the papers were filed, the marriage would be over."

"I did no such—" Nolan rose in one quick jerk and slammed a fist into his palm. "I don't believe it. He tricked me." This was his father's doing. He was certain.

He paced the patterned carpet, one hand scrubbing his jaw. Then he turned abruptly and came to sit beside her. "I swear, Hannah, the only thing I signed were papers to change my name in order to become Edward's heir. It was a large document and I didn't read every page." He paused. "It's entirely possible he included a hidden clause."

Hannah's lip trembled, and he knew what she was thinking—that they were no longer married.

He gripped her upper arm. "I am your husband, Hannah. No piece of paper will change that. We swore vows before God—that is what matters."

Before she could respond, he pulled her mouth to his. Even though she remained rigid against him, he wrapped his arms around her, relieved that she was finally back where she belonged. He relished the familiar scent of her, the taste of her warm lips.

Suddenly, she melted in his arms, her mouth responding to his, and he deepened the kiss. Nothing mattered except the sensation of touch. Her hair brushing his cheek. The velvet of her neck. Her soft lips.

A groan rumbled up through his throat. "Come back with me, Hannah. I need you."

A tear trickled down her cheek, yet her eyes bore the familiar gleam of love he'd so missed. He wiped the wetness away with the pad of his thumb, amazed to find his own eyes damp.

She opened her mouth to answer him, when a knock broke the silence.

"I hope I'm not interrupting. May I come in?" Iris peeked around the door.

Hannah didn't know whether to cheer or cry. "Of course,

Aunt Iris." She pressed trembling fingers to her lips in an attempt to hide the evidence of their kiss.

Nolan rose as her aunt came toward them.

"Might I have a word with my niece now?"

For a moment, Hannah thought Nolan might refuse her request, but good manners won out.

"Certainly." He gave a stiff bow and turned to give Hannah an intense look. "Remember what I said, Hannah. I meant every word."

A moment ago, overcome by passion, she'd been ready to go with him wherever he asked. But as his warm kisses faded, cold reality set in. She remained a mere kitchen maid, and he the son of an earl. Those facts would not change.

"Did you tell him?" Iris asked pointedly the moment he'd gone.

A flush heated Hannah's cheeks. "I—I didn't have the chance."

Iris leaned forward, her gray eyes earnest. "My dear girl, loath though I am to give advice, in this case I feel I must. No matter what mistakes your husband has made, he still has a right to know he is going to be a father." She reached over to take one of Hannah's hands in hers. "And as much as you might not care to hear it, this child comes from a great family line that he or she will have a right to be part of."

"The earl wouldn't accept me before. He surely won't now if our marriage has been annulled."

"Trust me, he'll change his tune if he learns you are carrying Nolan's child. Besides, other than a snippet of conversation, you have no evidence that an annulment has taken place."

Hannah pressed a shaking hand to her head, willing it to stop spinning. "Everything is happening too fast. I need time to think." But how could she think with Nolan's overwhelming presence swamping her senses? With everyone offering opinions from all sides?

Iris exhaled softly. "Nothing will be solved if you remain here and Nolan returns to Stainsby. You must be near one another to achieve a solution." She rose and paced across the room. At last, she turned, a determined expression on her face. "I believe I have an idea. I will accompany you and Molly back to Stainsby Hall. Perhaps I can be a mediator of sorts. An advocate on your behalf. After all, what good is my title if I cannot use it to help my niece?"

"Aunt Iris, I could never impose on you like that."

"Nonsense. Daisy and I are in need of a new adventure, and this will do quite nicely."

Hannah shook her head miserably. "But what about the earl? What will he think if you arrive with no invitation or warning?"

"As you may have already surmised, I pay little heed to social convention—sometimes to my own detriment." Iris helped Hannah to her feet and winked. "As for the earl's reaction, I imagine we'll find out soon enough."

Why did that not make Hannah feel better at all?

CHAPTER

20

Edward threw his hat and gloves onto a chair in the vestibule and yelled for his butler. "Dobson, where are you?"

When there was no immediate response, Edward growled. Dash it all, where was that man when you needed him?

Scurrying footsteps echoed in the hallway, and Dobson appeared. He bowed. "Here I am, my lord. What can I do for you?"

"Has my son returned yet?"

"As a matter of fact, he arrived not an hour ago."

"At last. Tell him to meet me in my study as soon as possible."

"But, sir—"

"Just do it."

"Very good, sir." Dobson bowed again and turned to climb the main staircase.

Edward blasted out a breath of frustration. Why did it seem as though the entire universe was conspiring against him? Nothing lately had gone according to plan.

But all that was about to change once he made it clear to Nolan how things stood.

Edward stalked down the corridor toward his study, the slap of his heels on the floor giving vent to his foul mood. As he strode past the parlor door, a shrill of female laughter met his ears.

Who in the blazes was that? Surely one of the maids wouldn't dare make herself at home in his parlor.

Edward stormed into the room. Someone had had the audacity to pull back the heavy drapes and let sunlight infuse the room. The sorry person responsible would get a tongue-lashing when he found them.

Slight movement by the fireplace drew his eye to the right. Instead of the expected maid, a woman he'd never seen before rose from the chair. If he'd been of a calm demeanor, he might have been polite, but all he could focus on was the large canine at her feet.

"Who the devil are you, and what manner of beast is this in my parlor?" Edward barked out the words before he had time to think.

The woman arched a brow and stared at him. Then she took two steps across the carpet toward him, her feet not making a sound. The beast rose as well, emitting a low bark.

"Good day, Lord Stainsby. I am the Duchess of Hartford. And this is my companion, Daisy." She inclined her head with a smile.

Egad, he'd just insulted a duchess. Through the fog in his brain, Edward fought for clarity. The Duchess of Hartford. Had he met her before? Surely he would have remembered someone so striking. How had he failed to notice her regal bearing, the sweep of her chestnut hair, the smoothness of her complexion? "Forgive my bellow, Your Grace. Edward Fairchild at your service." He bowed over her hand, trying to ignore the animal at her side, likely shedding on his carpet as he spoke.

"I'm sure you're wondering why I'm in your parlor." She laughed lightly.

"The thought had occurred to me—yes."

"I am here to visit with my nieces, Hannah and Molly."

He blinked, still not comprehending.

"I believe our families are connected in a somewhat loose fashion. Your son Nolan recently married my step-niece, Hannah Burnham."

His mouth dropped open. The kitchen maid had ties to the nobility? Impossible. "I-I'm afraid I'm at a loss for words." The ramifications of this latest news jumbled his brain.

Smiling, she moved forward and linked her arm through his. "Why don't you join me for tea, and I'll explain the whole story?"

He looked down into eyes the color of dove feathers, speckled with gold, and found himself being led to his own sofa while his guest poured the tea. A long-forgotten sensation moved in his chest as he accepted the offered cup, and his conversation with Nolan no longer seemed nearly as important.

In the second-floor corridor, Hannah waited as Nolan kicked open the door to his suite, his arms laden with her belongings. In three long strides, he crossed to the bedroom and dropped the load on the top of the great four-poster bed.

Hannah hung back, biting her bottom lip. Why did this feel like she was committing some type of sin? She'd lived in this mansion for eight years, yet she'd never once been on this floor.

Nolan poked his head outside the bedroom. "Why are you out there? Come inside."

She hesitated. "Maybe I should check on Aunt Iris."

"She's fine. We left her with refreshments, and she knows where her room is in case she grows tired."

"What if your father finds out?" She wrung her hands together, still standing in the hallway. Nothing was more fearsome to the Stainsby staff than the master's roar.

Nolan marched through the opening. "He *will* find out, because I plan to tell him as soon as I see him. You are my wife, and it's time we started acting like we're married."

Before she could discern his intention, he swung her up against his chest. His heart thudded under her hand, and the hard muscles there sent a thrill through her.

"I have been remiss in my responsibilities, it seems, Mrs. Price. Since this will be our quarters from now on, it is my duty to carry you inside."

With a flourish, he leapt across the threshold and kicked the door closed behind him. He whirled her into his bedroom and dropped her on the bed, among her belongings. While she laughed and caught her breath, he swept her bags onto the floor, a wide smile creasing his face. She hadn't seen him this lighthearted in weeks. Not since the few stolen days of their honeymoon.

"I think it's high time we christen this bed, wife." He grinned and pounced on her like a mischievous feline.

Her mouth dropped open. "It's the middle of the afternoon. Let me up right this minute."

Instead of obeying, he plied her neck with kisses. She writhed under him, trying to get away, until he raised himself on one elbow, and smiled down into her heated face.

"Nolan, stop. We can't do this now." Her voice was breathless. Why couldn't she sound more forceful?

He twirled a strand of her hair around one finger, a rakish look on his face. "Why not? Despite what you may have overheard about annulment papers, I choose to believe we are married. And other than our brief honeymoon, we have not gotten to enjoy this aspect of our union."

"But what will the staff think? What will my aunt think?"

"They'll think we're tired from the trip and that we're taking a nap."

She opened her mouth to argue, but he took advantage of the opportunity, effectively halting any objection. His kisses were like a drug to her system, dulling her senses. How she'd missed him—the warmth of his arms, the taste of his lips. She threw her arms around his neck and kissed him back with an intensity that astounded her.

Just when she thought she would swoon from lack of air, a thread of reason swam through her dazed brain. "Wait." She planted her palms on his chest, pushing him back.

"What is it?" His ragged breath stirred her hair.

How did she begin to voice the doubts and fears that had plagued her these past weeks? Fears that evaporated when he kissed her, but that reared their ugly heads again the moment she was alone. She pushed those thoughts aside and instead asked her most pressing concern. "What if your father has already annulled our marriage? Our love would be a sin."

"Never." The fierceness of his tone matched the fervor of the passion that blazed on his face. "Our love could never be a sin. We've made our vows before God. Filing a piece of paper doesn't change that." He brushed a tendril of hair from her cheek. "If we have to, we'll restate our vows in front of a magistrate. Whatever it takes to bind us together for life."

Oh, how she wished she could believe that the vehemence of his words would make everything turn out the way they wanted. "I'm so confused," she whispered.

"Trust me and trust your feelings. Let everything else go. Our love is all that matters."

His lips found hers once more, this time gentle and intoxicating. As he kissed her again and again, her concerns melted away, until a sharp rapping broke through the haze surrounding them.

"Wait here," Nolan said with a frown. "I'll get rid of whoever it is." He rose, adjusted his clothing and strode to the door. "What is it?"

Mr. Dobson's high voice rang out from the hall. "Lord Stainsby wishes to see you right away in his study, sir."

Ten minutes later, Nolan paused outside the door to Edward's study and attempted to tamp down his frustration at being summoned like a wayward schoolboy. He needed a moment to collect his thoughts before he confronted his father. If he didn't, he might do something he'd regret—like flail the man. He deserved as much after his treachery.

On a deep inhale, he knocked. No answer. He knocked again. After several seconds, he turned the handle and let himself in. Other than the remains of a fire in the grate, the room showed no sign of life.

Of all the nerve. Edward had interrupted his reunion with Hannah, and then hadn't bothered to be here when Nolan answered his order.

He returned to the corridor, about to head back upstairs to Hannah, when a female laugh caught his attention. But it was the distinctive male rumble that followed that brought Nolan up short. He'd wanted to be the one to introduce his father to Lady Hartford, but apparently Edward had bumped into her on his own.

Nolan gave a deep sigh and turned toward the parlor. Time with his wife would have to wait.

Edward's voice drifted from the open door. "Enough talk about Stainsby Hall. You must tell me how such a young woman as yourself became a duchess." His father sounded almost . . . flirtatious.

Nolan clenched his fists at his side and pushed into the room.

"I would love to hear this story as well," he said with forced cheerfulness.

Edward practically jumped off the sofa where he'd been seated beside Lady Hartford. The look of guilt on his face gave Nolan a brief moment of satisfaction, but he kept his features schooled.

"What are you doing sneaking about like that?" Edward scowled at him.

"I was looking for you since you summoned me to your study. Remember?"

A tint of red slashed the earl's cheekbones. "That was before I realized we had a guest. How could you be so remiss as to leave the duchess alone like that?"

The lady in question rose and placed a hand on Edward's sleeve. "You mustn't berate the boy. I insisted he take Hannah upstairs to rest after the journey."

Nolan cringed at his father's glare. He'd wanted to be the one to inform his father that Hannah and he would now be living together in his suite.

Lady Hartford gestured toward the table in front of the sofa. "Nolan made sure Daisy and I were comfortable and had refreshments."

Edward inclined his head. "Well, that is something at least."

"Please join us, Nolan. I do so want to get to know you both better now that we're all related through marriage."

Edward's features returned to their usual polite mask—the one Nolan had come to know so well after weeks of instruction on how to achieve the same look. Edward gave the duchess a stiff bow. "Forgive me, Your Grace. I need to speak to my son. A conversation long overdue."

"I agree." Nolan met his stare, granite on granite. "Excuse us, please. We'll have to get to better acquainted another time."

She nodded. "Of course. I look forward to it."

Nolan strode out the door and across the corridor to reenter his father's study.

The earl followed right on his heels. Edward slammed the door closed, marched to his desk, and slapped his palms down on the hard, polished wood. "In future, you will show me more respect, especially in front of such distinguished company. Not only am I your father, I am the Earl of Stainsby."

Too angry to sit, Nolan paced the rug in front of the fire. "I am quite aware of who you are. And, frankly, neither title impresses me."

They locked eyes. A toxic mix of emotions swirled in the air between them.

Edward broke the silence. "Do you know how humiliating it was to hear from a servant that my son had gone on a wild goose chase after a kitchen maid? From now on, you will do me the courtesy of informing me of your travel plans."

Nolan strode forward to face the earl on the opposite side of the desk, keeping the solid barrier between them so he wouldn't be tempted to physically lash out at his own father. "I think it's time we get a few things straight. Hannah is now, and always will be, my wife. I have met the conditions of our agreement, which is now fulfilled. I will not be the bait on your fish hook to lure some wealthy debutante for whatever despicable purposes you have in mind."

Blotches of red mottled the earl's chiseled features.

Nolan lowered his voice to a deadly whisper. "Now I demand the truth from you. Those papers I signed the day of the ball—what exactly were they?"

Edward's gaze slid to the left. "You know very well what they were."

"I thought I did." He leaned farther over the desk, his breathing uneven. "But that night, Hannah overheard you telling some-one that I had signed annulment papers. That's why she ran off." The horror of what Hannah must have felt at the time hit Nolan anew. "Is this true? Was there some clause buried in that paperwork?"

Edward raised his head, his eyes two blue slits in his face. "Yes," he spat out. "The document contained an annulment clause."

The truth slammed into Nolan like a fist to the gut. His own father had tricked him. Pretended to want a relationship with him, then lied and manipulated him without an ounce of remorse.

Nolan clenched his molars together to keep from yelling the obscenities that hovered on his tongue and swallowed hard to dislodge the ball of disgust from his throat. "You, sir, are an unfeeling, dishonorable shell of a man." He barked out a harsh laugh. "To think I pined for a father all my life. Now I thank God my mother saw fit to keep me from you. I'd rather have been raised without a father than turn out like you." He leveled a vicious glare at the man. "You will have this annulment rescinded immediately. If I do not see proof in the very near future, Hannah and I will leave Stainsby—and we won't be back."

Edward jerked upright. "You're asking the impossible. I doubt Mr. Grayson will be able—"

"I'm sure with your talents you'll find a way to make it happen."

Nolan held his gaze a moment longer, gaining immense satisfaction from the stunned look on the earl's face, then turned and strode from the room.

CHAPTER 21

Two days later, Hannah tidied her belongings in the large suite she now shared with her husband, still amazed at the size of the space. Their quarters made her former room upstairs look like a closet.

When she was finished, she glanced at her reflection in the mirror above Nolan's washstand. Her cheeks, still flushed from an afternoon encounter with her husband, glowed with a health that belied her constant nausea. Several strands of hair had come loose from her bun. She quickly re-pinned the pieces and walked out to the sitting area.

Nolan had gone out to the stables to check on his horse, and Hannah now found herself at a loss, adrift in unfamiliar waters. By all rights, she should be down in the kitchen helping Edna prepare the evening meal. But Nolan insisted that from now on she was to act as his wife, not one of the estate maids. And to do so, he thought it better that she avoid the servants' area belowstairs. How did she make this transition? What did one do with one's time if not working?

Hannah's thoughts turned to Molly. Though Aunt Iris had objected, Hannah thought it best that Molly return to her position in the scullery for now. Until matters got sorted out, it would give the girl something to focus on. And in case things didn't work out, there was no point in letting her get accustomed to living in luxury.

After stoking the fire in the hearth, Hannah made a quick decision to slip down to the kitchen before Nolan got back. She would check on her sister and Edna, then make sure Aunt Iris was faring well. She hoped her aunt was resting in the guest room, well out of the earl's way. Though his lordship's initial resentment at finding an uninvited duchess in his home had given way to polite tolerance, Hannah didn't trust him to remain cordial.

As she descended the stairs, Hannah recalled the way she'd left Stainsby Hall in such a panic, and a wave of remorse hit her. She'd surely worried poor Edna to death, springing her secret marriage on her in a fit of tears and quitting her post in one fell swoop. She owed the dear woman a well-overdue explanation and an apology. Edna would want assurance that she'd returned of her own accord.

The kitchen bustled with activity when Hannah arrived. Steam rose above the pans on the stove. The aroma of freshly baked rolls teased her nose, and despite her unsettled stomach, she found herself hungry for the first time in days.

Edna stood in the midst of the mayhem, cap askew, shouting orders at the other maids. Upon spying Hannah, she threw up her arms and rushed to embrace her. "Hannah, my girl. I was so happy to see Molly and to hear that you'd decided to return."

Hannah managed a genuine smile. She'd missed this down-to-earth woman more than she knew. "It's good to be back, though strange not to be helping you prepare the food. I'm sorry it's taken so long to come down and see you."

"Well, you're a grand lady now. You need to be learning the ways of a future earl's wife."

"All in good time." Hannah scanned the kitchen for her sister. Perhaps she was out in the larder.

"If you're looking for Molly, I've sent her up to the dining room to collect the silver. It needs a good polishing and will keep her busy for the evening. All she can talk about is the Duchess of Hartford and her dog. Head in the clouds, that one." Edna clucked her tongue. "She must be daydreaming up there. She should've been back ages ago."

Hannah patted the woman's plump arm. "Never mind. I'll go see what's keeping her and send her down straightaway."

"You're a good girl. Come back when it's quiet and have a cup of tea with me."

"I'd like that."

Hannah frowned as she made her way upstairs. What was Molly thinking? She should be paying more attention to her post and less time woolgathering. She prayed Molly had not broken any of the heirloom china or crystal. Maybe that's why she was taking so long to come back, afraid of the consequences.

Hannah quickened her steps until she reached the dining room. As she was about to enter, a deep voice floated out to her, chilling the blood in her veins.

"You are every bit as pretty as your sister, Miss Molly Burnham. How lucky we are to have you to brighten up the scenery." Timothy Bellows's chuckle held an ominous quality that made the hairs on the back of Hannah's neck rise.

She pushed open the door and looked from the dining table to the long sideboard. Timothy had Molly trapped against the cabinet, his lecherous mouth fused to her neck. Struggling against his arms, Molly's terrified eyes sought Hannah's.

A rush of intense anger burned through Hannah. "Take your hands off her, you rotter." She raced across the room and began to batter him with her fists.

She'd put up with the randy footman's advances for far too long, never wanting to make a fuss or jeopardize her position. But she would let no one harm Molly.

Hannah's fury climbed as she continued to flail his back. Finally the man's grip slackened, and Molly managed to break free.

With an angry roar, Timothy whirled around, swinging hard. His elbow connected with Hannah's head.

She screamed as the force threw her across the room where she landed with a sickening thud. Pain exploded in her skull, then everything went dark.

Nolan left the barn and headed up to the front door of the manor. He was still not completely comfortable using this entrance and half-expected Dobson to reprimand him for not utilizing the rear servants' door. Strange how one small detail could signify such a huge change in status.

As he entered the main hallway, a terrible scream split the air. *Hannah!*

His heart took off at a gallop as he raced down the corridor, trying to determine which direction the cry had come from.

Molly burst out of the dining room, her face wild with fear. "Nolan! Hurry! Hannah's been injured."

Nolan barreled through the door, coming upon a scene that chilled his blood. Timothy Bellows knelt over Hannah's limp form on the floor.

Murderous rage pounded in Nolan's ears. He stormed across the room, grabbed Bellows by the back of his shirt, and wrenched him away from Hannah. "What have you done to her?" he shouted.

Bellows stumbled and grasped the edge of the table, glaring at Nolan with undisguised hatred.

Fury pumped through Nolan's chest. The impediments that had previously held him back from dealing with the reprobate no longer existed. He was the earl's son, and he would not tolerate anyone threatening Hannah.

"You piece of scum." He charged, plowing his fist into Bellows's face, satisfaction soaring at the crunch of his nose.

Bellows roared, ignoring the blood that streamed from his nostrils, and lunged at Nolan. Nolan swung again, this time connecting with Bellows's jaw. The thug went down hard and lay unmoving on the ground.

Breathing hard, Nolan rushed to Hannah's side and gently lifted her head onto his lap. A large purple welt had already formed on her face, the only color visible against the deathly pallor of her skin. Blood oozed from a nasty gash over her ear. Desperate, he gripped one of her hands in his. The light fluttering of a pulse barely registered under his fingertips.

"Hannah, love, can you hear me?" He smoothed her matted hair off her forehead. With her lashes lying in wet spikes on her cheek, she looked like a wounded angel.

His chest heaved as he fought for air. *Please, God, don't take her from me now.*

The muffled sound of frantic voices came from the hallway, then someone came up beside him.

Lady Hartford's anxious face bent over him, her skin as pale as chalk as she took in Hannah's injuries. "You must call a doctor immediately," she said. "I believe Hannah is carrying your child."

CHAPTER 22

Nolan paced the hallway outside his suite and raked a hand through his already mussed hair. Tension banded every muscle in his body, aggravating the headache that throbbed behind his eyes. What was taking the doctor so long?

He stopped in front of a narrow window and laid his forehead against the cool glass. For a brief moment, the chill soothed his head as well as his battered soul.

Lord, I know I don't deserve your favor, but Hannah's done nothing to deserve this violence. Please protect her and the child she may be carrying.

Nolan smashed his fist against the wall, welcoming the searing jolt of pain that radiated through him. How had this happened? He was her husband. He should have been there to protect her.

Nolan moved away from the window, rubbing his raw knuckles from the blows he'd given Bellows. One thing was certain. Timothy Bellows would never bother her or any other innocent girl again. The authorities had arrived to take him away in shackles to the Derby jail. If Bellows did get out, he'd find himself without a job and without references to find another.

For the first time since learning of his paternity, Nolan found it advantageous to wield the power of an earl's son.

Down the hall, a door opened. Nolan strode over just as Dr. Hutton exited the room.

"How is my wife? Will she be all right?"

The doctor closed the door with a soft click and raised worried eyes to Nolan. "I hope so."

"What does that mean?"

"Your wife has sustained a rather serious head injury. I've stitched the gash, but she will have a severe headache for several days as a result of the concussion. Of course she'll have bruising, as well as aches and pains from the impact of the fall." He shifted his black leather bag from one hand to the other.

"There's another issue to consider," Nolan said in a low voice. "It's possible my wife is with child."

The doctor cleared his throat. "Yes, the duchess informed of this likelihood, and I concur. I believe your wife is in the very early stages. That's why it's too soon to tell what effect this incident has had. Mrs. Price is still unconscious. She should remain in bed for at least a week until we see if the pregnancy remains viable." He shook his head. "Only time will tell, I'm afraid."

The way the man's shoulders slumped, it didn't seem he held much hope.

An image of Hannah holding their child flashed through Nolan's mind, followed by a brief pang of sorrow, which he pushed away. There could always be more children. They had the rest of their lives for that. "As long as Hannah recovers, that's all that matters."

"Yes, well, keep a watch on her overnight. Unless her condition worsens, I'll be back tomorrow to check on her. Good day, sir."

"Good day and thank you, Doctor." He shook the man's hand and waited until he had started to descend the stairs before turning back to his suite.

"Nolan." Edward moved out of the shadows. "I'd like a word with you, please."

Tension stiffened Nolan's shoulders. He did not need his father's interference right now. "I don't believe we have anything to say to each other."

"On the contrary. We have a great deal to say, especially if I heard the doctor correctly. Did he say that Hannah is expecting a child?"

Nolan clenched his teeth together. The earl was the last person he wanted privy to this news. "That is a private matter between Hannah and myself."

Edward's eyes hardened. "That child is my flesh and blood as well as yours. If it's a boy, he'll be the second heir of Stainsby. Will you deny your son the heritage he deserves?"

"We don't even know if the child will survive." Nolan fought for composure. "Because of Hannah's injuries, we must stay here until she recovers. After that, I'm not promising anything. And I'm still waiting for those papers rescinding the annulment."

Edward relaxed his stance and stepped back, an unreadable expression on his face. "Give Hannah my best. I am truly sorry about this unfortunate occurrence. Be assured I will see Bellows gets the justice he deserves."

Nolan inclined his head stiffly, then left the earl standing in the hall alone.

Hannah fought to open her eyes, but her lids felt as though they were weighed down with stones. Every movement sent stabbing pains shooting through her skull. She groaned and reached for her head.

"Hannah, sweetheart, lie still. You've had a fall." Nolan's gentle voice met her ears through the haze of pain.

Her whole body ached as though she'd been kicked repeatedly by a horse. Warm fingers removed her hands from her head and laid them atop the coverlet. A moment later, a cooling sensation met her hot forehead. Someone was bathing her face with a wet cloth. She managed to open one eye. Her husband's anxious face hovered over her.

"Nolan. What happened?" she whispered.

"You fell and hit your head. The doctor says you'll have a headache for a few days, but you should make a full recovery."

She struggled to make sense of the flashes of memory that swirled through her mind. There was something important she needed to remember. Her muscles tensed as it came flooding back. Timothy Bellows with her sister in the dining room.

"How is Molly?" She shifted and tried to sit up, only to fall back on the pillow with a cry of pain.

"Hannah, you must lie still. Molly is fine, other than being worried about you."

"Thank goodness." She closed her eyes and exhaled slowly.

Nolan placed the cool cloth on her forehead. Stillness fell over the room. Hannah concentrated on keeping her breathing shallow so as not to aggravate the pain.

"Why did you not tell me?" Nolan's quiet voice broke the silence at last.

For a moment, she thought she'd dreamt the question. But when she opened her eyes, the wounded look on Nolan's haggard face speared her with guilt. How could she have forgotten the pregnancy?

"Is the baby all right?"

When he didn't answer right away, panic filled her lungs. She hadn't even had time to get used to the idea of becoming a mother, yet a wave of grief hit her hard.

"For now everything seems fine. But the doctor wants you to remain in bed for at least a week, so as not to jeopardize the child further."

Thank you, Lord. She bit her bottom lip to contain the threat of tears.

"Why didn't you tell me?" Nolan asked again.

Hannah's heart ached at the hurt in his tone. She'd ruined what should have been a beautiful moment between them. Her gaze slid past his face to the dark blue drapery surrounding the bed. "I wanted to be sure before I said anything."

"Is that the only reason?"

As hard as it was to admit, he deserved her honesty. She licked her dry lips. "I needed to be certain you wanted me for me . . . not just to give your father another heir."

Nolan jerked back as though she'd struck him. "Why would you think that?"

Did he not realize how it seemed to her? That he'd been doing everything he could to please his father? So much so that she no longer trusted her place in his life. Yet his injured expression tore strips off her heart.

"I-I'm sorry," she said. "Everything has been changing so fast. I'm so confused." Her excuse sounded lame even to her own ears. But now that everything was out in the open, there was no room for secrets between them. "I promise to make it up to you. To be a better wife once I'm recovered."

He raised her fingers to his lips with a sad smile. "And I promise to be a better husband." With a gentle touch, he smoothed back her hair. "You need to rest now. I'll have your aunt come and sit with you."

Why did it feel as though she were losing him, inch by inch? "When will you be back?"

"Later. Don't worry. You won't be alone." His eyes appeared haunted as he bent to kiss her cheek.

When the sound of his retreating boots met her ears, a sick sense of foreboding rose inside her, along with a wave of sorrow and loss that would not leave.

Would she ever feel secure in their marriage, or was their union doomed to fail?

CHAPTER 23

Nolan slipped into the stables through the back door and lit a lantern. He stood still for a moment, inhaling the scent of hay, horses, and manure, and at last some of the tension eased from his shoulders. Right now, he needed these familiar smells and sounds to ground him. To remind him of his roots and the truly important things in life.

Never had he felt so lost, so unsure of himself.

Life had been simple here in the stable. Growing up at Stainsby, even as a servant, he'd always had his rightful place in the world. He had his skill with the horses, the devoted love of his mother, and the faith she had passed on to him as a boy. The one thing he'd lacked was a father to look up to, though Bert had proven a wonderful surrogate. Then, by losing his beloved mother, he'd gained an enigma for a father, a man he might never come to understand.

His dream of one day marrying Hannah had come to pass, but not in the manner he'd envisioned. Now a child might be on the way, a circumstance he was in no way prepared for. How could he be a role model for a son or daughter when his sense of self had shifted so dramatically that he could no longer find his footing?

As though sensing Nolan's unease, King gave a loud whinny from down the corridor. Nolan smiled and made his way to the stall, where he greeted the eager animal. He stroked the long snout, then leaned his forehead against his sleek coat, while King nibbled the collar of his shirt. He pulled a piece of carrot from his pocket and held it up for the horse to take.

"If it weren't so dark, I'd take you for a long ride, my friend. Shake the cobwebs from my brain."

"And what cobwebs would they be?" Bert appeared out of the shadows.

Nolan started. "What are you doing here at this hour?"

"Just making sure the new lad's finished his job for the night. A shame he's got such big shoes to fill."

Nolan tried to smile, but his heart wasn't in it.

Bert set down the metal bucket in his hand and stepped into the glow of the lamp. "A better question would be, what are *you* doing here at this hour? What with a new wife waiting in your bed?" He winked and gave a jovial chuckle.

Nolan's jaw cinched into a hard line, remembering with sudden clarity the sweet playfulness he'd shared with Hannah earlier in the day, and the bruised, broken girl lying in their bed now.

Bert studied him. "You look like a man with a lot on his mind. Let's sit down a spell, and you can tell me what's bothering you."

The stout man pulled over two bales of hay and motioned Nolan to sit. He lowered himself onto the prickly seat and hung his hands between his knees, head bowed. "I've made a mess of things, Bert. And I have no idea how to fix it."

"Is this about the ruckus with young Bellows? Word has it you pummeled him pretty hard."

"Not hard enough, to my mind." Nolan absently rubbed the raw spots on his knuckles. "Not after what he did to Hannah."

"Is she all right?" Bert's thick brows pulled down over concerned eyes.

"Not really." Nolan dragged a hand over his jaw. "She has a gash on her head and enough bruises to rival a prizefighter. But the worst part is she may lose our child—a child I knew nothing about." An ache spread through his chest, radiating outward like ripples through a pond. He still couldn't fathom why she hadn't told him. Didn't a husband and wife share everything?

"She's with child already? Is that why she ran off to parts unknown?"

Nolan silently cursed the servant gossip mill. Nothing was private in a community like Stainsby Hall. He shook his head. "No. She got upset after seeing me all dressed up like a dandy at that daft ball, surrounded by a bunch of simpering females." He plowed his fingers through his hair and sighed in frustration. "And she overheard the earl saying I'd signed annulment papers. You can imagine what she thought."

"Aye. She's probably wondering how much you value this marriage."

Bert's underlying hint of accusation pricked at Nolan's pride worse than the pieces of hay at his backside.

"Not you too. I thought at least *you'd* be on my side."

"I'm always on your side, lad. But it doesn't make me blind to what's happening. You're bending over backward to please your father, not considering your wife and how she must be feeling."

Outrage propelled Nolan to his feet. "What about how *I'm* feeling? I'm the one whose life has turned upside down. Like I've been tossed into the ocean headfirst and can't find a way to right myself." He stalked down the corridor, dust flying up from his boots.

Bert followed, catching him at the door to Nolan's old quarters. His large hand came down on Nolan's shoulder. "I know this is difficult, lad. But instead of worrying so much about the earl, why not look to your heavenly Father for guidance? Trust Him to show you the way to make this right—for everyone involved." He gave him a squeeze. "I'll be praying for Hannah and the babe. You know where to find me if you need me."

Edward slumped in the hard wingback chair in his study, a tumbler of brandy dangling from his fingers. The loud tick of the mantel clock taunted him, reminding him of the lateness of the hour and that he was likely the sole person awake in the household. After the day's unsettling events, Edward knew it was pointless to even try to go to bed, since sleep would surely elude him. The only escape from the darkness invading his soul would be found in a bottle of brandy, the last dregs of which now swirled in his glass. It didn't matter that come the morrow, he wouldn't be fit for human company. What reason did he have to get up anyway?

He'd made a fine muddle of things with Nolan. His only son hated him and would most likely deprive him of knowing his first grandchild. If the babe even survived.

Edward closed his eyes, his lungs deflating with a weighty sigh. From the moment he'd learned Nolan was his son, he'd handled things badly. He'd presumed he could manipulate Nolan into doing things his way, never taking into account his son's dreams and goals.

Now Edward could see that he'd been playing too high-handed with Nolan, imposing his will on the lad. Taking away the farm his son wanted. Tricking him into signing papers that would end his marriage. Forcing Nolan into a maze with only one way out—Edward's way.

And now his tactics had backfired. Nolan's wife was expecting a child, Edward's grandchild and another possible heir. In all likelihood, if Mr. Grayson had followed Edward's orders, Nolan's marriage had been nullified, effectively rendering the child illegitimate.

Edward had to believe the situation could be undone. He would contact his solicitor and have him do whatever necessary to reinstate the marriage. Correction—he would wait and see if the pregnancy remained viable, and then he would have Mr. Grayson take action.

Maybe then Nolan would forgive him. Maybe then his son would come to regard him with something less than disdain.

The clock chimed loudly three times, breaking the utter stillness of the house. Edward raised the tumbler to his lips and drained it. Time for a refill. His legs, however, refused to cooperate with his brain. They remained sprawled out in front of him like useless logs. The empty glass slipped from his fingers and fell to the carpet with a soft thud.

"Do you always throw your tableware on the ground when you're finished?"

Edward jumped at the sound, knocking the table to his right. Slim fingers grasped the empty brandy bottle before it too could crash to the floor. Lady Hartford righted the container and regarded him with an amused expression.

"What the deuce are you doing—skulking around in the middle of the night?" With a mighty effort, he pulled his frame upright in the chair and turned to glare at her.

"I'd thank you to watch your language, sir. And I have never *skulked* anywhere." She moved around to stand between him and the fire. "Nolan relieved me from watching over Hannah, and I had to take Daisy outside. I'm afraid that with all the commotion today, I've neglected the poor creature. Once I got her settled, I found myself unable to sleep and came down for some warm milk."

Why couldn't the woman answer in two words or less? And how did someone look so appealing at this ungodly hour, dressed in a simple skirt with a well-worn shawl thrown over her shoulders? Her slightly disheveled chestnut hair framed her face with wispy pieces that had escaped her topknot. A soft pink color infused her cheeks and lips, hinting at the recent exertion of climbing the stairs.

She stared at him, her head cocked to one side, as though trying to decipher a puzzle. "I see you have chosen a different method to induce sleep."

"What I drink is my business." He scowled at her. "If you care to make yourself useful, you'll find me another bottle. I would get up, but my legs don't seem to be operating as they should."

"By all means." She crossed the room, and with a graceful tug, pulled the bell to summon the servant.

His mouth dropped open, astonished that she would comply so readily with his demand.

Several minutes later, the butler appeared in the doorway, looking rumpled from sleep. "You rang, sir?"

Lady Hartford moved toward the door. "Actually I rang, Mr. Dobson. I'm so sorry to bother the staff at this late hour, but the earl is in need of a pot of coffee, and I would adore some warm milk with a touch of nutmeg."

Dobson frowned and glanced over at Edward, as if seeking confirmation of this request.

"What I am in need of is another bottle of brandy." He hoped his words hadn't sounded as weak to the butler as they did to his own ears.

Shaking her head, the duchess laid a hand on Dobson's sleeve, and spoke in tones too low to overhear. "Thank you so much, Mr. Dobson."

"Very good, ma'am."

The infernal woman glided back and took a seat in the chair beside him, folding her hands gracefully in her lap. What did she think she was doing? He was not about to drink coffee, nor was he in the mood to chat. He sank lower in his chair and stared into the fire, ignoring her.

She moved not an inch until a maid appeared with the silver coffee service and a mug of milk.

The duchess smiled. "Thank you so much. I'm sorry to disturb you so late."

"No trouble at all, ma'am." The maid curtsied and backed her way out of the room.

"Are you always so blasted nice to the servants?"

"Why, yes. Aren't you?" She blinked wide eyes at him.

"Hardly. If I treated them with such deference, they'd take full advantage of my good nature."

"No fear of that, I'm sure."

If he weren't so inebriated, he would have been able to ascertain whether or not she was laughing at him. Yet her features remained composed as she poured coffee from the service and passed him a cup. Though he churlishly wished to refuse it, his deeply ingrained manners wouldn't allow it. He took it from her with hands that shook, making the cup dance in the saucer.

She steadied him with cool fingers. A rush of nervous energy sprinted through his system, jarring him from his near stupor.

Good heavens, had he been so long without a woman that the mere touch of a feminine hand made him skittish? No, it must be the drink.

She picked up her own mug and settled back in the chair

with a contented sigh. "Nothing better than warm milk and nutmeg in the middle of the night."

With a growl, he raised his cup to his lips, swilled down a large gulp, and burned his tongue on the scalding brew. He bit back a curse. "Feel free to take your drink upstairs, Your Grace. I don't need you to play nursemaid."

"Isn't it time you called me Iris? At least in the privacy of your home?"

He grunted.

She looked over at him and wiped a skim of white foam from her lips with the tip of one finger. Then she giggled like a schoolgirl. "Almost as delicious as whipped cream."

At his silence, she cocked her head. "Do you ever have any fun, Edward?"

"Fun?" The word was as foreign to him as washing his own clothes. "Who has time for fun? I have two estates to run and two daughters to oversee. Not to mention a stubborn son who refuses to accept my guidance."

"I also have estates to run," she said evenly. "And I know how much can be handled by competent staff members. Granted, I have no children to worry about, but then you haven't had the real day-to-day responsibility of children for many years." The duchess placed her cup on the side table. "As I understand, the girls went to live with your sister soon after your wife's death. And now, of course, Lady Evelyn is well married, with Lady Victoria about to announce her betrothal, if the rumors are true. I fear, my dear Edward, you have run out of excuses."

The audacity of the woman froze his tongue as surely as the coffee had burned it.

She smoothed her skirt, brushing some stray dog hairs from the fabric. "How remiss of me," she continued. "You do have another excuse not to enjoy yourself. You now have a grown son to educate in the ways of the nobility. An arduous task, most assuredly. Doubled with the horror of his marriage to a mere maid, and a possible pregnancy on top of that . . ." She waved a hand in the air. "It's no wonder you've taken to the bottle."

He sputtered, then clamped his mouth shut so hard his teeth clacked. Blood pounded its way to his temples, causing his temper to burst forth like a gust of steam. "Madam, you will leave me at once. I will not tolerate your rudeness one second longer."

Instead of cowering from his bellow, as his servants and daughters were wont to do, the infuriating woman threw her head back and laughed. Not a simple trill either, but a full-out, hearty guffaw. She took a handkerchief from her sleeve and dabbed her eyes, then rose and came to kneel before him. She cupped his face with soft fingers that felt like a cooling balm to his aching jaw. He couldn't seem to tear his blurry gaze from hers.

"From what my niece tells me, Edward, you have spent most of your life in sorrow and duty. Now you have the chance to forge a real relationship with a most worthy son. If you do not take advantage of the situation—this great gift you've been given by God—you may awaken one day to find yourself a very lonely old man. Take it from a woman with experience. It's not too late to change."

Then she leaned forward and kissed him full on the mouth. Her lavender scent swirled around him and mixed with the taste of cream and nutmeg on her lips. When she pulled her mouth gently from his, a cold breeze stirred the air between them.

"Good night, Edward. Sleep well." Her fingers rested on his cheek for a brief moment.

Then with a swish of her skirts, she was gone.

CHAPTER 24

"You are a very lucky young woman." Dr. Hutton replaced the stethoscope in his bag and patted Hannah's arm. "The child seems to have survived your ordeal, though it would be best to take precautions until the third or fourth month. Limit your activity and avoid all stressful situations."

From her bed, Hannah smiled. "Thank you for your care, Dr. Hutton."

He gave a slight bow. "You are most welcome, Mrs. Price. I'm relieved to also find you fully recovered from your head injury. You were wise to take the extra few weeks to heal." He paused at the door of the bedroom. "I'll let Mrs. Dinglemire, the local midwife, know of your condition, and perhaps you can meet with her when you feel up to it."

"That would be appreciated. Thank you."

After the doctor left, Hannah rose from her bed and rang for the maid for the first time in three weeks. With the girl's assistance, Hannah washed, dressed in a plain blue gown, and allowed the maid to style her hair in a sweeping chignon. Once the girl left, Hannah ventured into the sitting room of Nolan's suite where she got comfortable on the settee and took her breakfast alone. Physically, she felt much better, though her limbs were still somewhat weak. The bruises had faded, her head had ceased to throb, and the nausea had subsided at last.

As she sipped her tea, her hand drifted down over her abdomen. One thing her extended stay in bed had afforded her was plenty of time to think. To come to clarity of mind concerning her options and to make an important decision. A decision that the doctor had unwittingly reinforced earlier with his words of warning to avoid stress.

Almost losing her baby had brought things into sharp focus. The good Lord had entrusted her with the care of this precious life within her. Her most important job now was to protect it. And that task filled her with a ferociousness she'd never before experienced, shoring her courage and confidence. The earl might not like her, might not approve of her, but she was the mother of the future heir, and as such, deserved some respect.

The maid returned to clear the dishes.

"Could you please tell my husband I wish to see him, Ellie?"

"Yes, ma'am." The girl curtsied and backed out of the room with the tray.

Would Hannah ever get used to giving orders to the servants, or would she forever count herself among them? She sighed and sat by the window to wait for Nolan, asking God for the strength to impart her news to him. No doubt Nolan would be distressed by her decision, yet she had to remain firm.

She could not control Nolan's feelings for her nor his reaction to his father. Nor could she control the earl's displeasure at her marrying his son. The one thing she did have control of was her ability to protect the child in her womb. Though she loved Nolan with every fiber of her being, she would not sacrifice her health, nor that of her unborn child, to continue living amidst this battle of wills.

The baby's welfare must come first.

Heavy boots thudded in the hallway, followed by the creaking of the door.

Nolan rushed across the room to her side. "Hannah, you're up. Did the doctor allow it?" His anxious blue eyes searched hers.

"Yes, he did." She managed a bright smile. "He has pronounced me almost fully recovered. I still have to take care for a while yet though."

"And the baby?"

She squared her shoulders. "So far, everything appears to be well."

"That is wonderful news." The lines creasing his forehead relaxed. "You must join us for dinner in the dining room tonight. After all this time in your room, you must be tired of eating alone."

Yes, she was very tired of being alone. Nolan had been sleeping elsewhere while she recovered, and most times ate his meals with the earl. Her aunt had been more solicitous than Nolan in passing the long, boring hours, bringing Daisy for company and reading to Hannah from the Bible and from various works of poetry.

Was it the earl or Nolan's guilt that kept him away? Hannah worked hard to hide her resentment. She would not resort to guilt or coercion to win his attention.

"Nolan, I have made a decision that I need to speak with you about." She kept her regard even.

His dark brows drew together in a slight frown. "What kind of decision?"

"I'm returning with Aunt Iris to Hartford Hall for the remainder of my confinement." She clasped her hands together in her lap and awaited his reaction.

"I see. Well, that falls in line with what I had planned before the . . . accident." His face became animated. "I had already told Edward we would be leaving Stainsby—that I would not abide his interference in our marriage any longer. I hoped your aunt would see fit to offer me some temporary employment until such time that I can purchase a piece of land for us."

A lock of black hair fell across his forehead. Hannah had to restrain herself from brushing it back. She licked lips that had gone dry and gave a soft sigh. "You misunderstand my intention. I will be going to Hartford alone."

"What do you mean? You are my wife."

"Perhaps I am, perhaps I'm not. It depends on the status of those papers you signed. Has the earl given you an answer yet?"

Instant darkness crossed his features. "He says his solicitor is working on getting the annulment revoked, but there's been a delay in the courts. Which is why I planned to leave with you as soon as the doctor gave the word that you were recovered."

"So we're no further ahead regarding the status of our marriage."

Nolan grabbed her hand. "It doesn't matter. We can get married again. Find a magistrate, and—"

"No." Hannah pulled her trembling fingers free. "We married once in haste without fully considering the consequences. I won't repeat that mistake."

Hurt flashed over his features. "You view our marriage as a mistake?"

"Not the marriage itself, but the secretive way we went about it, yes. Our love is something beautiful that should have been celebrated by all our family and friends. Perhaps then we wouldn't be faced with this wretched situation." Tears burned behind her eyes, but she blinked them back.

"Hannah." Nolan shook his head, his tone full of regret.

"Can you deny it? From the moment the earl found out about our union, things have gone from bad to worse." She squared her shoulders. "In any event, two things have become clear to me. One is that the constant conflict in this house is detrimental to my health. The doctor said I must avoid stress, and right now my priority must be the welfare of my child."

Nolan's jaw hardened to granite, and his eyes turned dull. "And what is the other?"

"That you need to stay here and sort out your relationship with your father."

She could see the anger building in her husband, like a volcano about to erupt.

He jumped to his feet. "I don't care about my father. I don't even like the man."

She rose and placed a hand on his arm, aware of the strands of tension quivering there. "That is not true, Nolan. You care very much. Your whole life you've wanted to know your father, wanted to find out who he is and establish a connection with him. You have that chance now—under this very roof. How can you throw away this God-given opportunity?"

He didn't answer, but stared at her with eyes that seared her soul.

"Without me here as a constant source of conflict between you, perhaps you can both let down your guard and learn to be father and son."

He grasped her arms with desperate fingers. "I will not sacrifice you in order to become his son."

She held herself very still. "I hope it won't come to that. By the time our child's birth nears, I pray that you and the earl will have come to some clear decisions as to how you wish to proceed. At that point, we will reevaluate the situation, and if your father is willing to accept me into the family, I will be happy to return." She swallowed the lump in her throat. "We must pray long and hard to discern what God wants of us, Nolan, and the type of life He wants for this child."

With a soft moan, Nolan pulled her to his chest and laid his chin on top of her head. His every inhale and exhale became a quiet form of torture for her. She clutched him to her and breathed in to memorize his scent.

"There's nothing I can do to change your mind?"

The agony in his voice almost broke her resolve. But she took a deep breath. "I'm afraid not. If you choose me now over your father, you will always regret it, and might even come to resent me and our child. Take this time while you can." She pulled back and managed a smile. "Look at it this way. Establishing a better rapport with Edward will only make you a better father yourself."

He gave her a long look. "I hope you're right, Hannah. For I'm giving your fair warning—I will not allow our child to grow up without me."

Once Hannah apprised her aunt of her decision and convinced her of its merit, Iris sent for her carriage. Hannah was pleased that her aunt agreed with her request that Molly accompany them, but then again, Iris had never approved of Molly working as a scullery maid in the first place.

One of the footmen arrived to carry their bags downstairs, and after a tearful farewell with Edna, Hannah approached the earl's study, pausing to gather her courage. Despite her trepidation, Hannah could not leave without confronting Nolan's father. She had nothing to lose by speaking her mind. After all, she was carrying the man's grandchild, which meant, for the moment, she held the power in this game they were playing.

Still, her knees shook beneath her skirts as she knocked on the door.

"Enter." The barked word held no warmth of welcome.

She opened the door and walked inside. The room lay in shadows with no fire in the hearth, no candle lit. The earl stood at the window staring out at the circular stone pathway in front of the main entrance.

"I came to say good-bye," she said in a quiet voice.

With a startled jolt, the earl turned to look at her. "I am somewhat astonished that you would care to speak to me at all."

Hannah moved farther into the room. "Despite your low opinion of me, you are Nolan's father, and I do understand that you're only looking out for him."

"How big of you."

She winced at the sarcasm but did not let it detract her from her purpose. Whether her words would have any sway, she didn't know, but she would do her best to aid Nolan's cause. She inhaled and released a breath. "Actually, it *is* big of me. You see, I've loved Nolan for a lot longer than you. And I'm willing to put his best interests ahead of my own. That is why I am leaving—to give you time to get to know the wonderful man your son is. All I ask in return is that you show him your heart. Be a true father to him. The father he has longed for all his life."

The earl scowled, but remained silent.

She clasped her trembling hands together. "I will pray for the both of you, that you can forge a true connection, and that one day we may all be a family—you, me, Nolan, and your grandchild." She raised her head to look him directly in the eyes. "Until we meet again, I wish you good health and Godspeed."

No more would she curtsy or cower before him as a scared servant girl.

She was the woman carrying Lord Stainsby's heir.

A hint of vulnerability passed over his face. He opened his mouth as if to speak, then clamped it closed. Instead, he simply bowed.

With that, she turned and quietly left the room.

Edward stood at the window watching the footmen load the Hartford carriage. They were leaving—the bold woman with her dog, and the kitchen maid who had ensnared his son. Edward should be exulting in his victory. Why, then, did he feel so bereft? As though he'd just had to put down his favorite horse?

He was still standing at the window several minutes later when another knock sounded at his door.

Blast it all. Why couldn't everyone just leave him in peace?

Edward waited, hoping the person would go away, but instead the door opened. He turned to see Iris crossing the carpet. A rush of heat stole up his neck as he remembered what had transpired the last time they were in this room together. In the weeks that had passed since that night, he'd avoided her as much as possible, speaking to her only when necessary, usually involving exchanged niceties about the weather or inquiries about her health.

"I have come to bid you farewell, my lord." Looking as cool and composed as usual, Iris stood with that blasted beast at her side. "I wish to thank you for your hospitality during my stay here. It has been a welcome change from the solitude of Hartford Hall."

Edward blinked. Would there be no apology for the condemnations she had heaped on him that night, nor any mention of the kiss she'd laid upon him?

"I am overjoyed you had such a pleasant time here." *Especially since you weren't invited in the first place*, he wanted to add.

Iris ordered her dog to stay, and then ventured closer. "I see you have not forgiven me for my plain speaking the night of Hannah's accident." She ran a slim finger along the polished wood of his desk. "I suppose I should not have expected anything else. Although one can always hope for a miracle." Her lips tilted upward.

"Why did you kiss me?" The words were out before he could stop them.

Her smile widened. "Isn't it obvious? I wanted to shock you—to awaken you out of the stupor you've been living in." She tapped a finger to her mouth. "I could have slapped you, I suppose, but a kiss seemed a much more enjoyable alternative." Amusement danced in her eyes.

Audacious woman! He gave her his fiercest glare, forcing himself not to stare at those full lips and remember how they'd felt on his.

"Scowl at me all you want. It won't do you any good. For I know under all that bluster is a wounded heart—one that needs healing in more ways than one. I pray that getting to know your son will help in some small measure." She paused as if for emphasis. "Make good use of this time, Edward. And I hope one day we will meet again." She inclined her head and then turned back to her dog, who lay obediently on the carpet. "Come, Daisy. It's time to go home."

Dressed only in a waistcoat and shirtsleeves, Nolan shivered in the cool morning breeze as he watched the bags being hoisted on top of the Hartford carriage. Coal-gray clouds scurried across the sky, spraying the earth below with a fine mist. He focused his attention on the liverymen and the horses, on the gilded frame of the coach—anything to keep from dwelling on the fact that Hannah was leaving him.

The very thought sent spasms through his chest akin to heart failure. He supposed in a way it was fitting—for without her, his heart would surely cease to work.

The front door opened, and Molly and Daisy emerged. The dog bounded down the steps as though recognizing that the carriage meant she was going home. Then Hannah and Lady Hartford came out and descended the stairs.

Nolan's eyes locked onto Hannah, and he couldn't look away. She looked beautiful in her modest traveling gown. No queen could have looked grander. Her gloved hands clutched her skirts until she reached the ground, where she let them fall back into place. When her eyes met his, she stopped and stared.

Time seemed suspended as Nolan searched for something to say, some reason to keep her from going. If only he could fall to his knees and beg her to stay. But pride stiffened his spine, and he did nothing.

A subdued Molly bid Nolan good-bye and led Daisy into the carriage.

Lady Hartford came forward and pressed a kiss to his cheek. "Farewell, Nolan, until we meet again."

"And you, Your Grace. Take good care of Hannah for me."

"You know I shall." She gave him a thin smile, then boarded the carriage, seemingly to give him a private moment with Hannah.

He turned his attention to his wife, intent on memorizing every detail to store away for the months ahead. The cream of her skin, the pale tendrils of hair that curled down from her hat, the quiet dignity that was now part of her bearing. She'd changed from the timid servant girl he'd loved for so long, and now walked with the grace and self-assuredness of her own worth—a woman of quality.

She came slowly toward him. "Good-bye, Nolan." The words were a whisper, swallowed by the wind.

He shook his head. "I'll not say good-bye to you, Hannah. I'll only say Godspeed until we see each other again."

Tears stood out in her green eyes, mocking her outward composure.

He longed to reach out and touch her, but he dared not, fearing he could never let her go. "If you change your mind, I'll be here." It was as close as he could come to asking her to stay.

"I know, but I truly believe this is necessary if we've any chance of a future together." Her lips trembled. "Godspeed, Nolan." She hesitated, as though waiting for him to say something more, and when he did not, she moved toward the carriage. But once at the door, she turned and rushed back to him. Reaching up on her tiptoes, she laid her cool lips on his.

With a low moan, he grabbed her to him, claiming her in a fierce kiss.

A kiss he hoped she'd remember for a long time to come.

Her tears dampened his cheeks, and when he finally let her loose, she took a step back. "Do you remember what you said to me on our wedding day? That we would pray together every night?"

His throat constricted at the memory of those few idyllic days. "Aye, I remember."

"Will you promise to continue to pray every night? So that when I say my prayers, I can picture you doing the same, and in some small way, I will feel we're still connected?" More tears flooded her lashes and rolled down her cheeks.

He clutched her to his chest once again. "I promise," he whispered, the wisps of her hair teasing his chin.

"I love you, Nolan. Take good care of yourself."

He wanted to say he loved her too, more than anything, but the words got tangled up with his sorrow and lodged in his throat. He helped her into the carriage, and the footman closed the door with a loud click.

Amid a swirl of wind-tossed leaves, the driver whipped the horses into motion, and the coach sped off.

Nolan stood watching the road long after the carriage was out of sight and long after the rain had washed away his tears.

CHAPTER 25

Hartford Hall was as grand as Hannah remembered. Yet she arrived for the second time with dread roiling in her stomach. Once again, she had left Nolan behind to flee to the haven of this estate. She bit her lip to contain her emotions as she entered the vestibule. She'd made her choice, and now she would abide by her decision without giving in to constant tears.

"Welcome home, Your Grace." The butler greeted her aunt with a bow.

"Thank you, Carstairs. It's good to be home. Isn't it, Daisy?"

The dog's nails skittered on the tile floor as she bounded in beside Molly, wagging her tail.

Iris reached up to remove her plumed hat. "I trust everything has been fine while I was away?"

"Yes, ma'am. Although very quiet." He took her hat and gave another bow.

"No word from the duke?" Iris examined her reflection in the large gilded mirror, patting her hair into place.

"I believe there may be some correspondence from His Grace in the post that arrived during your absence."

"Very well. Bring it to my sitting room. We'll take our refreshments there."

The trip had taken more out of Hannah than she expected. Huffing out a weary sigh, she removed her hat, and she and Molly followed Iris into the sitting room. The room's soothing quality soon smoothed Hannah's frazzled edges. She lowered herself to the settee beside her sister, while Iris took a seat behind her spindled desk.

Carstairs arrived with a stack of letters, which he set down with a flourish. "The maid will be in shortly with the tea."

"Thank you." Iris took out a pair of spectacles and proceeded to sort through the post.

"Who is the duke you referred to?" Hannah asked once she was comfortable with a pillow behind her back.

Iris looked up. "My husband's uncle, Alistair. Being the only male relative at the time of Edgar's death, he was named heir. But Alistair is quite elderly now and in poor health. He never really wanted the responsibility of the dukedom and has always allowed me to run Edgar's properties as I wish. I do consult with him from time to time when in need of advice. He and Edgar's solicitor have been a great help to me."

Hannah was only beginning to understand the weight of such responsibilities. "You mentioned another property in the city?"

"Yes, in London. I never did care for that house. Old and drafty. And very noisy. I much prefer it here. I only go to London when absolutely necessary."

"I had no idea what it took to be a noblewoman," Hannah said. "It gives me a better understanding of what Nolan must be going through."

"Nolan is a bright boy. He'll pick it all up in no time, I'm sure." Iris returned her attention to the pile of letters. "Look here. It seems your mother has written to me."

"A letter from Mum?" Molly perked up faster than a newly watered plant.

Hannah had almost forgotten how attached her sister had been to their mother and how difficult it must be for her to be away from her.

Iris opened the envelope and removed the contents. "Yes, and there's a note inside addressed to you." She held out the paper for Molly, who rushed over to take it and then went to the window seat to read.

Hannah straightened on the sofa. "I hope everything is all right."

"Most likely your mother is asking after you." As Iris unfolded the page, the maid arrived with the tea. "Thank you, Maggie. Leave the cart and I shall pour."

The girl nodded once and retreated.

Scanning the letter, Iris came over to sit beside Hannah. "I was right. Ann was concerned for your well-being after Nolan arrived at the farm looking for you. She hoped you were well and that you had forgiven Nolan for his neglect."

Hannah frowned. "Why would she think Nolan neglected me?"

"Perhaps Nolan told her so when he was there. In any case, I will answer this straightaway and put her mind at ease." She looked at Hannah. "Unless you wish to do so."

"No. You go ahead." Hannah glanced at her sister on the plush window seat. "You must let her know that Molly is doing well. She will be worried about her."

"I'm sure Ann worries about *both* her daughters." Iris poured the tea and handed a cup to Hannah.

"Not really. Mum was more than happy to leave me at Stainsby Hall so she didn't have to trouble her new husband with my presence." Hannah lowered her voice so Molly wouldn't hear. "I often wonder what Mum would have done if Molly had been older and in better health." Hannah couldn't hide the wistfulness of her tone. Shame burned at her jealousy of her own sister, and she vowed to beg the Lord's forgiveness during her nightly prayers.

Iris sipped her tea, a thoughtful expression on her face. "I would dearly love to see Ann again. It has been too many years. And what better time for a visit than when both her girls are here? I shall issue an open invitation in my letter."

Hannah slumped against the cushions. She so wanted Hartford Hall to be a haven during her pregnancy. To have her mother here would surely disturb her peace of mind. "I doubt she will come. Mr. Fielding always requires her help with the house and the farm work."

"Perhaps once the winter is upon us and the workload lessens, we can persuade her to come. I'll send my carriage for her so it won't be a hardship."

Hannah sighed. A visit from her mother would certainly be a hardship for *her*, but if she were lucky, and her mother followed her usual pattern of behavior, nothing would come of the invitation. Best not to worry about something that likely wouldn't happen.

Molly bounced up from her seat. "Mum says that Mr. Fielding's daughter, Matilda, has broken off her engagement to the milliner. So now Mr. Elliott is going to marry her." Molly laughed out loud. "Mr. Fielding got what he wanted after all."

Hannah smiled. "I hope poor Matilda is happier than you were at the prospect."

"I hope so too. At least I'm not there to listen to her whine. Matilda is not a very cheerful person. Every night in our room, I'd have to listen to her complain about something."

Hannah reached out a hand to her sister, remorse arising

anew at her petty jealousy over the years. "I'm so glad we got you away from that place, Molly. I don't know what God has in store for our future, but together I know we can face anything."

Nolan entered the drawing room of his father's London townhome and once again admired the ornate furnishings and gilded walls. Fairchild Manor was every bit as grand as Stainsby Hall, only on a much smaller scale. Though Nolan favored the manor's cozier rooms, he did not like the setting. The city offered far too much noise and commotion for his taste.

This was his second trip into London since he'd learned he was Edward's son, and this time, he felt only slightly more at ease. The fact that Aunt Ophelia had not exactly welcomed him into the family had made his initial stay in London awkward and uncomfortable. Nolan hoped she'd had time to come to terms with the new addition to the Fairchild family.

Especially now that he'd decided to follow Hannah's advice and turn his full energy toward becoming the nobleman's son.

"Ophelia," Edward said. "Good to see you again."

"Edward." The tall, thin woman rose from the brocade settee where she had obviously been reading a letter. She offered her cheek for Edward to buss. "A second visit in almost as many months. To what do I owe this honor?" Her cold stare shifted to Nolan and back to her brother.

"I should think that would be obvious. I am continuing my son's instruction in the ways of the nobility and plan to show him around our holdings in the city." He stiffened and turned to Nolan. "I don't believe you've greeted your aunt properly, Nolan."

Nolan moved forward to bow over Ophelia's hand. "Forgive me, Aunt Ophelia. I hope you are well."

"Quite well, thank you." She turned to her brother. "How long do you plan to stay in town?"

"I'm not sure. A week, perhaps two. I'd like Nolan to get better acquainted with his sisters. And with you, of course."

Nolan had also hoped to meet with Mr. Grayson and see if Edward was telling the truth about the matter of his annulment being revoked, but Edward believed the man to be away on business.

Ophelia resumed her seat, and the men each chose a chair.

"You just missed Victoria. She's gone on an outing with her beau."

"Ah, the elusive Mr. Coverton. I take it he's gotten over his objections with the family since our last visit."

Nolan held his breath, recalling the initial hostility Sebastian Coverton had shown him. But once Nolan had assured the man of his good intentions regarding his sisters, Sebastian had let down his guard. He seemed genuinely fond of Victoria, though nowhere near as smitten as she. Nolan only hoped that their courtship had resumed its natural course.

Ophelia speared a haughty look at Nolan. "It appears Mr. Price's introduction allayed Mr. Coverton's concerns. Though there still has been no hint at a betrothal."

"Come, now, Ophelia. Surely you're in no rush for Victoria to marry, since you'd be all alone here, save the servants."

She frowned. "Not necessarily. Victoria plans to have her husband move in here once they are wed. I have plenty of room and would welcome a man around the house." Her arched look at Edward challenged him to disagree.

"I have given you free rein with the property, so I suppose I will have to trust your judgment on the matter. As long as the pup doesn't overstep his bounds and try to take over your place as head of the household."

"You know I'd never allow that." Ophelia smoothed her skirts. "Would you care for some refreshments?"

"Not I." Nolan was quick to respond. "I'd like to go to my room for a rest before dinner, if no one minds."

The earl threw him a quick glance. "Certainly. It will give me a chance to catch up with my sister."

Ophelia nodded. "Have the butler bring up your bag. I've given you the same room as last time."

"Thank you." Nolan bowed to them both as he exited the room, glad for a reprieve from his aunt's stern countenance. Would she ever forgive him for the manner of his birth?

After a brief rest atop the high four-poster bed, Nolan changed into more formal dinner attire and made his way downstairs. At the parlor door, he paused to gather his wits before enduring his aunt's frosty reception once again. During his time upstairs, he'd come to a decision: he would do his best during his stay to win over the austere woman.

Perhaps Victoria would be home for dinner. Of all his new relatives, Nolan had developed a genuine fondness for his youngest sister. She had been the most willing to accept him into the family, and maybe her example would soften his aunt. Even the presence of Sebastian at the table would be a welcome distraction. Nolan was sure if he got to know the man better, the two could become friends.

Voices drifted out into the hallway, causing Nolan to pause with his hand on the parlor's ornate doorknob.

"Could you please try to be nicer to my son?" His father's voice whined like a badly tuned violin.

"You expect me to welcome the product of your youth's folly into my home? If it wasn't for your gross misstep, I wouldn't have ended up a spinster who is subject to your whims."

"You still blame me for your idiot beau's fickleness?" Contempt dripped from his voice.

"And you still bear no responsibility for ruining the family name? If not for your elopement with a servant, Albert would have proposed as he intended, and my life would be completely different. I would be the Duchess of Milford."

Nolan inhaled as he tried to make sense of the conversation.

His father grunted. "Have you seen Milford lately? It seems I saved you from a life of servitude to a man who indulges his every whim. He's had two wives and at least a dozen mistresses, if the rumor mills are true."

"That's only because he's unhappy. Separated from his one true love."

A snort sounded. "True love, my eye."

Nolan pushed into the room. "Good evening. I hope I'm not late."

"Not at all," his father said smoothly. "We're still awaiting Victoria. Will you join me in some wine?"

"No, thank you." He gave his father an irritated glance. Edward knew Nolan did not indulge in spirits.

He crossed to the settee to sit beside his aunt. "How are you this evening, Aunt Ophelia? I hope our unexpected arrival has not put you out."

One brow rose. "Not at all. I welcome the company after such a long, dreary winter."

"I'm glad." He smiled. "I look forward to getting to know you, and if you are so inclined, learning more about our family history."

The woman seemed to preen in front of him. "Why, I'd be most pleased to apprise you of our esteemed heritage."

"Splendid. I'm sure your account will be infinitely more entertaining than my father's."

Aunt Ophelia gave him a true smile and her features lifted. "Most assuredly. Edward's head is filled with facts and figures, not the subtle nuances of his relatives' characters."

The door opened and Victoria swept into the room, Sebastian on her heels.

"Father! Nolan! What a pleasant surprise." Victoria smiled as she came forward. "What brings you into the city?"

Nolan bent over her hand, then offered a handshake to Sebastian.

Edward kissed his daughter's cheek. "I'm familiarizing Nolan with our city holdings."

Victoria looped her arm through Nolan's. "Wonderful. While you're here, perhaps we can spend some time together and get to know each other better."

"I'd like that very much."

"I hope you know what you're getting into," Sebastian said with a wink. "I don't think you understand how much your sister likes to talk."

Nolan laughed, his insides relaxing for the first time. Perhaps he might truly come to like this branch of the family after all.

The next day, after making the rounds to Edward's business associates in the city, and being shown other local places of interest, Nolan was relieved to find some time to become better acquainted with Victoria—without his father or Sebastian in attendance. And especially without Evelyn, whose overbearing presence dwarfed Victoria's sweet spirit. Thankfully, Evelyn and her husband were off visiting Orville's family for a few weeks.

Victoria had suggested a walk in the nearby St. James's Park, and Nolan readily accepted, eager for some outdoor activity. As soon as they were out in the fresh air, the tension in his chest eased, and his breathing became freer.

"How are you getting on with learning the ways of the nobility? I'm sure it must be a challenge." Victoria glanced at him from under her yellow parasol.

"A challenge indeed"—he made a wry face—"but I am slowly catching on."

She laughed at his expression.

"And how are things with Mr. Coverton?"

"Our courtship is proceeding nicely, thanks to you. I don't know if I properly thanked you for going out of your way to speak with him like you did. It was most generous of you."

"I was happy to help. I only wish I could find a way to win Evelyn's favor as easily."

She sobered. "I'm not sure Evelyn will ever get over this. Not with Orville fueling her resentment, though I do understand the reason for his displeasure. As Father's closest male relative, Orville would have inherited the earldom one day. I fear that's the main reason Evelyn wed him. To keep father's money in the family."

Nolan halted on the pathway. "You mean Orville was Edward's heir?"

Victoria turned to face him, surprise on her features. "Yes. Did Father not explain that?"

"He did not."

"How odd. Well, Orville is a third cousin on Father's side, and upon Orville's father's death a few years ago, he became the heir presumptive to the Fairchild title. Right about then, Evelyn's interest in the poor fellow grew by leaps and bounds."

"So learning of my existence . . ."

"Was quite a blow to both of them, yes."

Suddenly Evelyn's tirade after the ball made sense.

"But don't let that worry you. Orville and Evelyn will adjust to their new situation in time, I'm sure."

They continued to walk. Nolan kept his hands clasped loosely behind his back. "Are you very close with your sister?"

"We were close growing up. A bond forged by shared sorrow at our mother's early death and then being sent to live with Aunt Ophelia. We only had each other in our grief."

"Were you angry with your father for sending you away?" Nolan kept his tone gentle.

"Hurt more than angry. But Father is an unemotional man, never prone to show affection or praise, so we weren't entirely surprised."

"What about Ophelia? She seems quite fond of you now."

The girl's features instantly softened. "Oh, yes. She was glad to take us in since she was unable to have a family of her own. Although she appears crusty on the outside, she hides a soft interior. Evelyn and I were fortunate to have her and likely fared far better under her roof than we would have with our father."

The chatter of birds overhead drew Nolan's attention. When a bench came into view, he guided Victoria over to take a seat.

"If you don't mind, I'd like to know a little more about our aunt." He hesitated, choosing his wording with care. "I overheard her talking to Edward. It seems she blames him for her ruined chance at marriage."

Victoria's gaze slid to her gloved hands on her lap. "You may not wish to hear this story. I've only recently learned all that went on back then."

He took a breath. "I'm ready. Go ahead."

"Aunt Ophelia was betrothed to the Duke of Milford. He was considered quite a catch at the time, and from what I understand, Grandfather was overjoyed by the match."

Nolan braced for what was to come.

"Then Father, who was intended all along for our mother, became infatuated with a servant." She peered over at him. "Your mother."

Nolan set his jaw. "Mary was the woman who bore me, but Elizabeth Price will always be my mother."

Victoria's cheeks reddened. "Forgive me. I'm not saying this well."

"No, please go on. You are just repeating the tale as told to you, since you weren't even born at the time."

"You are most understanding." She gave him a fleeting smile. "Apparently word got out around the village that Father had eloped with a servant girl. Grandfather was apoplectic, and Grandmother took to her bed in a fit of nerves. When Father returned with his bride and told them she was expecting a child, matters grew even worse. Word got back to Duke Milford and he broke his engagement with Aunt Ophelia, saying he couldn't align himself with such a tainted family. Aunt Ophelia was devastated. For her, it was a true love match, and the heartbreak of his betrayal has never left her."

"I'm so sorry. That was most unfair." No wonder Ophelia resented him. He was the physical reminder of all that she had lost.

"Indeed. And the fact that Father has never really apologized for ruining her life has always rankled. However, I do believe his giving her Fairchild Manor was his way of atoning for his part in her unhappiness."

Nolan straightened on the hard bench. "Well, I will do whatever I can to make her life as pleasant as possible. Do you have any thoughts on how I could gain her favor?"

Victoria's brow rose. "You truly care about her feelings?"

"Of course. She is my aunt. I've never had much family,

though I had always longed for . . ." He was about to say a father, but quickly changed his mind. ". . . for more relatives. Now that I have them, I wish for harmonious relations with all of you, Evelyn and Orville included."

"Ensuring that Fairchild Manor remains in Ophelia's control will go a long way to earn you her good graces."

"Then I will make sure she knows I will never change her living arrangements."

Victoria studied him for a moment. "You continue to surprise me, Nolan. I do believe you will be an asset to this family."

"I sincerely hope so." He paused. "Just as I hope the family will come to accept my wife." He waited, wishing to gain one supporter in the matter of his union with Hannah. His heart squeezed with longing just thinking of her.

"Oh, are you to be wed then?" Pleasure brightened her features.

Nolan's stomach dropped. He thought Edward at least would have informed his daughters of the marriage. "I am already married," he said quietly.

Victoria gasped. "When did this occur?"

"Not long after my mother's death." He quickly relayed the events that had transpired.

When he finished, Victoria gave a loud sigh. "Oh, Nolan. You are in for quite a battle with Father, I'm afraid."

"But how do you feel? Could you accept Hannah as your sister-in-law?"

She smiled. "I am likely the one ally you may find in the family, for I have always been a romantic. And it's clear you love Hannah above all else."

"Aye. She is my very breath." His throat tightened, constricting his lungs, as though without Hannah he could not draw air. Being parted these many weeks, with only one rather impartial letter from her, was one of the hardest things he'd had to endure.

Victoria's gloved hand reached out to cover his. "Then she is a lucky woman, and I will do everything I can to facilitate her acceptance into the family."

Nolan nodded, his cinched vocal cords making speech impossible. At least he had one sister on his side, and perhaps her beau as well.

It was a start.

CHAPTER
26

Late October 1884

Hannah strolled around the grounds at Hartford Hall, the cool autumn air nipping at her cheeks. She relished her daily walks and would continue them as long as she could, since winter would soon be upon them, and her outings would then be severely diminished.

Molly and Daisy walked ahead of her at a much quicker pace. Watching her sister blossom into a confident, cheerful young woman these past months was the one thing that continued to bring Hannah a great sense of contentment. She placed a hand on her growing abdomen. That, and the knowledge that she would soon become a mother.

Hannah waved to Molly to let her know she was growing fatigued and would head inside. As per her sister's normal routine, Molly would likely stay outdoors with Daisy a while longer.

Iris came up to Hannah as she removed her coat in the hallway. "How was your walk, dear?"

"Very pleasant as usual, thank you, Auntie. I hope tomorrow you can join us."

"I'm sure I shall, now that I've finished all my correspondence." She withdrew a letter from her pocket. "This came while you were out." Her gray eyes shone with compassion. "It's from Stainsby Hall."

Hannah's heart leapt with both joy and trepidation. Would Nolan finally say that he had come to an understanding with his father and was ready for her to take her place as his wife? She breathed a prayer that this time it would be so.

With trembling fingers, she took the envelope and made her way into her aunt's sitting room. Lowering herself to the settee, she tentatively broke the seal and took out the sheet filled with Nolan's familiar script.

Dearest Hannah, I hope this correspondence finds you in good health.

Her spirits sank. Already she could tell this was another polite letter in which Nolan spoke of his comings and goings, but not of his heart. Still she forged on, ever hopeful that the end would contain an invitation to come home.

As per his usual fashion, he spoke of his father, their trip to London, his aunt and his sister, and the tedium of his studies. But nothing of his inner thoughts. No words of love, no longing for her return. And he signed it simply, *Nolan.*

Fat tears escaped down her cheek as she folded the paper. Had her leaving him at Stainsby severed the bond of their love? Would he become so embroiled in the life as a nobleman that he forgot her completely? Or was he waiting to find out if their child was a boy or a girl before he decided what to do about their marriage?

Her heart ached with immeasurable sorrow. She'd been naïve to elope with him, knowing how things were bound to turn out. But at the time, she simply hadn't had the fortitude to deny her love, and now she must face the consequences. She brushed away her tears and straightened her spine. No matter what the future held, she would trust in God's ultimate plan and continue to pray for patience.

Iris entered the room. "All is well, I hope?" Her tentative question told Hannah she had seen the tears on her cheeks.

"Nolan is fine. Still busy learning how to run such a vast estate."

"No mention of you returning?" Iris sat down beside her. Hannah shook her head.

"What is the lad thinking? It's high time he sent for you, or came for you himself. Why, this child will be here before he knows it."

Hannah looked over, surprised at her aunt's outburst. She had yet to hear Aunt Iris speak harshly about anyone.

Seeming to collect herself, Iris patted Hannah's arm. "Not to worry, my dear. We women have our own methods to bring about what we want." She rose and walked to her desk. "I believe I have a few more pieces of correspondence to take care of after all."

Hannah bit her lip to keep from asking what her aunt was up to. Instinct told her she might not want to know.

Seated across the desk from his father, Nolan pored over the estate's financial records, an activity that was doing nothing to dispel his foul mood. His ill-humor had started early that morning with the strange note his valet had brought to his bedchambers. The innocuous-looking piece of white paper had contained a chilling message.

*I warned you once, stable boy. Leave Stainsby while you
still can. This is your last chance.*

When Nolan had questioned Jeffrey, the man told him that
a young messenger boy had delivered the note at first light and
hadn't said who it was from, only that it was for Mr. Price.

The unsettling message had preoccupied Nolan most of
the morning, but he'd declined to tell Edward about it, certain
he would dismiss it as a prank. Still, Nolan planned to keep
an eye out for any trouble. The only person he could think
of who might be responsible for such a threat was Timothy
Bellows. Yet as far as he knew, Bellows was in jail. Tomorrow
Nolan would check with the authorities to make certain he
was still in custody.

He turned his attention back to the columns of figures that
made no more sense now than they had twenty minutes ago.
Nolan pushed the ledger across the desk with a disgruntled
huff. "Do you not employ bookkeepers for this type of work?"

It had been over five months since Hannah had left Stainsby
Hall. During that time, Nolan had thrown his energy into
learning everything he could about his father's world. Yet he
could not seem to master the intricacies of bookkeeping, a
chore he considered more tedious than pulling burs from a
horse's tail.

Nor had he mastered the art of dealing with a stubborn
father who seemed determined to confound Nolan at every
turn.

For these past months, Nolan had shadowed Edward on his
daily routines, riding out to survey the entire estate, meeting
with the tenant farmers and all those who depended on the
Stainsby estate for their livelihood. They had also made several
more journeys into London, where Nolan had endured endless

social rounds to visit with his father's peers. Nolan even found the trips to his father's clubs wearisome. He doubted he would ever fit in there.

Nolan released a weighty sigh. At least Edward hadn't tried to introduce him to any more flighty debutantes. That was one point in his favor. Another was the fact that they had at last agreed on the necessity of clarifying the status of Nolan's marriage. With a potential heir on the way, Edward seemed as eager as he to have the matter rectified and had pressured Mr. Grayson to get the affair settled once and for all.

Edward looked up from across the mahogany expanse and raised a haughty brow. "Of course, I have a bookkeeper. But if I'm not able to double-check the figures, how would I know if the man was cheating me?"

"If he would cheat you, why would you hire him in the first place?" Exasperation laced Nolan's voice. The mysteries of the rich remained unfathomable to him. Horses were so much easier to deal with. You knew exactly what they wanted by the way they stomped their hooves or tossed their heads.

Edward laid down his pen and rose. "A wealthy man must always assume that those beneath him are out to take advantage—to obtain some of the riches for themselves. I've been trying to teach you as much these past months."

"Is that what you think of your staff here? That they're all out to take advantage of you?"

Hands behind his back, Edward walked to the fireplace and stood, staring at the flames. "I suppose I do. Maybe not always in a monetary sense. But if I do not hold tight to the reins, they will run amuck, like untamed horses. Shirk their duties, become lazy. Which is another manner of cheating."

Nolan pushed to his feet and approached Edward. "In my experience, most of the people I worked with here are diligent, hardworking, and, for some reason, loyal to you. Though more out of fear than affection, I would say."

"You make it sound as if fear is a bad thing." Edward reached for the poker.

"Perhaps not. Yet the short time I was at Hartford Hall, I couldn't help noticing the difference in the workers' attitude where the mistress treated them with compassion and, dare I say, affection. Hannah said the duchess's staff all seem to adore her."

"The duchess is far too nice to the servants." Edward stabbed the coals, sending sparks shooting through the grate. "I suppose that is the difference between men and women. Most females are too soft to endure the harsh realities of life."

"Are you speaking of someone in particular?" Nolan studied him. "Perhaps Mary?"

Edward flinched and moved to the window. "Actually, I was thinking of my late wife, Penelope. Her parents pampered and spoiled her, and she expected me to treat her in the same fashion. Of the two women, Mary possessed the better character."

Nolan's thoughts turned then to the woman who had raised him. How he missed his mother's words of wisdom, and how he wished she were here to counsel him now. He approached the window, thrusting his damp palms into his pockets. "There is something I must know."

"What is it?" Edward's features became guarded.

"Did you truly love Mary, or did you marry her only because she was expecting a child?" Though the grotto built in Mary's honor attested to his devotion, Nolan wanted to hear his father speak the words.

A dangerous light gleamed in Edward's eyes. "I loved Mary with the folly of a young man's passion. In hindsight, guilt over getting her with child may have been a motivating factor in our hasty marriage, but I swear I had always planned to marry her—child or no." Edward rubbed a hand over his jaw, and when he looked up, lines of pain wreathed his face. "The day I learned of her death, something died in me as well. I lost the will to fight my father. Mary was dead and the child gone—or so I believed. What was the point in defying him? And so I took on the yoke of duty and agreed to marry Penelope."

"I take it the marriage was not a happy one."

"No." The terse word said it all.

Nolan couldn't imagine the kind of empty, loveless life his father had led. "Do you regret wasting your life like that—married to a woman you didn't love?" He didn't care if he pushed the limits of his father's tolerance. He needed to find out if Edward might be inclined to view his marriage to Hannah in a more favorable light and not solely as a means to legitimize an heir.

But Edward's expression instantly hardened, all softness erased. "I don't believe in regrets. You will soon learn, as I have, that regrets are nothing but a colossal waste of time."

Nostrils flared, he stalked from the room, leaving Nolan as frustrated as ever.

Two weeks later, Nolan entered the dining room for breakfast, surprised to find his father at the table. Most mornings, Nolan rose far earlier than Edward and finished his meal before his father even arrived downstairs. Used to rising before dawn, Nolan could not seem to adjust to the nobility's way of sleeping late.

Edward set down the newspaper. "Nolan, good morning. I was hoping to see you first thing today."

"Good morning." Nolan inclined his head. He made his way to the sideboard where the enticing aroma of eggs, sausage, and bacon drifted up from the silver serving dishes. He chose a plate and began to heap it with food.

"It's a beautiful day for late autumn. I thought we'd get a little fresh air and enjoy some hunting. It's one skill I can teach you fairly easily."

Nolan looked at the meat on his plate and fought back a shudder. In the past, he'd often readied the earl's horses for his hunting excursions, always glad he wasn't required to participate. "I'm afraid I cannot condone such a barbaric pastime." He set his dish on the table with a quick glance at his father's scowling face.

"All gentlemen partake of the sport."

"I'm sorry, but I consider killing animals for pleasure distasteful. Other than hunting for food, I see no point in it."

Blotches of red mottled Edward's cheeks. He opened his mouth, seeming prepared to blast Nolan for his uninformed opinion, but closed it. "Very well. We will give anything we hunt to the cook for our dinner tomorrow. Will that allay your objections?"

Nolan speared a piece of sausage and gave an inward sigh. Edward seemed to be reaching out in his own way, trying to share one of his pastimes with Nolan. The least he could do was accompany him. "I suppose I can live with that."

"Good. Meet me in the stables in one hour."

Despite his initial trepidation, Nolan ended up enjoying the time with his father. For once, Edward relaxed and let down his guard. Now, as they made their way back at a leisurely pace with two pheasants tied to the saddle, Edward relayed stories about his childhood, growing up at Stainsby. They had just crested a hill, affording them a splendid view of the estate below, when Edward pulled his horse up short.

"This view never ceases to inspire me." He spoke in a reverent whisper. The cool autumn breeze ruffled his hair about his forehead. "This land is your heritage, Nolan. Land is something you can count on. It never changes. No matter the people who might come and go in your life, the land remains constant. Steadfast."

Was it the wind or the sentiment that caused the moisture in his father's eyes?

Edward spurred his horse down the hill toward the stable. Nolan followed, and when the land leveled out, the horses' pace slowed. They rode in silence for a few minutes, until Nolan felt the earl's gaze shift to him.

"Have you heard from Hannah of late?"

Edward's casual question surprised Nolan almost as much as the show of sentiment moments earlier. "I received a letter last week. She appears to be doing well." He swallowed back the hurt that stabbed through him whenever he thought of his child growing in Hannah's belly without him there to witness it.

"And how is Lady Hartford faring?" His father's tone was almost too casual.

Nolan frowned and shifted in the saddle to look at Edward. "I thought you couldn't abide the woman."

Edward shrugged. "I wouldn't go that far. The duchess does possess some unsettling qualities, with her outspoken tendencies and her opposition to the norms of society, but all in all, I found her rather . . . charming."

Charming? Maybe Nolan's first impression that the earl had been flirting with Lady Hartford had been correct. "From what Hannah writes, her aunt is doing well. They are both busy making things for the babe."

The horses slowed as they approached the stables.

"Speaking of the child, when exactly is the expected date of birth?"

Nolan's suspicions mounted. His father had never once asked about Hannah or the baby since the day they left. "Why are you so interested all of a sudden?"

"This is my first grandchild. Of course I'm interested."

Nolan released a breath. "From what I understand, it will be another month or so."

"Before Christmas then?"

"Yes." The thought of bad weather at that time of year twisted Nolan's insides. What if he couldn't get there in time to be with Hannah for the birth?

"I would like my grandchild to be born at Stainsby, if at all possible. What arrangements have you made with Hannah?"

Nolan stiffened in the saddle. "We have no arrangements." That admission gnawed at him as much as the cold wind chafed at his cheeks. He'd hoped for word by now that Hannah was ready to come home. In every letter he wrote, he had to curb the impulse to beg her to return. But some remnant of male pride made him hold back. She was the one who left. It was up to her to determine when her self-imposed exile would end.

"Then I assume you will travel to Hartford Hall in time for your child's arrival."

"It looks like that will have to be the case." Nolan scowled as he directed King to the stable doors. He had every intention of being present when his child took its first breath. If he hadn't received word from Hannah by then, he would turn up at her aunt's estate—invited or not.

"I'd like to go with you—if you have no objection." Edward reined his stallion to a halt and swung a leg over the saddle to dismount.

A measure of unease surfaced as Nolan jumped down to open the stable door. What nefarious plan was Edward plotting now? "That may not be a good idea. Your presence might upset Hannah."

"In that case, I will write to the duchess and see how she feels about the matter. We still have time." The terse response erased the last few hours of camaraderie, bringing the usual friction back to the surface.

Edward led his horse into the barn, and Nolan followed with King. The new groom, a young lad named William, scurried to take the reins from his master. Nolan moved past them toward King's stall.

"Leave your horse for the boy." Edward bellowed the order down the corridor. "He can manage both."

Nolan shrugged off the irritation that crept up his back and continued down the aisle. "I'll take care of King."

Loud footsteps sounded behind him, and a hard hand clamped down on his shoulder. "You are no longer a servant," Edward hissed in his ear. "Act like the son of an earl."

Nolan turned. "As the earl's son, I choose to groom the horse myself."

They glared at each other, neither willing to back down. Tension swirled in the air along with the dust motes that danced in the streams of light. Nolan clenched his hands into fists, his jaw as hard as the packed floor beneath his boots.

"Master Nolan, is that you?" The anxious voice of Franny McTeague rang out from the rear of the stable.

Nolan unclenched his fingers. "Yes, I'm here, Franny." He looped King's reins around a post and went to find the woman.

She stood inside the back entrance, a frantic look on her plump face.

"What is it? Is there a problem?"

"It's Bert. He's had an accident in the smithy." Franny pressed a handkerchief to her mouth to contain a sob.

Alarm shot through Nolan's system. "What kind of accident?"

"He fell into the fire pit. His hands—" She could say no more due to the flood of tears that coursed down her cheeks.

"I'll be right there." He turned to Edward. "Send for the doctor. Have him go directly to the McTeagues' cottage."

Edward reached out to grab his arm, his features dark. "It's not your place to worry about the staff. When will you understand that?"

Nolan snatched his arm away. "For the last ten years, Bert McTeague has been the closest thing I've had to a father. I will do whatever it takes to ensure he's all right."

With a last glare, Nolan raced out of the barn, offering up desperate prayers for Bert's safety.

Edward ignored the tea ready for him in his study and headed straight for the brandy in his desk. Yanking open the bottom drawer, he removed the bottle and a glass. With a muttered oath, he poured a good quantity of liquid into the tumbler and downed it in one straight shot.

"Why can't he understand his proper place in this house?" Edward slammed the glass down on the desk and wiped his mouth with the back of his sleeve. Every time he made a bit of headway with Nolan, something set it back. His son was more stubborn than the stallion he'd been riding—always wanting to head off in his own direction.

Despite everything, they had managed to share a few moments of camaraderie today. Recalling the feeling of pride when Nolan had felled his first pheasant brought a smile to Edward's lips. Too bad such fleeting moments didn't last. He'd been trying to follow Lady Hartford's advice to get to know his son. Yet he continued to fail on a daily basis.

Edward swore and poured another shot of brandy. He had no intention of making the same mistakes with his grandson—for he was certain the child would be a boy. He would get to know the child right from the moment of his birth, and school him in the ways of the aristocracy. The child would grow up revering him, knowing that one day Stainsby Hall would pass to him.

The study door opened, and Nolan stepped inside, lines creasing his forehead. His blue eyes darted from the bottle on the desk to the tumbler in Edward's hand, and his scowl deepened.

"Care to join me?" Edward raised his glass in a mock salute.

"You know I don't drink spirits. They dull the mind and the senses."

"Exactly the reason I *do* drink spirits." He drained the tumbler again.

"I came to see if you'd sent for the doctor."

"One of the servants has gone to fetch him."

Nolan dragged the cap off his head and ran the edge around his fingers. "Bert's hands are badly burned. I did what I could for him, but he's in terrible pain. He may need a more specialized doctor."

Edward's fingers stilled on the bottle. "I see. And you expect me to pay for a specialist?"

"Bert has been a blacksmith here for thirty years. I think such loyalty deserves some extra consideration." Nolan practically snarled.

Edward bristled at the implication that he was anything less than a stellar employer. He'd always prided himself on the fact that his staff were well cared for. "You act as though I've treated him in some remiss fashion. I've afforded Mr. McTeague and his wife a nice cottage of their own. He has a piece of land for a garden. Have they not lived comfortably all this time?"

Nolan's combative stance did not change. "That is not the point."

Edward rose and moved around the desk to close the distance between them. A mixture of anger and despair darkened Nolan's eyes. He held himself stiffly—as though trying to contain the emotions vibrating within him.

A brief burst of jealousy flared. Would his son ever feel as strongly about him? Would he one day defend Edward with that same fierce loyalty?

Edward let out a resigned sigh. Balking Nolan on this point would not earn him any favor in his son's eyes. "Let's see what Doctor Hutton advises. If he feels the man needs further care, I will see that he gets it."

"Thank you." Nolan nodded, a half-smile gracing his lips. "I knew that a sense of compassion lurked under that grim exterior."

The tense muscles in Edward's chest began to uncoil. Perhaps his son didn't see him as such a black-hearted villain after all. Perhaps he was beginning to understand him just a little.

Nolan took his leave, presumably to go back and wait with the McTeagues.

Edward capped the brandy and returned it to the drawer, suddenly more interested in sobriety. He needed a clear head to figure out what else he might do to gain—and keep—his son's admiration.

CHAPTER 27

"I have splendid news." Iris bustled into the dining room, a letter in her hand. "Your mother has accepted my latest invitation and is coming for a visit after all. She will arrive within the week."

Seated at the long table, Hannah tried not to choke on her morning tea. In no way had she imagined her mother would ever accept any of Aunt Iris's repeated invitations. In all the years Hannah had been at Stainsby Hall, her mother had never once come to see her, claiming her husband couldn't do without her.

Iris stopped to watch her, a slight frown marring her features. "You don't seem pleased. I thought you'd welcome a chance to spend time with your mother away from Mr. Fielding's influence."

"Of—of course. It's most thoughtful. Thank you, Auntie." Hannah patted a napkin to her mouth, then laid it on the lap of her soft gray dress. Iris had commissioned her dressmaker to sew a whole new wardrobe for Hannah, one that could be altered once the baby arrived. "How did Mum manage to get away?"

"I'm not sure. But I'm delighted she can come." Iris stood at the sideboard and poured another cup of tea. The sun streamed in through the window, creating a halo effect around the soft sweep of her hair. "While she's here, I plan to invite a few more people and make an event of it."

"But Auntie, in my condition—"

"Nonsense. It will be extended family only." Her gray eyes brightened. "A family reunion of sorts. How splendid."

Her aunt seemed so excited that Hannah didn't have the heart to discourage her. With gentle fingers, she caressed her swollen abdomen. What would her mother think about becoming a grandmother?

A sudden suspicion struck Hannah. "You're not thinking of writing to Nolan, are you?"

"Why, yes." Iris blinked at her. "I plan to send an invitation to Stainsby. I'd like to invite Nolan—and his father."

The mere mention of the earl made Hannah's stomach clench. "I'd prefer that you not. I want Nolan to come here of his own accord because he wants me back. Not because of some invitation." She fought the sudden tremble of her lips.

"It appears to me that you and Nolan have reached an impasse, with neither willing to take action. Both waiting for the other to make some sort of declaration. If this brings your husband here so that you might discuss your situation and come to some sort of resolution, then I will not apologize for going against your wishes."

Tension seized Hannah's shoulders. Though she still was not ready to face Nolan, nor the possible demise of her marriage, her aunt would not be swayed. She sighed. Perhaps it was for the best. After all, time was running out before the baby would arrive.

She needed to find out once and for all the true state of her marriage, whether the earl had come to accept her as Nolan's wife, and most important, whether Nolan wished to continue their union.

The rest of the meal passed in silence, her aunt engrossed in the morning news, while Hannah's thoughts remained on the disconcerting tidings of her mother and husband's impeding visits.

Hannah wished for her sister's company to distract her from unwanted worrying, but Molly was already at work in the study with the tutor Aunt Iris had hired to catch the girl up on her lessons.

When Iris folded the newspaper in half and laid it down, the signal that the meal had ended, Hannah rose from the table and firmly pushed away all unsettling thoughts. For her child's sake, she needed to focus on nothing but happy things.

As had become their usual routine, she and Iris would take a brisk walk in the garden, after which they would sit in the parlor and work on the tiny baby clothes they'd been sewing. Molly would join them once she had finished with her schooling for the day.

A maid appeared with their wraps, while another led Daisy on her leash. The days had become much colder, a sure sign that winter was headed their way.

Iris held open the door that led onto the terrace, letting Daisy out first.

Hannah shivered with the bitter bite of air, pulling her cloak more firmly about her. The wind blew a flurry of dead leaves in a circular pattern over the walkway as they strolled. From the feel of the elements, Hannah wouldn't be surprised if it snowed soon.

Iris was unusually silent during the first lap around the garden. She let Daisy off her leash, then turned a rather grim face to her. "Hannah, I have a question to ask, and I trust you won't take it the wrong way."

Hannah frowned and slowed her pace. "What is it, Auntie?"

"You have been here for some time now. Almost half a year, in fact."

"Yes." Hannah swallowed a ball of fear. Did her aunt feel she was taking advantage of her kind nature? Would she ask her to leave?

"What exactly do you expect Nolan to do in order to let him back into your life?"

Hannah almost tripped on a raised stone in the walkway. "I don't know what you mean."

Iris looped her arm through Hannah's and led her back to their allotted pathway. "I think my question was clear enough. For all intents and purposes, you have left your husband, presumably for his own good, so he might forge a relationship with the earl."

"That's right." Hannah tried not to bristle at her aunt's implication that it was *not* for Nolan's own good. "I know how important it is to Nolan to have a father. Besides, the tension between them wasn't good for me or the baby."

"All very admirable reasons for running away." Iris shot her an arched look.

Heat rose in Hannah's chest. "I did not run away. You make me sound like a coward."

"Very well, then back to my original question. What must Nolan do to be allowed back into your life—and into your bed?"

Shock stole Hannah's breath. "Aunt Iris! That is a very personal matter between a husband and wife."

Iris pulled Hannah to a stop and took her gently by the shoulders. "My dear, what are you so afraid of?"

Hannah's mouth fell open. Her whole body began to shake uncontrollably, her legs almost giving out beneath the extra weight of her belly. Iris steered her to a nearby bench and sat down beside her.

Hannah's mind whirled with the sudden realization that not only was she afraid—she was terrified. And she wasn't sure what scared her more: loving Nolan or losing him.

Iris took one of Hannah's gloved hands in hers. "My dear girl, you are like the daughter I never had. I trust we've become close enough for me to speak plainly."

Hannah nodded, clutching the bench beside her as though to anchor her there lest she give in to the urge to flee.

"It seems to me you are deathly afraid of giving yourself completely to your husband. Of letting Nolan love you. Why would that be?"

The gentleness in her voice brought the rise of tears to Hannah's throat. She shook her head, unable to answer.

"Do you think yourself unworthy of Nolan because of his father's station?" With the tip of one finger, she raised Hannah's chin. "Or do you think yourself so unlovable that you doubt his feelings?"

Unlovable. The word echoed in her mind, spinning its ugly truth like an insidious web. The lump in her throat became a sob that burst forth in a gush of tears. She collapsed against Iris's shoulder.

Her aunt hugged her tightly until the spasms subsided. Then she pulled out a handkerchief to dab at Hannah's face. "There, there. I can speak with absolute certainty when I say that you are the least *un*lovable person I know. Not only are you a beauty on the outside, you are more than beautiful on the inside, and I, for one, adore you. Can you at least believe that?"

Hannah looked into Iris's sincere eyes and nodded.

"Good. And I hope you also know that your heavenly Father loves you unconditionally and without limit. You are a treasured child of God, most worthy of all goodness that comes into your life. And definitely worthy of a fine man like Nolan."

Hannah stared at her lap and shook her head.

"What is it that makes you feel so undeserving, dearest?"

Hannah slowly raised her head to meet her aunt's gentle gaze. She attempted to speak, then stopped, her mouth dry.

"It's all right to say what's in your heart." Her aunt gave her an encouraging squeeze.

Hannah nodded and forced herself to admit the truth. "Ever since Papa died and Mum left me with Mrs. Bridges, I felt there must be something lacking in me—a reason why everyone leaves me. I must not be good enough, flawed in some way. People start out loving me, but then it fades . . . and they forget about me." She bit her lip, once again feeling like the scared thirteen-year-old girl watching the carriage take her mother away. "Mum chose to keep Molly and not me. I wasn't good enough."

"That can't be true." Iris clasped her hands over Hannah's fisted ones. "Your mother must have believed she was giving you a better life than you would have had with Mr. Fielding and his brood."

Hannah shook her head, sadness seeping through her soul. "After losing Papa and our little brother, all I wanted was to be with my mother and sister. Nothing else mattered. I thought I must have done something terribly wrong for her to punish me that way."

"Oh, my darling girl." Iris pulled her back into an embrace. "I'm so sorry you had to go through that. If only I hadn't been so sick at the time, I would have gladly taken you all in. I'm sure my Edgar would have loved having the house full of family." She sniffed, and Hannah was surprised to find her aunt's eyes damp as well. "You mustn't let your mother's desperate actions determine your self-worth. I have to believe it was all part of God's plan for your life. That there was a purpose for bringing you to Stainsby. One we have yet to learn." She inhaled deeply. "Come now, let's continue our walk."

They rose to resume their place on the path. Daisy dashed ahead, eager for the rest of the outing. Iris remained silent as they walked, lost in silent contemplation. As they neared the end of the path, she looked over at Hannah. "I think this family reunion is long past due. I will continue to pray that God will heal old wounds and bring about a true reconciliation."

Hannah wished she could share her aunt's optimism but feared it would take a miracle for that to come to pass.

Nolan paced the dirt floor of the McTeagues' cottage, his attention fastened on the closed bedroom door. Any time now, Doctor Hutton would emerge after tending to Bert's hands. Nolan prayed that this time he'd have better news for them.

Franny sat at a scarred table by the hearth, paring potatoes for their next meal. Every so often, she stopped to stare into the fire, her knife paused in midair. Nolan knew she was trying hard to be stoic, hiding her worry as best she could from her husband.

Nolan had had plenty of time since Bert's accident to recall his friend's words of advice in the smithy. *Think of the good you could do for the servants and the tenant farmers. What better advocate could we have than someone who's lived in our shoes?* As Edward's son, Nolan would make sure Bert and Franny were taken care of, even if he had to bully his father into doing what was right. This incident brought into sharp focus the plight of many of the older staff whose health might prevent them from being able to do their jobs. What would happen to those loyal workers?

Steam spewed from the copper kettle on the range. Franny

pushed her frame up from the table and moved to take it off the heat.

"Please have a seat, Master Nolan," she said with a frown. "You'll create a dust storm in here with your pacing." She poured boiling water into the teapot.

"I can't sit doing nothing. Why don't you put me to use around here while we wait?"

She rolled her eyes. "As if I'd ever let his lordship's son do labor in my home."

"Forget about my title, Franny. I'm still the boy you used to chase out of your garden for stealing carrots."

Despite her gruff countenance, her lips twitched. "And I'll do it again if I catch you now."

The bedroom door swung open, and Dr. Hutton emerged. Nolan went to meet him. "Any improvement, Doctor?"

"Not much, I'm afraid."

It had been three days since Bert had taken a dizzy spell and fallen into the fire. The doctor had been back every day to apply new dressings and change the bandages.

"Will he be able to use his hands again once they've healed?"

"It's hard to tell." Dr. Hutton shook his head as he fastened his bag. "All we can do is wait and see. I wish I could give you better news." He retrieved his overcoat, and after imparting some further instructions for Franny, he left the cottage.

Franny sank back onto her chair, softly weeping. "What if he can no longer work, Master Nolan? What will we do then?"

She voiced the very thing that troubled Nolan. He couldn't picture Bert anywhere else but in his smithy.

Nolan patted her broad back. "Try not to imagine the worst. We must be optimistic for Bert's sake."

"But the master won't let us stay here for free. Where will we go?" She dabbed the corner of her apron to her eyes.

A ferocious determination welled in Nolan's chest. No matter what his father said, Nolan would do whatever he could to ease the McTeagues' fears and ensure they were taken care of.

A loud knock tore Nolan's attention from the troubled woman. "You sit. I'll see who it is."

When he opened the door, he could only blink.

Edward stood on the other side, his top hat in hand.

"Hello, Nolan," he said. "I've come to see how Mr. McTeague is faring."

Nolan swallowed his surprise and stepped aside for Edward to enter the small abode.

Edward greeted Franny, who rose to curtsy.

"The doctor just left," Nolan said. "Bert's improving slowly, but it will be some time before we know the outcome."

"I see." Edward glanced at Franny and back to Nolan. "I'd like to see him, if I may."

Nolan hesitated, trying to decipher his father's motives. From his shuttered stare, Nolan could tell nothing. "Very well. But only if you promise not to cause him any distress."

"That is not my intention, I assure you."

Nolan pointed to the bedroom.

Edward knocked lightly before stepping inside the room. As Nolan followed him in, the smell of unwashed body hit him full force, and he winced at what his father must think. Nolan hovered by the doorway, unwilling to leave Edward alone with Bert, ready to step in if necessary.

"Hello, Mr. McTeague," Edward said. "I've come to make sure you're as comfortable as possible."

An expression of disbelief flitted across Bert's face. "Your lordship. This is an unexpected surprise." He went to lift a bandaged hand and flinched. "I'm so sorry, sir. I don't know how this happened. One minute I was tending the fire, the next I was in it."

"There's nothing to apologize for. Is the pain bearable at least?" Edward stood at the foot of the bed, hat clasped behind his back, looking as out of place as a vicar in a brothel.

It occurred to Nolan that this was likely the first time Edward had ever visited the McTeagues.

"Aye. Thank you for sending the doctor."

"It was the least I could do." Edward shifted, seeming uncomfortable with the praise. "I want you to know that I intend to hire a temporary replacement until you are well enough to return to your post. You're not to rush your recovery."

"Thank you, sir." Bert's beard trembled.

"And you're not to worry about money. Everything will be looked after until you're back on your feet." Edward straightened. "If you need anything at all, please let me know."

Bert's mouth hung open. If the situation were not so serious, Nolan would have laughed out loud at his shocked expression.

Edward cleared his throat. "That is all. Get well, Mr. McTeague. We will miss your fine work." He nodded in Bert's direction and returned to the main living area. "Mrs. McTeague, be sure to let us know if you require anything as well."

The plump woman bobbed to her feet and rushed forward to grasp Edward's hand. "Oh, thank you, my lord. Thank you. You don't know how relieved I am."

Edward's cheeks reddened as he discreetly pulled his hand away. "You're welcome. Good day." He put on his hat, nodded to Nolan, then strode out the door.

Still unable to trust his father's sudden show of generosity, Nolan followed him outside. He caught up to him at his horse, placing a hand on the stallion's bridle. "That was a very decent thing you did in there. What made you change your mind about helping Bert?"

Edward would not meet his eyes. He flung himself into the saddle, grabbed the reins, then finally glanced down at Nolan. "One might say I've been forced to look at things in a new light as of late." His mouth twitched up into a semblance of a smile.

Then he tipped his hat, clucked his horse into motion, and rode off.

CHAPTER 28

Ann Fielding's arrival caused a flurry of excitement at Hartford Hall. Molly practically danced down the steps to greet the carriage with Aunt Iris right behind her. Hannah, however, hung back from the open doorway, shivering under her shawl. She'd worn her favorite dress for the occasion—lilac silk trimmed with lace and imitation roses. Her aunt's maid had curled Hannah's hair in a most becoming fashion, looping the ringlets to frame her face. Hannah made a mental note to have the girl re-create the same hairstyle whenever she would next see Nolan.

Her heart tugged at the thought of her handsome husband—if he indeed was still her husband. It had been so long since she'd seen him, she wondered if she could still remember his features. Once etched with precision on her memory, his face now blurred like an image in a distorted mirror. She thrust her hand into her pocket and fingered his last letter, which she'd kept with her since it arrived. A very nice note, one she could recall with word-for-word accuracy, but not filled with the declarations of love and pining she longed for.

Was Nolan missing her at all? He sounded so busy with all

his duties and taking care of poor, dear Bert that it seemed he barely had time to give her a passing thought.

Hannah's hand drifted over her now expansive abdomen where the babe kicked and squirmed. She welcomed these stirrings of life inside her. Each day, she came closer to holding her child in her arms. A child who would love her with an unwavering devotion. And whom she would love equally in return.

Perhaps then she would at last feel whole.

"Hannah, dear. Here is your mother." Iris ushered Mum through the door into the vestibule.

Hannah took a moment to observe her. Though younger than Iris, hard work outdoors in the elements made her mother appear years older. Her faded brown hair, streaked with gray, framed a plain face, lined from years of worry and hardship, yet her eyes sparked with a light of welcome as she came forward to greet Hannah.

She pressed her cheek to Hannah's, then stepped back to study her. "My word, look at you dressed up like a real lady." In contrast, Mum smoothed down her brown cotton dress— most likely her Sunday best. Moisture filmed her eyes. "You're beautiful, Hannah. As I always knew you would be."

Hannah's heart swelled. "It's good to see you, Mum." For once the words were true. Somehow here, without the fear of Mr. Fielding looming over her shoulder, her mother appeared lighter, happier.

Mum turned and held out a hand to Molly. "And look at my wee Molly. You seem all grown up too."

"It's the lovely clothes Aunt Iris ordered for me. Underneath, I'm still the same." Molly laughed.

Iris threw her arms around them and squeezed. "Come, darlings. Let's get comfortable in the parlor with a nice cup of tea."

For an hour, Hannah and Molly listened politely while her mother and aunt caught up on years of news.

At last, Mum set her cup down and turned her attention to Hannah. "Now where is that handsome husband of yours?"

Hannah licked lips that had suddenly gone dry. "Nolan is at Stainsby Hall."

"What? Why would a man not be with his wife? Especially at a time like this." She looked pointedly at Hannah's abdomen.

"Nolan is getting to know his father," Iris explained. "And learning the ways of the nobility, while Hannah is resting and taking care of her health, away from any potential conflict."

"What sort of conflict?"

Hannah kept her gaze trained on the delicate patterns in the carpet. "The earl does not approve of our marriage and, in fact, may have"—she swallowed—"had it annulled."

Her mother gasped. "This is terrible. Your poor child will be a—"

"I'm quite aware of that."

"I'm sure it will all get worked out before long," Iris added quickly. "In the meantime, Hannah and the baby are always welcome here—marriage or no marriage."

"That is most generous of you, Iris." She shot Hannah a frown of disapproval. "But what have you done to drive Nolan away?"

Barbs of pain lodged in Hannah's chest. Of course, it had to be all her fault. Just like everything that happened during her childhood with her siblings. From a bruised knee to a broken cup, it would always be Hannah's fault.

"The doctor has recommended that Hannah avoid stress," Iris said. "She's only following orders. I'm sure Nolan will show up very soon to remedy matters."

Would he? Sudden tears burned Hannah's throat. Other than

a few impersonal letters, Nolan had not initiated contact. Had never indicated that he missed her or that he was ready to resume their marriage.

Just as Hannah feared, it seemed she didn't matter enough.

She pushed to her feet, clutching her stomach. "Excuse me, please. I think I need to lie down for a while."

And before anyone could deter her, she rushed out the door.

Nolan strode into the drawing room where his father had requested his presence. They didn't often use this room, since it was smaller than the formal parlor and decidedly more feminine—perhaps decorated by Penelope Fairchild or Nolan's late grandmother. The room afforded a grand view of the Stainsby gardens, now mostly dormant due to the cold weather.

Edward stood at the long window, staring at the bleak landscape.

Nolan paused in the doorway. "You wished to see me?"

"Nolan." He turned with a brief smile. "Come in. I have news."

"What kind of news?" Nolan crossed the floor. Fragrant bouquets of flowers from the Stainsby hothouse sat atop the piano, lightly scenting the room.

"I have received an invitation to Hartford Hall."

The mere mention of Hannah's place of exile made Nolan's pulse sprint. "From whom?"

"From the duchess herself. It seems that Mrs. Fielding is visiting and Lady Hartford wishes to host a gathering in her honor. A type of family reunion, I believe, is how she put it."

Nolan's thoughts swirled. Hannah's mother at Hartford? Surely he would be invited too. "Did Lady Hartford mention my presence at this gathering?"

Edward moved to a table beside the piano where he picked up a square of vellum paper. He scanned the missive. "Yes, your name is here as well."

"Was there any note from Hannah?"

"No. Just the invitation and a short note from the duchess."

His stomach fell. Why wouldn't Hannah have sent a personal message, indicating her wish for him to come? Hadn't he honored her request and kept away, giving her the space she claimed to need? How much more time did she require?

A cloud of frustration pushed Nolan to pace the carpet. "Edward, I need to know once and for all the true state of my marriage."

Several weeks back, when Nolan had mentioned the annulment again, Edward had mumbled something about the matter taking more time than Mr. Grayson expected. And once again, Nolan had let the matter drop, loath to damage the fragile bond they had established. Why hadn't he followed up more forcefully? "Did your solicitor manage to overturn the annulment?"

"No, he did not," Edward admitted after several seconds.

Nolan's heart sunk. So they were no longer married after all. "I thought you said things were in the works to rescind it."

"I may have . . . misrepresented the matter." Edward's glance slid away.

Nolan's nerves stretched as tight as violin strings. "What exactly does that mean?"

It occurred to him now that his father could have been stalling all along on purpose. Perhaps he'd never had any intention of having the annulment overturned. Perhaps Nolan had been a fool to trust him.

Edward walked to the other side of the piano, hands clasped behind him. "The truth is . . . Mr. Grayson never filed the papers in the first place. After I learned of Hannah's condition and discovered that he still had the document, I told him to hold off."

"You what?" Disbelief roared through Nolan as he struggled to take in the meaning of his father's admission. "Why didn't you tell me? Why lie to me all this time?"

Edward looked Nolan in the eye. "I feared if you knew, you would have no reason to stay. As long as this legal entanglement hung over your head, I could keep you here." He let out a sigh. "It was wrong of me, and I apologize."

A mixture of emotions swirled though Nolan's system. Outrage that Edward had purposely misled him all this time and blessed relief that an annulment had never taken place.

"So Hannah and I are still legally married?"

"As far as I know, yes."

"And my status as your heir?"

Edward winced. "Still unofficial." A hint of fear flashed through his eyes.

Did his father not believe that after all Nolan had been through these past six months that he had accepted his role as Edward's son? Too many secrets and ambiguities remained between them.

Edward came around the piano to stand beside Nolan. "I deeply regret any harm I've caused." He lifted a hand as though to touch Nolan's shoulder, then let it drop. "I want you to know how much this time with you has meant to me. I only hope you can one day forgive me." His eyes were shadowed with sincere remorse.

Nolan ran a hand over his jaw. As the stress of the past several months faded, so did his anger. Holding a grudge against his father would serve no purpose. Would do nothing toward helping Nolan achieve his goal of a reunion with Hannah.

But one major hurdle remained. Hannah had said she

wouldn't return until she had Edward's blessing. He lifted his head to meet his father's uncertain stare. "May I ask if your opinion of my marriage has changed? Or do you still oppose it with every breath?"

Edward hesitated, then gave a slight shrug. "A funny thing has occurred over these past months. I have been forced to reevaluate many things in my life and during this time of introspection, I have come to realize that your wife gave us both a great gift when she left."

"How so?"

Edward's lips twitched, as though recalling something amusing. "I never told you that Hannah came to see me the morning she departed. She advised me to use the time to discover what a wonderful man my son was. At the time, I was glad to be rid of her and did not think much of her words. But I've been giving the matter a great deal of thought as of late."

He turned back to the piano, fingering the note from Lady Hartford. "The duchess has given me some recent written counsel as well. She asked me to think about what I wanted my future to look like. Did I want a family filled with resentment and bitterness? Or did I want a united, loving family that would provide a nurturing environment for my grandchild?" He straightened and gave Nolan a pained glance. "You once asked me if I regretted my life, and I answered untruthfully, for I could not admit to making a mistake. The truth is that I do regret it—most grievously. I regret those lonely, wasted years that caused me to harden into a man I did not recognize." He moved closer and placed solid hands on Nolan's shoulders. "I do not wish to see you repeat the same miserable life, nor do I wish to see my grandchild grow up without a father."

Nolan's chest squeezed. "Nor do I," he said quietly.

"I have watched you do your best these many months to

conform to your new role, doing all I have asked of you and more. I now wish to return the favor. Come with me."

Edward strode out into the corridor. Nolan followed somewhat tentatively. They entered his study, where Edward pulled open a desk drawer. With a flip of his hand, he removed some papers. "These are the documents you signed so long ago. Do with them as you wish. I've already advised Mr. Grayson to draw up new papers regarding your status as my heir."

Nolan stepped forward to take the document, warring emotions churning in his gut. "Does this mean that you are finally willing to accept Hannah as my wife?"

Edward's gaze remained steady. "From what I've observed, I believe her to be a woman of substance. Anyone who would sacrifice her own happiness to give her husband the opportunity to figure out his place in life is a worthy woman indeed."

Nolan's mouth fell open. The words on the pages bled together into one black mass—as dark as his sordid soul. How had he not understood her true motives? "Hannah did say something to that effect, but I didn't listen. I was certain she was using it as an excuse to punish me."

"Punish you for what?"

"For neglecting her." A wave of shame rolled over Nolan, making his cravat feel much too tight. "For not putting her needs ahead of mine. For not protecting her from that beast Bellows and allowing possible harm to come to our child."

Edward moved closer, his eyes solemn. "I believe that is your own guilt talking. I sincerely doubt Hannah viewed it that way at all."

Pride goeth before destruction, and a haughty spirit before a fall.

One of his mother's favorite Bible verses came to mind with startling clarity. Nolan raked his fingers through his hair. "I have allowed my pride to keep me away all this time. Nursing my resentment and anger at her for leaving me." His throat clogged with an uprising of emotion. "I've been a first-class fool."

Forgive me, Lord, and let Hannah forgive me as well. I forgot to put God in the middle of my marriage as Reverend Black advised. Perhaps if I had, things wouldn't have gone so awry.

Edward draped his arm across Nolan's shoulders with a rare grin. "I fear my son takes after his father in more than just looks."

Nolan stiffened. Was it true? Was he really as arrogant and prideful as his father?

Edward stepped back and clapped a hand on Nolan's shoulder. "It's not too late to rectify this mess. Come with me to Hartford Hall and make amends with your wife. I'm sure if you grovel enough, she'll forgive you and take you back in time to see your child born."

Sudden energy surged through Nolan. "You're right. It's long past the time for action. And the first thing I will do is this." He grabbed the papers from the desktop, strode across the room, and flung them into the fire. With great satisfaction, he watched them curl and blacken.

As if in concurrence with Nolan's actions, the mantel clock chimed the hour.

"I will go to Hartford. But I will go on my own. There's an urgent matter I need to take care of first."

The earl blinked, brows hiked. "Very well. I plan to leave at first light tomorrow. When I arrive, shall I tell them to expect you?"

Nolan smiled his first real smile in months. "No. I think I'd prefer the element of surprise in my favor."

CHAPTER

29

Daisy barked a loud greeting as the Stainsby carriage pulled up in front of Hartford Hall. Standing at the open front door, Hannah smoothed the fabric of her green silk dress over her bulky front. Her stomach hadn't roiled this much since the early days of her pregnancy.

She squeezed her eyes shut, a desperate plea echoing in her heart. *Please, Lord, let Nolan be here. Please let him come to claim his family.*

Seconds later, her anticipation floated away like dead leaves in the wind when the carriage door opened and the earl emerged—alone. Hannah remained focused on the coach, praying Nolan would alight, but the driver stepped up to close the door.

Nolan was not inside.

Still, a small flicker of hope remained that perhaps he had chosen to ride King instead of being confined in a carriage. She waited, holding her breath, as the earl mounted the steps to the front door.

"My lord." She curtsied as low as her belly allowed.

He was impeccably dressed as usual in a black frock coat, striped cravat, gloves, and top hat. His silver-winged sideburns had been trimmed in a precise line, his hair slicked back beneath his hat.

"Good afternoon, Hannah." He bowed over her offered hand. "I see you are keeping well." He glanced at her abdomen and then back to her face.

"Very well, sir." She worked to contain her surprise. He greeted her as though she were his peer rather than a servant. Perhaps it was due to her new wardrobe.

"I'm pleased to hear it." He peered over her shoulder, a brow lifted. "Is our hostess not here to greet me?"

Light footsteps tapped across the inside tiles, and a flustered Iris appeared. "Here I am. Please forgive my tardiness, Lord Stainsby. An issue with one of my staff." She paused to catch her breath, a blush staining her cheeks. She patted several stray hairs into place and made an effort to compose herself. "Welcome to Hartford Hall."

The earl's mouth tipped up in a smile. "Lovely to see you again, Your Grace." He took Iris's hand and slowly brought it to his lips.

For the first time since Hannah had known her, Iris appeared out of her element, staring at the earl as if every thought had left her head. "P-Please do come in."

Eyes still trained on her face, he took her arm in his, and together they walked through the entrance.

Hannah remained on the top step to scan the road as far as she could see, but no telltale signs of a rider came into view. She blinked hard to hold back the threat of tears, squared her shoulders, and reentered the house.

Molly appeared in the hall, and together she and Hannah joined their mother, the earl, and Aunt Iris in the parlor.

"Where is Nolan?" Iris asked as they took their seats. "Was he unable to join you?"

Hannah perched on the settee, her back ramrod stiff.

The earl flicked a quick glance in Hannah's direction. "He had some urgent business to attend to, I'm afraid."

"I'm sure he'll do his best to be here." Iris gave Hannah a sympathetic smile.

Hannah's insides quivered, and she bit her lip to keep her distress from showing. Nolan's absence spoke louder than any words. Clearly, she and their child were not important enough.

When the refreshments arrived, Iris rose and the earl turned his attention to Hannah. "Nolan tells me you are well. At least from what he ascertained in your letters."

"As well as can be expected." *Without one's husband.* She frowned. Why was the earl suddenly so interested in her? It had to be because she carried a possible Fairchild heir.

Anger swooped in to replace the tide of hurt. Anger at this man for dashing her dreams into pieces. She lifted her chin to glare at him. "Tell me the truth, sir. Did you succeed in having my marriage to Nolan annulled? Is that why he no longer wishes to see me?"

Her bold question did not seem to faze the man, as his expression did not change, save for the slight rise of one brow. "I believe that question will be best answered by Nolan himself." Then the Earl of Stainsby winked at her and rose from his chair.

What on earth did that mean?

Flummoxed, Hannah stared as he crossed the room to Iris's side and prayed that Nolan would show up soon to clarify the situation once and for all.

Sometime later, after freshening up in his guest quarters, Edward descended the impressive Hartford staircase to the hallway below. While the duchess took care of some estate business, he planned to check out the late Duke of Hartford's library as Iris had suggested earlier. According to her, it was a private collection without equal.

Following the directions she had given him, he made his way down a back corridor to the double-paneled doors. He entered the library, surprised to find a fire burning in the hearth.

He gazed around the room, which consisted of row upon row of books, organized in floor-to-ceiling mahogany shelves. Iris wasn't exaggerating—it was a fine library indeed.

Edward hoped he wouldn't have too much time on his hands for reading, since he was looking forward to enjoying the company of his hostess. Other than her unusual bluntness, he found her to be charming and capable, a woman of extreme intelligence, as demonstrated by her running of such a vast estate—also further evidence of her flying in the face of social convention.

He scanned the rows of shelves, searching for a volume to catch his interest. As he reached out a hand to choose one, a low bark sounded near his feet. Edward froze. The mud-colored canine blended right into the carpet. He would have stepped on the creature if it hadn't moved.

The dog sprang to its feet and leaped up, its front paws landing on Edward's chest.

"Get down." He pushed the animal aside and moved back, tripping over the edge of the settee and landing in an undignified heap on the floor.

A youthful giggle met his ears as he twisted to right himself. On his hands and knees, he glared in the direction of a wing chair, where the wide eyes of Molly Burnham peered at him from behind her book.

"What the deuce is so funny?" His most ferocious earl voice failed to intimidate her, as her shoulders shook with silent glee.

Another burst of laughter erupted from the doorway. "Why, I think that should be obvious, Edward." Iris made no attempt to conceal her mirth at his predicament.

How much had she witnessed of his disgrace? With as much dignity as he could muster, Edward pulled himself to his feet and tugged his waistcoat into place.

Daisy trotted to her mistress's side as though bearing no fault in his humiliation.

He jabbed a finger in its direction. "That beast should not be allowed loose."

Another stifled giggle came from Molly.

Iris laid a hand on Daisy's brown head and sighed. "This will never do. Please sit down, Edward."

He clenched his teeth together and reluctantly obeyed.

"Molly dear, would you go and check on Hannah for me? I need a word with the earl in private."

"Yes, Auntie." The girl grabbed her book, gave a quick curtsy, and left the room.

"Daisy, come." Iris settled herself beside him on the sofa, while Daisy padded over to sit in front of them, tongue lolling, watching her mistress with adoring eyes.

It took all of Edward's concentration not to flinch at the drool dripping from the sides of its mouth. Edward had never had pets. The only animals he tolerated were his beloved horses, as well as the dogs he kept for hunting, and the occasional barn cat to keep the mice population under control. As far as he was concerned, dogs belonged in the barn, not shedding hair and slobbering over the furniture and carpets.

"First of all, Edward, you need to relax. Animals can sense your dislike. Now give me your hand." Iris's calm gray eyes held his as she waited with her palm up for him to comply.

"Why?" He eyed her with suspicion.

"Do you trust me, Edward?"

"I fail to see—"

"Yes or no."

"I suppose so, yes."

"Then give me your hand." The dog remained unmoving at her feet.

Edward swallowed once and placed his hand in hers. Her smooth fingers sent chills up his arm, and he forced himself not to snatch his hand away.

"The first thing you must do is let Daisy learn your scent and let her know you like her. That you're trustworthy." Her grip on his hand tightened as he tried to jerk it back. "Relax. The more you resist her, the more annoying she will become in trying to win you over."

Edward huffed out an annoyed breath. "Fine, if it means she will leave me in peace."

Iris held their joined hands out to touch the animal's cold, wet nose.

All at once, his focus moved from the dog to Iris's thumb moving in mesmerizing circles around his palm. Heat blasted up his neck. He turned to find her face very close to his.

"That's not so bad, is it?" She gave him an angelic smile.

His eyes fell to her upturned lips and unexpected, inappropriate thoughts—like the desire to kiss those lips again—seized his brain.

Daisy let out a yip and nudged their fingers.

Iris turned her attention to the dog, moving Edward's hand to the top of Daisy's head. Together they stroked the dog's silky fur, and her tail began to wag.

"Good girl. You see, Edward is a friend."

Though his gaze stayed on the dog, Edward's entire being remained attuned to Iris's every breath, the touch of her hand, the brush of her elbow against his side.

If it wouldn't have been horribly rude, he would've jumped up and dashed from the room. Away from the onslaught of emotions swirling through his system. Away from the uncomfortable sensation of being caught in a snare.

A very attractive, wonderful-smelling snare—but a snare nonetheless.

After dinner, which Hannah barely picked at just to be polite, Iris moved the small party into the parlor for some entertainment. Her aunt announced she would play the piano, followed by a Bible reading from Molly and, if interest persisted, a reading of poetry. Though Hannah wasn't in the mood to socialize, she reluctantly rose from the table with the rest of the group.

The earl—or Edward, as he suggested they call him—escorted Iris from the dining hall. "Tell me, Lady Hartford, do you play chess?"

"As a matter of fact, I do." She smiled up at him. "My late husband taught me to play early on in our marriage. We often enjoyed a game in the evening by the fire."

"I hope you'll indulge me with a match during my stay. Even though I've tried to teach Nolan, he isn't partial to the game. It's been forever since I've faced a good opponent."

Inside the parlor door, Hannah's state of anxiety heightened. Perhaps it was the way her mother and Molly had become inseparable since her arrival, or perhaps it was seeing the stirrings of a romance between the earl and her aunt. Whatever the reason, Hannah found she could not abide an evening as a fifth wheel—ignored and invisible once again—all too aware of the gaping hole of Nolan's absence.

She begged everyone's pardon, claiming fatigue, and bid them good evening. No one dared challenge her, given her delicate condition. Instead of heading upstairs, however, she slipped down the corridor to the garden doors that led onto the terrace, making sure to keep away from the parlor windows. She craved the cool evening air to whisk away her tortured thoughts and the blackness of the evening to shroud her grieving soul.

Hannah leaned against a stone pillar looking out over her aunt's darkened gardens, shivering in the damp evening air. She should have taken time to retrieve her wrap before coming out, but she'd forgotten it in her room, and the thought of climbing all those stairs seemed daunting. With her added weight, she tried not to use the stairs more than once a day.

She rubbed a trembling hand over her belly where the child kicked under her ribs. *Where is your father, little one?* Nolan should be here, sharing her wonder and joy at this life growing within her. Did he care so little for his unborn child that he'd abandon them both?

Hot tears welled in her eyes and, with the dark solitude of the night surrounding her, she allowed them to spill freely down her cheeks. She was tired of being strong and sensible. Tired of waiting for her husband. If it hadn't been for her condition, she would have sought him out long before this. But traveling at this stage of pregnancy would be inviting disaster. Time was slipping through the hourglass, and soon their babe would be born. Would Nolan leave his child without a father, when he knew the harm it could cause?

A hot flash of pain seared her side. She clutched her belly and held her breath. A few seconds later, the spasm subsided, and Hannah released a long gust of air. Yet, a thread of fear wound its way around her heart.

Please, Lord, don't let the baby come now. It's too early. I couldn't bear to lose Nolan and my baby too.

Another pain shafted through her abdomen. She let out a cry and doubled over, clutching the pillar to keep upright.

"Hannah, what is it?" Quick footsteps sounded on the terrace, and her mother's warm hands grasped her shoulders.

"I . . . I'm having pains, but it's too early."

"Come inside. We need to get you off your feet." Her mother wrapped a strong arm around Hannah's waist and steered her back inside to her aunt's drawing room. She laid her gently on the sofa, placed a pillow beneath her head, and unfolded one of her aunt's knitted throws over her.

"What were you thinking, staying outside without a wrap? You're chilled through."

Her mother's disapproving frown made Hannah want to weep anew.

"I'm going to get Iris and ask the maid to make you some chamomile tea. I'll be back in a moment."

Hannah closed her eyes and shivered, waiting for her mother to return.

At last, she arrived with a hot brick wrapped in flannel, which she place at Hannah's cold feet. "The maid is bringing the tea. It will warm you and soothe your nerves. You must let go of all this worry, Hannah. It will harm the child."

Her mother pulled a chair closer to the sofa and took Hannah's chilled hands, rubbing them to bring the blood back. Minutes later, the maid arrived with the tea. Hannah allowed her mother to help her sit up and sipped from the delicate cup. The hot liquid flowed through her cold, stiff body, infusing a trail of warmth.

If only her heart could thaw as quickly.

"How are the pains now?"

"They have subsided."

"That's a relief. Though I must say it saddens me to see you so unhappy, daughter." Her mother's features pinched.

Hannah frowned, about to refute her mother's claim.

"No need to deny it. I could tell the moment I arrived you're not yourself. What can we do to rectify this situation with Nolan?"

Hannah shook her head. "There's nothing you can do. I thought Nolan would come, but it's clear he will not. I will have the baby alone and find some type of employment to support us. Aunt Iris has kindly offered to let us stay with her."

Her mother's thin lips flattened. "I never imagined you'd end up raising a child on your own. And to think, all I ever wanted was for you to have a better life than I could give you."

Hannah stared at her mother in disbelief. "Is that why you left me alone at Stainsby, tore me away from the only family I had left? To give me a good life?"

At one time, Hannah would have been shocked by the bitterness and hostility of her voice, but today, with her feelings so close to the surface, nothing surprised her. She wanted to lash out, to make someone else share her pain.

God suffers with you, my child. He counts every one of your tears. The minister's words from her father's funeral sprang to mind. Once again, the words failed to console her.

"What are you insinuating?" Her mother's face was pale.

"That you chose Molly over me. That you chose your husband's wishes over your own child. How could you leave me with strangers?"

Her mother's eyes grew wide. Silence hung in the room.

Then a new searing pain ripped across Hannah's midsection, eliciting a scream that echoed out into the hall.

Iris rushed into the room. "Hannah dear, shall I send for the doctor?"

"No, no. I'll be fine." Her breath came out in pants.

The earl appeared beside her aunt. "Call for the doctor, Iris. I will not have the life of my grandchild jeopardized." He turned stony eyes to Hannah's mother. "If you are causing your daughter distress, madam, I suggest you leave immediately."

Mum nodded meekly. "We'll talk again when you're feeling better, Hannah. I'll be in the parlor if you need me."

Dr. Greenley, her aunt's physician, arrived within the hour. He examined Hannah, felt her abdomen, and told her she was having early contractions. "In most cases, these are harmless. Merely the body's way of preparing for the labor to come. In some instances, however, they continue to progress, and the babe is born prematurely. I hope this will not be the case."

Hannah twisted the edges of the throw between her fingers. "What must I do, Doctor?"

"For starters, you must stay off your feet. For several days at least. Secondly, you must avoid becoming upset. Try to remain calm so as not to trigger any further contractions."

Hannah nodded. "I will do whatever I must."

The doctor patted her arm and snapped his bag closed. "I will leave you a tonic that is known to help stave off labor pains. Take two doses daily." He straightened. "Now, someone will need to assist this young lady to her bed. If anything further develops, do not hesitate to send your boy for me, Your Grace. I will be back to check on Mrs. Price in two days' time, barring further developments."

"Thank you, Dr. Greenley. We are most grateful for your assistance." Iris ushered him to the door.

Hannah closed her eyes and breathed a prayer of thanks to God for stopping the contractions. She vowed, with His help, to keep her emotions firmly in check for the duration of her pregnancy.

When she opened her eyes, Iris had returned with the earl in tow. "Edward, would you please carry Hannah to her room? I'll show you the way."

Heat infused Hannah's cheeks as the earl reached down and lifted her as though she weighed no more than a feather. She held herself stiffly within his arms, wishing it were Nolan carrying her upstairs instead.

"Relax, Hannah." The earl's low voice rumbled through his chest. "Contrary to popular belief, I do not bite." He glanced down at her then, his features softening. "If it's Nolan that's causing your distress, you needn't worry. One thing I'm certain of is that he loves you and will be here as soon as he's able. "

"Truly?"

"You have my word."

A measure of despair lifted from Hannah's spirit, easing the tension in her muscles. She breathed a quiet sigh of relief. Who would have thought the earl would be the one to provide her comfort?

After a full day of rest and no recurrence of the contractions, Hannah was allowed out of bed. Iris asked Edward to bring Hannah down to the drawing room to lie on the settee. Molly and Daisy kept her company, while Molly sewed the final ribbons onto some of the baby clothes Hannah had made.

In the afternoon, Aunt Iris accompanied Hannah's mother into the drawing room.

"How are you feeling today, Hannah dear?" she asked.

"Much better, thank you." Hannah tried to muster a smile. For although she had mended physically, her heart and her spirit had not.

"If you feel up to it, and if it is not too distressing, your mother would like a word with you."

Hannah released a small sigh. Her outburst the other night had been made in the heat of emotional turmoil, and now in the calm light of day, she regretted her accusations. "I would like that. Thank you."

Her mother crossed the room, and like a bird looking for a perch, seated herself on a high-back chair near Hannah. Iris took a seat at her desk on the opposite side of the room.

"Mum, I need to apologize for the other evening. I wasn't in my right mind and spoke harshly. I hope you can forgive me."

"It is I who owe you an apology, Hannah, for my distance all these years. I'm afraid my motives for bringing you to Stainsby were never made clear to you."

"Your motives?"

She nodded. "When I agreed to marry Robert, he told me he could not afford to take on my children as well as his own. I saw the type of conditions his children lived in, and I did not want that for you—or Molly, for that matter. By leaving you at Stainsby Hall with Edna, I truly believed you'd have a chance at a better life." Her mother's eyes grew damp.

Hannah fought to control her emotions, hardly daring to believe her mother's words. "So it wasn't because you preferred Molly over me?"

Mum reached forward to clutch Hannah's hand in her own work-worn ones. "No, Hannah. I love both my daughters equally. Molly's age and her fragile health were the only things that colored my decision. It almost killed me to leave you. You may not believe that until you're a mother yourself. Maybe then you'll understand the lengths a parent would go to for her child's well-being."

Hannah caressed her abdomen. Would she be able to make the same type of sacrifice her mother had made? She hung her head. "I'm so sorry for thinking the worst of you."

"It's not your fault. I should have explained my actions better. It's just that I could seldom get away from the farm." She paused and let out a long breath. "That's not entirely true. The truth is, it was harder to see you and have to leave you again. Keeping my distance was a way to avoid the pain." Tears formed in her eyes. "Can you forgive me for not being the mother you deserved?"

Hannah's heart expanded in her chest, as though a stopper had uncorked, and a flood of affection poured forth. Her mother had loved her after all—had only meant to save her from suffering. She never knew she had unwittingly caused Hannah such grief, or that Hannah had thought herself unloved and abandoned.

"Of course I forgive you, Mum." Hannah opened her arms to receive her mother's embrace, their tears mingling on her cheek.

"I love you, Hannah."

"I love you too," she whispered.

In the comfort of her mother's arms, Hannah's heart began to heal at last, and the seed of a thought began to sprout. Perhaps she was worthy of love after all.

CHAPTER 30

Nolan straightened his cravat as he stepped from the carriage in front of Hartford Hall. His stomach tightened, and his palms grew damp despite the cool temperature. How would Hannah receive him? With love or contempt? With forgiveness or fury?

He would have been here days sooner, if not for the schedule of the man who shared his carriage.

"Wait here until I send for you," he said to his traveling companion. "I hope it won't take too long."

"No rush. This is a most comfortable carriage." The man settled back against the cushioned seat and closed his eyes.

Another coach would arrive shortly with Victoria and Aunt Ophelia. Nolan hoped that Evelyn and Orville would be able to make the trip as well. It was time they all came together as a family. Yet the fact that the pair had gone out of their way to avoid him did not bode well.

Nolan frowned. Another piece of news added to his edginess. He'd had a note from the constabulary in Derby, stating that in light of Nolan's previous inquiry about Timothy Bellows and the possible threat made against Nolan's family, they wished to inform him that Bellows had recently escaped from jail. Though the authorities doubted he'd have the gall to come anywhere near Stainsby Hall, they advised the earl and his family to take whatever precautions they deemed necessary. Nolan set his jaw, vowing to do so as soon as he returned home. For the present, he was relieved that Hannah and Molly were nowhere near Stainsby.

Nolan shook off his thoughts and started up the stairs to the front door. How differently he approached the great ivy-covered mansion on this occasion. His first time here, he had stormed in full of anger and pride, demanding to see his wife. Now he arrived in humility, coming to beg his wife's forgiveness, his pride in tatters around his feet.

Once again, Mr. Carstairs answered Nolan's knock.

Nolan gave a bow. "Good day. May I speak with the Duchess of Hartford—in private, if possible?"

"Please come in." The man's pinched features belied his polite words.

"Thank you." Nolan followed the butler inside.

"If you'll wait here, I'll see if Her Grace is available." The older man shuffled off down one of the corridors.

Nolan paced the vestibule, praying for the Lord's guidance. He needed to ensure that he acted with complete respect and sensitivity for Hannah's feelings, as a true husband should.

A few moments later, the duchess herself came out to greet him. "Nolan, thank heaven you've come at last." She leaned forward to kiss his cheek, moisture skimming her gray eyes.

"It's good to see you again, Lady Hartford. Is everything all right?"

"Please, you must call me Iris." She smiled. "Come and we'll speak in my husband's old study. We'll have more privacy there." She led him down a corridor toward the back of the house.

At the end of the hall, she opened a door and entered a dark, musty room.

He waited while she threw open the heavy draperies to let in the sunlight and motioned him to take a seat in front of a carved desk.

"I'm sorry this room is a little stale. I haven't come in here much since Edgar died." She took a seat beside him. "I wanted to speak to you about Hannah before she knows you're here."

"Why? Is something wrong?" Tension banded like steel across his shoulders.

She laid a comforting hand on his arm. "Everything's fine now, although we had a scare the other day."

"What kind of scare?" His heart galloped faster than King racing through a field.

"Hannah started having early labor pains, but the doctor gave her a tonic that managed to stop them. She's only been allowed out of bed since yesterday."

Nolan lunged to his feet, ready to charge through the house to find Hannah.

Iris gripped his arm with surprising strength. "Please sit down. There's more you need to know."

On a deep inhale, he resumed his seat and prayed for the patience to handle whatever else she had to say. "Go on."

The duchess kept a light hand on his arm as though she didn't quite trust him. "Hannah has been very distressed lately. She seems to be wrestling with some sort of inner demons that she won't speak about. Part of the issue has been her mother's arrival. In fact, it was during a rather heated conversation with Ann that Hannah's pains worsened."

Nolan gripped the wooden arms of the chair as though he might snap them in two. As soon as he could, he would speak to his mother-in-law about the deplorable way she treated her daughter.

Iris must have seen the anger on his face, for she quickly added, "They have made their peace now, thank the Lord. However, the doctor told us that Hannah must remain calm in order to avoid the contractions starting again. If you wish to see her, you mustn't upset her. It could cost her the baby—as well as her own life."

A cold ball of fear lodged in Nolan's chest. The possibility of losing Hannah was something he could not even let his mind consider. He raised his gaze to Iris. "What do you want me to do?"

"We must take this reunion with extreme caution. First, I must prepare her for your presence. The shock of seeing you without warning would surely send her into labor."

Nolan bowed his head over his clasped hands. So much for surprising his wife, but perhaps this way was better. His head jerked up at the recollection of the man waiting outside in the carriage and the entourage Nolan expected any moment.

"Perhaps I'd best explain my whole plan, Iris, for I'll need your help to make it happen."

Hannah paused at the bottom of the staircase, proud to have managed without the earl's assistance. She'd awoken with a new determination today, a new strength. The mending of her relationship with her mother, as well as the earl's unexpected support, had put things into a new perspective. She wasn't proud to admit it, but she'd been wallowing in self-pity, a most unattractive state, and one she vowed to rectify immediately. And so she had started her morning with a prayer of thanksgiving to God and a resolve to put her trust more firmly in Him. She had to believe that everything would work out as the Lord intended. And that Nolan would find his way back to her.

To that end, Hannah had at last taken matters into her own hands and penned a truly honest letter to her husband. One that apologized for any hurt she had caused and for her fear that had kept her from him for so long. She wrote of her unwavering love and that no matter what he decided for his future, whether it included her or not, she would bear him no ill will. That he would always have a place in his child's life, and that she would continue to advocate for his happiness.

Hannah patted the letter in her pocket, which she intended to have her aunt post this very day. Just committing her true feelings to paper had lifted a terrible burden from her soul and filled her with peace.

She headed down the hallway, suddenly aware that an odd hush surrounded the house. She'd expected to hear Aunt Iris's voice in the parlor, or Molly's precious chatter, but only silence met her ears as she made her way to the dining room. Even Carstairs was noticeably absent.

Because she'd risen much later than the rest of the household, breakfast would be long over. She would ask the cook for some toast and tea.

The unexpected sight of her aunt at the dining table made her smile. "Good morning, Auntie. How are you today?"

"Very well, my dear. You slept well, I trust?"

Hannah removed a lid from the silver platter on the sideboard, pleased to note some scrambled eggs remained. "Yes, though I fear I stayed too long abed." She chose a sausage and some toast to complement the eggs.

"Nonsense. You need all the rest you can get before the babe arrives." The teacup in Iris's hand trembled on its saucer.

Hannah set her plate on the table with a slight frown. "Is everything all right, Auntie? Why are you not with Edward this morning?"

"He is out walking with Molly and Daisy. Come and sit beside me. There is something we need to discuss." Her aunt's normally sparkling eyes remained solemn.

Hannah's heart clutched as she took a seat next to her.

"You must promise to remain calm at what I'm about to tell you. It's not bad news. At least I hope it's not."

Hannah swallowed. "I'll do my best."

Her aunt pressed her lips together, then exhaled. "I've heard from Nolan."

Despite her promise, Hannah's pulse quickened. Why had he contacted her aunt instead of her? Her mouth went dry and she licked her lips to moisten them. "What did his letter say?"

The clock on the sideboard ticked loudly in the silence.

"I didn't receive a letter." Her aunt reached out to cover Hannah's hands with her own cool fingers. "Nolan is here, Hannah."

The air whooshed out of her lungs, while the room's floral wallpaper swirled around her. Her heart threatened to leap from her chest.

Nolan was here—in this house—at this very moment!

"You don't have to see him if it will cause you distress. I have explained your condition, and he understands."

Hannah inhaled deeply, thinking of the letter she had written him only hours earlier. Nolan had come to her at last. She owed it to him and to their child to face her future with courage.

Iris had risen to pour her a glass of water. "Here, dear. Drink this."

Obediently she sipped the cool liquid, grateful for the relief to her parched throat.

She met her aunt's gaze. "Could you have Nolan meet me in the parlor in five minutes?"

"Are you certain you won't be putting the baby in jeopardy?"

Hannah straightened her spine against the back of the chair.

"Not knowing where I stand with my husband would be worse for our child. I need to resolve the situation one way or the other."

"Very well, then. Five minutes."

In the musty study, Nolan paced the length of the carpet until he feared the pattern would wear away. What on earth was taking Iris so long? Had Hannah refused to see him?

His insides twisted more with each passing minute.

At last, the door opened and the duchess entered. She smoothed the skirts of her blue dress and came toward him.

Nolan met her halfway. "Well? How did Hannah take the news?"

"She was shocked, naturally, but she wants to see you. She's asked for a few minutes to prepare herself." Iris clasped his hand and squeezed. "I will be praying for you both. That God will grant you the wisdom and strength to heal your marriage."

"Thank you. I've been praying for that same outcome myself."

Five minutes later, Nolan stood outside the parlor, palms slick with sweat as he knocked on the door.

"Come in." Hannah's sweet voice met his ears.

The voice he hadn't heard in six months.

He ran his fingers over his hair and straightened his waistcoat.

Lord, if ever I've needed your guidance, it's now. Give me the grace to win back my wife's affections—without causing her any distress.

He stepped through the door. The sunlight streaming through the large rectangular windows blinded him momentarily. He blinked to refocus, then turned to the settee where Hannah sat like a queen on her throne.

Nolan forgot to breathe. He drank in her beauty like a thirsty man finding an oasis in the desert. She was more beautiful than ever with her blond locks curling down over one shoulder. Instead of servant's garb, she wore a gown of the softest yellow that rivaled the sunbeams dancing over the carpet.

"Hannah." Her name was a whisper on his lips.

"Hello, Nolan. It's good to see you." She held herself rigid on her seat. Her calm green eyes gave away nothing.

His gaze dropped to her waistline, and his jaw dropped. Gone was the slim maiden he had fallen in love with. In her place, a mature woman bloomed with health, ripe with the new life within her. Her hand moved to cover her abdomen as if protecting the child from him. The pain of that small motion cut through him like a lance.

"You look beautiful." He wanted to move closer, but his feet rooted themselves to the floor.

"Thank you, though I feel like a lumbering ox most times." Her lips tipped upward into a smile. "You look very nice too. Like a true gentleman."

He forced his feet to move across the floor and took a seat on one of the armchairs where he could look her in the eye.

Hannah twisted a handkerchief between her fingers. "Before you say anything," she said. "I need to ask your forgiveness—for leaving the way I did. I realize now how unfair it was to you."

"You needn't apologize, Hannah. You were protecting our child. I understand that."

She lowered her head. "I was also running away. And for that I'm truly sorry."

Frustration built an uncomfortable pressure in his chest. He wanted to shout his feelings from the roof, not weigh each word before he spoke. But for her sake, he would contain himself. "I'm the one who needs forgiveness, Hannah. Not you."

Confusion clouded her eyes. She opened her mouth to speak, but he held up a hand to stop her. "Please," he said. "I need to say a few things without interruption. After that, you can tell me whatever you wish."

"Very well."

He fisted his hands on his lap, then forced them to relax, splayed loosely on his knees. "These past months, I spent every day sitting through instructions on what the nobility eats, wears, and thinks. Though mad with the tedium, I did it for you—or so I told myself—all the while congratulating myself on how noble I was in giving you the space and the tranquility you said you needed. I waited patiently for my wife to come to her senses, to let me know she needed me, wanted me with her, yet nothing but a few polite letters arrived." Unable to remain seated, he pushed to his feet and paced in front of the settee. "I told myself I was doing the right thing, honoring your request, and patted myself on the back for it. It took my father to make me realize I was suffering from a severe case of pride."

A slight frown creased her forehead, but she remained silent.

"I was too proud," he continued. "Too angry and hurt to follow my heart and come for you. I have been steeping in sin all these months, letting it fester inside like an infected wound, instead of trying to see the situation from your viewpoint." He came to kneel in front of her, taking one of her hands in his. "Can you ever forgive me for being such a fool?"

"Oh, Nolan. I have felt so alone." Tears brimmed on Hannah's lower lashes. "So afraid that you didn't want me now that you were getting used to life as the earl's son." She held the handkerchief to her nose. "I feared you would only want the child—and not me."

Nolan hung his head. "It's because I left you alone too long."

"To a degree. But for the most part, it was my own insecurity." She paused. "Ever since my mother left me at Stainsby, I have felt undeserving of love. If my own mother didn't love me, or want me, why would anyone else?" More tears flowed down her cheeks.

Restraint gone, Nolan moved up to the settee and gathered Hannah into his arms. "Hush. You mustn't upset yourself." He drank in the familiar feel of her in his arms, the wondrous scent of her hair. When she seemed calmer, he held her away from him to study her.

She gave him a tremulous smile. "It's all right. I've finally made peace with Mum, and I feel better about things now."

"I'm glad to hear it. Though there is one more thing that has weighed on my mind." He hesitated, a clutch of trepidation gnawing at him. "I fear that I rushed you into marriage before you had time to consider it fully. I didn't give you a chance to refuse. Didn't take time to listen to what *you* wanted."

"That's not—"

"So I am asking you now with the sincerest humility—Hannah, do you wish to be married to me?" His heart thudded, awaiting her reply. What would he do if she wished to end their relationship?

"Are we not already married? Or did your father succeed in annulling our marriage?"

"That's not the point." With effort, he reined in his frustration. "If you were a free woman right now, would you still wish to marry me?" Perhaps it was pride, perhaps insecurity, but he needed to know that despite everything, she would still choose to share her life with him.

She stiffened within his arms and raised her chin. "Only if you truly love me. Not for the child I carry, but for who I am inside."

His shoulders slumped with the enormity of her question.

How could he ever convince her of that? Get past her emotional scars and make her see the truth?

Speak from your heart, an inner voice urged.

He swallowed the last remnant of his pride and allowed his heart to take over. "I have always loved you for who you are, Hannah. It doesn't matter to me if you wear a servant's apron or a gown of the finest silk; if you're as slender as a reed or large with child. It's your soul that I love. You are a woman of courage and faith who keeps me grounded." He took one of her hands in his. "I thought my life would be complete once I knew my father, but I was wrong. My life is only complete with you there to share it. It has taken me this long to figure out that I am worthy in my own right of such love, not because of who my father is, but because I'm the man my mother raised me to be. The man my heavenly Father shaped me to be." He paused to wipe the tears from her cheek. "And this man, with all his flaws, wants you to share his life—whatever that turns out to be." He waited for her response, not daring to breathe.

Misery swirled in her eyes. "What if I don't fit into your new life?" she whispered.

"Then we'll go elsewhere. Live the simple life we'd originally planned and raise our child to be a kind, considerate, faith-filled person."

"You would give up your inheritance for me?"

"I will do whatever it takes to make you happy. I only wish I had done so up until now." He raised her hand to his lips.

A tremulous smile broke through her tears. "In that case, Mr. Price, I would be honored to be your wife—again. For better or worse."

"So I haven't destroyed your love for me?"

She reached out to cup his jaw. "I'll never stop loving you, Nolan. My heart doesn't know how."

His vision blurred with tears of his own as he pulled her to him, his mouth claiming hers at last. Their breath mingled, entwining their souls in a long-awaited reunion. He placed a gentle hand on the swell of her abdomen, on the miraculous embodiment of their love.

A ripple under his fingers made him jump. "What is that? Have I kissed you too hard?"

Hannah's rich laughter pealed through the room. "No, that is your son or daughter claiming our attention. I have a feeling this little one will be very demanding, based on all the trouble he or she has caused already."

Relief coursed through him, as did the sudden recollection of the rest of his plan. "I have one more surprise, if you think you can handle it." He searched her face for any sign of fatigue or discomfort, but all he saw was his own joy reflected back.

"What kind of surprise?"

"I fear our wedding was a rather rushed affair. More of an elopement, and not likely the ceremony you'd dreamed of having."

"Nolan, no—"

He placed a finger against her lips. "Since we have most of our family here in one place, would you be willing to repeat our vows?"

"Now?" Her green eyes widened.

He grinned, liquid happiness spilling through his veins. "As soon as you can get ready. I fear we've kept the good reverend waiting long enough as it is."

CHAPTER
31

Hannah glanced at her reflection in the drawing room mirror and arranged the lace veil her aunt had insisted she wear. It had been Aunt Iris's bridal veil, and she'd kept it packed away in the attic all these years, carefully wrapped so that the ivory fabric appeared as fresh as the day she'd worn it. Hannah hardly dared to believe all that had happened in such a short space of time—that Nolan had come to declare his love at last, and that now they would reenact their wedding in front of all their loved ones, even some of his new relatives.

Nolan was right—she hadn't realized what she'd missed out on the first time around. Grateful tears dampened her eyes at all the trouble he'd gone to, finding Reverend Black, waiting for him to bury a parishioner, and bringing him to Hartford.

Hannah smiled at Molly, who had changed into her best dress. Delighted to be a bridesmaid, she'd helped Hannah don her ivory silk gown, one of the new ones made for her widened waistline that she hadn't yet had a chance to wear. Iris had provided lengths of pink ribbon to adorn both girls' gowns and had fashioned a small posy out of some dried roses.

"You look radiant," Aunt Iris exclaimed once the veil had

been secured in Hannah's hair. "I'm so happy I get to see your wedding after all."

"No happier than I." Hannah's mother did not bother to stop the tears streaming from her eyes. In a rose-colored dress borrowed from Iris, her mother had transformed from a farm wife to a lady of status. Even her face looked more youthful. She squeezed Hannah in a warm embrace. "You are certain you want to do this?"

"More than anything."

"This is so romantic," Molly sighed. "I hope someday I'll marry a man as handsome as Nolan and get to wear such a beautiful dress."

Iris patted her cheek. "All in good time, Molly dear. Now let's not keep the gentlemen waiting."

With a flourish, she opened the door into the hallway, and they all filed toward the parlor. Her mother and aunt slipped into the room, which had been set up with extra chairs facing the mantel. Iris's housekeeper, who had a passable talent on the piano, had been asked to play a lilting tune while Hannah entered the room. When everyone was ready, Molly led the way with Hannah a few steps behind. Dressed in his robes, Reverend Black stood in front of the hearth, Nolan and the earl to one side.

When Hannah's gaze locked with Nolan's, the nerves dancing in her stomach settled. This was the man she had adored since she was a girl. In his eyes, she saw the light of his love shining with such purity that she couldn't look away.

It seemed to take forever to reach him, her legs trembling with every step. He moved toward her, hand outstretched. Smiling through her veil, she placed her hand in his. Together, they turned to face the minister, whose ruddy face beamed at them.

"As most of you might know, I performed this couple's marriage ceremony several months ago. I am most pleased to be here today to witness the renewal of their vows in front of their family and friends. Without further ado, let us begin."

Hannah gave Molly her posy and joined hands with Nolan.

The minister opened his prayer book. "I'd like to begin with a verse from Genesis. 'And the rib, which the Lord God had taken from man, made he a woman and brought her unto the man. And Adam said, This is now bone of my bones, and flesh of my flesh: she shall be called Woman, because she was taken out of Man. Therefore shall a man leave his father and his mother, and shall cleave unto his wife: and they shall be one flesh.'"

After a significant pause, Reverend Black looked up. "Do you, Nolan, in sight of God and these witnesses, take Hannah to be your wedded wife, to love, honor, and cherish her till death do you part?"

Nolan looked deep into her eyes. "I do."

"And do you, Hannah, in sight of God and these witnesses, take Nolan to be your wedded husband, to love, honor, and obey him till death do you part?"

She looked into Nolan's handsome face, eyes the warm blue of a summer sky. "I do."

"Then it is my honor once again to pronounce you husband and wife. What God has joined let no man put asunder."

Nolan smiled as he reached into his pocket and took out the simple wedding band Bert had fashioned for her all those months ago. "I think it's time we put this back on—for good." He slipped the ring onto Hannah's finger.

She gave her husband a trembling smile. At last her doubts had been laid to rest. She belonged to Nolan, and nothing would change that. Their child would be brought into this world secure in that knowledge.

Nolan lifted the veil from her face before he winked at the

minister. "If it's all the same to you, Reverend, I intend to kiss my bride." He cupped Hannah's face with both hands and laid his lips on hers.

Hannah's heart filled with such love that she feared it would soar past the roof and up to the sky.

When Nolan released her, a round of applause broke out, and everyone stepped up to embrace them. Even the earl appeared moved, gripping Nolan's hand and kissing Hannah on the cheek. Nolan introduced her to his Aunt Ophelia, a dignified woman who welcomed Hannah into the family.

And Nolan's sister Victoria beamed with happiness as she embraced Hannah in a tight hug. "I'm so happy to have another sister. I truly hope we can become friends."

"I'd like that very much."

Victoria turned to Nolan. "I'm afraid I couldn't get Evelyn to change her mind and attend the ceremony. But don't worry. She'll come around in time."

Nolan simply smiled. "I hope so. But I don't intend to let her ruin this happy moment."

A beaming Iris turned to her butler, hovering in the doorway. "Carstairs, please bring us a bottle of our best champagne and enough glasses for everyone. This is indeed a cause for celebration."

Nolan's hand sought Hannah's, entwining their fingers together. "I fear I may become a nuisance, Mrs. Price. I don't intend to let you out of my sight for the foreseeable future." He rested his free hand on her abdomen. "I also intend to spoil you until this wee one is born." He leaned over to kiss her soundly.

"Oh, Nolan. I am so happy. I have to pinch myself to make sure it's real. Thank you for this beautiful day. It's exactly what I needed."

"You are most welcome." He gave her a tender smile. "I

thank God for allowing me come to my senses in time. I love you more than anything, Hannah Price, and I plan to spend the rest of my days making sure you never doubt that again."

Hannah opened her eyes to find her husband leaning on one elbow, studying her features, and couldn't keep the smile from her face. In the days since their marriage renewal, life had settled into a comfortable routine at Hartford. Their wedding guests had long since departed, all except Edward, who opted to stay on. Hannah's mother had wanted to stay as well to be here for her grandchild's birth, but she didn't wish to upset her husband by staying away longer than agreed. Hannah had assured her she could come for a visit whenever she was able to get away again.

Hannah and Nolan existed in a cocoon of joy, using the time to get reacquainted, talking about all that had happened over the last months. Nolan was wonderfully attentive and spoiled Hannah with his doting, as though trying to atone for his absence. Hannah was relieved to learn he had no intention of returning to Stainsby without her, which meant he would have to stay until their child made its appearance.

"I've forgotten how nice it is," she said, "waking up with someone in the same bed. Not to mention having someone to keep me warm during the night."

"And I don't even mind those cold feet against my legs." Nolan grinned, reminding her of the mischievous youth he'd been when they first met.

Warmth from the newly-stoked fire had begun to spread through the room, easing the morning chill.

Hannah fingered the quilted coverlet. "I'm sorry we haven't been able to repeat our honeymoon. But I don't wish to jeopardize the baby."

Nolan shook his head slightly, lifting a strand of her hair and running it between his fingers. "Nor do I, especially when I think about the scare you had. I couldn't bear it if I lost you, Hannah."

"You won't lose me. It's the baby I'm worried about."

Concern darkened his blue eyes. "You've felt fine since then? No more pains?"

"Not a twinge." She patted Nolan's warm arm lying across her belly. "It shouldn't be too much longer. Another two weeks or so according to the doctor. I can hardly wait to hold our child."

"Speaking of which," he said, lightly caressing her abdomen, "shouldn't we discuss names for the baby?"

"I suppose we should. Do you have any preferences?"

His hand found hers on top of the blanket. "If it's a girl, I'd like to include my mother's name." His voice faltered for a moment, giving evidence to the grief he still suffered.

"I was thinking the same thing. How about Elizabeth Ann, after both our mothers?"

His eyes softened. "I like that. We could call her Lizzie."

"What about a boy? Will the earl want a say in his name?" Hannah presumed that as a member of the nobility, Edward would have certain stipulations for naming his grandson and future heir.

"He's already hinted about it. What would you think of Edward Nolan Price-Fairchild?"

"That is an honorable name." She paused. "However, I'd like to add George, after my father too."

"Edward George Nolan Price-Fairchild. That's quite a name for such a tiny creature." Laughter rumbled in his chest. "I think it's perfect."

"Maybe a nickname would be a good idea. Teddy perhaps?"

"Teddy? I like the sound of that." His face broke into a grin. "But I bet my father will hate it."

She laughed with him, and he kissed her, then jumped up from the bed.

"Speaking of my father, he plans to leave for Stainsby today. I'd best go and see him off." Nolan pulled on his trousers and shot her a rueful look. "He's not happy that I'm staying here. He wanted me to return for a week or so and come back closer to the expected birth date."

"Why?"

"I'm not sure. Some business matter he feels I need to be privy to. However, I have much more pressing business here." He dropped a light kiss on her nose and snatched his jacket off the chair.

Hannah shifted on the bed. "Wait a moment and I'll come with you." Good manners dictated that she should go down and see Edward off as well. Besides, she didn't want to risk harming their tentative truce.

As she reached for her robe, a strange sensation rippled through her abdomen, followed by a gush of liquid. She gave a loud cry and clutched her belly.

Nolan rushed to her side. "Hannah, what is it?"

She bit her lip hard and clutched his arm. "I think the baby may be coming sooner than we planned."

CHAPTER 32

Edward stood in the foyer of Hartford Hall, awaiting the appearance of Lady Hartford and his son. His bags had been stowed in the boot of the carriage. Now all that remained was to say good-bye.

Why was he so reluctant to take his leave? He'd already stayed far longer than he'd ever anticipated. Yet somehow he couldn't seem to tear himself away from Iris's intoxicating presence. Being around her, the void in his life disappeared. He felt young again, vital, a man worthy of her respect and admiration.

The clip of nails on the tile floor alerted him to the dog's arrival. Iris came into view, leading Daisy on a leash, apparently ready for their usual morning stroll. A wave of regret moved through him that he would no longer be here to share that pleasant ritual with her.

"There you are, Edward." Her lovely face was wreathed with unusual lines of worry. "Have you looked at the weather? My groundskeeper told Carstairs that a severe snowstorm is expected. Perhaps you should put off your departure for another day."

Warmth tumbled through his chest that she cared so much

about his welfare. Or perhaps she merely wanted a reason for him to stay longer. "It's only a few flurries right now," he said. "I'll be fine. I have complete confidence in my driver."

She patted Daisy's head in an almost unconscious manner. "I suppose you could always stop at Derby if the roads become impassible. Stay at the inn overnight until the worst of it passes."

"My dear Iris. I have been traveling the roads in this area for years and have fared just fine. I'm not worried."

Her anxious eyes told him that she wasn't convinced. "You must think me overly fretful. I'm not normally one to fuss so. It's just that I had a strange dream last night that's left me out of sorts this morning."

For some unfathomable reason, he almost bent down to kiss her, to distract her from her troubling thoughts. But with the butler lingering in the shadows, and Nolan likely to appear at any moment, he held himself in check. "I'll be back in time for the birth of my grandchild. I look forward to seeing you again then."

A lovely blush stole into her cheeks. "And I you as well."

A moment of awkwardness descended. How would he take his leave? With a handshake? Too formal. A hug? Not his style. A kiss on the cheek would have to do.

The swirl of her lavender scent surrounded him as he brushed her silky cheek with his lips. He lingered, perhaps a moment too long, for he heard her sharp intake of breath.

She pulled back an inch, her mouth close to his. "Edward," she whispered.

His pulse thundered in his ears, and his breath went shallow. If he didn't take a chance now, when would he have another opportunity? He moved toward her lips, hovering there for an instant—

The pounding of feet on the stairs brought reality crashing back. He jerked upright and took a step back.

Nolan rushed toward them, a look of panic on his face. "Send for the midwife. Hannah has gone into labor."

Pain like a hot knife ripped through Hannah's abdomen. She tried to inhale, but the air clogged in her lungs. How long had this misery been going on? It felt like days, not just hours.

When at last she was able to draw a breath, it did nothing to lessen her misery. Something had to be wrong. Giving birth should not be this horrific.

Someone wiped her face with a wet cloth. She writhed, trying to ease the tightness across her abdomen, but no matter how she turned, the pressure would not lessen. Another wave of pain began, mounting in intensity until Hannah could not bear it. Sweat poured from every pore in her body, her chemise clinging to her damp skin. The pain eased up only long enough for her to grab one or two normal breaths, before the fire took hold again.

Dear God, help me. Please.

With the burning pain so all-consuming, she couldn't even form a proper prayer. On the periphery of her consciousness, she heard voices arguing, rising and falling. Where was Nolan? Shouldn't her husband be with her at this dire time?

"Let the midwife do her job, Nolan." Her aunt's voice seemed to come from a distance.

Sounds of a scuffle followed, then the slam of a door.

Hannah had no time to wonder what was happening. Another contraction started, and a blister of pain seared through her. She opened her mouth to scream, to call for help, but a surge of blackness swept her away.

The opening of a door snapped Edward to attention. He pushed away from the corridor wall where he, Nolan, and Iris had been keeping vigil. Molly had grown impatient and had gone to her room to study. Just as well since she didn't need to hear her sister's screams.

The midwife emerged from the room, wiping her hands on a towel, her face grim. "The babe should have come by now. You'd best send for the doctor."

Edward's insides clenched. Surely God wouldn't punish him for his selfish ways by taking Hannah's life and his grandchild with her?

Nolan shot a worried glance at Iris. "Will your doctor travel in this weather?"

"I don't know. The roads may not be passable."

Edward stiffened, his resolve firming. He'd do whatever necessary to get the man here, even if it meant trudging on foot through miles of snow. "We have to try. I won't sit around and allow my grandchild to die." He strode to the staircase. "My carriage is still here. I'll go for the doctor. Just give my man the directions to his house."

Iris followed him. "I'll go with you. Dr. Greenley will be more likely to come if I'm there."

Edward looked down into her anxious face and weighed his options. "I'm sure if you send a note—"

"I'll only worry if I'm not with you. Besides, it will make me feel useful instead of just pacing the floors."

Though he was loath to risk her safety, arguing with the stubborn woman would prove futile, as well as a waste of valuable time. "Very well, let's be off." He turned back to meet his son's tortured gaze. "Hannah needs you to be strong now, Nolan.

Go and tell her everything will be all right. We'll be back with the doctor as soon as we can."

Within minutes, they had donned their outerwear and ventured outside to the waiting carriage. The chill of the winter wind sliced through Edward's greatcoat. He shuddered and pulled up the collar with gloved fingers. Inside the carriage, warm bricks at their feet would serve to keep away the cold, for part of the journey at least.

He scanned the sky, frowning at the darkening clouds in the distance, and prayed that the weather wouldn't worsen so they could reach their destination without undue trouble.

Edward helped Iris into the carriage. Propriety dictated that he sit across from her, but as he moved to take a seat, she patted the bench beside her.

"Edward, you must sit here so we can share the warmth of the blanket."

Nerves swirled in Edward's stomach. Much too intimate for his liking. After the moment earlier when he'd almost succumbed to the temptation to kiss her, Edward wasn't sure he trusted himself. "I'll be fine over here."

She shrugged one shoulder under her fur-trimmed pelisse. "Suit yourself."

The first leg of the journey passed with agonizing slowness. Too chilled to relax, Edward rubbed his hands on his legs to keep the circulation going. The warmth from the brick at his feet did little to help. The panes of glass in the carriage had frosted over, making it impossible to see outside. He reached over to scratch a hole in the ice with his thumbnail, affording him a tiny opening. A vortex of white surrounded them. It appeared they were traveling into the heart of the storm.

Though not usually a praying man, he sent a plea heavenward to grant them safe passage.

Iris leaned forward. "Edward, your lips are blue. I insist you move over here and share this blanket."

Despite his near-frozen state, he gave a fierce shake of his head.

"You can come here, or I will go there. Your choice." She began to move the covers aside.

He exhaled loudly, creating a blast of steam in the enclosure. "You are the most stubborn woman I have ever encountered." Begrudgingly, he unfolded his cold-stiffened limbs and crossed the carriage to take a seat beside her. When she wrapped the blankets about him, her lavender scent mixed with the lingering warmth from the covers to envelop him.

Her hands gripped his under the blankets, and she swiftly stripped off his gloves.

With surprisingly warm hands, she began to knead his fingers, urging the blood to flow again. Her haughty gray eyes flicked to his face as she worked. "Is it so distasteful to sit near me that you would rather suffer such discomfort?"

He huffed. "It's not distasteful. Just the opposite in fact. I find it too . . . distracting."

Iris continued her massage, a slow smile tipping her lips. She arched a brow at him. "You find me distracting?"

Edward scowled. "I believe that is what I said." Could the woman not take a compliment and remain silent?

Still smiling, she slid a hand to his wrist. A pleasant warmth worked its way up his arm and invaded his chilled torso. When at last she stopped, she kept her hand resting in his, and he made no move to disengage his fingers.

"For the record, Edward," she said softly, "I find you distracting as well."

She looked up at him, and the air seized in his lungs. Eyes locked on hers, he lowered his face toward her—

The carriage lurched to a sudden halt, tilting at a precarious angle that sent Iris slamming into him. He steadied her, then moved the blanket aside.

"Wait here," he said. "I'll go and see what the trouble is."

He pushed out the door and landed shin-deep in a snowdrift. The driver had jumped down and was at the horses' heads, trying to pull them back onto the road. If he could even tell where the road was.

Edward motioned to his man to help him push the back of the carriage. With their combined efforts, they finally managed to get the vehicle back onto level ground.

The driver blew on his hands. "Shouldn't be much farther, my lord. Get back inside and stay warm." Tiny icicles had formed on the man's eyebrows.

Edward frowned. He pulled off his overcoat and handed it to him. "Here, take this."

"No, sir. I couldn't."

Edward draped the cloak over the driver's shoulders. "I have a blanket inside. I'll be fine." He opened the carriage door and pulled himself up, relieved to find that Iris appeared no worse for their ordeal.

"Goodness, where is your coat?" She sidled toward him on the bench, tucking the blanket around him.

Edward shivered. "The driver needed it more than I."

"That was most thoughtful of you." Her lips curved in a smile. "If you're not careful, Edward, you'll lose your reputation as an ogre."

As the carriage jerked into motion, Iris lifted a corner of the blanket and began to wipe the moisture from his face. She dabbed at his forehead and cheeks, then reached up to brush the snowflakes from the hair on his brow.

His breathing grew shallow at her nearness. He brought

his hand over hers to still her fingers, and when her eyes met his, all coherent thought left his brain. He dipped his head to capture her lips with his. The warmth of her mouth melted the coldness of his, shooting heat straight through his system. His heart bucked like a runaway stallion. She lifted a warm palm to his cheek, and he pulled her closer, intensifying the kiss.

This is what he'd missed, what he'd craved since the loss of his beloved Mary so long ago. He'd forgotten what it was like to be so in tune with another human being.

Forgotten what it was like to be loved, and to love in return.

When Iris drew back a few seconds later, her eyes danced. "What a perfectly delightful way to get warm."

"Indeed. I believe I could use a little more thawing out."

And he drew her closer to kiss her once again.

CHAPTER
33

Nolan paced the hallway outside his room. With Hannah's every scream, impotent fear filled his lungs, making the simple act of breathing near impossible.

Please, Lord, help Hannah. Don't let her die. I can't lose her again now that I've just gotten her back.

When Edward and Iris left, he'd gone in to sit with Hannah, holding her hand while she labored, until the pain got even more intense and the midwife had shooed him out of the room, claiming she couldn't work with him in the way. Now he seethed with frustration at his helplessness to aid his wife and child.

Nolan descended the great staircase and peered out the front door, willing his father's carriage to appear, but masses of swirling snow impeded his vision. He closed the door and paced the area inside. What was taking them so long? They'd been gone for hours. Hours that Hannah had writhed in agony. Nolan didn't know how much more she could take—or he, for that matter.

At last, he made out the sound of horses' hooves and carriage wheels crunching over hardened snow. Nolan opened the front door as his father emerged from the carriage. He helped Iris out, and a man soon followed.

Edward entered the house, shook the snow from his overcoat, and removed his hat. "How is Hannah?"

"In tremendous pain. Is this the doctor?"

The man nodded. "I'm Dr. Greenley. I understand your wife is having some difficulty."

"Yes. She's on the second floor."

The man shrugged out of his bulky outerwear, grabbed his bag, and followed Nolan upstairs. Nolan entered the bedroom with him, determined that no matter what the midwife or doctor said, this time he was not leaving Hannah's side.

His wife needed him, and he would not let her down again.

Edward removed his wet boots and accompanied Iris into the parlor where they took seats by the fire.

At the sight of her anxious expression, he reached for her hand. "It will be all right now. The doctor will ensure the baby is safely delivered."

"Dr. Greenley is an excellent physician. I know he'll do all he can." Yet lines of tension still creased her brow.

Edward's pulse quickened. He wished he could take her in his arms and kiss away her anxiety. Since when had it become his sole purpose in life to make this woman happy?

Iris squeezed his hand. "Would you do something for me?"

Edward gazed into those arresting eyes and nodded. If it was within his power, he would do anything she asked of him.

"Would you pray with me? It's the one thing we can do right now for Hannah."

Surprisingly, he did not find the idea at all aversive. In fact, he welcomed the opportunity to pray with Iris. He bowed his head over their clasped hands. "Of course. Why don't you begin?"

After giving Dr. Greenley time to examine Hannah, Nolan quietly reentered the room, his eyes trained on the bed where he and Hannah had awoken earlier that day. The midwife stood by the headboard, wringing out a cloth. Nolan's stomach fell as he caught sight of his wife.

Hannah lay unmoving against the pillows. Her usually lustrous hair hung in lifeless strands over the linens. The thin chemise clung to her chest, damp with perspiration. Suddenly, her whole body convulsed, and she let out a low moan.

Attempting to swallow his panic, Nolan moved forward to grasp her hand. The only other time he'd felt this helpless was at his mother's deathbed. At that time, he'd asked God to spare her, but the Lord had chosen not to grant his request. Would He now?

When the pain receded, she opened her eyes and gave him a weak smile. "Nolan. You're here."

"Yes. And I won't leave again." Nolan turned to the doctor at the foot of the bed and lowered his voice. "Is the baby all right?"

Dr. Greenley raised his head. "From what I can ascertain, everything appears normal." He shrugged. "I don't know what to tell you. Some women have a harder time than others."

Nolan gripped the bedpost. "What can I do to help?"

"It's almost time to push. You can support your wife and lend her your strength once she begins."

Nolan nodded and, ignoring the midwife's disapproving scowl, climbed up beside Hannah. "All right, sweetheart. We're going to bring our child into the world. Together."

If only he felt as confident as he sounded.

I need you, Lord. Let me be Hannah's strength now. Use me to help her deliver our child.

"On the next contraction, Mrs. Price, you must start pushing." The doctor's firm voice roused Hannah.

She opened her eyes and nodded. "I'll do my best."

When the next pains began, Hannah gripped Nolan's arm with the force of ten men.

On a burst of energy, he helped raise her upper body as she pushed. "That's it, Hannah. You can do this."

Her breath came out in panting gasps, then she fell back with a thud. "No. I can't."

"Yes, you can. Focus on my voice."

She lay weakly against him for several seconds until her whole torso stiffened, and another contraction started.

"Again, Mrs. Price," the doctor ordered.

"Push now, Hannah." Nolan hoped she would obey without question and that instinct would take over.

She bore down, grunting with exertion, then fell back against him when the contraction ended. With each new pain, she struggled until he thought she would swoon from the sheer effort it took.

How many times had he seen a mare deliver a foal and watched sheep, cows, and even barn cats give birth? Most times the process happened with barely a grunt from the animals. Why was it so difficult for humans? If Nolan could, he'd take every ounce of pain in Hannah's stead.

Finally, the doctor beckoned to the midwife. "Bring me a clean sheet."

The woman hurried to do as he requested.

"That's it, Mrs. Price," the doctor said. "One more big push should do it."

Hannah's groans indicated how hard she was straining. She stiffened, then collapsed against Nolan.

His heart stilled in his chest. "Hannah? Don't give up on me now."

Just then a lusty cry split the air.

"Congratulations, Mr. Price," Dr. Greenley said. "You have a son."

One thing Edward hated was feeling helpless. Powerless. Out of control.

His grandchild's life hung in the balance, and there was nothing he could do about it. He stood outside the bedroom waiting for Iris, who at his request, had gone inside moments earlier to check on the progress, since he feared he would go mad if he didn't know what was happening.

At the sound of a baby's wail, Edward jumped away from the wall. His heart pumped at a furious rate. Crying was good, wasn't it? It meant the child was alive at least.

For a moment, Edward's sole focus centered on the door that hid the secrets of life and death behind it. The child's cries quieted, and Edward's palms grew slick with sweat. When he thought he couldn't stand still another moment, the door opened, and Iris emerged carrying a bundle in her arms.

Tears streamed unchecked down her face, but he couldn't tell if they were tears of sorrow or joy. Repressing a fierce urge to gather Iris in his arms, he took a deep breath to steady himself for whatever was to come.

"Edward," she whispered. "Meet your new grandson." A tremulous smile quivered on her lips as she moved the cloth away to reveal a tiny, wrinkled being with a shock of black hair.

Edward stared down at the closed eyes, fringed with impossibly small lashes, the bud of a nose, and miniature, pouting lips. He swallowed past a lump in his throat the size of a hen's egg. "Is he . . . all right?"

"I don't know much about infants, never having had one of my own, but he appears to be fine. The doctor said his color is good, and he's breathing well." Iris raised wide eyes to him in what looked like awe. "I've never held anything so precious and . . . new."

He reached out a finger to touch the petal soft skin of his grandson's cheek. "I barely remember my daughters being this small." He frowned. "Why isn't he with his mother?"

"Hannah lost consciousness when he was born. Nolan won't leave her side." Iris's chin quivered.

Alarm shot through Edward's veins. How would his grandson survive if his mother perished? "What is the doctor doing for her?"

"He's trying to stop the bleeding."

Edward raked fingers through his hair. "We have to do something."

"All we can do now is pray. Let's take the baby to the parlor by the fire. Keep him warm."

Helplessly, Edward followed Iris down the staircase and into the parlor. She took the seat closest to the hearth and motioned him to sit beside her.

"Would you like to hold him?" she asked.

Nerves roiled through his stomach. He'd never held a newborn before, not even his own daughters, and had no idea how to support such a fragile thing. He opened his mouth to refuse, but Iris laid the blanket on his lap.

"Support his head in the crook of your arm," she instructed.

His arms stiffened like two pieces of firewood as he looked down into the face of his progeny. Gradually the warmth of the small body seeped into Edward's muscles until they relaxed.

He looked down at the tiny creature cradled there. Never had he experienced such joy and wonder. On this child rested the future of the earldom—a new generation of Fairchilds.

Molly entered the parlor. "Aunt Iris? Did I hear a baby?"

"Yes, dear." Iris smiled. "Come and meet your nephew."

Molly rushed over and knelt in front of Edward to peer at the child. "He's beautiful."

"Yes, he is. A miracle from above." Iris held out a hand to Molly. "Now let's pray for Hannah and this beautiful boy." She bowed her head.

Edward glanced from the face of the child in his arms to Molly's fair head bent in prayer. Then he fixed his eyes on Iris. With her eyes closed, her mouth reciting the soothing words, she had never looked more beautiful.

Edward's heart swelled. This is what had been missing in his life. This bond, this sense of connectedness. Even in the midst of a crisis, Edward had never felt more part of a family than he did right now.

He bowed his head and joined in their heartfelt prayers.

Hannah drifted out of sleep, slowly coming back to consciousness. Her body felt both hot and cold at the same time. She tried to open her eyes, but her lids refused to cooperate. Somewhere in the distance, an animal cry could be heard. The noise grew louder and more insistent until Hannah felt an odd tugging in her breasts.

Fighting the urge to sink back into sleep, a deep instinct urged her to fully awaken. She forced her lids open as the crescendo of harsh sobs climbed.

Her baby!

"Nolan." She tried to speak, but her voice was a whisper. She cleared her throat and tried again. This time footsteps clattered across the floor.

Nolan's concerned face appeared in front of her. "Hannah? How are you feeling?"

"Tired. But how is the baby?"

Nolan leaned over the bed and smiled. "Our son is perfect. But he needs to nurse. Do you think you're up to trying?"

Hannah moved a hand to her chest, felt the wetness there, and realized what had happened. Her body had answered her child's cries. A rush of joy filled her soul. "Bring him to me."

Nolan reappeared seconds later with a swaddled bundle in his arms. "The midwife will help if you need her."

Very carefully, he brought the baby down to her level. He moved the blanket aside to reveal a very red-faced infant.

A lump rose in Hannah's throat. This was their son.

She untied her chemise and brought the baby to her breast. After a few unsuccessful attempts, the child finally latched on and began to suckle. She marveled at the way the baby and her body knew instinctively what to do.

Tears slid down her cheeks. "He's so beautiful, Nolan." She glanced over at her husband, who had been so strong through the whole ordeal, and saw tears in his eyes as well.

"Yes, he is. And so are you." He pressed his lips to her hair, his shoulders shaking.

"Nolan, is everything all right?"

He smiled at her through water-rimmed eyes. "Thanks be to God, it is now."

CHAPTER
34

Three weeks later, Hannah sat in her bedroom back at Stainsby Hall, rocking her son. Though Edward had insisted on equipping the newly furnished nursery with everything Teddy could possibly need, Hannah preferred to feed the baby in her own room where she felt most comfortable.

After the baby's birth, they had spent more than two weeks with Aunt Iris until Hannah felt strong enough to make the trip home. Now, settled back at Stainsby, Hannah's world was perfect. She gazed down at her son's precious face, relaxed in sleep. How blessed was she to have such a wonderful husband and child?

She kissed Teddy's downy head one more time before reluctantly handing him to the waiting nanny who would put him down for his nap. When the woman left, Hannah released a sigh of pure happiness. Her son should be settled for the next while, so perhaps she'd go and see if Molly's lessons were over. Now that Edward had accepted Hannah into the family, they all agreed that Molly need not work as a maid, and that she would be better off completing her schooling.

Edward had been most accommodating in hiring a tutor for her sister.

Nolan entered the bedroom just as Hannah finished fixing her clothing and re-pinning her hair.

"Our son looks quite content." He dropped a kiss on her cheek. "I peeked into his room on the way here."

"He's always content with a full belly." Hannah chuckled.

Nolan's arms slid around her waist. "Like father, like son, it appears. Though there are other appetites I look forward to satisfying." His lips caressed the area of her neck below her ear.

She shivered. "All in good time, my love. You must be patient a while longer."

He turned her around within the circle of his arms and winked. "At least there are no restrictions on kissing."

"None at all," she murmured as his lips claimed hers. Her heart nearly burst at the intensity of his embrace. As much as Hannah adored being a mother, she also yearned for the love of her husband.

Before things got too heated, she stepped out of Nolan's arms. "When will Edward be leaving for London?"

"I'm not sure. After being away from Stainsby for so long, he has things to take care of here first." Nolan frowned. "Speaking of London, I'd hoped Evelyn and Victoria would have come to see their new nephew by now."

"Not many people enjoy traveling in the winter, even by train." Hannah laid a hand on Nolan's arm, wishing she could ease his insecurities concerning his siblings. "I'm certain with time Teddy's birth will bring this family together. Look at how he's changed your father."

"You're right." Nolan laughed. "I've never seen a man so besotted by a grandchild."

"Teddy will have the same effect on his aunts once they meet him." She kissed Nolan's cheek and crossed to the dresser to retrieve a handkerchief. With the baby, it seemed she was always in need of a clean one. "Perhaps when Teddy is a little older, we can take a trip into London and visit both your sisters. Or there's always the christening. I'm sure they'll come if you invite them."

"Of course. There will be plenty of opportunities to win them over." He grinned. "And even if *my* considerable charm doesn't work, they won't be able to resist my beautiful wife and son."

Hannah laughed, having no doubt that God would answer her final prayer and that the Fairchild family would ultimately be healed, united by ties of affection and mutual respect.

Sometime later, Nolan walked toward the barn and, despite the sleet that fell from the leaden sky, lifted his eyes to the heavens in sincerest gratitude. Never could he have imagined such happiness, such a feeling of rightness in the world.

He was home again with his wife and newborn son. And though his relationship with his father was not perfect, Edward had made remarkable progress over the last few weeks and had finally accepted Hannah into the family. Giving Edward a grandson had gone a long way toward cementing their bond. Naming the child after him hadn't hurt either.

Nolan entered the stables to check on King, fed him the apple he'd brought from the larder, and then headed over to Bert's cottage. Nolan had been back at Stainsby for two days, and with having to catch up on estate business, he hadn't had a spare moment to come down to the barn or the smithy. Now, with Edward gone into Derby on some personal business and Hannah spending some time with Molly, Nolan could at last see how his friend was faring.

Franny McTeague answered his knock. "Master Nolan. Come in, come in." She beamed at him, easing the tension in Nolan's shoulders. If she was smiling, Bert must be doing better. "Bert will be so happy to see you. I understand you have some wonderful news to share."

"Happily, yes. Hannah and I have a new son."

"Ach, congratulations, lad." Bert's hearty voice boomed through the cottage as he emerged from the bedroom. "I knew you'd come to your senses. Finally begged your wife's forgiveness, I see."

Nolan grinned. "Not only that, I married the girl all over again."

Bert chuckled as they took a seat by the fireplace, and Franny scurried off to tend the stove.

"You're feeling better, I take it." Nolan glanced at the bandages still partially covering Bert's hands.

"Aye, but I won't be able to work for a few weeks yet."

"I'm glad to hear you're improving. And I wanted to thank you for your advice. It took a while for it to sink into my hard head, but between you and God and even Edward, I think I'm on the path the Lord intended for me."

Bert nodded. "Sometimes we have to hear God's message several different ways before it finally takes root."

"Especially in someone as stubborn as me." Nolan laughed again, marveling at the lightness of his soul.

"Would you like a bowl of stew, Master Nolan?" Franny asked. "We'd just finished our meal before you arrived."

"Thank you, but I've eaten as well. Though I'll take a cup of tea, if you have it."

"You know the pot's always ready in this house."

She soon set a steaming mug in front of him and freshened her husband's cup as well.

"How are you getting on with the earl?" Bert asked as he stirred his tea. "Have you come to terms with your new station in life?"

"I believe so. Things aren't perfect with Edward, but at least now he understands that Hannah will always be part of my life. Of course, giving him a grandson has made a huge difference in his attitude."

"Aye. I imagine his lordship must be busting his buttons."

"You're right. I've never seen a man so smitten with a babe before." Nolan took a long swallow of tea. "I want you to know that I haven't forgotten our conversation in the smithy. As soon as things settle down, I plan to speak to Edward about increasing the workers' wages and possibly starting a retirement collection for the more senior servants. Then I'll look into how to improve things for the tenant farmers."

Bert gave him an approving nod. "Just knowing you're on our side is a great comfort."

A loud rap on the front door interrupted them.

"Who could that be?" Franny frowned and went to open it.

"Is Nolan here?" Molly's anxious voice drifted inside. "I need to speak to him right away."

Nolan rose from his chair as the girl entered. "Molly? How did you know where to find me?"

"Hannah sent me." An expression of terror haunted her pale features. "You have to come quickly, Nolan. The baby is gone, and Hannah is beside herself."

A bolt of alarm shot through Nolan's body, but he struggled to remain calm. "I'm sure everything's fine. The nanny likely has him."

Molly shook her head, tears standing in her eyes. "Nanny said she left Teddy's room for only a few minutes, and when she came back, he was gone." Molly held out a crumpled piece of paper. "She found this in his bed."

Cold chills raced up Nolan's spine as he took the note.

If you want to see your son again, stable boy, come to the gatehouse on the Wexford estate at dusk. Don't contact the authorities. And come alone or the baby is dead.

The words swam before him, the sinister meaning sinking in. Someone had kidnapped his son!

CHAPTER 35

Hannah's knees ached from the time she'd spent on the floor at her bedside in desperate prayer, her eyes almost swollen shut from her storm of weeping. She still couldn't grasp the enormity that someone had stolen her child.

How could she have left him in the care of a nanny who clearly didn't have the same diligence that his own mother would have? And how could God allow this to happen after everything Hannah had been through to have her baby?

She squeezed her hands together so hard that her nails bit into the flesh of her palms, breaking the skin.

Dear God, please keep Teddy safe and bring my baby back to me.

The heaviness of her breasts told her that her child would be hungry by now. Hungry without her to feed him. Crying, missing his mama.

Oh, Lord, how will I bear it?

She stifled a sob, barely taking note of the door opening. If the kidnappers had come back, they might as well kill her, for without Teddy, she had no desire to go on living.

"Hannah." Nolan swept her up from the floor, hugging her tightly to his chest.

She clutched the fabric of his shirt, shaking with the force of her grief. "He's gone. Our baby is gone."

His arms tightened around her. "Not for long. I'm going to get him back. I promise."

"Y-You're going to do what they ask?"

"Yes, but I had to see you first."

She pulled herself upright, drawing in a long breath to calm her quivering body. Purpose filled her and renewed her strength. "I'm going with you." She reached for her shawl at the foot of the bed.

Nolan placed his hand on hers and turned her to face him. "No, Hannah. I'm going alone. I won't subject you to such danger."

"But I can't stay here doing nothing."

"You must." He brushed the stray hairs from her cheek. "I swear by everything in me, I won't fail you. I'll find Teddy and bring him home."

Hannah looked into his determined face and nodded, forcing herself to be strong. "Aye, Nolan. I trust you with my life. With our son's life."

He pressed a fierce kiss to her cold lips and strode to his dresser where he took out a pistol from the top drawer.

Shudders whipped through her. Since when did Nolan keep a gun?

"Be careful," she whispered. Hannah didn't know what she would do if she lost him too.

"I will. Stay here with Molly. If my father returns, let him know what's happened. I'll be back as soon as I can." With a last intense look, he rushed from the room.

334

Banking down his irritation, Edward entered the front hall and removed his hat and gloves. His fingers and cheeks still stung from the raw wind and sleet on the trip back from Derby.

"Dobson," he barked as he shrugged out of his greatcoat. Where was the man when he needed him?

If Edward were being honest, he'd have to admit it wasn't only the bad weather that had him out of sorts. His sour disposition had more to do with missing Iris. Had it only been a few days since they'd left Hartford Hall? It felt more like years. Without her, he already felt himself slipping back into the curmudgeon he used to be.

His thoughts turned to their parting. When he'd taken her hand in his, he'd been shocked at the emotions swimming through his system—especially his regret at having to leave the woman who had become as vital to his life as air to his lungs.

"I'm sorry you have to go," she'd said. "I've enjoyed our time together."

"As have I. More than you know." He lifted her hand to his lips. "I hope you'll come and visit us soon."

She smiled, and a trace of pink colored her cheeks. "With my new grandnephew as enticement, I'm sure you'll soon tire of my visits."

"I doubt that very much." Edward captured her lips in a lingering kiss, wishing he could find some way to delay his departure, or to entice her to Stainsby for an extended stay. "Until we meet again, I wish you good health."

"Godspeed, Edward. You'll be in my thoughts and my prayers." Her eyes shimmered with emotion.

If he concentrated, he could still feel the warmth of her kiss. Did he dare hope she might feel as strongly about him?

"Here I am, my lord." Dobson rushed into the hallway.

"About time. I need coffee in my study right away."

"I'm afraid a situation has come up that I need to apprise you of first."

"Can it not wait five minutes?"

"No, sir. It cannot."

Edward came to an abrupt halt. He peered at Dobson, taking in his pinched features. The unflappable butler looked decidedly perturbed. "What is wrong?"

"Something terrible has occurred, your lordship. I don't know how—"

Pounding footsteps echoed from the staircase. A wild-eyed Nolan raced into the hallway and snatched his overcoat from the hat stand.

"Nolan. Whatever is going on?" Edward demanded. He'd only been gone a few hours. How had the household fallen into chaos so quickly?

Nolan shot a desperate look over his shoulder as he slid his feet into a pair of boots. His mouthed formed a grim line. "Someone has taken Teddy. They've left instructions for me to meet them at the Wexford estate."

The blood drained from Edward's brain. His mouth flapped open, then he snapped it shut. "A kidnapping?"

"It appears so."

A cold ball of rage formed in Edward's stomach. "How much did they ask for?"

"They didn't." Nolan thrust a crumpled bit of paper at him.

Edward scanned the scrawled message and looked up. "I'm going with you. But we should bring some money just in case." He turned and marched down the hall.

Seconds later, Nolan entered the study behind him.

"Close the door." Once Nolan had done so, Edward crossed to the safe in the corner behind his desk. He glanced at Nolan. "I suppose this is a good time to show you where I keep a sizable amount of cash for emergencies." He took a key from his desk drawer and unlocked the safe. Edward reached in, grabbed several stacks of bills, and closed the door. He brought the cash to his desk, where he withdrew a leather satchel and began stuffing the money inside.

Nolan watched silently, his eyes wide. "I can't let you come with me," he said at last. "You saw what the note said."

"You don't expect me to sit here doing nothing while—"

"I expect you to protect my wife and Molly in case the thugs come back."

Edward latched the case, then reached into a drawer for his pistol. "Don't be foolish, Nolan. It's suicide going there alone."

"Some of the stable hands are going to hide in the woods near the gatehouse. I'll have help if I need it."

"You think you're better off with stable hands than with me?" A wave of frustration washed through Edward. Why wouldn't his son accept his help?

Nolan closed the distance between them. "You're the only one I trust to keep Hannah safe. Will you do that for me?"

An untold emotion clogged Edward's airway. He stared into his son's anxious face and saw absolute trust. "Very well."

"Thank you."

"Here. Take the pistol."

"I have the one you gave me. You might need yours here." Nolan glanced at the window. "I have to go if I'm to be there by dusk. I'm not sure how long it will take."

Edward fought the rush of fear that filled his chest. This might be the last time he saw his son alive. He handed Nolan the satchel. "Be careful, son. Bring our boy home." He pulled Nolan to him and clapped him on the back.

Nolan cleared his throat. "I'll be back with Teddy as soon as I can." He paused. "Give me an hour's head start, then send word to the authorities. By then it shouldn't matter if they show up."

Once Nolan had gone, Edward went upstairs to find Hannah and Molly. Both women were red-eyed and grim. He convinced them to come down to the main level, saying they would be safer near him. Now the pair sat huddled together on the sofa in the parlor, watching him as though he held the answer to their dilemma.

As soon as things settled down, he'd fire that nanny for leaving Teddy unattended. He didn't care that he was being irrational. Someone had to pay for losing his grandson.

How Edward wished for Iris's calming presence. She'd know what to do, what to say to comfort these girls. All Edward could do was murmur platitudes and pace in front of the hearth, watching the minutes tick by on the brass mantel clock.

When the maid arrived with the coffee he'd ordered, he found he had no stomach for it. Instead, he excused himself and went across the hall to his study to write a message for the constable. He'd have one of the footmen deliver it as soon as possible and pray that the man would understand the need for extreme discretion. If the kidnappers discerned the presence of the authorities, heaven only knew what would happen.

Edward's hand shook as he wrote, smearing the ink, and he had to start the note a second time.

Quick footsteps sounded in the hall. For a moment Edward's heart leapt in the hope that Nolan had returned, even though he knew it unlikely.

Seconds later, a boy rushed through the open doorway. Snowflakes glistened on his cap and jacket.

"Your lordship." The lad's breathing came in gasps.

Edward jumped up and came around from behind the desk, just as Dobson appeared, frowning. "I'm sorry, my lord. He ran past me."

The boy came forward, holding out an envelope. "An urgent message, my lord. From Lady Evelyn."

Edward took the envelope and peered at the lad. "You're Langley, from our London house."

"That's right, sir. Lady Evelyn arrived last night, very upset. Gave this to me. Said to deliver it straight to your hands and no one else. Been traveling since then. Had to change horses twice."

"Dobson, take the boy below and get him something warm to drink and some food. And see that his horse is being cared for."

"Very good, my lord." Dobson led the boy out of the room.

Edward sank onto one of the armchairs. With unsteady hands, he broke the seal and slid out a note in his daughter's handwriting. He scanned the page, barely comprehending what he was reading until one line jumped out at him.

Father, you have no time to waste. Nolan's life is in jeopardy.

Sitting atop King on the crest of the hill that overlooked the Wexford mansion, Nolan patted the weight of the pistol in his overcoat pocket. When Edward had insisted he keep a weapon in his chambers, claiming that men in their position couldn't be too careful, Nolan had balked at the ridiculous idea. But then he'd remembered the threatening notes he suspected were from Timothy Bellows and realized Edward had a point. Having the gun with him now gave him added courage. As did the leather satchel of cash. If the kidnappers wanted money, he'd gladly give them the amount Edward had provided. But somehow Nolan's gut told him this had nothing to do with money and had everything to do with the threats he'd received.

As though sensing his master's trepidation, King gave a loud snort and tossed his head.

"Steady, boy. We've a ways to go yet." With a cluck of his tongue, he guided the horse down the slope, officially crossing onto the Duke of Wexford's property. Though they were technically neighbors, acres of woods and field separated the lands. Rumor had it that the duke never visited his country estate, and from the look of the house below, it appeared to be true. The dilapidated building cried out with neglect. What would the smaller gatehouse be like?

Nolan would soon find out.

His hands slicked with sweat as he reached the flat ground. He kept to the shelter of the trees to stay out of sight. He'd come alone as requested, but that didn't mean he wouldn't take precautions and attempt to gain the upper hand on these thugs—whoever they were. Nolan was certain that Bellows must be behind it. And if so, he would make sure the lowlife never got out of jail again.

Bert had wanted to accompany Nolan, but he and Franny had made him see there was little he could do without the use of his hands. He'd relented once he learned that Mickey and Will would keep hidden in the woods. Knowing they were there gave Nolan a small measure of comfort.

When the rear of the gatehouse came into view, Nolan pulled King to a halt. From the looks of it, no one had lived here for some time.

He slid from the saddle and wrapped the reins loosely around a bush, so King would be ready for a speedy departure, but not close enough that a whinny might give away his presence.

As Nolan crept along the edge of the woods, his footsteps muffled in the soft snow, he lifted a silent prayer. *God be with me in my hour of trial. Guide my steps and let me bring our son safely home. You helped David fight Goliath and be victorious. I'm asking for your help in facing this unknown adversary. Amen.*

He reached the back of the gatehouse and stopped to listen. Nerves slicked his shirt against his back. Inside, the faint cries of an infant could be heard. Nolan's chest constricted, and he had to fight the urge to burst into the building to retrieve his son. He needed to be smart to outwit the criminals.

Nolan moved to a small window and peered into the gate-keeper's kitchen. No signs of life. He ducked back down and made his way around the side of the building. What was he supposed to do now? Knock on the front door?

Before he could decide his next move, the cold press of metal against the back of his neck shocked him upright, his heart slamming into his ribs.

"No sudden moves or you won't see the kid again."

Nolan's pulse thundered, and his gut clenched. With supreme effort, he reined in the instinct to strike out. Instead, he held up his hands in surrender and awaited further instructions, concentrating on the push and pull of air from his lungs.

He had to stay calm. Teddy's life depended on it.

The man patted down Nolan's side and whipped the pistol from his pocket. With a grunt, he tossed it into the bushes. "Get inside." The gruff voice was accompanied by a shove at Nolan's back.

Nolan stumbled, then regained his balance and walked toward the door.

"Open it." The forced roughness of the man's voice made it difficult to recognize.

Could it be Bellows? Until he saw his face, Nolan couldn't be sure.

Nolan reached for the latch, pushed the door inward, and then stepped cautiously into a narrow hall. The wails of his son grew louder. Nolan's throat thickened. Teddy must be frantic for his mother. He swallowed hard and forced himself to scan the area for anything that might serve as a weapon.

"What do you want?" Nolan ground out.

"You'll see."

The man shoved him down the corridor and into a sitting room. Years of neglect coated the furniture in white dust. Nolan looked around for other possible cohorts, but the room was empty. On the floor by the grate, a wrapped bundle kicked and cried.

Teddy!

Setting his jaw, Nolan turned to finally face his captor.

A scruffy man with a dark cloth tied over his face glared back at him. Though he no longer resembled the man who had worked at Stainsby, there was no disguising those hate-filled eyes.

"Bellows. I figured as much." Nolan straightened to his full height. "You failed to mention a ransom amount in your note. How much will it take to get rid of you once and for all?" Despite his bravado, sweat trickled between Nolan's shoulder blades. He prayed that a large sum of cash would satisfy the fugitive's demand.

Bellows sneered. "That's not what this is about."

"Then what? You want me dead? If so, why drag me out here, and why involve my son?"

"I'm not the one who wants you dead, though it won't hurt my feelings any." He leveled the pistol at Nolan. "Aren't you even curious to know who hired me?"

A sick feeling of dread weighed heavy in Nolan's stomach. Something far more sinister was at play here than simple revenge on the former footman's part. "Who?"

Teddy's wails increased.

"A relative of yours. One who doesn't think too highly of having a servant take his place as heir." Bellows smirked. "That's right. Your sister's husband wants you dead. And your son as well."

CHAPTER
36

Edward had never ridden a horse so hard in his life. Nor had he beseeched the Almighty with such desperate prayers. He couldn't allow himself to imagine the horror of what was taking place at that gatehouse. He only prayed he would make it in time to save Nolan and Teddy.

Evelyn's note explained how she'd only just learned of her husband's vile plot to secure the earldom for himself. She'd overheard him telling one of his cronies that he'd hired a common criminal to kidnap little Teddy in order to lure Nolan away from home, where the thug had orders to murder Nolan and the child too. Everyone would assume it was a kidnapping gone wrong, and Orville would remain the heir to Stainsby. As soon as she'd been able, Evelyn had escaped to Fairchild Manor and penned the urgent note to Edward.

Edward could not believe that he'd underestimated Orville to such a degree. He'd known the man was lazy, entitled, and much too fond of spirits and gambling. But murder? He'd never have imagined Hugh's son capable of such treachery.

Fueled by an indescribable anger, Edward had ordered a footman to ride into Derby and fetch the constable, while he headed to the stable for his horse. Nothing would stop him from doing whatever he could to save Nolan and Teddy.

Now Edward's muscles burned with fatigue from the hard ride, but he would not slow down. Finally, Wexford Manor came into view. He dug his heels into the horse's side and pushed on until he saw the gatehouse. Then he dismounted, prepared to walk the last bit to keep the element of surprise in his favor.

Heedless of the snow and slush that tugged at his feet, Edward made his way toward the building. The closer he got, the faster his heart sprinted. *Please, merciful God in heaven, spare my son and keep my grandson safe.*

As he paused by the bushes near the front door to get his bearings, his thoughts swung to Iris. If things went badly, there was a chance he might never see her again. Regret lodged in his chest—regret that he'd never found the courage to declare his feelings. Other than a few stolen kisses, he hadn't revealed his heart.

Forgive me, Iris. If I get the chance to see you again, I promise to remedy that fact straightaway.

Nolan inched across the room, away from the baby, who had fallen silent. He prayed Teddy was all right, but his silence was preferred at the moment. Nolan had to catch Bellows off guard and get control of his gun before the hooligan could use it.

"So, how long have you been working for Orville?"

The man pulled the rag from his face. "Ever since you became the newest heir of Stainsby. Mr. Orville paid me to spy on you and leave you threatening notes. Until I went to prison, that is. Then he must have got someone else to deliver his messages." He swiped a sleeve across his mouth. "If you'd been smart and listened to those threats, all this might have been avoided." A hint of fear flashed in the man's beady eyes.

"Listen, Bellows. I have cash. A lot of it. You can have it all if you leave us now. Disappear and don't come back."

He squinted at Nolan. "How much?"

"A sizable sum." Nolan removed the satchel from his shoulder.

Bellows went to grab the bag, but Nolan held back. "Not until I have my son and you give me the gun."

"You think I'm stupid?" He cocked the pistol and yanked the bag from Nolan's hand. "This will be a nice little bonus."

Nolan's heart thudded hard in his chest at his miscalculation. He had to keep the man talking. Distracted. Appeal to his compassion for Hannah and the baby. "Look, I know you never liked me, but surely you don't want to stoop to murdering a nobleman and his son. You'll hang if you're caught."

Beads of sweat appeared on the man's grimy forehead.

Nolan inched toward Teddy.

"Think of what this is doing to Hannah. She's out of her mind with worry over the baby. I know you'd never want to hurt her." Nolan took another small step. "If you take Teddy back to his mother unharmed, I'll do whatever you ask."

A snarl erupted from the man. "You need to shut up. I'm the only one leaving this place alive." The gun wavered in his hand as he aimed it at Teddy.

Icy chills shot through Nolan's limbs. In a burst of desperation, he sprang at Bellows, knocking his arm. The thug's eyes bugged out, but his grip remained firm on the weapon. Nolan shoved the man, knocking him away from Teddy. They both fell to the ground with a thud, Bellows landing on Nolan's chest.

The gun went off, and a streak of heat ripped through Nolan's side. He ignored it and clutched the man's hand in a desperate attempt to loosen his grip on the pistol. Teddy screeched louder in the background, grinding Nolan's nerves to an even sharper edge. Despair seeped through him as his strength waned.

Lord, help me. Please.

Using all his might, Nolan heaved upward and knocked Bellows off him. The two rolled across the floor, dust flying with their struggle. In the melee, the gun clattered to the floor. Bellows scrambled over, snatched it up, and trained the weapon at Nolan. "You won't win this time, stable boy."

The loud report of a gun echoed in the room. Amid a haze of smoke, Bellows's eyes went wide. He slumped forward and fell facedown on the floor.

Nolan pushed to his knees. What had happened? He stared in shock at the unmoving form. Then his gaze moved to the man standing before him, pistol in hand.

"Father. Thank goodness." Nolan's muscles went lax. He gasped for air, his lungs not cooperating.

Footsteps sounded, and Mickey and Will burst into the room just as Edward kicked Bellows's body over with his foot. Blood saturated the front of his stained coat.

Teddy's frantic wails increased in volume. Nolan crawled over to pick up his son. With shaking hands, he pulled the cloth away and peered at the tiny face, swollen from crying. "It's all right, son. Your papa's here."

Nolan attempted to stand, but the searing pain in his side intensified. Sweat dripped from his forehead.

"Nolan! You're hurt." Edward shoved the gun into his pocket and strode forward.

Nolan blinked. The room swam before him like a changing kaleidoscope as he passed the baby to Edward. "Bring Teddy to Hannah. She needs to know I kept my promise." His legs gave way beneath him, and he slid to the floor. He pressed a hand to his side where a hot, sticky sensation met his palm.

"Hang on, son. You're going to be all right."

But as the edges of Nolan's vision grew dark, he feared his father was wrong.

"Tell Hannah I love her," he whispered. "More than anything."

CHAPTER

37

Hannah shook her head at the mug of broth Mrs. Bridges slid in front of her.

"Come on, dearie. Just a few sips. You want to keep your strength up for when the bairn gets back."

Hollow-eyed with no tears left to cry, Hannah lifted the cup to her lips. Edna was right. She had to think of Teddy. She had to believe Nolan would bring him home.

"That's it. A bit more. There you go." Mrs. Bridges took the mug Hannah handed out to her. "We have to have faith. God will prevail against whoever dared to do this evil thing."

"Will He? How do we know for sure?" Hannah hated that in this time of crisis her faith wavered. Would God help her if He sensed her doubt? If only she could find a way to reach deep for the cornerstone of her faith.

I'm sorry, Lord. Help me to be strong. Give me your shield of armor to surround me in my weakness.

A Bible verse drifted through her mind, one her father often quoted in his sermons. *My grace is sufficient for you, for my power is made perfect in weakness.*

"Thank you, Papa," she breathed. For she was sure he'd

brought the verse to her mind right when she needed it to give her a burst of strength. She would not give up; she would endure no matter the outcome.

Seated beside Hannah in the kitchen, Molly silently squeezed her hand, giving comfort without words. Hannah held on until her knuckles turned white.

The clatter of feet on the stone floor shattered the stillness. One of the maids rushed in. "Come quick, Mrs. Price. The master is home."

Hannah leapt from her chair, unsure whether the girl meant Nolan or Edward. It didn't matter, as long as someone had news of Teddy.

Please, Lord, please, was all she could think. Her legs shook as she flew up the stairs.

"Nolan?" She raced into the parlor and stopped at the sight of Edward standing by the fireplace.

When he turned, her focus riveted to the bundle in his arms. A soft mewling noise could be heard.

She let out a cry of joy and rushed forward. "Teddy!"

Edward nodded, his eyes filled with unspoken messages. Why didn't he seem happier?

He handed the baby to her. She pulled the cloth away, and Teddy's beloved face looked up at her. With a strangled cry, Hannah clutched him to her and sank onto the sofa. Tears streamed down her face unchecked as she rained kisses over his face. She rocked back and forth, inhaling the scent of her son.

Thank you, Lord. Thank you.

After several seconds, she became aware that Edward had not moved, and in fact stood staring at her with stark sorrow in his eyes.

A chill of foreboding ran through her. Where was her husband?

She lifted her questioning gaze to her father-in-law.

Edward slowly shook his head. "I'm so sorry, Hannah."

A flood of heat suffused her chest. "Where is he?" she demanded. "Tell me."

"Nolan's been shot." Edward moved forward to lay a hand on her shoulder. "The constable showed up right after it happened and insisted on taking him to the infirmary."

The air in her lungs thinned, and blood pounded in her ears. "Is he alive?"

"For now."

She held back a sob that caught in her throat. "You must take me to him."

He stared at her, his anguish as palpable as her own, and finally nodded. "I'll have the carriage sent around. Meet me out front."

Teddy let out a wail that pierced Hannah's soul.

"Give me a few minutes. I need to feed my son first."

"The infirmary is no place for a new bairn." Mrs. Bridges hovered in the hallway with Teddy in her arms as the maid helped Hannah on with her coat.

"I just got him back. I'm not letting him out of my sight." Hannah set her jaw. Nothing would stop her from bringing Teddy to see Nolan. He needed to know they were both safe and that they were there to help him get better.

For he would recover, if Hannah had anything to say in the matter. She would not let Nolan leave her now.

Hannah plucked the child from Mrs. Bridges and kissed her cheek. "Keep praying, dear Edna. We'll be back as soon as we can."

Hannah had no idea how long it took to get to Derby. She

prayed and rocked little Teddy the whole way. Thankfully, the baby was content to sleep after having nursed.

When they arrived, Edward helped her alight at the entrance. The minute they reached the desk inside, Edward barked orders to the staff. A nurse appeared and led them down a corridor to a private room.

"You may go in one at a time. The patient needs quiet."

When she disappeared down the hall, Edward looked at Hannah. "You go first. It's you he'll want to see."

The respect in his eyes gave Hannah added strength. "Thank you, Edward."

Tightening her grip on the baby, she entered the dim room and approached the bed. Nolan lay very still beneath the sheets, his face as white as the pillow.

Hannah bit her lip and reached out to brush tender fingers over his forehead. "Teddy and I are right here, Nolan. We're both fine. Now you just have to get better and come home to us."

No response. Not even an eyelid flickered.

Hannah pushed back her fear and dragged a chair over to sit by her husband's side. She would wait as long as it took.

Nolan fought through a misty haze to open his eyes. He blinked and squinted, trying to focus. Where was he? He shifted slightly, and searing heat shot through his side. He groaned as a rush of memories came flooding back.

"Teddy." He grasped the metal rail of what he realized was an infirmary bed and attempted to pull himself up.

"Nolan, lie still. You mustn't move."

He blinked, and Hannah's face came into focus. "Hannah. Is Teddy . . . ?"

"He's fine. I have him right here." She raised the bundle in her arms and moved the blanket from the baby's face. The child appeared to be sleeping peacefully.

"You're sure he's all right?"

"He's perfect. Thanks to you." A tear hovered at the corner of Hannah's eye. "You saved our son. Just as you promised." She pressed a kiss to Nolan's forehead.

Relief trickled through every one of Nolan's muscles. Hannah and Teddy were safe.

And he was alive. *Praise God.*

Warm fingers squeezed his hand. "The doctor said the bullet went right through your side without damaging any organs. He expects you'll make a full recovery."

Nolan was glad, but he needed to know the threat was truly over. "Is Bellows dead?" He had a vague recollection of the man lying unmoving on the gatehouse floor.

"Yes." Her lips tightened into a flat line.

"What about Orville?" Nolan's throat scratched. "And Evelyn?"

"Evelyn's safe with Ophelia and Victoria. She wanted no part of her husband's crime, and as soon as she learned of his plan, she alerted Edward and the police. That's how Edward knew you were in such danger." Hannah's voice quivered. "I thank God for allowing him to get there in time to save you."

Nolan nodded. Never had he been happier to see anyone at that moment.

"The authorities have Orville," Hannah continued. "He's being held in prison until his trial. With Evelyn's testimony, he should be put away for a long time."

As the truth sank in that all was truly well, gratitude seeped through every cell in Nolan's body. Never again would he take one minute with his family for granted. He raised a hand to rest on his wife's cheek. "I thank God for the gift of you, Hannah.

You are my heart and my life. Without you, nothing matters." He tugged her toward him for a brief kiss, tasting the salt of her tears. "From now on, Mrs. Price, if it's agreeable with you, I would like to live a perfectly boring life at Stainsby, enjoying our married life and raising our son."

Hannah's beaming smile illuminated the dingy room. "I like the sound of that, Mr. Price. Very much indeed." She leaned down to kiss him again, her soft lips lingering with a promise of more to come. A lifetime, in fact.

Their son's contented gurgle seemed to indicate that he agreed with his parents on all accounts.

EPILOGUE

"Do you really think we should leave Teddy alone with them?" Hannah frowned as she arranged the knitted blanket around the infant in his cradle, his adorable little face relaxed in sleep. Her heart swelled with more love than she ever thought possible. She turned to face Nolan. "After all, how much do either of them know about babies?"

"It's one night, Hannah. They'll be fine." Nolan moved across the carpet of the Stainsby parlor, where they had temporarily moved Teddy's bed, to drape an arm over her shoulder.

The physical contact sent shivers down Hannah's arms, reminding her of the evening to come.

Iris had been staying at Stainsby Hall since Christmas, helping Hannah with the baby while Nolan recuperated. He had been released from the hospital on Christmas Eve, and Edward had kept the festivities to a minimum so as not to overtax Nolan's strength. But now that he had recovered, Iris had insisted on giving them a night off. She and Edward would take care of Teddy so that Hannah and Nolan could have some time alone. As much as Hannah longed for private time with her husband, she dreaded leaving her child for the first time since his kidnapping three weeks ago.

"Molly, keep an eye on Teddy until Iris comes in, will you?" Nolan motioned to Molly, who sat reading by the fire, a loyal Daisy at her feet.

"I'd love to." Molly smiled over the rim of her book. "Don't worry, Hannah. We can manage without you until tomorrow."

Nolan steered Hannah out of the parlor into the hallway. "There's a whole staff of women here to give advice if need be—Edna being first in line." He took her by the hand, his boots ringing on the floor, until he came to a stop in the foyer. "We have a nice dinner waiting for us at the Thornbridge Manor Inn, not to mention the plans I have in mind for later." The heat of his look scorched Hannah's cheeks.

He leaned down to tease her lips with his, igniting in her a passion she'd almost forgotten. "Yes, it has been too long," she murmured against the demand of his mouth.

"There you are." Iris's cheery voice had them breaking apart as if they were still unmarried servants. Her skirts swished as she walked briskly down the hall toward them. "Edward would like a word with you before you go. He's in the study."

Hannah followed her aunt into the room, taking note of the subtle changes in the space. Most days now, the drapery was opened to let in the bright sunlight. Vases of fresh flowers adorned the side tables and the mantel over the hearth, filling the room with a subtle promise of spring, even though it was a few months away. Even Edward himself was lighter, less brooding, and his more colorful clothing matched his new attitude.

"All set to go?" Edward smiled as he rounded the desk to greet them. He kissed Hannah's cheek and clapped Nolan on the back.

Once again, Hannah thanked God for Edward's change of heart. Ever since Teddy's birth, he'd been supportive and welcoming. The miracle of their son had gone a long way toward bringing them closer as a family.

"Other than Hannah's nerves and your summons, nothing is holding us back." Nolan grinned at his father.

Edward laughed. "Well, let's get right to it then, and you can be on your way. I'm looking forward to spending the night looking after my grandson."

Iris cleared her throat and raised a slim brow.

"Correction. I'm looking forward to assisting Iris as she looks after my grandson."

"That's more like it." Iris laughed as Edward motioned the group over to the sitting area.

"Please have a seat for a minute. I have some news to share with you."

Hannah's curiosity spiked as she and Nolan perched on the settee. Had something happened between her aunt and Edward? But Iris's questioning expression as she took a seat in one of the wing chairs told Hannah she had no idea what Edward was about to say.

Leaning an elbow on the mantel above the blazing fire, Edward glanced at all of them. "I received a letter from Victoria today. First and foremost, she tells me that Evelyn is doing better and has filed for a divorce. She believes there should be no impediment to her request, now that Orville is in prison for the foreseeable future."

Hannah nodded. "It's for the best. Evelyn deserves a fresh start with an honorable man."

"One can only hope," Edward said. "As for Victoria, it seems congratulations are in order. Her suitor Sebastian has at last asked for her hand in marriage."

"Took him long enough." Nolan chuckled. "I thought he'd have proposed long ago."

"From what I gather, swiftness is not one of Sebastian's prominent personality traits. His motto is more along the line of 'slow and steady wins the race.' Still, Victoria is very happy now that she, Evelyn, and Ophelia can begin planning the wedding."

"I do love weddings." Iris sighed, her expression euphoric.

Edward moved across the carpet to stand closer to the threesome. "On that note, I have one more piece of business to attend to." He glanced at Nolan and cleared his throat. "It's no secret that my life has changed tremendously over the last year. Before I found out you were my son, I was a lonely, bitter man who lived a hermit's existence, rarely leaving Stainsby. I owe you all a great debt of gratitude for bringing me out of that darkness and back into the land of the living." Edward laid a hand on Nolan's shoulder. "The greatest gift I've ever received is learning I had a son. Because of you, Nolan, I've become a better man."

Hannah looked at her husband, her heart swelling with joy for him. At last he had the father he'd always longed for.

"Thank you, Father." Nolan's voice was gruff. "I must admit I had my doubts that we would ever form a real bond. But I truly believe God has helped us overcome our differences."

"I couldn't agree more. Which brings me to my next point." Edward turned his full attention to Iris. His gaze bore down on her as though Hannah and Nolan were not even in the room. "I must confess, Duchess, that when I first met you, I found your outspoken ways to be most annoying."

Hannah stifled a gasp. Iris, however, did not seem offended in the least. Her lips tipped up in an amused half-smile.

"But the more I came to know you, the more I realized what a wise and admirable woman you are."

"Oh, Edward." Iris blushed. The flames in the hearth added to the glow on her face.

Hannah's pulse quickened as she suddenly guessed where this conversation might be heading.

Sure enough, Edward dropped to one knee before Iris's chair and took one of her hands in his. "My dear Iris, you are a woman of great beauty—both inside and out. When I'm away from you, my life is not complete. To my utter amazement, I have found myself in love again at this late stage of my life, and I wondered if you might do me the great honor of becoming my wife?"

Tears rolled down her aunt's cheeks. The love that radiated from her eyes told Hannah what her answer would be.

"Nothing would make me happier, Edward." Iris leaned forward to meet him in a kiss.

Edward wrapped his arms around her and pulled her against him in a passionate embrace.

Nolan leaned over to nuzzle Hannah's cheek. "Look what we've started." He chuckled softly.

Hannah smiled as she moved back to look into her husband's eyes. "You don't mind sharing your father?"

"Not at all. My father is entitled to happiness after all the misery he's been through. And I think Iris is more than a match for him."

Hannah laughed. "I think you're right." She rose, pulling Nolan up with her, and they went to offer their congratulations.

Edward beamed, his wide smile splitting his face as he hugged them both.

"I'm so happy for you, Auntie." Hannah kissed Iris's cheeks.

"Thank you, Hannah dear. You'll never know how grateful I am for that fateful day you and Molly knocked on my door. Since you came into my life, I've gone from a lonely widow to a woman blessed with more family—and more love—than I ever could have imagined."

Hannah looked at Nolan and smiled. "I think the Lord knew we all needed healing in one way or another and brought us together for that purpose."

"How wise is our God," Iris murmured.

"Amen." Edward dropped his arm possessively around his Iris's shoulders and kissed the top of her head.

Nolan tugged Hannah's hand. "And on that happy note, my dear wife, let us be off before these two decide to elope."

"No worries there. I think this family has had enough elopements for one lifetime." Edward winked at them.

A burst of laughter followed Hannah and Nolan out the door, and she marveled once again at the power of love to bring about such astounding changes. Who would have ever believed that the formidable Earl of Stainsby could turn into such a doting father and an eager husband-to-be?

And who would have ever believed that a stable boy—*her* stable boy—could turn into a most noble heir?

Proof once again that with God and with faith, all things are possible.

LETTER TO THE READERS

Dear Reader,

Some books are born from pure imagination, but some are born from true life events enhanced by imagination. *A Most Noble Heir* falls into the second category.

I've always loved reading any type of romance novels, but when I first started penning my own stories, I wrote strictly in the contemporary genre. I used to say, "I could *never* write historicals. Imagine the research involved." Well, as I've discovered many times in my life, never say never!

During the 2006 Christmas holidays, my mother made a comment that sparked a journey I never could have anticipated. She said she wished she'd asked her mother more about her family history, because she knew nothing about her background. She didn't even know the names of her maternal grandparents. My mom's mother, Iris Irene Colver, had been told by the aunt who raised her that her mother had died in childbirth, and her father followed soon after from a broken heart. Despite my romantic nature, I instinctively knew that George Colver did not die of a broken heart. And so I took it upon myself to uncover the secrets of my ancestors. My instincts proved correct, and I learned that my great-grandfather had indeed been alive all that time, remarried with another family. My grandmother never knew she had a living father, as well as a stepmother and half-siblings. Would that have made any difference in her life? Sadly, we'll never know.

Needless to say, I was fascinated with the questions that arose from my research. But the most intriguing story I uncovered was that of my great-great-grandfather, Charles Henry Colver, who I learned was a stable hand at a great English estate called Stainsby Hall. He married a girl named Mary Hannah Burnan, a kitchen maid at the same estate. I had great fun imagining how their romance had unfolded. Unfortunately, their love story had a tragic end when Henry's early death left Mary Hannah a young widow with two babies.

Nevertheless, their tale sparked my imagination and became the seeds of Nolan and Hannah's romance. Of course, I couldn't give them such a sad ending, so I started imagining different scenarios. What if one of the stable hands at Stainsby Hall was actually the heir? What would happen to his love for the kitchen maid then? That led me into the world of English aristocracy, and once I started the research, I found I rather liked it!

Thank you for taking this journey with me back to Derbyshire, England, in 1884. I hope that you enjoy Nolan and Hannah's story and that my characters will do justice to the real Charles Henry and Mary Hannah who inspired this book.

Warmest wishes,
Susan

ACKNOWLEDGMENTS

This book has had quite a journey from conception to publication, much like the ancestors who inspired it.

First, I must give thanks to God for His divine inspiration—for taking the whispers of my ancestors and turning them into a story that will hopefully entertain and encourage others.

Second, I have to thank my agent, Natasha Kern, who, when she discovered I had this completed manuscript hidden away, said something to the effect, "That will never make you money sitting on your computer!" Thank you for making me take it out, dust it off, and eventually get Nolan and Hannah's story out for the world to enjoy.

I'd also like to thank Sue Brower, who first bought the book for Gilead Publishing. Thank you for believing in this story, despite it being a somewhat unconventional romance. I'm sorry things didn't work out with Gilead, but it was wonderful to know you loved the story and that it had merit. I also wish to thank Amy Drown, a freelance editor, who made me rewrite the beginning six chapters of my book and challenged me to make the story so much stronger.

Thank you to my amazing critique partners, Sally Bayless and Julie Jarnagin, for your wonderful insights and suggestions. I wouldn't be the writer I am without your input. And my sincere thanks to my former critique partner, CJ Chase. An expert in all things pertaining to English nobility, she was the first to point out some serious errors I'd made concerning inheritance laws and the aristocracy and offered great suggestions to make the story work!

A big thank you to David Long, my editor at Bethany House, who eventually bought this book and saved it from going back to the slush pile! Thanks for taking a chance on something a little different from my normal stories and giving it a good home. And thanks to Jen Veilleux, whose keen eye during the editing process really made the story shine.

Thank you to my family, to my husband, Bud, and my children, Leanne and Eric, who support me through all the ups and downs of this crazy business.

Last, thank you to my wonderful readers, who are so encouraging with their support and praise. We write for an audience, without whom there would be no stories, no characters, no spiritual journeys, or happily-ever-afters. Thank you for spending your precious time with my characters. I appreciate you all so much!

Susan Anne Mason describes her writing style as "romance sprinkled with faith." She loves incorporating inspirational messages of God's unconditional love and forgiveness into her characters' journeys. *Irish Meadows*, her first historical romance, won the Fiction from the Heartland contest sponsored by the Mid-American Romance Authors chapter of RWA.

Susan lives outside Toronto, Ontario, with her husband, two children, and one rather plump cat. She loves red wine and chocolate, is not partial to snow even though she's Canadian, and is ecstatic on the rare occasions she has the house to herself. Learn more about Susan and her books at www.susanannemason.net.

Sign Up for Susan's Newsletter!

Keep up to date with Susan's news on book releases and events by signing up for her email list at susanannemason.com.

More from Susan Anne Mason

At Irish Meadows horse farm, two sisters struggle to reconcile their dreams with their father's demanding marriage expectations. Brianna longs to attend college, while Colleen is happy to marry, as long as the man meets *her* standards. Will they find the courage to follow their hearts?

Irish Meadows, COURAGE TO DREAM #1

More from
Susan Anne Mason

Maggie Montgomery has come to America to visit her brother Rylan and his wife but secretly plans to stay for good. Rylan warns her to keep away from Adam O'Leary, yet her heart pulls her toward him. Will Adam's past—and other obstacles—prove too much for Maggie to overcome?

A Worthy Heart, COURAGE TO DREAM #2

When her mother suffers a stroke, Deirdre puts her medical career on hold and persuades Dr. Matthew Clayborne to help her treat Mrs. O'Leary at her family's farm. But since the doctor has no intention of leaving his life in Canada, and Deirdre has sworn off marriage altogether, how will they deal with the undeniable spark between them?

Love's Faithful Promise, COURAGE TO DREAM #3

You May Also Like

After a night trapped together in an old stone keep, Lady Adelaide Bell and Lord Trent Hawthorne have no choice but to marry. Dismayed, Adelaide finds herself bound to a man who ignores her, as Trent has no desire to connect with the one who dashed his plans to marry for love. Can they set aside their first impressions before any chance of love is lost?

An Uncommon Courtship by Kristi Ann Hunter
HAWTHORNE HOUSE
kristiannhunter.com

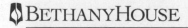
BETHANYHOUSE

You May Also Like

At the outset of WWI, high-end thief Willa Forsythe is hired to steal a cypher from famous violinist Lukas De Wilde. Given the value of his father's work as a cryptologist, Lukas fears for his family and doesn't know who to trust. He likes Willa—and the feeling is mutual. But if Willa doesn't betray him as ordered, her own family will pay the price.

A Song Unheard by Roseanna M. White
SHADOWS OVER ENGLAND #2
roseannawhite.com

In 1772, Lady Keturah Banning Tomlinson and her sisters inherit their father's estates and travel to the West Indies to see what is left of their legacy. On the island of Nevis, every man seems to be trying to win Keturah's hand and, with it, the ownership of her plantation. Set on saving their heritage, can she trust God with her future—and her heart?

Keturah by Lisa T. Bergren
THE SUGAR BARON'S DAUGHTERS #1
lisatbergren.com

Vivienne Rivard fled revolutionary France and now seeks a new life for herself and a boy in her care, who some say is the Dauphin. But America is far from safe, as militiaman Liam Delaney knows. He proudly served in the American Revolution but is less sure of his role in the Whiskey Rebellion. Drawn together, will Liam and Vivienne find the peace they long for?

A Refuge Assured by Jocelyn Green
jocelyngreen.com

◆ BETHANYHOUSE